F

MW00963204

Plaistow Public Library
85 Main Street
Plaistow, NH 03865

FIC D7323bl

THE BLIND PIG

A NOVEL

ELIZABETH DOUGHERTY

SCHOOL
STREET
BOOKS

Plaistow Public Library
85 Main Street
Plaistow, NH 03865

The Blind Pig
by Elizabeth Dougherty

Copyright © 2010 by Elizabeth Dougherty

Published by School Street Books
Northboro, MA

All rights reserved. Without limiting the rights under copyright reserved above, no part of this publication may be reproduced, stored in or introduced into a retrieval system, or transmitted, in any form, or by any means (electronic, mechanical, photocopying, recording, or otherwise) without the prior written permission of the copyright owner.

This book is a work of fiction. Names, characters, places, brands, media, and incidents are either products of the author's imagination or are used fictitiously. Any resemblance to actual events or locales or persons, living or dead, is entirely coincidental.

ISBN: 978-0-9845513-1-6

Library of Congress Control Number: 2010907020

Cover design by Luke Strosnider
Copyright © 2010 Luke Strosnider
http://www.lukestrosnider.com

For all who eat.

1

Angela waved her wrist over the scanner and held her breath, hoping that the NArc wouldn't punish her for having an extra drink last night. It wasn't even an extra, really. She'd had three before with no points, no fines. But she'd been younger then. And the NArc had been dumber. She tapped her toe. Did the meal assembly always take this long? She couldn't afford more points. Not this month. Not with the way things had been going at work. She needed at least one thing in her life to be stable.

Within seconds her meal slid out of the hatch. No penalties attached. Just a small compostable box. Relieved, she trailed the crowd in front of her and juggled the container to peek inside. An Ediball. Ordinary on the outside, but uniquely for her on the inside. As she eyed the simple tawny ball, its crunchy surface rough yet reflecting an oily sheen, she once again marveled at the NArc's ability to molecularly assemble every meal to meet each diner's individual nutritional needs. With a satisfied smile, she flipped the lid shut and made for the exit.

As she stepped out the door, she felt a tug on her shoulder. "Angela Anselm?" a voice whispered. Angela turned and saw a young woman, face taut, eyes darting left and right. The urgency in the woman's expression made Angela stop. The woman seemed normal enough—well-dressed and clean—except for the fear in her eyes. Angela felt inclined to help her, but then thought better of it. Few people recognized her face. Those who did sought her out, and they were rarely her fans.

"Sorry. In a hurry," Angela muttered as she side-stepped the stranger.

"Please," the woman insisted, and not just with her voice. She grabbed Angela's elbow and pulled back hard. "Please. I'm desperate. And you're the only one who can help me."

Angela pulled away and gave the woman a doubtful look.

"I'm *Marty*," the woman hissed. She cornered Angela in a nook just out of the way of the foot traffic streaming from the NArcCafe door. She used her hand to shield her lips from passers by. "A follower."

Angela shook her head. The name didn't register. How could it? She received hundreds of messages each day, from people all over the world who followed her nutrition column, The Well. She made a move to escape but a surge of pedestrians blocked her path. The woman pulled her collar up around her chin and ducked down. She seemed so convinced that she was being watched that Angela half expected to see someone peeking out from behind a doorway nearby. "Who are you hiding from?" she asked, wondering if this woman might really need help.

"Not who. *What*. It's the NArc. The NArc is supposed to keep me well. That's what you always say. But I feel awful." She ducked even lower behind her collar and leaned in closer. Angela shrunk from the sickly sweet smell on the woman's breath. "I stopped Cheating right away. Months ago. But I just keep getting worse—"

"Look, I'm sorry." Angela gently cut her short. She didn't have time to chat with Cheaters about their ills. Not today. "I'm just a reporter, I can't—"

The woman gripped Angela's arm tightly and pleaded. "But you're an *investigative* reporter. And an expert on the NArc. *Please.* You can find out what it's prescribing me. There's no one else who knows this stuff like you."

"Look, I really do have to get going." Angela wrenched her arm from the woman's grip again and discreetly groped for her sanitizer. "Marty, you said? I'll take a look, okay?" Angela felt her stomach knot and tried to ignore the disappointment on the woman's face. She forced herself to turn away. She'd lied to the Cheaters who pestered her before and she'd do it again, but that didn't mean she had to like it. Sometimes she had no choice. Cheaters think they can stop and they'll be okay, she told herself. They don't realize how long it might take to repair the damage they've done. And then they come running to me with their conspiracy theories. And their illness. It's as if they think I've got a personal line to the NArc. It's as if they've forgotten that the NArc is inside of them. It's inside all of us.

Angela had hoped that by the time she reached the news office she'd have forgotten Marty, but the desperation in the woman's eyes still haunted her as she rode the elevator to her editor's floor. It never felt good to put people off. Especially people who looked to her as an authority. She resolved to look Marty up just as soon as she got home. At the very least, Angela figured she might be able to convince the woman to give up Cheating for good.

That settled, she took a deep breath and knocked on her editor, Stewart Oakham's door. She peeked in and saw him sitting at his desk. He looked the same as always, eyes baggy, khaki pants and button-down rumpled. He reminded Angela of the old-time movie star who played one of the Watergate journalists. What was his name? Redmond? Redford? Stew managed, artlessly, to keep both feet in the twentieth century even though he had spent only a few of his 65 years in it.

"Hi Stew," she said.

"Angela, right on time," he replied, closing the files on his screen one at a time.

Angela shook her head. Stew sometimes acted as if he'd just gotten his computer last week. Knowing his file fidgeting would take some time, she started to rummage around in the box of cables he kept next to his desk. Not only had he failed to master the basics of desktop management, he also had refused to update his hardware. Instead, Angela had to buy a special adapter to make her wireless handheld display on his outdated monitor. As she disentangled the connectors, trying to free the one she needed, Stew said, "Now, what was it you wanted to talk about?"

Stew knew as well as she did that the hit counts for The Well were down again last month. And they weren't coming back up. Angela was still adjusting to the downturn and her inability to reverse it. She'd been writing the column for years, keeping her readers up to date on all the latest engineered food and nutrition news, dissecting the science, explaining the technology, and touting the benefits. But recently, her stories had fallen flat. The whole thing was eating away at her confidence and making her second guess every word she put on the page.

"I wanted to review my story with you. I'm hoping to get this series started off right," she said, trying to sound more professional than desperate. She slipped her computer out of her pocket, plugged in the clunky cable, and projected her story onto his screen.

Stew mumbled aloud as he read.

"Nice title. 'Decadence without the Guilt.'" He flicked his fingers in the air as if he were setting the headline in bold type. "Let's see now. 'Nutritional Architecture System…plans to bring authentic taste back'—I like authentic, but it's a big claim. We'll have to see." He rubbed his chin as he continued reading. "'Americans willingly traded flavor for fitness'—also nice. Blah, blah…'next-generation Neermeat adds flavors without the evils'—Good."

Stew's reactions sounded positive, but the bland look on his face told a different story. Something was missing, only she had no idea what. "Citation, blah, blah—wait. Hang on. 'The chicken blend tastes just like chicken?' Is that a real quote?" He looked up at her, puzzled.

"Yeah. Like it says, she's a taste tester. And old enough to remember the Old Ways. She was pretty excited about it." Angela had never heard of a taste tester before. She thought the concept sounded fantastic. "It's a great quote, isn't it?"

"Uh, well, not exactly. How old are you again?"

"I just turned forty."

"Too young, I guess. See, 'tastes just like chicken' was one of those things people used to say. Uh, so if a person ate something unusual, like alligator, they'd say 'tastes just like chicken' because chicken used to taste pretty much like nothing. It tastes like what you put on it. So alligator bits in batter taste like chicken bits in batter."

Angela stared back at Stew, horrified. "Alligator?"

"Point is, you need to get a different quote. Can you substitute? 'The blueberry blend tastes just like blueberries.' Something like that?"

"Not really. I mean, according to Arthur Short at SynEngra, the only flavor they have so far is chicken. None of the others are ready yet. And the taste tester didn't really say anything else. It seemed so perfect, I just went with it. Do you really think people will notice? I mean, how old is this joke? Do you think people will remember it?"

"Maybe not."

Angela could sense his disappointment. "Stew, I'll call her right now. I'm sure I can get a new quote."

He waved her off. "You're probably right. People won't notice." He rubbed his chin and shook his head. "Thing is Angela, this is a fine story. Fine, clear writing. But to get readers back, especially with a topic like this, you need to *take* them back. Help them remember the taste of chicken. Or better. Strawberries with cream. A perfect peach on a summer afternoon." Stew leaned back, hands clasped behind his head. He rocked there for a minute, apparently still savoring his imaginary peach. "I'd sure read a column like that."

"But do you think enough people remember? I mean, people were mostly eating processed food long before the NArc mandate. Sure, people my age remember food. But it's like it was a different world. The taste of a peach just doesn't seem as interesting as a perfectly balanced meal that's *tasty*. To me, going back seems, well, backward."

"You sure about that?" He eyed her critically. "The latest NArc stats I saw said between 10 and 20 percent of people cheat. That's a lot of readers. And don't forget that we have readers on the Outside and in Vermont—"

"So you think this could be a service piece," she interrupted, thinking about Marty. "This series could be a way to help convince Cheaters to stop? Maybe it could help get them back on the NArc?"

Stew had spun his chair around and was staring out the window. "That's one idea…"

He seemed lost in thought until Marcus, the managing editor, poked his head in. He gave Angela a quick nod then asked, "Stew, can I have a minute?" Turning slowly back to face the door, he nodded and followed Marcus down the hall.

Alone in Stew's office, Angela stood up and walked to the window. Stew had once made a point of telling her that he liked his view. He had a sentimental attachment to it. By modern standards, and by Angela's, it didn't have much to offer. His fifth-floor office overlooked the Greenway, a narrow swath of shaggy vegetation that half a century ago had been a raised highway. He had told her that, beyond the trees, he could still make out the old storefronts in the flooded remains of his old neighborhood, their walls stained with high-water marks. Leaning on the window sill and gazing through the plate glass, Angela screwed up her eyes. She tried to trick herself into slipping back in time the way Stew said he did. She tried to picture a scene from her own past, from the short time she had with her mother, before everything changed. But she couldn't see through the drizzle. Nor could she see past the reality of her own modern city, now a megalopolis stretching from north of Boston as far south as the eastern seaboard would take it.

"Angela?"

Stew's voice had an edge to it that made her reluctant to face him. When she finally did, the look on his face confirmed her fears. She leaned against the window and gave him a pathetic smile. She knew what was coming. She just hoped he'd get it over with quickly.

"Marcus gave The Well one more week. Next Friday, if there isn't anything fresh, I'll have to reassign you." He looked down. "I'm sorry." She nodded and made for the door. She could feel her eyes burning and wanted to get out of there as quickly as possible. As she walked past him, he put his hand on her shoulder. "Take the weekend to mull things over. I know you'll come up with something."

Angela meandered the skywalks, making her way home. At first she'd felt defeated. But the further she got from the gloomy old news building and the closer she got to her own neighborhood, the more determined she was to keep her column. He's giving me a shot, she told herself. One more week. But where to begin? She'd been through Stew's idea a hundred times in her head. It wasn't going to work. It couldn't. Take them back to what? The old miserable days when food was contaminated? When disease was crippling the economy?

She refocused. Take them back to remember tastes, he'd said. It made logical sense, except for the fact that most people her age had grown up on fruit leather and energy drinks with designer chemical tastes. Natural taste was as elusive to her as illness. Still, she knew that Stew had great intuition. Problem was, he hadn't kept up with his audience. He didn't know what young people wanted to read about.

But then again, neither did she.

When Angela finally arrived back home, it was late and she was tired. But not too tired to work. Back at her desk, she fired up a stream of headlines and sorted it by hit rate. "What are people reading right now," she murmured. At the top of the list for the Northeast City was a local story from the Food Police blotter: Woman Dies Cheating. Angela closed her eyes. Please don't let it be her, she thought as she opened the link.

Woman Dies Cheating

Northeast City, May 4, 2063 — This evening, a woman collapsed after eating banned food products at an alleged illegal speakeasy. Emergency responders scrambled to save her, but her condition deteriorated rapidly. The woman, twenty-nine year old Martine Sinsky, died en route to the hospital.

"Cheating is a dangerous game. Illegal foods are not safe under any circumstances," said Lieutenant Henry Potente, Food Police, at the scene of the incident.

Martine Sinsky. Angela looked at the attached photograph and shook her head. *Marty.* Marty is dead. So young. The NArc wouldn't have scheduled termination for at least another sixty or seventy years. And if the longevity numbers keep going up, maybe not for another hundred.

She swallowed the lump in her throat. With everything that had happened, Angela had forgotten about her decision to help the woman. And now, it was too late. She read the article again and frowned. It contained so little information. What was Marty doing in a speakeasy? Had she really stopped Cheating, like she'd claimed? But Angela knew the woman had been sincere. She may not have made much sense, but she hadn't been lying. No. Angela knew who the real liar had been. Maybe if I had done more, she thought. Maybe if I'd really offered to help, she wouldn't have taken this chance—

Angela pushed the thought out of her head. She scrolled away from Martine Sinsky's innocent smile, and scanned the comments. New entries flooded in as she skimmed. Conspiracy theories. Rumors. Sympathies. Questions. Everyone was talking about what happened to Martine Sinsky.

2

The next morning, Angela walked into an old concrete building and hit the elevator's up-arrow. She had a meeting with Lieutenant Henry Potente, Food Police, the officer quoted in the Sinsky story the night before. Frank from the crime section of her news outlet had helped her get in with him on short notice. When she walked into Potente's tattered cubicle, she immediately wished she hadn't.

"It's Saturday morning, and I'm not happy to see you," he grumbled as he dragged an unwelcoming but sturdy chair over to his desk. Tall and grizzled, his hair a grey halo over a furrowed ebony face, Potente had the look of a veteran. He had worked the Food Beat for over a decade and, according to Frank, homicide before that. His gruff manner had Angela frozen in his doorway. "Sit. This had better be good or Frank's going on my shit list."

Angela didn't know what to say. Frank had told her that Potente was a good guy. A friend. She felt suddenly unprepared. She hadn't spoken to the police in a long time. The scientists she interviewed made it so easy. Sometimes they would talk for hours with the slightest prompting.

"Well? What is it that couldn't wait? Out with it, sweetheart."

"I'm here about Martine Sinsky."

Potente waved his hand, prompting her to continue. He obviously had no idea what she was talking about.

"The woman who died last night. The Cheater. Martine Sinsky." Angela fed him the information, prodding him with her eyes.

"Look, if you want answers, you need to ask questions. That's how it works. You ask. Maybe I answer."

"I just want to know if there's more information." Potente huffed and rolled his eyes. "For instance," she added quickly, "Where did she get the food she ate? Who did she eat with? And how did it kill her?"

"Very good. Now, why do you want to know?"

"This woman, Martine Sinsky, she contacted me yesterday. She'd been sick for a long time and wanted my help." After reading the news bit the night before, Angela had dug Sinsky's old comments out of her recycling bin. Sinsky had written that she'd been feeling sluggish for weeks and she wanted Angela to look into it, to see if the NArc had a flaw. She'd admitted to cheating but had dismissed it as a cause of her ills. Angela remembered that that was why the comments ended up in the recycling bin in the first place. The woman was obviously in denial. "She told me she'd stopped cheating but she still wasn't getting any better. I told her I would help her." When Potente raised his eyebrows at this, she added, "I guess I wasn't very convincing."

Potente eked out an apologetic look. "I see," he muttered. "If it makes you feel any better, there's not a thing you could have done. Why don't you stick to your strengths? The Nutritional Architecture System's your game. Or the NArc as you kids call it." Potente smirked. "I always liked the sound of that."

"Right now, I just want to know what happened." Angela felt tears welling up in her eyes and fought to keep her cool.

"Ok now. Don't get all bent out of shape," he sighed and rubbed his eyes. "Look, I don't know what to tell you. She wasn't someone heavy in the Cheater world. Never seen her before. I can't tell you what she ate, where she ate it, or with whom. I just don't know. No one does. But I *can* tell you she cheated yesterday. I saw the labs." Potente fiddled with the files on his desktop, signaling that the interview was ending. "That's all I can say. I suggest you put Martine Sinsky behind you. Go back home, go about your business, and in a few days, you'll have forgotten all about her."

Angela stood her ground. If Potente had stopped with the facts, she might have backed down and done just as he'd suggested. She might have put this all behind her. But his patronizing tone irked her. He was either too lazy to do his job thoroughly, or he was trying to get rid of her. It didn't matter to Angela. What mattered was that she wanted some answers. "What, specifically, did the labs say? I mean, they can tell what she ate, can't they? What about the people she ate with? Isn't anyone else sick?"

Potente shook his head. "There's nothing else I can tell you because there's nothing else to tell. In a case like this, there simply isn't any more information than what I'm giving you."

Angela slumped in disappointment. "Won't you be investigating?" she asked, giving the cop a puzzled look. She didn't understand why this death wasn't causing a stir.

Potente laughed. He seemed genuinely amused. "Why don't *you* investigate the Cheaters if it's so important to you. If you find something, you let me know. Alright?"

Angela stared at Potente as he stood and offered her his hand, still chuckling. Instead of taking it, she smiled enthusiastically. "That's a great idea. Now, where can I find those lab reports?"

Later that day Angela rounded a corner and, using a building as a windbreak, tried to capture her stray tangles in a clip. Peering through the fog, she checked down a vacant alleyway for signs. She'd been walking for blocks with no luck. But she hadn't lost hope yet.

She'd decided to take Potente's advice seriously and had started her investigation immediately. After leaving Potente, she'd gone to the hospital where Sinsky had died. But the emergency responders had filed bare bones reports. The "labs" consisted of two computerized lines that read "Foreign Contaminants: PRESENT" and "Treatment: ABORT." According to the doctors, the NArc scans the body, performs the diagnosis and administers the treatment. It's more efficient that way, they explained, because the NArc has all of the latest scientific data about bugs and drugs. "We don't know much about it," said one doctor. "It's just too much information for a human to keep up with."

Instead the doctors provide care, handle disposal, communicate with families and manage billing. While most care is free, they told her that Marty's case will cost her family thousands even though she died before receiving treatment. "It would have been worse if she'd lived," one of the more callous doctors had added. "Cheating automatically invalidates insurance."

Angela concluded that there was nothing new to be learned about Sinsky on the inside. But here, on the streets, she had a shot. If she could make contact with other Cheaters, maybe she could retrace Sinsky's final hours. Maybe she could find out where she ate and who she ate with. Maybe others were sick and needed help.

Even though Angela hadn't believed Sinsky at first, she'd had to admit later that what the woman described sounded strange. She'd stopped Cheating for months, but the NArc hadn't made her better. This didn't add up. Angela had seen the NArc improve chronic conditions within weeks, even conditions caused by Cheating. She'd done a profile of a habitual Cheater once, years ago, and chronicled his journey from infirmity to wellness over an astonishing 8-week period. If anything, Sinsky should have recovered faster if she had really been an occasional Cheater. Unless Cheaters were catching something more serious. If they were, now *that* would be a story people would want to read.

Angela scanned the left-hand side of the alley. No signs. When she crossed to the other side and looked back, she spotted it. Across the way was a hotel service entrance. There was nothing unusual about it. It was just a grey door, set inside a concrete wall painted the same dull shade. But just above the highest hinge someone had scrawled a rudimentary acorn. To the casual observer, it looked like a stain. But based on her research, Angela felt confident the mark was intentional.

After several seconds of standing in the early-spring drizzle, too stunned by her good fortune to move, she decided to knock. No answer. She tried the door, but it was locked. So she positioned herself in a nearby nook of recycling bins. She stamped her feet to warm up and then checked the time with a wave of her fingers over the test-tube sized computer hovering just over her eyebrow. The metal arm jutting out from her ear to support the device looked clunky and awkward, like the stem of an old-fashioned pair of eye-glasses. She'd been saving for a newer, sleeker model but still didn't have enough money to make the purchase. In response to her finger wave, her eyepiece projected a clock onto her retina. Seeing it was earlier than she'd thought, she decided to wait an hour.

She examined the acorn again and then navigated from the digitized projection of the time to the CheaterChasers website she'd found earlier. Most of the posts there denigrated underground food and suggested community action to quash it. But they were also unwittingly helpful to those who wanted to find it. Angela checked the site's legend of Cheater symbols again. Her mark was definitely a Cheater mark. According to the site, though, the scrawls came and went. They, like the Cheaters, moved on an erratic schedule and, while present, were not always active. This made it difficult for the food police and activists to stage busts. Angela had been lucky to find this mark. But now, staring at the acorn, she wondered if it was a decoy. She stamped her feet again. Just one hour. If nothing happens by then, I'll move on.

After several minutes, Angela stood up to stretch. She needed fresh air. The garbage surrounding her smelled sharp and rotten. She tried to ignore the fact that the smelliest bits of this trash would be recycled right back into the nutritional manufacturing system to be used as fertilizer and fuel to feed the food chain. She put the sights and smells out of her mind as she took in a deep breath of the clean air just above the bins.

As she did, the sound of footsteps made her shrink back into the acrid nook. Peering between the bins, Angela watched a man approach the door. He glanced right and left, then slipped inside. She considered following, but her feet wouldn't move. After a few minutes, she stood on wobbly legs and ventured out to try the door. Locked. Her only hope was that the man would come out the same way he went in. She scuttled back to her hideout.

Twenty agonizing minutes later, the man emerged and strode down the street, his backpack bulging. Angela waited for him to round the corner, then dashed out of the nook and followed him. She'd barely seen his face and didn't want to lose sight of him—that backpack wasn't distinctive enough to help her pick him out of a crowd and the rest of him appeared nondescript. Average build. Brown hair. Blue jacket. Out on the street, he'd slowed his walk and was only half a block ahead. She trailed him for two blocks until he stopped to wait for a train to pass.

Angela decided it was now or never. She crept up beside him. Without turning her head, she whispered, "Is there any room left at your table?" She'd read on a different website that this was a sort of pass phrase. She felt his eyes sizing her up and got the feeling that her attempt at contact had somehow worked.

"I'm Logan," he whispered.

"Angela," she replied, sensing him move a step closer.

"Eight tonight. Sharp. Upper Kennedy Square," he instructed. As she nodded, she felt his hand on the small of her back. It lingered. Even after he had darted across the road and vanished, she could still feel the imprint of its unwelcome warmth on her skin.

Wading through piles of rejects, Angela reached for the mustard-colored wrap top she'd started with. Paired with the aubergine meditation pants, she felt smart yet casual, young but not immature. Plus, these odor-free soytek fibers breathe well, she thought. She had enough to worry about tonight, she didn't need to be thinking about sweat rings. Scrunching her damp hair, she eyed herself in the mirror and tried to breathe evenly. But her jitters were getting worse. She had no idea what she was getting into. Logan had seemed harmless, but was he? Even if he wasn't dangerous, what about the load in his backpack?

"Hello!" called Molly, home from work at seven sharp, like every other Friday. Before Angela knew it, Molly stood at her door; two quick strides had carried her the length of the common room, her functional clogs silent on the carpet. She poked her head in. "Going out?" Molly asked, taking in the scattered garments and looking her friend up and down. "Those colors look nice on you."

"Thanks. I've tried a million things, but I think this works." Angela turned and checked the view from the rear and scrunched again, trying to avoid eye contact with her friend. "I picked the soytek over the hemp, which looked kind of sloppy. This drapes better, I think."

"Where are you off to? You don't usually spend so much time in front of the mirror," Molly commented.

Angela hesitated. She'd hoped to get out of here before Molly got home. She didn't have time to explain her plans and Molly wouldn't understand without a precise justification—the one thing Angela was sure she didn't have. She decided to dodge the question. "A party, but I've got to run. I need to meet them on time. They told me they won't be able to wait."

Angela stepped toward the door, but Molly, who was blocking the exit, didn't move out of the way. "Wait. Whose party?"

Angela knew that Molly wouldn't relent. All through college, Molly had kept track of Angela, almost as if Angela had been one of her lab projects. At first, Angela thought it was smothering. And creepy. But it wasn't long before she ended up needing Molly to rescue her from a situation she should have known enough to avoid. Too many boys. Too much booze. The refreshing thing about Molly was that she'd never seemed to pass judgement on Angela's lack of self-control. She just observed and, when Angela needed it, she offered a helping hand. By the end of their first year in school, Angela knew she had a lifelong friend. Looking back now, she couldn't believe that twenty years had gone by, they still lived together, and Molly still felt the need to keep track of her.

Angela decided to come clean. She walked to her desk and brought up the Sinsky story then waited, picking at her fingernails while Molly read it over.

"Sounds like she got food poisoning. It happens, but hardly ever these days," said Molly, shrugging. "Are you thinking about a historical piece? About how risky eating used to be?"

"Sort of," said Angela. "This woman, well, I saw her yesterday." Angela filled Molly in on the encounter. "She wanted me to help her. I wonder if, if maybe… Maybe if she knew it was the Cheating that made her sick and not the NArc, maybe she wouldn't have kept doing it. So, I guess I'm thinking of doing a piece on how risky eating is *now*."

Molly stared back at her friend, her eyes steady ovals under her inky matchstick bangs. "Angela, what does this have to do with tonight? You aren't going underground already. Are you?"

"I am."

Molly blinked. "But it's so dangerous. You do realize this woman is dead, don't you?"

"That's *why* I have to go. I need to find out what happened to her. People Cheat because they just don't get it. I obviously can't help her, but maybe I can keep this from happening to other people."

"Angela, food outside the NArc is illegal. What if you get caught?"

As Angela transferred her lipstick into a small bag woven with concealed recording electronics, she shrugged. Straight as an arrow, Molly had never once had a NArc violation. Like most people, Angela budgeted for the occasional fines she racked up. She didn't think of it as criminal. She told herself she wasn't the least bit worried about getting caught, even though she couldn't ignore the hollow feeling in her gut. What Molly didn't know was that Angela had to take this chance. In this line of work, the only stories worth pursuing are the risky ones.

"Or what if you get sick," Molly added, her eyes moving back to the screen, back to the photograph of Martine Sinsky. "Don't you remember what we learned in school? Food outside the NArc is nutritionally unbalanced. And some of it is addictive. If you don't get poisoned you'll develop a chronic condition. Don't you remember the statistics? One in two people overweight, and that was by the old health standards—"

"I admit it, okay? It's dangerous," Angela interrupted. She didn't have time for one of Molly's lectures. And she, of all people, knew about the ills the NArc had eliminated. After all, she had lost her own mother to obesity and diabetes. But seeing the concern on Molly's face, she took a deep breath. "Sorry. You know I'm nervous. But you also know I have to do this. It's what I do." As she spoke, Angela realized that her hands had steadied. She hadn't felt this alive in years. She smiled at the thought. "I'll be careful, okay? And I'll check in later. Now I've really got to get going."

Angela arrived at Upper Kennedy Square a few minutes before eight. The "square" was an intersection between two twelfth-floor walkways in a neighborhood along the river just west of her own. The walkways were wide enough to support the hanging trains speeding in opposite directions beneath them. They connected four towers built during the Migration, when the end of oil forced people to move en masse out of the countryside and to cram into engineered cities. The tunnels joined together inside a five-story sphere, the top of which housed a rotating bar. On a quiet morning the glassed-in tunnels, covered with a bramble-like structure that supported flowering vines, gave walkers the impression that they were treading a garden path in the countryside. But the surging Friday night crowd and the vibrations of the hurtling trains made it hard for Angela to forget that she was suspended by steel and concrete a hundred feet in the air.

Before reaching the entrance to the sphere, she paused at an overlook to take in one of her favorite views. Jutting out from the left was the south-facing slope of the building she had just exited. Its ever-widening tiers shimmered green in the dying evening light. Though there were skyfarms like this all over the city, it was hard to find an equal to this view. The greenery rippled down over the tiers in a cascade that looked almost natural, especially since the steel struts and all the other automated rigging was partially obscured by the building's glassy outer covering. On one of the floors she could see blooms in an orchard that reminded her of the rooftop park in her own building. When looking for a place to live, she and Molly had agreed that park access was key, though neither of them ended up spending much time in the orchard kitty-corner to their apartment. In fact, in the spring the park's 25th-story orchard had turned out to be a nuisance. The hum of swarming robotic pollinators had woken Angela on several mornings, making her wish they had chosen a place overlooking the park rather than sitting next to it. Then again, she did enjoy the snowfall each January. The artificially-induced cold lasted a few weeks each year, just long enough to harden the trees and get them ready to bear fruit. Just long enough for her to make a snow angel and take a romantic walk at twilight.

Though Angela couldn't see the windmills and solar collectors atop the pyramid-shaped tower, she knew they were there, electrifying the complex. Across the river, she could make out a row of brownstones, the last remains of the old city. When the Migration started, the mayor tried to preserve the city's heritage by saving certain neighborhoods. The old brownstones were at the top of the list. They kept as many old walk-ups as possible, filling in the alleys behind them with hulking steel-clad and glass-walled buildings. The modern materials were supposed to reflect the character of the neighborhood, their surfaces either mirroring the brown blocks or vanishing into the sky. Angela thought the combination of old and new was ingenious and had wanted to live there. But to Molly the buildings looked too much like cages for lab rats.

When a nearby clock tower began its 8 o'clock chimes, Angela merged back into the crowd and stepped into the glinting metal and flashing neon of the sphere. She chose a spot at the northwest edge of the intersection with a view of the storefronts along the eastern block: the retro karaoke place, its entrance fronted by a tiny sign-in counter, but its core a maze of hallways and booths stretching two stories above and below the main level; the angry club, its music scrambling the thoughts of passers by; and in the distance, the blues bar. She had always felt comforted by its threadbare sofas, dim lighting, and crackly vocals on a dreary afternoon. Part of her was tempted to go curl up in there right now.

Angela scanned the intersection for her contact. She hoped she would recognize him. But when she spotted him, it wasn't his face she remembered. It was the feeling of his fingertips pressing on her spine. She found herself arching away from it. As Logan walked toward her, he winked. Traveling with him were two other couples. They looked young. Too young. Dressed in too-tight pants and a snug t-shirt, a look popular among twenty-somethings and students who hadn't yet launched their adult lives, Logan tossed his hair and gave her a practiced half-smile. The group slowed as they reached the corner. Without stopping,

Logan slung his arm over her shoulders and drew her into the fold.

$\neq$

Ten minutes later, Logan pulled Angela into his apartment and led her by the wrist through a throng of students slopping drinks and crunching on orange-powdered sticks and dusty red triangles. This is all wrong, she thought to herself as Logan dragged her to a room in back, closed the door, and faced her.

"Hi Angela. I was hoping you'd show," he breathed, lightly tugging one of the curls dangling at her chin. Angela froze, her eyes glued to the wispy mustache under his narrow nose. His hair hung limp on his forehead. "I've got some stuff I don't want to share with anyone but you." From his bag he pulled out a waxed-paper log of toasted rounds and a jar with a red screw cap. He lined up the rounds on a plate, opened the jar, then spread a dollop of orange goo on top of each one. He beamed at her through his reedy bangs and lifted the plate as if it were a religious offering. "These babies are so hard to get," he crooned.

Angela half-smiled back and took a round. It splintered as she bit into it. She cringed as a rush of salt mixed with the grainy topping like a mouthful of sea and sand.

"So good," he mumbled with his mouth full. He grabbed two more and ran off to get drinks.

While he was gone, she checked his bag. She opened the front pocket first. Out spilled several foil-wrapped NArc-vended snacks. She shoved them back inside and tugged at the zipper. It wouldn't close. Her hands shaking now, she rearranged the packets neatly and pulled the zipper slowly shut around them. She glanced back through the door. No sign of Logan yet. So she dug into the main compartment and immediately found a photo ID that showed he was a second-year grad student at Tech. Silently thanking the NArc for keeping her looking young—he obviously hadn't noticed their age difference—she dug deeper. The bag contained more so-called food. Sugar-packed, salt-laced Junk. She considered pocketing some of it for Molly to analyze at work, but decided to check Logan's whereabouts again first. Good thing she did. She ran into him just as he reached the door. He greeted her with another wink and a brimming cup. She reluctantly nodded her thanks and sipped at the neon-red syrup as she followed him into the crowd.

The room, warm and smelling of farts and sweat, was divided in two by a tortured sofa with crusty stains and a broken leg propped up with what looked like a petabyte storage device, the green LED on its front fluttering with activity. She snaked between the sofa and a clutch of girls who were corralling a young woman with wide eyes and a scanty mood dress that glowed an icy blue. "Just drink more. That'll turn your dress red," advised an exotic, almond-eyed woman, her mottled crimson tunic stretched over generous hips. It had never occurred to Angela to use alcohol to manipulate the mood fabrics. Wondering if it would work, she made eye-contact with the girl in the center. A mixture of fear and defiance flitted across the girl's face as she tilted her head back and finished her drink in one gulp, dribbling orange liquid down her chin. Before Angela could detect any noticeable changes in the color of her dress, the crowd lurched and pushed her away.

When Angela caught up with Logan, she turned on her recorder with a sly flick of her wrist. The conversation centered around getting more Junk for next week's bash. "There's a party at Ray's, Lo. We need a re-up on the goods." "We're gonna need a bump. Can you swing it?" And so on. Angela could tell that he liked the attention. Each time a newcomer joined the circle, Logan leaned in to introduce her, his breath awash with salt and goo.

During a lull in conversation, she decided to probe him for information. "So where does all this stuff come from?" she asked, touching Logan's elbow lightly to bring his attention back to her. When he smiled and inched closer, she wondered how she could stand herself.

"Junk labs all over. The big ones are set up Outside. They run under the radar in old abandoned factories. All the stuff in nice wrappers comes from them. Good quality control. Same stuff every time. Makes good business sense."

"Is there stuff that's not in nice wrappers?"

"Hell yeah. Hard to get, but this one guy makes these things called 'fried rinds.' So awesome. He's got a whole setup in his apartment. He's got these burners from an old school science lab. The whole place looks like it's straight out of Dr. Jekyll and Mr. Hyde. Ancient. The guy's little too. And mean. Just like Hyde. Man, but those rinds…" Logan rubbed his belly and closed his eyes.

"What are they made of?" Angela channeled her inner four-year-old and blinked at Logan.

He shrugged. "Never thought to ask."

"Have you actually been to this guy's lab? It sounds so *dangerous*." She couldn't tell if it was the sugar, the salt, the alcohol, or the ease of her bimbo act that was making her head pound.

"Naw, no. I've got an in. A guy I know tells me about raids, so I don't get caught in one. In exchange, I tell him about bad Junk. Sometimes we get a stash that's rank. I mean *nasty*. We test it usually, 'specially before a big party. Kiefer takes a sample to his lab and does a spec on it. Don't want a bunch of people keeling over, you know? Like that chick in the papers last night."

Angela stared at Logan. "Did you know her?"

"No, but it's big news when someone our age kicks it." He shrugged. "Stuff like that happens if people aren't careful." He looked at her sideways. "You ask a lot of questions. C'mon, let's dance. Or maybe let me get you another drink." As he took her half-full cup and turned away, the wide-eyed girl Angela had seen earlier, her icy blue dress now an unflattering pea green, flew by in a coltish twirl and elbowed Angela in the ribs.

Angela contemplated leaving. The pounding in her head was getting worse and she was worried that she'd pushed Logan too far. But then she had just gotten started. Just go easy, she coached herself.

"Nice bag," said a voice behind her.

Angela spun around and found herself staring into a pair of deep brown eyes that peered out from behind curtains of sleek chestnut hair.

"Model NCR-250? I've got a 500. In navy. Ochre's good for you though." The woman held Angela prisoner with her gaze and Angela felt her heart start to race. "My advisor designed the original." The woman eased her visual grip with a deliberate blink and a toss of her hair. She settled in next to Angela. They both leaned against the back of the sofa and looked out into the room. "Cop or reporter?" the woman asked casually. Angela still didn't say anything. She was too busy looking for an escape. "I'm only asking out of self-preservation. I won't out you if you don't out me. Name's Courtney by the way."

Angela breathed out a sigh of relief. "Angela. Reporter. I'm investigating a death. Martine Sinsky. Last night."

The woman raised an eyebrow and turned to look at Angela. "What're you doing here, then?"

"Do you know something about her death?" Angela countered.

The woman calmly reached over, opened Angela's bag, and switched it off. "I didn't know her, but she wasn't a Junkie. Junkies don't keel over like that. Junkies who aren't careful end up like those creeps in the corner." She nodded to an isolated group huddled in a dark nook, their bodies misshapen, skin pallid, eyes vacant. They ate mindlessly, discarding their wrappers on the floor. One of them nodded off in what Angela guessed was a kind of food coma. "We—at least around here, anyway—we try to watch out for each other. Make sure the Junk is pure. Make sure people's stats read clean. The right dose of exercise pills, fat burners, hydrators. You know the drill." Her eyes flicked back to the corner. "Some hard cases you just can't help."

"So if Sinsky wasn't eating this stuff, what do you think she did eat?"

Courtney smirked. "You're kidding, right? Isn't it obvious? She ate food. Real meat. From animals. Plants grown in the soil. Infested with bacteria. Parasites. Allergens. Compared to that, this stuff is candy." She popped a Junky snack in her mouth. As she chewed and delicately brushed the dust off of her lips, she tipped her head to the opposite side of the room. "Looks like I'm not the only one who's onto you."

Angela glanced behind her and saw Logan huddled with two other guys. She sucked her breath in through her teeth. They were gesturing in her direction.

"Don't worry. I'll get you out of here," she heard Courtney say.

Angela looked around again for a nearby exit. She couldn't see one. She glanced behind her. Logan was heading towards her, a drink in each hand and a phony smile on his face. When she turned back, Courtney had vanished. Angela scanned the room for her, craning her neck to see over the crowd. All she could see were Logan's two big friends flanking him. She decided to fess up to Logan and talk her way out of whatever it was she'd gotten herself into. But she didn't get the chance. From out of nowhere, the girl in the mottled pea-green dress flew across the room and flung herself at Logan. Angela didn't see what happened next— Courtney had grabbed her elbow and dragged her into the hallway. "Cruel but necessary," she said to Angela as she maneuvered them through the crowd. "Bound to humiliate herself anyway." From the sound if it, the girl had knocked into Logan so hard that he fell backwards and both drinks splashed behind him. When Courtney reached the door, she shoved Angela out and shut the door behind them. Pointing left, she said, "Staircase. Two floors down you can catch the express elevator to Lower Kennedy. Ground floor. No one would ever think to go there. Can you find your way home?"

"Yeah," Angela breathed. "Thanks."

"Anytime," she said with a wink. For the second time that night, Angela credited the NArc for what was starting to feel like eternal youth. She really needed to get out more often.

An hour later, Angela walked into a bar on the 10th floor Avenue that cut through her own apartment building. Instead of waving in, she avoided the NArc and keyed in a straight SuperCleanse. It would cost her. Better to be safe, she thought. She spotted Molly and their friend Nate in a back corner and waved hello. As she approached, Nate gave her a cool nod, his blonde hair flopping into his eyes. "One week, six days and, uh, 12 hours to go," he said. "Cheers!" He lifted his mug, grimacing as the steam from his moss-colored tea filled his nostrils. Then he took a swig.

"Probation?" she asked him. Nate had more than once been fined for drinking too much. Angela had always felt sorry for him. He wasn't a bad guy. In fact, he was definitely a good guy. He just couldn't seem to keep himself in check.

"Worse. Happy hour after work last week did me in. I must have lost track," he said sheepishly. "Landed myself in Food School." As Nate swallowed another gulp, his face twisted into a scowl. He smacked his lips in distaste and said, "It wasn't as bad as this detox tea." He smiled, but his expression withered under Molly's disapproving gaze.

Angela, however, was intrigued, especially since her current project was taking her precariously close to a similar sentence. "What was it like?"

With less drama in his voice, he continued. "The Food School in my neighborhood is in this old piano factory. You're assigned a room based on your offense. I ended up being late"—this comment caused Molly's frown to deepen—"No, you see, I was on time, with time to spare, but then the walk from the registration desk took fifteen minutes. This building is like one long Escher hallway. Nothing is flat. Each level looks the same, with these old wooden floors coated with about a hundred layers of lacquer, the plaster dingy and peeling. Hardly any rooms are labeled. I ended up trying three different doors before I found the right one. And you know me. I'm good at navigating through spaces."

Molly's face softened, encouraging Nate to continue. "Well, the rest is just boring. You sit in a very small, hard chair in front of a desk that crushes your knees. They give you a workbook and a dull pencil, probably left over from decades ago, and the instructor walks you through the lessons. For eight hours. And its not like you're thinking. The teacher literally tells you what to write in each space. If you don't write it, he humiliates you. If you do write it, he taunts you."

"For what?" asked Molly.

"For being so stupid as to break the law. For following his instructions blindly. For anything he can think of. A talent for mindlessly berating people is the only qualification for that job. That and knowing how to game the system. Because that's what it's about. By the end, I'd learned at least two new ways to avoid

Food School. I think they want to maximize the fines. Fines make more money."

Molly huffed. "If you broke the rules, they have to assume you don't know them. That's the premise of something like Food School. Of course they're going to walk you through them, slowly, so you will understand them better," said Molly. Then, more conclusively, she added, "Studies show that rehabilitation works better than retribution for repeat offenders."

Nate slumped back a bit and Angela felt his embarrassment at being a "repeat offender."

A robotic arm cut the tension as it descended from overhead and placed Angela's drink order in front of her, distracting all of them from Nate's humiliating story. Angela was grateful for the delivery too; she had no idea what had been in the foods that Logan fed her, and she wanted whatever it was out as quickly as possible. One whiff of the muddy concoction made her wish the new taste profiles were further along. She'd considered asking the woman at the party for one of her Junk remedies. But then everything had happened so quickly, she never had the chance. Just as well, she thought. Who knew what was in *that* stuff.

As the arm retracted into the groove in the ceiling to join the other automated wait-staffers, Angela noticed that Nate was taking advantage of the interruption. She watched his eyes trace Molly's nose, its tip pointing slightly upward, then her lips, a crimson heart offset by her ivory skin. She had to admit that her friend was striking. Flawless, even. But so exaggerated in Nate's mind that she had become unattainable. She knew he resented her for intruding on his evening alone with Molly. Not that he would have taken advantage of the opportunity, she thought. He'd been in love with her for so long, if he hadn't mustered the nerve to act on it yet, he probably never would.

"So how are you feeling? Can you tell us what happened at the party?" Molly asked Angela, oblivious to Nate's attentions.

Angela nodded and started by telling them about the Junk and the people she saw eating it. She paused to take a sip from her glass, but ended up gulping at it. Wiping her mouth, she said, "You know, I wanted to grab some of the Junk for you to analyze, but then I had to rush out. I'm dying to know what's in it."

"Probably better that you don't know," commented Nate.

"I am shocked that these students are taking such risks with their health," said Molly. "The ones in the corner? Don't they know the consequences? It really shows that we've gotten too comfortable with our good health. Angela, I agree with you. We do need to keep educating people about the dangers of Cheating. Only I'm not convinced you need to put yourself at risk to do it."

"I wonder about the risks," Angela said, leaning in on her elbows. "Most of these kids just binge on weekends. They've got all kinds of evasion strategies. I mean, the Junk dealers aren't just selling Junk. That woman was slipping people exercise pills to burn off the bad stuff. She told me that if you take them at the right time, your NArc stats read clean the next day. And I'm pretty sure some of them were bingeing and purging. It was only a small minority of them that looked sick."

"It sounds even more dangerous to me now. Tell me you didn't take any of that stuff." Molly placed the back of her hand on Angela's forehead and peered into her eyes. "No. Tell me exactly what you did take," she added, frowning. When she reached for Angela's wrist to check her pulse, Angela pulled back.

"I'm fine. I barely ate anything," she assured her friend.

Molly continued to eye Angela, looking for signs of illness. "I'm not sure you should keep going with this investigation," she said. "I know you're looking to push the boundaries, but I don't think you should sacrifice your health to do it. These Cheaters aren't worth it."

"Probably not," Angela agreed. "But these aren't the Cheaters I'm looking for."

"What do you mean?" Molly asked. "Cheaters are Cheaters."

"I don't think so," Angela replied. "Logan told me they test to make sure the Junk isn't tainted. So maybe what that woman said was right, maybe it *is* the real food that's the problem. Especially now that no one is policing it. It was bad when it was legal and inspected. Imagine how bad it is now."

Nate raised an eyebrow. "You've come up with some wild ones in the twenty years I've known you, Ange, but this tops them all. You're telling me that in less than six hours, you've penetrated the Cheater network, ruled out Junk as an issue, and now you're going to investigate an underground world you don't know anything about? All because some Cheater that you don't even know keeled over?" His tone started out deriding, but changed. By the end, he started to sound concerned. "I know you like adventure, but Molly's right. You need to figure out what you're getting into before you get so far in you can't get out."

"I agree. You should take the time to do some research—"

"Stop." Angela whispered, her head slung low. "Just stop. Please? There is no time." Her head was still pounding and her tongue felt like sandpaper. She looked up and met their eyes, trying to sound matter-of-fact. "I don't have any time. If I don't have a fresh story by Friday, I'm bound for the city desk. Or worse. Stew told me yesterday." The pity in their eyes made her squirm. It was exactly why she hadn't wanted to tell them in the first place. They had secure jobs working for SynEngra, building next-generation Neerfoods and designing faster NArc diagnostics. She had always been the one with an uncertain future. She had always been the one scraping to survive in a dying industry. She picked up her drink to take a swig, but her glass was empty.

"Maybe Nate can help," Molly offered. "He can do some digging for you. Maybe he can find something a little more, uh… sophisticated?" Molly looked as if she'd just had the idea of the century. Out of the corner of her eye, Angela could see that Nate wasn't any more keen on this suggestion than she was. But she knew that Molly would get her way. Nate wouldn't dream of disappointing her. And Angela had to accept the help. She had no logical argument against it.

Nate walked home alone.

Right after Angela had somehow tangled him in her scheme, she'd left. Molly had insisted on going home with her. "To keep an eye on her, don't you think? I'm worried," she'd whispered to him. He hadn't argued even though he thought Molly was overreacting. Angela had hardly eaten any of the Junk. In fact, Nate remembered a summer eating almost nothing but junk food when he was ten. A drought year. The garden had fizzled and his parents couldn't afford much else. He'd skimped at meals to make sure there was enough to go around. Then he'd used the spare change he made doing odd jobs to fill up on chips and cookies. A lot of cookies. Today's Junk wasn't much different than that crap. But he could hardly tell Molly to ignore her friend just so he could have a few more minutes with her. He'd waited this long. He could wait a little longer.

He began to think of how he could arrange to see Molly again without being too obvious. Maybe this thing with Angela will help me out, he thought. At the least, it'll give me something to talk to Molly about besides work.

When Nate arrived home, he slid into his chair and put on his gear. He thought about Angela's theory that real food had killed this Sinsky woman. It sounded reasonable. He'd seen enough of farming to know that real food wasn't all that clean. He'd seen enough of it that he didn't want to see any more. His parents had put off Migration for so long that they had been among the last to leave their town. When Nate finally got to the city, he couldn't believe what he'd been missing. An early approximation of the NArc at school made everything so simple. He couldn't believe he'd wasted all those years fighting weeds and bugs and eating endless piles of potatoes and zucchini and still feeling starved. Meanwhile he could have been in the city, working on just about anything else and not spending his time hungry. Well, it made him angry enough that these days he dreaded the holidays with his family. He couldn't stomach their stories of the old times or their food. He would never be able to bring Molly to meet them, that was for sure.

But at least he knew what he was getting into with this food stuff, he thought as he ambled into cyberspace. He navigated directly to a virtual bar he'd been frequenting for the past five years. He went there because it was a good place to play pool and listen to the jukebox. He also liked the people. Unassuming. Unpretentious. It wore on him working in a sterile office all day running simulations and talking about engineering. He came here to escape, to go someplace that hadn't been designed but instead had just, over time, come to be.

"Hey Joe," said the bartender as Nate's avatar slid onto a stool. The bartender called everybody Joe. "What can I get you?"

Nate leaned in. "You know anyone I can see about some goods?" he whispered. He looked at the bartender for signs that he'd crossed a line but didn't see any. "Edible goods?"

The bartender assumed an easy pose, leaning on the bar with both hands spread wide. "'Fraid we don't have that on tap tonight. Might want to head over to Willy's, down behind the ballpark. Fred there, he'll be able to help you. Just tell him I sent you." The bartender wiped down the space in front of Nate.

"Thanks," said Nate as he tossed a tip on the bar.

Minutes later, Nate stepped into Willy's. A black-hatted cowboy that answered to the name Fred tended bar. When Nate told him what he needed, Fred nodded to a staircase in the back of his bar. Nate waded through a slough of cigar smoke, card tables, and loose women. He knew he looked out of place in his jeans and t-shirt, but he didn't mind. As he climbed the steps, he engaged the cloaking program he'd designed. He smiled, congratulating himself. It was one of his better pieces of work.

The stairway led to a long hallway of closed doors. Fred had held up two fingers with his left hand, so Nate walked to the second door on the left, opened it, and stepped inside.

Two men sat at a table in front of a map. "What the hell?" one of them said as he snapped his head to look at the wide open door. "Who's there?"

"It's nothing," said the other, waving it off. "Just a software glitch. Sometimes stuff like that just happens."

The first man looked dubious. "Stuff like that doesn't just happen," he said. He got up and checked the hall, then closed the door.

On his way back to the table, Nate ensnared him.

"Whoa! Where did you come from? What are you doing in here?" the man demanded. "This is a private room."

"I'm interested in a trade. Food for this," Nate said, gesturing with his hands at the space around him.

"For what? What the hell are you talking about? Who let you in here?" The man was getting angrier. "Can you believe this guy?" He looked over to his friend, but the other man appeared to be oblivious.

"He can't hear you," said Nate.

"Dude, get back in here!" the second man called out. "Let's finish this up before it's tomorrow already."

"Can't see you either. It's a cloaking algorithm. It's got other features too, but for now, it shouldn't be hard for me to convince you that this"—he gestured again—"is better than hiding out in a virtual brothel. And a cheesy theme-park one at that." He eyed the lace curtains, the rumpled quilt on the bed, and the hay poking out of the mattress. "With this, you can make plans anywhere, anytime, completely undetected."

The man narrowed his eyes. "Exactly what is it that you want from me?"

A little while later, Nate left Willy's flying. He'd gotten Angela exactly what she needed. And he'd had fun doing it. Busting in on those guys, seeing the looks on their faces, the whole thing had him revved up. He could still feel it and didn't want it to stop. Instead of disconnecting, he ducked into a club he'd never been to before. He sat down next to the prettiest girl he could find and made them both disappear.

3

Angela sat alone in the quietest NArcCafe in her living complex. The other breakfasters had long since moved on, heading out for a Sunday afternoon of diversion from the long work-week. She had spent the morning searching the digital library system for clues about old-ways food. She didn't find much. The public libraries had digital copies of all books published after 2020. But before that, collections were spotty. Some copies were stored in old formats that she didn't have a reader for. Others just hadn't been scanned yet. Even some digitized books were scarce. The ones with low hit counts got aged out of the indexes to speed the searches. She would need to request retrieval and possibly conversion. One of the more exclusive university libraries had bound copies of books about food, but it would take days to get approval to access them. She was filling out her fifth archive request form when Nate pinged her. "Got something," he wrote.

Molly's appeal to him the night before had bugged her, but at this point any help was welcome. She snapped her computer into monocle-mode and attached it to her headgear so it hovered just above her eye. Nate picked up her video connection almost immediately. Angela noted that he looked ruffled, as if he'd just rolled out of bed. "What've you got?" she asked him.

"Good stuff. But first, did you know that Sinksy didn't cheat that much? Only once a month or so."

"How d'you know that?"

"I went back and read her comments. Marty, right? In the first one, she said she started to feel sick and decided to stop Cheating. She didn't want to interrupt the NArc's efforts to make her better. In the second one, she asks straight out, is it possible for Cheating to make you sick two weeks later? So it sounds like there was a pretty big gap between her Cheating and her illness."

Angela frowned. She'd reread the comments too, but she'd missed these. They weren't in her recycle bin. She must have approved them, so they were still attached to her online articles. "That does sound odd. A parasite could take that much time to affect someone. So that doesn't really rule out Cheating as the cause of her illness, does it? I'm guessing the NArc would have fixed it eventually. That is, if Cheating hadn't killed her in the end."

"Probably," replied Nate, but he didn't look convinced.

Angela cocked an eyebrow. "Do you have another theory?"

"It's a long shot, but the NArc could have been at fault. I used to code the diagnostics, remember? Coders make mistakes."

"So you think a software bug killed her?"

"No, maybe it just made her feel not so good. I mean, she might not have been sick at all. People are so used to feeling well, they overreact when things are the slightest bit off."

"If that were the case, though, wouldn't lots of people be feeling not so good? I mean, there aren't separate diagnostics for each and every person, are there?" As she said this, Angela was trying to remember exactly how the NArc did work. She'd done a story once on some mathematical reduction that allowed the NArc code to run in real-time, but the details hadn't stuck. One big leap had been Fast Genomics, technology that didn't just read a person's genes, it also watched them as they activated and deactivated. She remembered a scientist explaining it by likening old-fashioned genomics to knowing the frequency of a radio station. "Modern genomics is like *listening* to the station while watching the equalizer bars bounce," she'd said. Angela also remembered her reaction: Radio? The other big leap was Nanobiognostics, massively parallel yet nanoscopic detectors that screened blood, spit, urine, and breath for signs of illness. But the logic that brought all of this data together had always mystified her.

"Good point. I'm actually not sure how it all fits together, now that I think about it." Nate shrugged again. "Just thought I should mention the possibility. It's better to know the limitations than to make assumptions. Anyway, want to hear what I found?"

"Yes. Definitely." She paused. "Should we be on a secure line or something?"

"No, I'm not worried about that. The main checkpoint is the NArc—it's always spying on us. As long as we—and mainly I mean you—stay in line health-wise, we'll be fine. Unless of course you decide to become a dealer."

"Yeah, I can see that happening. Alright, tell me what you've got."

Nate had learned about two underground portals that had food drops coming up in the next week. At first, Angela was excited by the breakthrough. But as Nate spoke, her excitement waned. "My source says there are hundreds of pick-up and drop-off sites," Nate explained. "Everything is individually arranged. It's a loose network. There's no hierarchy. Just people trading with people. It's hard to break in unless you make a friend."

Angela groaned. This was bad news. Her success stories in the past had come from scaling organizations from the bottom up. How would she climb a network that had no top? "Where'd you get the info?" she asked, groping for some insight.

"A couple guys willing to trade information for one of those cloaking programs I wrote. Seemed solid," he replied.

"Wait a minute. Why was this so easy for you when I didn't know where to start?"

Nate messed up his hair, thinking about the question. "People like you and Molly, no offense, but you don't know what regular people are like. You spend all your time with scientists. NArcists. Regular people, well, they aren't as strict. So maybe they talk about Cheating, and that conversation leads to another and they eventually just find a contact. Someone in their circle. Regular people just know who to ask."

At first, Angela *was* offended. But then, he had gotten in and she hadn't. Besides, she knew he ran in a lot of different circles. He knew all kinds of people. Maybe, if she stuck with him on this, she'd eventually know too. "Okay Sherlock. I get your point. Now tell me about these drops."

Nate explained that on Monday morning in an isolated neighborhood across town, the Cheaters would be trading cheeses and meats smuggled in from Vermont. The idea of food from Vermont made her feel good. The state had seceded during the Migration. Now it was one of the few places left that maintained the Old Ways culture. Its farmers sustained themselves with their crops. A whole country still ate this food every day. *Legally*. If it really was dangerous, she rationalized, it wouldn't be legal. Even in Vermont.

The drop after that, Tuesday afternoon in her own neighborhood, involved illegal Outsider goods. Rumor had it that lots of these foods were contaminated with metals, bacteria, and genetic material from the industrial crops outside the city walls. The one thing she felt confident about was that the engineered crops were well controlled. She had seen them. Their color-coded domes dotted the landscape Outside and housed huge plantations of pharma, fuel, and industrial replacements as well as mass-produced engineered grains for the NArc. New agriculture was one of the biggest businesses in the country and it was run almost completely outside the walls of the urban network. But as far as the other concerns, she wasn't so sure. Even though the country had stopped burning coal and oil, metals most likely still polluted the water and soil. And even with the elimination of animal farms, the bacteria the old factory farm lagoons had spawned probably still thrived.

She knew that eating Outsider food was a big risk. A risk she didn't want to take if she didn't have to. I need to get in on Monday, she thought.

Angela watched the taxi slip away from the curb, its electric engine inaudible over the sound of its tires on the concrete surface. The ride had cost a small fortune, but it was the only way to get to this part of town this early in the morning. Alone on the sidewalk, she tried to remember what it had been like back when road use was free and public transit wasn't. Rushed and hectic were the words that came to mind.

Moonlight peeked between the buildings, tracing long shadows and painting the sidewalk with pale light. Angela shivered and tightened her scarf against the wind. She wasn't used to being outdoors, let alone before daylight.

She trained her thoughts on her destination. As she walked the deserted streets, clenching and unclenching her gloved hands for warmth, she used her headset to navigate. The image projected into her eye showed a simplified but accurate sketch of the streets and instructed her at each turn. Soon, the route took her off the main surfaceway and into a maze of narrow streets lined with old brownstones.

As Angela approached an intersection just few blocks from her destination, she noticed a cluster of people lined up along the sidewalk. She craned her neck to see what they were waiting for. Maybe a NArcCafe? But she'd never seen one that wasn't open 24-hours a day before. Then again, she'd also never walked this many blocks without seeing one at all. Still unable to see the doorway, she smiled and turned to the people in line. But her smile quickly faded. One glance revealed a man's pouchy eyes and a woman with yellowing skin. Even though not everyone looked ill, Angela quickened her step anyway. She passed quietly by the ragged, the aged, and the afflicted, trying not to call attention to herself, then hurried across the street. Curiosity made her look back at what they were all waiting for. But she already knew. This was one of the neighborhoods that the NArc had left behind. These people were waiting for handouts of NArc scraps, random bits of nutrition and lumps of sustenance. People outside of the health insurance network didn't have chips in their wrists, so they weren't linked to the NArc's prescribed Nutrition. These people had no hope for preventing or treating their ills. And since the NArc had all but replaced the diagnostic and treatment ends of the medical system, there was no clinical infrastructure to keep them from falling through the cracks.

When Angela reached the midpoint of the next block she stopped to catch her breath. She stared for a moment at the trim silhouette cast before her by the rising sun. Then a chirp from her headset reminded her that the drop site wouldn't remain open all day. So Angela checked her map. With only a block to go, she stowed her gear. The side streets had become uneven enough that she needed both eyes to keep her footing.

The shop appeared just as Nate had described it. The FootPad stood three doors down from a quiet intersection.

Above the door hung a grimy neon sign that looked as if it hadn't worked for decades. Just before the door, an old brickwork alley led to a side entrance. A delivery vehicle obscured the door.

Nate's informant had said that inside the door and across the stock room, she would see a grey metal door to the far right. Knock twice fast, pause, then twice slowly, he'd instructed. They'll be watching through a peep hole. A voice will say, "The store is closed. What brings you here at this hour?" He told her to respond: "chow" and to raise her left hand, holding a folded $10 bill.

She flipped open a compact and glanced behind her. She was alone on the block. She removed her gloves, placed them carefully in her bag, and pulled a bill from the side-pocket. She turned down the alley and Bam! Two steps off the street she ran head-on into a petite woman with a full tote bag over her shoulder. The woman stumbled back but caught herself just as Angela tried to reach out and grab her. "I'm so sorry. Are you okay?" breathed Angela.

The woman wrenched her arm away. "Fine," she mumbled as she scurried off.

Angela straightened herself and resumed her march, this time creeping a bit more cautiously past the truck. At the bumper, she peered around back and into the open doorway.

Instead of a deserted stockroom there were five or six people chatting as if they were at a cocktail party. She snapped back her head and froze. She wasn't prepared for this. With a quick breath, she walked around the bumper and stepped into the room, stopping just after crossing the threshold. Her ten dollar bill hung limp between her thumb and damp palm as she stood there, dumb, waiting for a cue.

The group continued its chatter as the seconds crawled past. Finally a reedy young man broke away. "The store is closed. What brings you here at this hour?" he asked casually.

Lifting her hand, Angela croaked a feeble "chow."

"This must be your first time here. C'mon in. I'll show you the ropes." He put his hand on her shoulder and guided her toward the grey metal door. "I'm Sean," he said, smiling. She smiled back.

But as she followed him through the doorway, her smile faded. The room smelled. She couldn't place the odor, but horses came to mind. Two women in aprons were deep in conversation on the far side of a long rectangular table. On the table, in between a metal box and a propped up chalkboard, was the source of the smell. A plate of something runny and yellow and the remains of a mangled baguette.

"Today's your lucky day. We've got a bunch of great cheeses. We've broken into the Teleme, of course. Who wouldn't?" he laughed. "Feel free to try some. We've also got some great Elk sausage and a few Reds left." He waved at one of the women behind the counter. "Millie, you still got those Rhodies?"

The woman nodded but kept talking. "She'll be with you in a minute," Sean assured her. "Whatever you're looking for, just ask." He leaned over the table and patted one of the coolers, its size diminished by the imposing shelves of synthetic shoes behind it. "We may not have it in stock today, but we can get it. The charm of the underground—you can get anything you want, just not *when* you want it," he joked, grabbing a chunk of bread. He used it to scoop up a wad of cheese and popped it into his mouth. "Thanks for coming in," he added, then retreated to the entrance hall.

Though Sean had treated her like a trusted friend, Angela felt more like an outsider than she ever had before. She had no idea what to do. She didn't dare try the Tele-whatever on the counter. It looked as if it had never been refrigerated and the bread had been manhandled by several too many people.

She turned her attention to the chalkboard and looked up at the scribbled list. None of the words made any sense. *PTomme; Blythedale C.; Grf. Ched. 7mo/2yr; TCBrie; RIRed; Pcs.* Were these servings or whole dishes? And of what? She wasn't sure how much to order or how much any of it might cost.

Whatever hazy visions Angela may have had about this drop, she hadn't expected this. She hadn't expected to encounter an alien culture complete with its own language and inside jokes. With its own kind of impenetrable sophistication.

Behind her, a man came in and approached the table. Out of the corner of her eye, Angela saw him dip into the pool of cheese. "Mmmm," she heard him say. The woman, Millie, made an agreeable noise and asked him what he wanted. Angela strained to listen as he rattled off a list, but she couldn't match his words to the scribbles. Before she knew it, Millie had assembled a package for him and he had left.

"What can I get for you?" Millie asked with a voice that wasn't as friendly as Sean's.

"Ummm…," Angela started. Millie shifted her weight to one hip. "I'm sorry," she finally admitted, "but I'm new to this. Could you recommend something?"

The woman's eyes narrowed slightly, but then she shrugged, opened a cooler, and pulled out a small round wrapped in white paper. "This one's mild," she said. "It's a good introduction." She pulled a short baguette from below the table. "Try it with this. You can just break pieces off," she said, pointing to the mangled loaf on the table. "What've you got to offer?"

Angela looked at her quizzically. "I, uh, I only have cash. Is that okay?"

Millie smiled and nodded. "Yup. Cash or barter. We make all kinds of deals. Let's see, that'll be sixteen fifty."

Angela paid Millie and thanked her, then stuffed the items into her bag.

On the way out, Sean intercepted her. Still smiling, he asked her, "Did you get what you needed?"

Angela blushed and looked down at the ground. "I should tell you that this is not just my first time here. It's my first time. Ever." She looked up at him. "I should have told you earlier, but I guess I was overwhelmed. By the smell and, well, everything. I've been trying to learn. I just don't know that much about the Cheater world yet."

Sean's face darkened, and a heavy silence filled the room. Again he placed a hand on Angela's shoulder, but his grip was now firm. He led her to the exit. "I'm sure whoever told you about this place will give you another shot, but next time, do your homework." Now a safe distance from the others, he whispered, "It's Foodies, not Cheaters." Angela stood in the alley and watched the door shut.

When Angela got home, she pulled the illicit goods out of her bag. She put them on her desk and sat staring at them. She decided to start with the bread, but it was too hard to bite into and she didn't have a knife. So she tried to pull it apart. When she was done wrestling with it she was left with a pile of crumbs and two flattened pieces. How had she managed to crush the whole thing?

She bit into one of the chunks. The sharp crust stabbed at the roof of her mouth as she pulled at the stretchy insides with her teeth. She closed her eyes and chewed. She scratched her head. Good, I guess, she thought.

She eyed the cheese. She had to open it. But that smell. What if this cheese is no different? I won't be able to hide an odor like that from Molly. Or my neighbors. And I won't be able to eat it. Anything with that kind of stink can't be good for you.

She pulled open the white paper wrapper and flattened it on the desk. No smell yet. Taking a crusty piece of the baguette, she poked at the dusty white disk. The rind broke. The creamy white insides weren't as runny as the Tele-stuff. In fact, they held together nicely. And the smell was sweeter. Definitely not as overpowering. Mimicking Sean, she scooped out the insides and popped the cheesy bread in her mouth. Not bad, she thought. At least, not nearly as bad as she'd feared.

When she balled up the package to toss it, she realized it wasn't empty. At the bottom of the bag was a single sugar cookie. Angela held it up between two fingers and eyed it with suspicion. She hadn't ordered it. Had it been packed by mistake? Or was it some kind of attempt to get her addicted and coming back for more? She dared to smell it and instantly felt herself salivating. She hesitated, then took a bite. A wave of sensation swept over her—butter, sugar, a hint of spice—followed by a vivid flash of memory. Her mother in the kitchen. Herself standing on a chair. Both of them giddy. Before them on the counter, a tray of cookies still too hot to eat. Angela's eyes welled up. She had been ready for the unexpected flavors, but not for the visions. Before her mother's unhealthy diet and not so resilient genes conspired to take her away from her young daughter, she had one surefire remedy for skinned knees and hurt feelings. She had one reward for good grades and a cleaned room. Freshly baked cookies. They had tasted just like this one.

The next morning, day four of the seven days Stew had given her, Angela walked into the old concrete building and hit the elevator's up-arrow again. She had another meeting with Lieutenant Henry Potente, Food Police. She wanted to know why getting food had been so easy for her, even if she couldn't have done it without Nate's help. She wanted to know, if Cheating was so rampant, why weren't they cracking down? Why weren't they investigating the Sinsky death? When she walked into Potente's tattered cubicle, the first thing he did was shake his head.

"It's Tuesday morning, and I'm not happy to see you," he said.

Angela smiled. She liked Potente despite his gruff exterior. She could see in his eyes that this tough cop bit was just an act. "Do you show up for work grouchy every morning?" she asked.

He reclined in his chair and looked back at her. "Ever since Food's been a beat," he said. His eyes crinkled but the rest of his face remained stern. "I heard about your gaff at the FootPad, by the way. Impressive, how far you've gotten already."

Angela's eyes widened. "How did you hear about that?" she asked. "And why?" She began to worry that Potente might slap her with a ticket right then and there.

"Settle down. It's just coincidence. We had an officer peek in as a routine checkpoint and good old Sean accused him of sending in a new undercover cop. And an incompetent one, at that."

Angela reddened. Then frowned. "Wait. You sent in a cop who talked to Sean. But no one got arrested? They're trafficking illegal food! Why didn't the cop take them in?"

Potente nodded. "You're doing much better with the Q&A today. You're a quick learner." Potente shuffled some papers around his desk, evading the question, but Angela didn't budge. She wanted an answer. He finally relented. "Look, we spend most of our time raiding Junk labs. The kids can't get enough of the stuff. It's an epidemic. We're seeing more and more kids in the emergency room. More and more kids with chronic diseases. It's getting so it's just like it was in the old days. That's the city priority. In fact, we've got a new campaign in schools. Trying to show kids what the Junk's made of. A chemical stew fried up in a big pot of lard. Flabbies with greasy hair shaking off the excess fat. Scares them out of their pantsuits," he joked.

"So you just let these Foodies get away with it. I don't understand why. They're Cheaters too. I've heard that their food is more dangerous than the Junk."

Potente sat back in his chair and regarded her over tented fingers. "Off the record?"

She nodded.

"Ok then. It's not a question of what's more dangerous," he finally said. "It's not that simple. There are a lot of things we worry about. There are a lot of bad guys we do go after. But if the food isn't tainted and they aren't shooting each other, we're not gonna get our panties in a bunch over a few folks smuggling in salads and baguettes. There are better ways to keep things in check than arresting people."

"But what about Martine Sinsky? According to the news report—and to your statement—she died eating this food. So it *is* tainted." Angela waited for his reaction.

Potente cupped his chin in his hand and looked at her. "I expected you to give up easier. But since you didn't, I have to warn you about what you're getting into. You are chasing after an organization. A gang. They operate an underground business that plays by different rules than you're used to. You need to tread their turf carefully."

"Right. They're a gang. A mob so dangerous that you and your officers don't do anything to stop them. I'll keep that in mind." Whether she liked Potente or not, she'd had enough of his excuses.

"Not everyone is who they say they are. Not everything is what you think it is."

"Well, that's helpful," she spat. As Potente leaned back in his chair, she realized she had alienated her only contact. Yet she couldn't hold her tongue. "Whatever it is you're not telling me, I'm going to find it. I'm not just going to go away."

Potente nodded. "I know. Just keep your eyes open, Angela. And your mind."

She headed straight from Potente's office back to her own neighborhood. Nate had told her about two drops and the second window was opening down the street from her apartment in a few hours.

Nate had tried to cheer her up after the cheese fiasco. He listed all the things she knew now that she hadn't before. But she knew it wouldn't be enough for Stew. For him to let her continue, she needed a contact. So far she hadn't made any friends. It hadn't helped that Nate didn't tell her to call them Foodies. When she confronted him about that on Monday afternoon, after she'd convinced herself that the cheese she'd eaten wasn't going to kill her, he just laughed. "Geez Ange, I thought everyone knew they were Foodies. You know it's a throwback term, right? I thought it just went without saying." She'd heard him trying not to laugh. "I can't believe you called them Cheaters. A whole room full of them. On their turf."

It still riled her to think about it. But then, Nate had given her some helpful advice, too. He'd explained how he'd gotten the information in the first place. "You need to try to connect with these people. On their terms. Offer them something they might be interested in," he'd advised. So she'd come up with a plan.

When Angela got close to the drop, she switched off the music she'd been listening to. She didn't bother to stow away the headgear, deciding that she'd look more out of place here without it. She followed the crowd, each person splitting his or her attention between moving with the flow and monitoring the sights and sounds piped into their heads. Some attended conference calls as they walked, making chopping motions with their hands for emphasis as they talked into space.

Without breaking her stride, Angela stepped into a pharmacy and up to the sign-in window. The attendant asked her what brought her in today. Angela replied according to Nate's instructions. "I'm feeling run down. I need something special. Perhaps a natural remedy?" The attendant handed her a number and told her to wait.

She took a seat and passed the time trying but failing to distinguish the Cheaters from those waiting for their monthly scans. She'd always thought of the scans as a stop-gap, just in case the NArc-injected nanobots in her bloodstream missed something like the early signs of a growing tumor or a deteriorating joint. She shuddered to think that someday she would leave her scan with a referral to one of the regen hospitals for parts replacements.

"Number 57," called an attendant. Angela hesitated. "57," she called out again. Angela slowly stood.

The expressionless attendant led Angela into a small chamber with bare white walls, white tiled floors, a second doorway, and one hard black chair. She sat for ten minutes, waffling between running away and staying. She wondered if the pass phrase had worked. Part of her expected one of Potente's guys to burst in and take her away. She still couldn't believe they never arrested anyone for illegal food trafficking.

Angela was about to stand up and pace when a woman walked in and shut the door behind her. Her heels clicked as she walked across the room. She handed Angela a clipboard and said, "Mark what you want. Limit 5 pounds. Pick-up's at the window."

Angela scanned the sheet and breathed a sigh of relief. Beets, garlic, carrots, asparagus, greenhouse herbs—a list she could understand! She checked off a few things that sounded exciting. Beets, herbs, and some garlic. As she handed the sheet back to the attendant, she smiled and tried to make a connection. "I'm working on a collection of recipes to share with other Foodies. I wonder if you could help me. Do you have a favorite recipe? Or is there someone that I could talk to that might have some ideas to share?"

As Angela spoke, her heart sank. Her words ricocheted off the woman's sharp angles and bounced ineffectively around the tiny chamber. The woman folded her arms across her chest and narrowed her eyes into two charcoal slits framed by a helmet of hair. Her milky skin blended into her starched white lab coat. As the last syllable faded, the woman clicked back across the room, her face an impenetrable mask.

Angela sat, immobile, staring across the empty room. She waited, hoping that the woman would send someone out to talk to her. Minutes passed. Finally, the door she entered through opened and the blank-faced attendant leaned in. "Your prescription is ready," she said, gesturing back down the hall to the waiting area. Angela dragged herself out of the chair, her hips and knees stiff, and hobbled down the corridor.

Angela had been dying to unwrap her package the whole trip home. As soon as she arrived, she sat down at her desk and ripped off the paper wrapper. She pulled out the vegetables and searched the rubble, hoping to find another surprise, another thread to connect her with her memories of a past long forgotten.

But it contained only what she'd ordered: a pile of ruddy globes, a bouquet of wilted greens, and one head of garlic. She stared at the lifeless vegetables and tried to imagine cooking the bundle of beets. She poked her finger at it, dislodging a clump of dirt onto her desktop. I'd have to wash them first, she decided, crinkling her nose. Then what? Boil them? What about the leaves, she thought, lifting them then letting them drop. She sniffed the bundle. It had a sweetish smell. She also detected a hint of decay. What a hassle, she thought. Why would anyone bother?

Even though Angela's mother used to cook, she'd never brought home raw ingredients like this from the store. Cans and shrink-wrapped containers had filled her bags. Of course, she knew that those foods had started out raw and unwashed. By the time food reached people's plates back then, it had traveled a long road. From "farm to fork" her food texts called it. The NArc had changed all that. The new road, a much shorter and more direct one, went from nutrient to nutrition. By design, Neerfoods produced specific nutrients in abundance. Today's engineered tomatoes—the textbook example—carry as much lycopene and vitamin C as they can handle. The automated harvest funnels the foods into a processing stream that converts everything into uniform media—pastes, syrups, juices—that the NArc uses to infuse nutrition into a meal. The path isn't as short as the one this beet traveled, she thought. But then, this beet isn't even remotely ready for her fork.

She looked at her illicit goods again. What compelled someone as sick as Marty to eat something like this? Frowning, she picked up the freshest and cleanest looking beet leaf and took a bite. She instantly gagged on the bitter taste and gritty texture and ran to the bathroom to rinse out her mouth. Disgusted, Angela left the food on her desk and, after scrubbing her hands, headed down to the NArcCafe. As she picked up her personalized meal, a vitamin-infused starch wrap filled with Neermeat, fiber, and a bioactive blend, she wondered again what it was that moved people to Cheat nowadays. Things were so different now. Why would anyone choose the laborious, inefficient, and chancy Cheater world over the simplicity of the NArc?

Without a contact, without some sort of guide to the underground, her story was as dead as Martine Sinsky.

4

Angela reported to the office again late Wednesday afternoon. She had two days left before the deadline Stew had set for her, and she had to impress him with her interim report. If she did, he might be able to coax Marcus into giving her more time. She felt good about her progress and knew that if she had one more week, she might just crack this Cheater network. If she did that, who knew what stories she might find.

Stew listened as Angela reported her progress. When she finished, Stew blinked, his face inscrutable. Angela braced herself.

Finally, he spoke. "Interesting. So this is supposed to be a story about someone named Sinsky who met her end by this food somehow. Sinsky is your hook into a series on the dangers of Cheating. Sounds like you've found a lot of information about the food network. But what more have you got about the dead woman? If I recall, that news bit was scant."

She nodded and filled him in. "There hasn't been an update on Sinsky in the news. The doctors who saw her just after she died didn't have much to add either."

The doctors had told her food poisoning happens more often than people think. "Most people just get better on their own after a day or so," one doctor had told her. "With some cases though, it progresses too quickly. There's nothing we can do." They'd mentioned that it was curious that one person got sick when others didn't. Typically, they get groups wandering in with milder cases. But they'd shrugged it off. It wasn't their job to investigate. Angela knew all too well that the police, who should have investigated it, weren't going to.

"After hearing all of this, I decided that I needed to focus on getting underground," Angela explained. "That's where the information is. The Foodies are the people who know about these bugs. They self-police themselves. They know what the real risks are. They'll know what happened to Sinsky." At least, I hope someone will, she thought to herself.

"Okay," said Stew slowly, rubbing his temples. "It sounds like you could use some help. Did you try talking to Frank on the crime desk?"

It seemed that Stew wished Angela would just go away. She ignored the sinking feeling in her stomach and tried to to re-engage him by nodding enthusiastically. "I did. Frank connected me with a cop on the Food Beat. I've talked to him a couple times now. Apparently they don't crack down on the Foodies because they just aren't that big of a problem compared with the Junkies. He also said it isn't simple, which tells me I'm onto something interesting. And I'm starting to get inside. Word of me had gotten back to him. It's a question of time. Which is what I need more of if I'm going to break this thing."

Stew sighed. Angela could tell he didn't like the direction this was going. The sigh was not a good sign.

"The Sinsky thing was a decent but now stale hook," said Stew, uncharacteristically thinking it through out loud. "And Frank's food crime stories never caught on, either. But then, Frank's stories never mentioned dark alleys or secret passwords. This bit about the pharmacy intrigues me. I go there for my monthly scans. I trust the people who work there. Now I wonder if, while I'm laying there in the scanner, people are trading tomatoes in the exam room next door." He shook his head, but then stood up and left the room.

Angela fidgeted for a few minutes in the empty office, then spied a framed photograph on Stew's desk. She turned it slightly. The woman staring back at her had large, childlike eyes and a perky haircut that defied her age. More than once, over a few beers, Stew had told Angela his stories about Melanie. During the years before the Migration had started, but after the more severe climate shifts had begun, he and Melanie had tried to make their weather mishaps fun. Miss Adventure, his wife had called herself. Instead of griping when sudden storms flooded their streets, they'd stayed in swanky hotels and pretended this was their first visit to the city. One time, they paid a water taxi to navigate the streets and drop them off—"As if we lived in Venice," Melanie had said. He'd smiled when he told the story and Angela had noticed that his hand moved, as if his whole body were remembering the way he'd helped his wife climb into their third story window. She'd never been able to think of him or her city the same way since.

Angela turned the picture a little more to get a better look at this woman that she'd never met. She knew it still hurt him to think of her. From the way he looked at the picture, she could tell that it was the kind of hurt he didn't want to let go of. Every time he told her a story about Melanie—the way they met one night playing barroom trivia, the foot of snow that fell on their springtime wedding, the pumpkin pie she made with peanut butter in the crust—his eyes got glassy. Angela felt sad too, but a sympathetic kind of sad. She'd had plenty of boyfriends, but she had never felt as close to any of them as Stew had been to Melanie. She wondered what it was that made two people decide to marry. And she wondered if whatever it was would ever happen to her.

She was about to reach out and pick up the picture when Stew walked back in. He leaned against the doorjamb and scratched his chin.

"Do you remember when we covered the NArc Mandate?" he asked. Not waiting for an answer, he continued. "We covered it and no one cared. It barely registered. The state criminalized eating, and no one blinked an eye." He shook his head. "You were crushed. You'd made such a big splash with that Neermeat story, documenting the first sustainable and edible artificial meat, I think you expected to just keep ratcheting up. But you didn't stay down for long. That flop fired you up. You bounced back and took the NArc head on when they announced their prohibition plans."

He was talking about the biggest stories of Angela's career. The first Neermeat. The NArc Mandate. And "Twenty-First Century Prohibition."

By the time of the Mandate in 2050, the NArc had matured into a personalized nutrition delivery system. One-time typing had turned into real-time monitoring, made possible by injected nanobots and implanted chips. The bots watch everything that's watchable and record the changes. At each mealtime, people scan in. The NArc reads their chips and whips up personalized meals—meals made possible by the advent of locally-manufactured Neerfoods, like Neermeat.

In the first years after the mandate, people still cheated, but the NArc kept them coming back by keeping them well. Plus it devised a progressive penalty scheme modeled after traffic violations. Cheaters racked up fines and points on their health care records. Repeat offenders faced Food School. Tedious, uncomfortable, and humiliating, Food School made you pay in tears.

The NArc mandate had required everyone to stay within the national health bounds. The government set the standards and appointed the NArc to enforce them. She had thought people would celebrate the story, almost like a war victory, but instead the public shrugged. Voluntary adoption of the NArc had already brought the country back from the brink—children obese and chronically ill, bankruptcy looming over the healthcare system, food recalls leaving supermarket shelves empty. The public saw the Mandate as a natural, uneventful next step.

A few years later, though, the NArc overstepped it's bounds.

"I can't remember how you found out about that ban. Some bartender, was it?" asked Stew.

"Yeah, I was chatting with one of the bartenders in my living complex. He had heard a rumor from a brewer he knew out west."

She remembered the story well. After the thirties, a decade that saw deaths from food poisoning triple, people started to welcome government intervention. No one protested when, throughout the forties, more and more old-ways foods joined the prohibition list. After the Migration, with the countryside abandoned and the farms converted into fuel, fiber, and pharma factories, animal protein had become scarce anyway. Hardly anyone missed it. Neermeat seamlessly took its place. As earth-bound vegetables—too often polluted with bacteria and too fuel-intensive to grow—phased out, engineered replacements phased in. With each new ban, an engineered equivalent appeared in its place.

Instead of balking at the changes, people reveled in the ingenuity. The way Angela told the story, no one had ever felt deprived.

But alcohol was different. The Nutritionists saw an alcohol ban as an obvious next step. Only they had no backfill plan.

Intoxication of any kind was on the chopping block. Angela couldn't imagine life without a drink with friends on a Friday. She imagined that her readers would feel the same. It didn't take her long to uncover the decades-old studies that showed the benefits of alcohol in moderation. The experts she interviewed called the old science archaic and dismissed the evidence. But Angela felt compelled to write about it anyway. She and Stew battled back and forth. He wanted at least one modern scientist to back her. But when the scientists refused to even discuss the old science with her, he relented.

"I took a big risk with that story," said Stew. "If I remember correctly, almost no one backed you. You wrote it on your own authority."

"And the historical record," she reminded him. And I was right, she thought. Because of her story, public pressure forced the scientists to take a hard look at the old data. A year later, results of modern studies made headline news: small amounts of alcohol are harmless. The evidence left the Nutritionists with no alternative. They folded the data into the NArc. Drinks are just another set of personalized rules in the database. A few too many, and the NArc prescribes a detox diet. Many too many and the fines and points stack up.

Angela could almost see the gears turning in Stew's head. He knew she could pull this new story off, but it meant taking another big risk. "Take it," she silently willed to him. "We've got nothing to lose."

Stew scratched his chin again and nodded. "Let's talk again on Friday," he said.

By late Friday afternoon, Angela's headgear reported that she had walked ten miles and burned 1000 calories. She'd spent all of Thursday and most of Friday walking the streets and looking for signs. But in all that time, she had seen only two Foodie markings. One was scrawled on a concrete sidewalk in front of a vacant lot. The other was on a door that looked as if it had been sealed shut for a decade. Though she suspected they were decoys, she staked them out anyway, but didn't see a soul approach or depart. She revisited the shoe store and wandered the surrounding streets hoping to catch a glimpse of Sean, the only person who seemed as if he would help her. He never appeared. She went back to the pharmacy, but no one there looked familiar.

She was ready to admit defeat as her time had all but run out. Until Nate called.

"I've got one," he said into her earpiece, catching her on her walk home. "Seven tonight on the western edge of the city. But I don't like it."

"What do you mean you don't like it?" Angela walked faster, hoping to get to someplace quieter than the busy skywalk.

"My informants have been clamming up. I guess they don't like unescorted newbies at the drops. You've got people kind of freaked out. Everyone's trying to figure out who leaked the info. Thing is, the guy who told me about this drop seemed eager to pass on the details. Too eager." Nate paused, then cautioned, "It might be some kind of setup."

Angela didn't like the sound of it either, but she had no choice. If she failed tonight, it would all be over.

She did an about face and headed back to the subway station. As she walked, she scanned the map Nate sent. She calculated that the 6 pm maglev—the high-speed express trains servicing the outskirts of town—would leave her time to spare. Just as she finished working it out, the subway train arrived. She filed in and found standing room near the door. She lifted her toes, trying to work out the knots in her calves. The train screeched around a bend, its modern technology straining against the limits of the country's first subway tunnels.

She arrived at the maglev station at the height of rush hour. The place bustled with passengers heading to their homes out west. The local city stretched thirty miles from the hub in all directions save eastward into the ocean. An old highway that used to ring the city now formed its outermost border. During the Migration, people from miles around—from cities, towns, and rural areas—flooded the space inside the ring and left the Outside nearly vacant. As they did, they abandoned their possessions, shedding their 3000-square-foot lifestyles and adapting to snug, minimalist, city living. She had never understood the lure of the suburbs when they existed and understood even less the desire to live in the urban sprawl of the outer city. It lacked the character and basic amenities of City Central, like skywalks and tunnels. Sure, the apartments were larger, and some even had nature views or outdoor spaces, but residents also had to go outside every time they wanted to go somewhere. In fact, the commuters shuffling in front of her seemed outfitted as if they were headed out on a grand expedition. It just didn't make sense, she thought as she stepped onto the waiting train.

As Nate instructed, Angela got off at the last stop. The modern station seemed oversized for what lay beyond. It seemed the Migration had not quite finished here. In between the modern living complexes were decaying spaces and old-fashioned houses filled with the forsaken stuff of lifestyles unsustainable.

Outside the station, Angela followed Nate's map. She walked past makeshift stuff stores hawking the Migration's detritus, their insides resembling long-neglected attics, with stacks of boxes packed three layers deep. Through grimy windows she could see that access to the rooms inside was often completely blocked by old appliances, window sashes, and furniture.

Having arrived early for her rendezvous, she ducked into a store and mustered the courage to ask about old food books. The proprietor, an elderly nearsighted woman, was friendly enough, but not very helpful. She led Angela to a pile of water-damaged textbooks. At the next store, the owner showed her a rusty pile of cast iron pans.

Angela walked into the last store on the block—her designated meeting place—feeling a little more relaxed after braving these other places. She spotted the owner huddled in his office fiddling with the dials of a shoebox-sized metal device. To her ears, the box produced little more than static and the occasional sound of a foreign and oddly distant voice. He hunkered down and pretended not to see her as she moved past the door. Nate's instructions said that an agent would greet her inside, so she assumed the owner wasn't her contact. She looked around, but the three-room store appeared deserted. Finally here, her new-found courage deserted her and she felt a shiver zip up her spine. When her hands started trembling, she decided to try to distract herself by shopping. After poking around in the store's main room, she moved on to the back room and unearthed a box labeled "kitchen" from beneath a pile of antiquated electronic equipment and a bin of baggies filled with nuts and washers. In the box, she found a promising looking book. The author's name sounded familiar. She had a vague notion that this Julia Child person had lived somewhere near her own apartment building almost a century ago. Angela flipped through its pages and began to read.

Twenty minutes later, she looked up from her book. At some point she had sat down on the cushion of nuts and washers and leaned against the hulking copy machine behind it. She had completely lost track of time. She stood and looked frantically from room to room. She must have missed her agent. It was now fifteen minutes past her meeting time. Had he come and gone? Had he not seen her? She ducked her head into the owner's office. "Did you see anyone? I was supposed to meet a friend here."

He shook his head. "You're the first person I've seen in a week, lady. You gonna buy that book?"

Angela paced the storefronts, watching until all the doors had locked and the lights had dimmed. With little choice but to give up, she dragged herself back to the station and slumped into her seat on the maglev.

Dispirited as she was, she felt the book she'd bought tugging at her, begging her to read more. She pulled it from her bag and cradled the fragile volume for a moment, hoping to savor these last few minutes of her foolhardy adventure. She opened the book and let her new friend take her away, perhaps for the last time. The musty sweet smell of the paper transported her out of her seat and into a distant world over a century away, to a time when people faced daily trials of cooking, cleaning, and even living, as Julia had in Paris, without heat or phones. From page one, everything about this book—the weight of it in her hands, the rough fabric caressing her palms, the heady smell, the tales of culinary delights she could only pretend to comprehend—stirred her imagination. She closed her eyes for a minute and imagined the open air market places, with stacks of vegetables, cartons of eggs, and glass-fronted meat cases. Behind them, she saw vendors smiling, eager to sell the fruits of their labors. She tried in vain to imagine the smells or even the colors, textures, or flavors. Then, her stomach growled.

Embarrassed, she checked to see if anyone else had heard. That's when she noticed them. The eyes of a man across the aisle. They weren't watching her. Rather, they were glued to the cover of her book. When he looked up, she met his gaze through the gaps between the other riders. Just then, the train lurched to a stop and shuffling bodies obscured him. She craned her neck to find him. When the shuffling stopped, he was standing next to her.

"Enjoying your book?" he asked quietly, peering down at her. "It's one of my favorites." His voice broke the silence of the magnetically-propelled train and the lack of chatter between the other passengers.

Angela didn't know what to say. She stared, mouth agape, into the eyes of her contact. It had to be. Who else would go around wearing work boots and jeans and what looked like a leather jacket? Clothes like that that hadn't been sold in the States for decades. And who else but a Foodie would care about this book?

"I'm entranced," she finally said, keeping her voice down. The man was tall but didn't seem intimidating even though he loomed over her. She noticed that his skin appeared furrowed in a way that she had not seen in a long time. His dark eyes were set into crinkled purple lids and tucked under thick salt and pepper eyebrows that matched his hair. They seemed friendly, but with a touch of sadness. Hardly the eyes of the gangsters Potente warned me about, she thought. "Because of this book, I think I've missed an important meeting."

"Mmmm." he said vaguely, nodding while leaning on the back of the seat in front of her and glancing around the car. "What kind of meeting?"

"I was hoping to…to meet someone who would give me the chance to live like this," she said, patting the open pages. The words came easily, and as she heard them she knew they were true. "Just for one afternoon, to see what it was really like." It wasn't just the book, enticing as it was to read about Julia Child's discovery of food in France. It was that she'd thought she'd lost the chance to experience it at the very moment that she'd understood how much she wanted to. Stew had been right. Julia Child had taken her back. That cookie had taken her back. And she wasn't ready for the return journey to begin.

The train slowed to a stop and Angela stood up to let the person next to her out. When she sat back down again, the man nudged in next to her. "Mind if I join you?" he asked with a wry smile. He leaned in close to her and spoke in a hush. "I know you're trying to break into our network. I know who you are and I've read your work. So Angela, what are you after?"

"Usually I'm the one asking the questions," she whispered back, trying to buy herself some time to think. She decided to play it straight. There wasn't time for much else. "I'm interested in what happened to Martine Sinsky. She died a few days ago. They say she died from eating tainted illegal food. But the story has some holes in it, so I'm investigating."

"Why?" he asked. "A few holes in a Cheater's story doesn't seem like enough to get someone like you interested." She noted a hint of alcohol on his breath and smoke on his clothes and she started to wonder if Nate had been right to be worried about her meeting up with Cheaters on her own.

Angela sighed. "The thing is, she came to me for help. I'm ashamed to say that I didn't give her a minute's consideration. She had some strange ideas about the NArc, so I ignored her, but now I'm not so sure. I guess that, even though it's too late to help her, I'd like to find out what happened to her. Maybe it will help someone else out there." And maybe it will help me, too, she thought to herself.

"So do you have any ideas?"

"I know she died Cheating. At some point earlier she'd stopped Cheating because she felt sick. But then the NArc never made her feel better. I want to understand why. I want to understand the details. I thought putting a finger on the risks of Cheating would be easy, but so far, it hasn't been. So far, nothing has met my expectations. That usually means that my instincts are right. There's a story here. I just don't know what it is yet."

"Everything in life has its risks," he admitted, still quietly, but as the train emptied, he became less cautious. "No doubt Sinsky knew that…" Before Angela could ask if he knew her, he started talking again, but not about Sinsky. "Most Foodies agree that the risk is overblown. We eat this food for a lot of reasons. It's delicious, and we also believe it's safe and nutritious—"

Angela interrupted. "I'm not sure how you can say that. All of the evidence for the last twenty years points to the opposite. Neerfoods are designed to be nutritious. Balanced. *Personalized*. And they're guaranteed to be safe. Real food can't possibly win by those measures."

"Wow," the man chuckled, shaking his head. "Sounds like you've already got your scorecard filled out." He made a move to stand up but stopped short. "I thought journalists were supposed to be more open-minded."

Taken aback, Angela tried to recover. "I… No, I…I haven't worked it all out yet. This book makes the food sound wonderful. Sensuous. Irresistible. And tasting the food made me remember things…" Angela hesitated. Where was she going with this? She motioned for him to lean in closer. "This might not make sense," she started again, more slowly, "but I think my mother was a cheater. A cheater in her time. She rejected the NArc. She rejected diets. My dad begged her to join the NArc, back when it was just starting, but she wouldn't hear it. She loved to cook. She loved food. But food is what killed her. I was only ten and, well, I never forgave her for being so selfish." She looked at this stranger through teary eyes. He had sat back down and turned to face her, his knees jutting into the space between them, his chin enticingly close. Angela felt surprised at their sudden intimacy yet she didn't check herself. "I still don't understand what drove her to eat like that. And I don't understand what drove Martine Sinsky either. The food I brought home this past week? Well, I know it was limited, but it seems impossible to be able to craft the kind of Nutrition the NArc provides from these bits and pieces. It's just so much *work*. So I'm hoping to learn what it is that makes it worth the effort. And worth the risks."

The man eyed her for a minute and she held his gaze. She hadn't talked about her mother like that with anyone. Ever. It suddenly occurred to her that she didn't even know the man's name. When he reached inside his jacket, she tensed.

"It's okay," he said gently as he pulled out a pen and a card. He scribbled something on the back and handed it to her. "Meet me there at five tomorrow," he said. "I'll send instructions. For now, though, go home and get some rest. And tell your editor to give you one more day."

She looked down at the card in her hand. He'd scrawled an address on the back of an old-fashioned business card bearing his name: Josh Salter. When she looked up again, he smiled. She wanted to say something. To thank him. Or to find out how he found her. But the car had stopped again. A wave of commuters flooded the compartment and jostled for seats and handholds. He tipped his head and fell back into the crowd, slipping out of the car just as the doors clamped shut.

At home the next day, Angela sat across from Molly at their regular table in the corner of the NArcCafe nearest their apartment. Molly faced the window, but rather than looking out at the view across the river she stared into a palm-sized flexscreen, her fingers drifting over its surface.

Angela faced the room. It was a typical Saturday afternoon. Most of the tables were full, though few of the diners interacted. She could make out one side of several distinct conversations. The other sides were piped directly into the diners' headsets. The headgear had seemed awkward when it first came out, but now nearly everyone traveled around with one ear plugged and one eye obscured. At a nearby table a guy appeared to be playing a game while also talking with his mother. The girl across from him chattered away, her lone eye staring at a point in space as her head bobbed and her sensor-gloved hands gestured in the air. She seemed to be dancing. Probably on a virtual first date, Angela figured. An odd hour, but then she'd squeezed in virtual dates at off times too. That was one of the great things about cyberlife; it could be whatever, whenever, and wherever you wanted it to be. Young people, embedded in their own virtual lives, all seemed oblivious to one another's real life existence. Angela still found it strange. Sure, she'd been on plenty of cyber-dates, but she still liked to meet her close friends face-to-face.

Case in point, Angela had spent the morning reading aloud to Molly from her new but now-treasured book, *My Life in France*, trying to make sense of the stories it told. As Molly took a break to catch up on some work, Angela watched the midday crowd thin. A clutch of thirty-somethings lingered in the back corner. They stared at a wall of streaming sports and news projected from their own personal devices. Random cheers and jeers erupted as they each responded to their own programs.

Angela marked the time. Five hours to go before her first meal. Josh had invited her to a friend's house for a home-cooked dinner. She had no idea what to expect. Still plenty of time to learn, she told herself, looking back down at the open book in front of her. It instantly sucked her back in. "So, I'm trying to imagine this. This woman, Julia Child, a self-proclaimed nobody in the food world at the time—not just that, a nobody in France—walks into a restaurant, orders something called beurre blanc, and then gets invited to a private cooking lesson in this woman's kitchen. What I don't get is what's so special about this sauce. She explains how to make it in one sentence. One sentence!"

Angela paused to spoon a scoop of her now cold but still frothy noodles into her mouth. She slurped the rubbery strings through her lips, hardly pausing to chew them, and continued her commentary.

"Then later, she has this picture of a page from her book, her cookbook, with this woman's recipe on it. See? It's marked 'Top Secret.'" She held up the book and waited until Molly lifted her eyes from her own screen and nodded. "If this French woman is willing to show anyone how to make this beurre blanc stuff, how can it be Top Secret?" She waited for Molly to share her bewilderment but also hoped for insight.

Angela knew that Molly had been half-listening all along, but half-listening for Molly was almost as good as full attention from most people. She waited as Molly closed her work.

"One second…" Molly said. Then, "Let's see… Here we go." With her access to the corporate and university libraries, Molly had the answers to most every question at her fingertips. "That sauce is actually mentioned in some of my food technology texts. It's a basic emulsion." When she looked up, Angela gave her a blank look. "Fat and water don't mix," she explained. "You can get them to mix, but you have to do it right. The goal is to get the oil or the water to turn into tiny droplets that get suspended in the other liquid. It's funny, because the NArc does the exact same thing today when it makes things like the froth you're eating and the dressing I have." She pointed to a squirt of green topping a flaky white triangle. "The NArc uses lots of basic kitchen techniques during processing to turn engineered nutritional components into a variety of meal formats. It's easy to do. Take the emulsion. The system first adds elements that hold the droplets together. Then the machines add just the right amount of heat and agitation. It's basic chemistry. But back then, it must have seemed like magic. If you don't do it right, the sauce never blends."

"So if it was like magic, why was this woman blabbing about it to someone who went on to make a fortune blabbing about it to anyone with a bowl and a whisk?"

Molly thought about this for a minute. "Maybe this woman was just happy to be asked. Maybe she just wanted to share something she knew about. Kind of like me being happy to tell you about how we do it today."

Angela raised her eyebrows. Sometimes Molly surprised her with her insights into human nature. Slurping up another mouthful of noodles, she tried to imagine taking the risk of cooking something that might not work. She wondered what they did with food that didn't work out. Did they just throw it away, even after taking so long to grow it? And if they did, where did they put it?

Flipping through the pages, she asked, "Do you remember eating things like this sauce?"

Molly shook her head no. "Eating food that isn't controlled has always been this big unknown. To me, it's like playing roulette. But it's not just that it's dangerous. We need good nutrition and old-ways food is such an inefficient way to get it."

Molly's parents had both worked in bioengineering. She had grown up in a building that was a model for future living complexes. Their apartment featured some of the first glass-wall gardens. They ate meals made from early versions of engineered foods. As a result, it seemed to Angela that Molly couldn't help but think of everything in terms of cells and molecules.

"So what *do* you remember?" Angela asked.

"Well, the cafe in our building made these shakes. I used to love the peach melba." Molly smiled with what looked to Angela like a hint of guilt. "Of course, it wasn't made with real peaches and probably tasted nothing like them, but I liked it. It was only available in summertime, as a nod to seasonal food limitations. That used to annoy me. But later I realized that the restriction was what made it special."

Angela thought back to her own childhood. "I remember toast with butter and cinnamon-sugar. I went through a phase where I wouldn't eat anything else. So my mom would make it for me for breakfast, for lunch, for snacks. It was salty and sweet, crunchy and soft." She closed her eyes and her mouth watered as she thought about it. "Looking back, it wasn't very healthy for me. Or for Mom. But boy did we love it." Angela took a moment before opening her eyes. "After Mom died, Dad jumped at every new food gimmick. He took me to get tested, to figure out my type. Remember those old nutritional types? Mom thought it was all bunk and would never let him take me. I was so excited when I found out I was a Wanderer and Dad was a Puzzler. In hindsight, I guess she was right. Those early types were pretty silly, weren't they?"

Molly nodded. "My mother was skeptical too, but from a scientific viewpoint. She thought the whole idea was a kludge, a clumsy model of genetic data cobbled together with duct tape and string. Dad agreed as far as the science went, but from a business perspective he thought the contrived types were a good start. He says good technology always starts with awkward and experimental solutions. Until people use it, you don't really know what you need."

Angela had never thought about it in quite this way before, but it *had* taken time for the technology to catch up. The power of today's NArc is in its ability to gauge an individual's health as it unfolds. The power of today's Neerfoods are their specificity.

Each raw good has specific nutrients designed in and each meal combines just the right blends to keep an individual's health moving in the right direction.

"I remember my very first NArc meal," she told Molly. "Dad took me to one of the first-generation NArcCafes. The inside gleamed like a spaceship, but somehow it seemed inviting. I had to stand on my toes to slide my card. Then a hatch opened and our meals skidded out. 'One Wanderer, One Puzzler,' it announced. I was literally jumping up and down." Her father had smiled down at her, pointing out the kaleidoscope of colors on her dish, encouraging her, perhaps for the first time ever, to clean her plate. She remembered his meal, a pale mound of protein with a slash of red sauce. She could recall everything about that day in vivid detail.

Except the taste.

For the first time, the enthusiasm she felt for the NArc that day felt like a betrayal. Her mother had reveled in cooking and eating and she'd wanted Angela to as well even though neither of their bodies could tolerate it.

Angela looked back down at her book and flipped through the pages, raising a cloud of dust that made Molly sneeze. She stopped flipping at the last marked page. "Did I tell you about the bread?" she asked, turning the text toward Molly and sliding it across the table.

Molly puzzled over the photograph taking up the entire right-hand page and after a minute asked, "Is he baking bread in shorts with no shirt?"

Angela nodded. The photo showed a small man in a dank Paris basement, leaning his naked torso into a brickwork oven.

Molly groaned.

Angela laughed. She had been to Molly's lab. No one was allowed into the Synganium hold without a full costume of gloves, slippers, coat, cap, goggles, and face shield. Any contamination of the Singers—the synthetic-organic beings that grow Neermeats for harvest—could shut production down for days.

"Oh, shoot. What time is it?" Molly pushed the book back. "I have to visit my grandmother. Her time has come. She found out yesterday. I've got to get there soon if I'm going to make it to the lab this afternoon."

Angela stared blankly at her friend. Neither of them had gone through the scheduled mortality process yet, so she wasn't sure what it entailed. The concept had been around for several decades out of necessity. When the country couldn't afford to keep people alive, it had phased in scheduled terminations as a cost savings measure based on an actuarial cost-benefit analysis. No one had liked it at first. Everyone feared that people would misuse it to eliminate people for financial gain. But in the end, it hadn't worked out nearly as badly as people expected. Cases of fraud were few and far between. And studies showed that the program slashed both costs and human suffering many fold. By the time of the NArc mandate in 2050, scheduled termination had become a way of life.

"Can't the lab wait? I mean, you don't need to be there yourself do you? Can't your team handle a day on their own?"

"I like to be at the lab," Molly replied. "There is too much at stake right now for me to let things run unattended. I don't want to waste time fixing their mistakes." Molly finished the last two bites on her plate and stood up to go.

"But doesn't your grandmother need you too?"

"My parents will be there for her. And my grandmother will understand. She was working every day herself until a year ago. She doesn't expect anything different from me. And she wouldn't want it either. We've had our time together. Very special times. But now it's time for her to go."

Molly gave Angela a reassuring smile, as if she were comforting a little girl. Angela nodded in response, but she couldn't help wondering if Molly and her grandmother had really had their time together.

Before walking away, Molly stopped at the edge of the table and her eyes grew stern. "I know there is nothing I can do to stop you from going tonight, so I won't lecture you." Angela let out a sigh of relief. She had been dreading Molly's safety lecture all day. "But I do think you need a reminder. You set out to do this for Martine Sinsky. So what happened to her wouldn't happen to other people. But now you seem to have forgotten all about that. I just want you to know that I haven't."

Angela watched Molly walk away. For a person who often seemed to be devoid of emotions, she had a way of making Angela acutely aware of her own. She knew Molly was right. She knew she'd become obsessed with these foods and indulging in the memories they conjured. But she hadn't forgotten about Martine Sinsky. Not completely.

As the cafe emptied, Angela finished her cold soup. She couldn't afford to feel run-down tonight. As she swallowed the last frothy mouthful, she made a silent offering of thanks to the NArc and its ability to keep her well.

5

"Where did you say you met her?" June asked Josh, rapping a dripping spoon on the edge of the saucepan. He watched her frown at the wall behind the stove, now spattered with sauce.

"I told you, on the maglev," Josh replied. "Look, she's fine. I'm sure of it." Josh saw that his friends were giving one another sideways looks.

His hosts, June Peterson and Ken Fischer worried most about newcomers because they had the most to lose. They lived in an older house, a rare stand-alone as far from city center as a person could go and still get basic services. They shared the house as much out of friendship as practicality. She had style and knew how to cook. He had tools and knew how to use them. They still had a kitchen, though its appliances were by law disconnected. Ken spent part of each Saturday rigging up a generator to power them. He ran that using fuel he bought through his business, not wanting the appliances to cause spikes in the household meter.

This evening, the only other guest was Parrish Knight. Josh had never warmed to Parrish, but he had to admit that the man brought an important skill to the table. Parrish made sure their

NArc implants never betrayed their extracurricular noshing. It was a skill he had gained from his above-board life working for the NArc on the human-machine interface, a life that, like the rest of them, he kept as separate as possible from his Foodie life.

Josh always looked forward to these weekly dinners, filled with bright conversation punctuated by chopping, slicing, and simmering. In between these meals, Josh kept himself sane by doing underground work with the same group. Under Josh's supervision, they smuggled illicit goods into the city. Josh relied on all of them and an army of others to keep the traffic moving. He needed Parrish for help with quality control. And Ken for shipping. Ken's construction business took him all over the city as well as Outside. With his utility vehicle and his easy passage through the urban borders—a possession and a privilege only enjoyed by licensed contractors—he was indispensable for moving goods. And June. June brought a human element and a historical perspective that had helped Josh close deals with all manner of people. And Josh knew that they needed him too. He had the connections, the cash, and the clout to keep the whole system together.

The special excitement he had brought with him this particular evening, however, was now mixed with a twinge of unease. Josh didn't like to see his friends look uncomfortable when they'd taken such big risks for him. Normally when he looked at them, and in truth, whenever he ate a meal his network made possible, it made him feel a little less guilty. He wasn't sure he'd ever get over the fact that his own work on robotic pollinators, done years ago in what seemed like a different lifetime, had helped marginalize food. He'd seen the bee-bots as a stop gap at the time. They were intended to give compromised crops a boost. During the height of climate change, he imagined they would help offset the loss of live bees to unexpected frosts, heat waves, and droughts. He thought they would give traditional farms the resilience they needed to survive. He never imagined that his alma mater would sell the patent to the highest bidder, especially not after the entire team had agreed to license the technology for free to anyone who gave discounts to small farmers. But then again, he hadn't foreseen the depression, either. Once the farmers were priced out it didn't take long for the new owner of the patent to use it to corner the vegetable market with designer plants grown in artificial urban farms. The engineer in Josh still marveled at the design that went into these indoor farms. And the rebel in him enjoyed spending every penny of his royalty income trying to undermine it.

June, still tending the sauce, turned the heat up a notch. "Well I don't like it Josh. We agreed to screen newcomers as a group. Ken and I don't like sticking our necks out so you can get laid or indulge in your rebellion fantasies." A teacher by trade, June was a master of withering faces. The one she shot him as she jabbed a spoon at his chest sent him right back to grade school.

Josh frowned and crossed his arms to shut her out. It seemed to work. He heard her sigh and withdraw the menacing spoon. After the others wandered away to attend to their prep work, he grabbed a knife and started to slice potatoes for the gratin. "You know, she is pretty hot," he admitted to June sideways.

She elbowed him hard and then laughed. "You know I trust you Josh, but I get nervous. Ken won't say anything, but he'll ride you out on a rail before he risks losing this house," she said. "Even if it means no more food," she added under her breath. She pinched some dried herbs between her fingers and sprinkled them over the sauce, then leaned in for a whiff. "What do you really see in her?"

As he sliced, Josh recalled his meeting with Angela. He wasn't ready yet to tell June about her interest in Martine Sinsky.

And he definitely didn't want to tell her that the entire meeting nearly fell apart. So he improvised. "I think she could be perfect. For one thing, she may be the only person in this city who is qualified. She understands science. And she works for the only independent news outlet left." In his lifetime, Josh had watched newspaper after newspaper shutter its doors. The reporters had little choice but to take public relations positions, many of them in big corporate and academic outfits. In his opinion, it had gotten so that almost no one knew the difference between reporting and propaganda anymore.

"That doesn't make her immune from influence you know," June said tartly.

"I know. And she's not. She thinks in terms of nutrition. She looks at a long life as the only measure of a full one. She values efficiency over quality. She's going to have to work hard to be objective. The good news is, she knows it."

June shook her head. "What I don't get is, if you think something's going on, why not get the authorities involved. Seems to me like you need a cop, not a reporter."

"Right. I'll call the cops. Oh. Wait. Who do they work for? The state. And who runs the NArc? The state. Besides, what cop is going to work with me? They put up with me, with *us*, but you know what they think of me." He stopped slicing and looked at June, giving her his best puppy dog, feel-sorry-for-me eyes. "They think I'm a mobster."

"Ha. A mobster." She pointed her spoon at him again. "You need a hat. And an accent."

"No sympathy at all." Josh went back to slicing. "Anyway, I read her stuff. She's smart. And curious. I think she's a little bored with the NArc. When she gets here, she's not going to know what hit her. I think, once she sees what's happening, she'll see things our way. She'll want to tell the world what we know."

June gave the sauce one last whiff and turned the heat way down. She faced Josh, leaning one hip on the counter and placing her free hand on the other hip. "And just what is it that we know, Josh?" she asked, though Josh knew she didn't want an answer. She put the spoon down and opened her mouth to say more, but two small raps at the door interrupted.

As June started for the door, another small rap followed, then a quick rap and a firm knock. June raised an eyebrow at Josh and, after another pause, another firm knock followed.

Josh grinned and June shook her head. As she walked out of the kitchen, she said, "You've been reading too many spy novels. You and Parrish, both."

Angela stood at the door, her hair tied back and her chin tucked into her scarf. She was biting her lip and counting to ten. As she lifted her hand to run through the knock sequence again, a woman opened the door, smiling tightly.

"Hi Angela. Come on in," she said, ushering her inside and scanning the street for followers. She led Angela into a room in the front of the house, showed her a seat, and asked her to wait.

The first thing Angela noticed was the smell. Sharp yet mellow. She couldn't place it, but the aroma made her think of autumn, with piles of golden leaves and long shadows across a lawn. Breathing in again, she still didn't recognize it. So she scanned the room, a room so large she figured the entire apartment she and Molly shared could fit inside it. She then realized that she hadn't been in a house in 25 years, since her own migration to the city with her father.

She judged the house to be old. Not just pre-Migration old, but pre-eletricity old. Maybe even pre-civil war. The wood-plank floors sloped toward the back of the house and the ceiling dipped in the center to form a bowl. Her chair felt scratchy, as if it were upholstered with woolen fibers. Through a doorway in one corner she could hear a vaguely familiar clanging. Baking pans. She smiled at having another chance to remember making cookies with her mother. They would taste each round as they cut it off the store-bought cylinder of dough before cooking it. "Just to make sure it's still good," her mom would say, beaming. Angela could almost taste the sticky sweetness on her tongue. But not quite. Its absence sent her eyes searching the room again to fill the empty space with something tangible, something to bring her back to the here and now.

She was about to stand up to look at a photograph on the mantle when a man walked in. Dirty blonde hair fringed his grey eyes, carved cheeks, and stubbled chin. He leaned against the doorframe and gazed at her, but said nothing.

She stood to introduce herself, extending her hand and a warm smile. His chin tipped in an almost imperceptible nod, but his hands remained in his pockets. She filled the yawning silence. "This is a lovely home—"

He sat down, cutting her off with his body language, and gestured for her to sit opposite him. Leaning forward, he said, "Angela, my name is Parrish Knight. Josh has vouched for you, but for me, that isn't enough. A great many people put themselves at risk to make nights like tonight happen. I need to ask you to make a promise. I need for you to promise me that you will not put our hosts in jeopardy by revealing telling details. I trust you can learn what you need to learn and write about it while still protecting your sources."

Angela responded, her tone professional. "I keep my sources confidential. I always have. My work is to observe and report, but never to jeopardize. You have my word." Angela had to assume that Parrish and Josh had both heard about her through rumors about her efforts to break into the underground.

She felt confident that she had shown integrity throughout, so if they had heard of her, they couldn't possibly suspect her intentions. But Parrish clearly wasn't satisfied with second-hand reports or with his friend's judgement. She could tell that he needed to see it in her eyes. Meanwhile, she couldn't place just what it was that she saw in his.

They stared at each other for several seconds. Parrish's face remained cold and stony. Angela willed herself to project her years of experience as a reporter. She had come here to learn about underground food, not to spoil it. Unless, of course, she had to. She could still hear Molly's sharp reminder from earlier that morning running through her brain.

Angela felt a shiver coming on when Parrish nodded decisively. He stood, opened a roll top desk tucked in behind his chair, shifted a pile of yellowed envelopes, and pulled a small tool out of a hidden compartment.

"We'll need to adjust your chip," he said without looking up from the desk. "I'll just send in a time-release override that will protect you this evening. If you decide to continue with your investigation, we can talk about next steps."

Angela's eyes widened. She hadn't thought this through at all. "I thought I'd just take the fines. Is that an option? To just Cheat and pay the consequences?"

"No, that's not an option," he replied, sitting back down across from her and reaching for her left forearm. "Tonight's meal won't just generate fines. It will raise the kind of alarms that will put you on a surveillance list. Maybe you think you can handle that?" He raised an eyebrow and looked Angela in the eye.

She frowned back at him. "The Food Cops won't even investigate a death. Why would they start watching me?"

"You don't think they'll put two and two together? You're planning on writing a story about this, right? I'd recommend you publish it using a pseudonym. You need to protect yourself." He reached for her forearm again and grasped it gently but firmly. "And we need to protect ourselves. This isn't optional. Do you understand?"

"I understand," she replied.

"Ok then. This won't hurt a bit." He pushed up her sleeve and rubbed his thumb along the pink skin just above her wrist. Then he pressed the end of the tool—a metal tube with a lever on the side—and squeezed the trigger—

KaChunk!

Angela flinched. But the injection hadn't hurt a bit. She looked at Parrish quizzically.

"Air gun. It forces a sequence of coded particles into the chip. They feed in a signal to suspend monitoring temporarily. No side effects. By the time you finish dessert, you'll be back to normal."

Parrish patted Angela's knee and she couldn't help but notice the satisfied look on his face. He could have warned her. But she wasn't going to complain. She was in. And she was safe.

Parrish smiled. "Smells good, doesn't it?" he said, suddenly acting as if they ate together every night. He stood up and beamed at her, motioning for her to follow. "Come on in, Angela. We're cooking up some of my favorite dishes tonight. You're really going to enjoy this."

Angela felt compelled to follow. Eager, even. As she trailed behind him, she shed her irritation and anxiety. With each step, and with each of Parrish's friendly overtures—a touch on the sleeve, a mimed whiff of the food—the feelings faded further, displaced by a sense that Parrish had accepted her into the fold. When he opened the hidden door that led into the kitchen, she smiled back at him and stepped across the threshold.

≠

The first thing that hit her was the heat. Steam rose off of pots boiling on the stove and she felt a warmth radiating from a pair of ovens mounted into the wall to the right of the door. The room bustled with activity. June, tall and slender, tended the stove. Josh stood next to her, slicing what looked like carrots. Another man had just taken something out of the oven. He rustled underneath its foil tent. As Parrish made a quick round of introductions, the man named Ken, burly and painfully shy, nodded at her as he returned the foil-covered pan to the oven, causing another wave of heat to wash over her.

As she stood there on the threshold, she tried to take in the rest of the room. She wanted to register her first impressions, to log them in her brain so she could jot them down later, after everyone had gotten comfortable with her intrusion. But she was quickly overwhelmed; the cluttered mess was too much to absorb all at once. Without witnessing it herself, she never would have believed the number of different food items and gadgets strewn about. At Josh's feet was a ceramic pot filled with brown and blonde ribbons and green ferns attached to orange nubs. Potato peels and carrot tops, she guessed. June stirred something shiny and unidentifiable, and next to the stove were bottles of what looked like juices and syrups. On the island were several jars of dried greens that looked like shriveled versions of some of the herbs she had tossed in the trash earlier that week. There were also two off-white hunks with crumbles around them.

Angela was still trying to figure out what the hunks were when June addressed her. "Well Angela, I've got a job for you." June pointed to the far corner of the island with the tip of a large knife. There sat a mound of something covered with a dish cloth. "Give your hands a wash and I'll show you how to knead the bread."

Angela gulped. She looked at Josh for reassurance. It wasn't that she didn't want to help, she just wasn't sure how. He pointed to the sink and said, "Will work for food. That's our motto."

"That's right," said June. "This is a community effort. We all pitch in. You won't understand us unless you participate." She pulled the cloth off of the dough and showed Angela how to dust her hands with flour. "Now, gather the dough in your hands and press down with your palms."

As her hands plunged into the tacky mass, she abandoned all hope of note taking.

An hour later, Angela slid into a chair in the dining room. To her right sat Ken, who had vanished with Parrish after fiddling with the oven. To her left, at the head of the table, sat June. She faced Josh, and Parrish sat next to him. She looked at the silverware. She was so accustomed to using compostable all-in-one sporks that she couldn't remember the last time she'd used flatware, let alone a collection that included a knife, two forks, *and* two spoons.

Ken passed her a bowl of carrots. "It's hot," he cautioned. They may have been the only words he spoke to her all night. She took the bowl and snuck a peak at his plate to see how much he had taken and where he had put it. She copied him and then passed the bowl to June. "It's hot," she added, though June had already taken the dish and started scooping herself a serving.

With the plates full, Angela looked for a sign. She didn't want to be the one to start. Besides, with the lump in her throat and the remains of her lunch doing flip-flops in her stomach, she wasn't sure she could eat at all.

To Angela's relief, June raised her glass. "To food," she said. "To food," the group echoed. "And to each of you. To Ken, for finding that high-speed oven at the junk store. I just love being able to bake bread in 15 minutes. To Josh, for the wine. This is one of my favorites. To Parrish, for keeping our records clean." June gave each of them in turn a personalized look of appreciation. Then she cast her gaze on Angela. The expression on her face appeared more uncertain than unfriendly. "And to our guest. May you enjoy your meal now and remember to protect us later."

Angela reddened, but she tipped her head and took a sip of her wine. When it hit her tongue, her eyes widened. She pulled the glass away from her lips and stared at it. She had never tasted anything so smooth yet so complex. She didn't know where to begin to describe it.

"Good, isn't it?" Josh remarked. "It comes from upstate New York. They used to make passable reds. But now, with the new weather patterns and their expertise in plant breeding, they make some of the best in the world. We're lucky. Being close by, it's not so hard to get."

Everyone had started to eat. They were Mmming and Ahhing over each bite and exchanging knowing glances. Angela's stomach growled, but she wasn't sure where, or how, to begin. Part of her wanted to follow up on this news about wineries in New York. But she didn't want to be rude. She needed to eat. Only, there were just so many different things on her plate. "June," she began, trying to convince herself that she was reporting, not stalling. "Could you tell me about what we're eating? It's just, I haven't seen this much variety on one plate since, since... Well, maybe since never."

"Take a bite," June urged her with her mouth full. "Before it gets cold. And I'll tell you what we've got tonight. If you're lucky, Parrish will tell you why it's good for you. And Josh might even tell you where we got it. Sound okay?"

Angela looked down at her plate. She picked up one of her forks and a knife and cut into the roast beef, its brown and crusty edges rimming a blood-red center. She sawed off a small bite and lifted it to her mouth. She could feel them all watching her, waiting. June encouraged her again, and then she met Josh's eyes. He lifted a similar forkful and said, with a wink of encouragement, "Bon appétit."

As Angela ate, she learned that the shiny stuff was a maple, mustard, and orange glaze that now coated a pile of carrot medallions on her plate. The foil tent had concealed a roast beef. And the white hunks she had seen on the island earlier were blocks of cheese—hard aged cheddar cheese—that had been transformed into a sauce for the bubbly and browned potatoes gratin.

"Did you know that cheese was one of the first illegal foods?" Parrish asked her. Angela shook her head. "People used to eat raw milk cheese all the time. But in the mid 20th century, people in America decided the bacteria in the milk was too dangerous. So they banned cheese made from unpasteurized milk. They made exceptions, of course. Aged cheeses like this cheddar were okay, for example. The whole thing turned into a bureaucratic nightmare that was only marginally grounded in science."

"I remember reading about children dying from contaminated raw milk," said Angela. "So it seems like at its core the rule did make the food supply more secure."

Parrish laughed and shook his head. "In actuality, it didn't. It just gave people a false sense of security. After the law passed, as cheese making got more and more industrial, studies showed that the worst outbreaks of bad cheese came from big manufacturers using pasteurized milk." As Parrish paused to chew on a forkful of potatoes, Angela noted that his argument sounded compelling, the same way Molly always sounded so convincing. It made her wonder what she was missing. "You see," he continued, wiping his mouth with his napkin, "the small farmers didn't take chances. If they made illegal cheese, they made sure their raw milk was clean. But the big guys got cocky. They pushed the limits of the technology. They took big risks—milking sick cows and leaving milk-filled trucks without refrigeration for days—and people died as a result."

"But that's not the technology's fault," Angela said, frowning and trying to think it through. "I don't understand why the small farmers wouldn't jump at the technology, at the chance to eliminate risks. Pasteurization is so simple. And if it doesn't change the cheese—"

Angela could hear the whole table chuckling under their breath. Except Josh. He tried to explain. "You wouldn't have any way of knowing it, but it does make a difference." He took another sip of wine and paused for an instant to enjoy it before continuing. "You'll see. Maybe not in tonight's cheese sauce. But a small batch of fresh goat's cheese carries with it a sort of local essence. Each farm is different. It's *that* complexity, *that* richness, it's the local flora and fauna that make real food so…well…so irreplaceable."

Flora and fauna. Fungi, yeasts, and bacteria. She knew that standard strains of microbes were used in NArc foods, but they somehow seemed cleaner than wild bacteria. Predictable. Controlled. After all, they were designed that way. To avoid thinking about the local, incorrigible bugs teeming inside those blocks of cheddar, she lifted her fork away from the cheesy potatoes and eyed the slice of holey bread.

Angela admired its thick honey-colored crust. She had spent more time with that bread before it was baked than she normally spent eating an entire NArc meal. As she'd kneaded it, June had told her that the mother dough had come from the 20th century. "Mother dough?" Angela had asked. "The sourdough starter," she'd replied "It's the wild yeasts in my kitchen that make it unique. You'll not find another loaf like it anywhere." Is that what's special about this food? she wondered, shaking her head. She'd never thought of bread or cheese as quite so alive before. All of this thinking was making it hard for her to concentrate on eating.

She looked around the table again and watched Josh's friends compliment one other on their cooking. So far, she'd eaten only that first bite. She had to start somewhere, so she stabbed her fork into a pile of carrots. As she chewed, she began to share in these exchanges. She smiled at Parrish and exchanged nods with Josh. When June lifted a hunk of bread in Angela's direction, as if toasting her, Angela returned the gesture. As she chewed, she felt something she couldn't describe. A kind of warmth mingling on her tongue along with the gravy-soaked hunk of bread. It spread across her face, down her throat, and all the way into her gut.

Angela let the sensations wash over her. She watched the others and mimicked them, breathing in the wine as she sipped it, letting it entrance her. She let the meat and cheese linger on her tongue and chewed the carrots slowly, until there was nothing left. Her notebook sat untouched next to her plate. She didn't have the vocabulary to put words to paper, and she felt too overwhelmed to think. Instead, she just let the tastes come and then, reluctantly, she let them go.

At the end of the meal, Angela took stock of the table. It was littered with empty serving trays and plates. She leaned back in her chair feeling sated. She no longer needed her hosts to explain why they took such risks for food. But she still didn't understand how they did it. "That was delicious," she said to the table in general. Glancing at the last few crumbs of her chocolate dessert, she couldn't stop herself from picking them up with her fingertips and popping them into her mouth. "But where does it all come from? And how do you get the ingredients you need?

And how do you even know what you need to make these dishes?"

Josh laughed. "One question at a time!" He leaned back, too, and sipped a cup of strong coffee. "You've seen parts of where the food comes from—the drops. There's more to that story, but before you learn about the network, you need to understand some of the history."

"So where do we start? With the NArc mandate?" she asked.

Josh smirked and shook his head. "We'll need to go back further than that. Back before Neermeat. Before the first NArciTypes. Maybe even back before you were born. You'd better get yourself a fresh cup of coffee."

Sunday night, minutes before her deadline, Angela filed her story. She hit send, then sat alone at her desk staring into space. She was still staring blankly ahead several minutes later when her chat icon beeped. Stew. She let it beep three times, her stomach queasy, then rushed to answer. She hadn't been this nervous about a story in ages.

"You have some explaining to do," he deadpanned.

She hesitated, unable to read his face. "You don't like it. I went too far, didn't I?" She pinched the bridge of her nose between her fingers and closed her eyes. She knew it was too late to go back and change it now. But when she opened her eyes, she saw that Stew had a wry look in his eyes.

"I love it. Now, tell me, who is this Sage Weaver person."

Angela sat up straight, knowing that at the very least she'd bought herself another week. She started to explain. "I got in with this group because one person trusted me. Now I've had to convince a whole group of people to trust me. They made it clear that their identities need to be protected. It only follows that mine needs to be protected too. But from what, I just don't know yet."

"Unorthodox. But not unreasonable…" Stew scratched his chin. "You're right that this isn't what I expected. What happened to Martine Sinsky? Did you give up on that story?"

"No, not at all." Angela had been thinking about Sinsky all day. She'd tried to find a hook, some way to bring her in. But the simple truth was that she didn't have one. Yet. "My contacts know something about Sinsky. I'm sure of it. But they aren't ready to talk about it yet. What I do know is that this underground world is big. I figured, now that I'm in, I should see where this takes me. Maybe something about Sinsky will shake out. If not, worst case, I figured I should try to get some traction on this taste story line, like you suggested."

She had spent hours thinking this strategy through. Was it ethical? Was she using Josh and his friends? She had decided that she was being as honest with them as they were being with her. But Stew's silence was making her think again. She took a deep breath and, when Stew still didn't step in, she said, "Look, this is the fresh start we were looking for. It's exactly what you wanted. And it has a chance to be huge. Ditch the old Well and run this. I promise you, there's plenty more where this came from."

Stew smiled. "It'll be up first thing tomorrow."

6

The First Bite
RealFood, by Sage Weaver

Northeast City, May 21, 2063 — The first bite nearly made me gag. Translucent fat glistened around one edge of the slice of meat. Blood-red liquid oozed from its center and dripped onto my plate. As I held up my fork, I stared at the sinews lined up in rows, the muscles that had supported this animal, this cow, and allowed it to walk, to stand, to breathe.

They were all staring at me. The people who bought this meat and cooked it were already chewing, moaning with pleasure, mopping the drippings on their plates with the next forkful of flesh. My eyes met the chef's and she nodded. "It's okay. Just try it," she said. I forced open my jaws and slipped the dangling morsel between my teeth. The fat melted, coating my tongue, and my throat closed. My eyes popped. "Chew," said my hostess. I closed my eyes and mashed the meat between my molars.

That was when I noticed it. The flavor. Something tart, perhaps the lemon juice squeezed over the steak just before serving. Something hot, most likely the crushed pepper rubbed on before roasting. Something meaty, a heft, a fullness, that I had never tasted before. And the blood? Everyone at the table called it "juice." In a way, that's exactly what it was.

After that first bite, I had to force myself to eat slowly. I wanted more. With each bite, I breathed in the flavors. The sweetness of spring in each maple-glazed carrot, the potatoes au gratin as rich and sharp as any food writer ever described them.

I thought to myself that eating meals this delicious everyday, I would never fit into the clingy attire we are all so fond of. Yet, as I glanced around the table, I took in the fact that everyone around it appeared healthy. Glowing. Some of them dined underground only once a week, but others admitted to more frequent meals, sometimes going under more than once a day. "It's the most fulfilling thing I do," one diner said as he mopped up the last of the cheese sauce, pink "juice" and maple glaze with a piece of homemade bread.

I kneaded that bread. It is the closest to food that I have ever been, strings of tacky gluten stretched between my fingers. The dough yielded less and less to the pressure of my palms with each fold and delivered my first whiff of yeast, alive and thriving inside the pale mass. My hostess taught me to cup my hands around the ball of dough and pull up, to create a "skin" that would form a crust. I looked askance at her, then lifted my hollowed palms. The mass slipped underneath as the outer coating clung to my fingers. I lifted again then pinched the top closed. Later, that crust contained a stretchy, chewy sponge perfect for cleaning our plates.

The final course, a dense chocolate cake, was made with eggs laid by chickens just a few days ago. One narrow slice brought out the fruit flavors in the red wine and blasted my tongue with cocoa and berries. After the final bite, I leaned back in my chair, eyes closed, hands on belly, and sighed.

The after-dinner conversation turned quickly to the obvious. Why is such food illegal? We all know the standard answers. We had an unsafe food supply, contaminated with chemicals, metals, and bacteria. We had unhealthy food habits that caused epidemics and public health crises. And we had an unsustainable food industry that was too costly in terms of energy, space, and pollution. We had no choice is why.

Speaking for myself, the trade-off we made was a soulless one. We have gained much, but what we have lost in terms of flavor, texture, variety, in terms of bliss, cannot be measured. We let these intangibles slip away, most of us in ignorance, never having had them in the first place. This new column will bring them back to you, even if just for a few fleeting minutes. And perhaps it will help us all learn to appreciate the power of our senses.

Angela went into the office again the morning her new column went live. Stew had guided her old column to success. Now she wanted his input on this one. But before she had a chance to find space in the Pit, a sunken galley of desks surrounded by the editors' offices, Frank intercepted her.

"So 'Sage,'" he said, mocking her with quote fingers. "Who is she? Who is this Cheater you hooked up with?" He leaned against the far wall, his arm and his wide shoulders blocking her path. She saw in his face the assurance of someone who was used to getting his way.

Angela had never liked Frank's bullying. He had a reputation as a hack reporter who didn't bother to think for himself. Her own reporting style was at the other extreme, and she knew her way had its own pitfalls. She couldn't deny that she sometimes got too personally involved in her stories. But on the other hand, people opened up to her because she put so much of herself into her work. She had tried to explain this to Frank once before. He told her it was her wavy hair and green eyes that opened doors, not her brain.

Frank shifted under her stare, easing back a bit, but not laying off. "Who did Potente set you up with?" he asked again. "I hooked you up with him. Now it's your turn. Way I see it, you owe me one."

She considered ducking under his arm, but at the very least, she owed him a response. "You know I can't tell you that, Frank," she replied, taking advantage of the space he created by moving into it slowly and resuming her course to the Pit.

"Throw me a bone, Ange. I've been wallowing in Junk. I need a new line. Now you've got your story, set me up. Let me cover the trafficking. There's more than enough fodder for both of us here."

"Sorry, Frank. I gave my word," she said, a touch of sympathy mixed in with her determination. As she walked away, she heard his fist slam against the hollow wall.

That same Monday morning, in an apartment building several miles west, Arthur Short opened his eyes. The sound of soft music filled his ears as the room brightened with artificial light to simulate the rising sun.

Arthur slid out of bed and, as he selected a brown suit from his closet, he thought about how lucky he was to have a job that made a difference in the world. For as long as he could remember, Arthur had wanted to become a doctor. But by the time he'd finished college, the medical profession had changed.

Bureaucracy made it impossible for doctors to focus on patients. At the same time, medicine had become so data intensive that computers did most of the real work. Arthur had had little choice but to find an alternate career.

Prescribed nutrition had seemed like the most promising choice. He had turned out to be right. Early on he had helped test some of the NArc's food preparation technologies. Then, he'd managed the project that brought the first Neermeat to the market. He'd even worked with the press, to get them to back the prescribed nutrition movement. And now he ran all of engineering for SynEngra, one of the biggest suppliers to the NArc. He loved his job and believed in his work, and today, like almost every other day, he looked forward to a solid day at the office.

Arthur got dressed and clipped his headgear in place. He flipped through the morning news, scanning the most popular headlines. The top story stopped him in his tracks. "The First Bite: a story about real food and real living." He opened it up and started to read.

Halfway through, his stomach growled. Since Arthur was alone, he allowed himself a few minutes to indulge in his memories. What he missed most were backyard barbecues. He could almost taste the tender steaks and the tang of sauce rinsed down by a cold beer on a hot afternoon. He glanced at the author's name: Sage Weaver. He didn't recognize it. Whoever this new Sage woman was, she did a great job. Too great.

Before Arthur had a chance to think about it, his earpiece beeped, reminding him that it was time to leave. He headed for the skywalk to the elevated express train near his apartment complex. He arrived in time to stop at the NArc stand before boarding. The energy shake it prescribed would stop the grumbling in his stomach if not in his mind.

On the train, shake in hand, Arthur's demeanor changed. At home, it was fine to dabble in food fantasies, but out here, he needed to start thinking about how to contain this situation. If this story could tempt him—someone deeply and professionally committed to the NArc—then it would certainly tempt those with more pedestrian concerns. Arthur liked to think that the NArc and Neerfoods thrived because people cared more about health than about taste, but he knew their continued success hung in the balance between fear and convenience. What maintained this balance, in part, was the fact that most people were taste blind. They'd lost all sense of the flavors of real food. One story wouldn't open their eyes. It might amuse them. Perhaps tempt a few to venture underground for a meal or two. One story was nothing.

But this was a column. She promised more. Making taste more alluring than wellness could tip the scales. It could bring back people's desire for real food. People might begin to believe that their lives, their choices, their meals, were also soulless. Arthur knew that recent news of the untimely Cheater death had knocked down interest in the underground, but it wasn't going to prevent the flood that would come from this.

As Arthur walked into his office at SynEngra, Josh stepped into his home office, a windowed corner looking out over a marsh on the southern edge of the city. He donned his sensor-studded gloves and logged into cyberspace. As his avatar ambled into the 'SpaceCafe, his physical self breathed in the aroma from the steaming mug of coffee in his hand. He'd brewed it himself from beans grown many hundreds of miles south. A couple from the Carolinas smuggled the beans north. They followed a rugged path just west of the Appalachian mountains that used to be a gun and drug trafficking route. He closed his eyes and took a sip, wondering how people got through the day without it.

Once inside, Josh spotted June and sat his avatar down across from her. She had been waiting for him to arrive. "So, what do you think?" he asked.

"You were right. She is good. And she didn't betray us. At least, not yet." June's avatar, a Barbie-shaped vixen with spiked yellow hair clad in a black dress and boots that climbed above her knees, crossed her legs slowly. "You never did tell me what you have in mind for her."

At his desk at home, Josh laughed out loud. June was naturally pretty in real life, but online, she took her appearance to an amusing extreme. He especially loved her get up, as if her avatar had not yet made it home from a night out on the town. "You know as well as I do that there are suspicious things going on," he answered. "But we have no evidence of foul play. And we can't call the authorities. Our new friend doesn't have those same limitations."

"So you're using her," said June, warming her hands on a cartoonishly large mug.

"Let's first remember that she came to me. Then let's remember that she wants to break this story. Or, at least, a story. Remember that she's an inv—" Josh stopped and chose more prudent words. He always assumed someone was listening in, watching him. He didn't worry so much about his own safety but he didn't want to put Angela in jeopardy. "Just remember that this is what she does. She's succeeded in getting this far, and that tells me a lot. I'm not using her. I'm working with her to help her get what she wants."

June's avatar smiled with half her mouth. "Mmm hmmm. But you're not being completely honest with her. I'm sure you have your reasons. You need to remember that not everyone wants what you want. Depending on how things go, we might not be there to back you when you need us."

He had heard this from June before. Despite her appearance online, she was conservative. She didn't like the unknown. But Josh felt confident that, in the end, she would want the truth to come out. Her principles outweighed her fears. Otherwise, she wouldn't have stuck with him for as long as she had already. He let her words hang for a minute, then said, "Let's just see how it unfolds, okay?"

If things turned out to be anything like what he suspected, she would continue to back him. He was certain of it.

Angela's story had topped the reading charts all day. She'd received more comments in the first few hours of the morning than she'd received for her last three stories together. Having finally struck a nerve, she wanted to enjoy her success for a little bit longer before trying to figure out if it was the right one. But as she walked into the bar she'd told her friends to meet her in— an up-scale place on the top floor of the tallest tower in her living complex—she could see from a distance that Molly and Nate were in no mood to celebrate.

The rest of the place was quiet, typical for a Monday evening. No one but the bartender—a rare human interface to refreshment—and a loner on a stool. As Angela paused at the bar to order her drink, she sized up the other patron. He wore a next-gen computing vest with sleek, integrated headgear. His fingers drifted in the air, controlling an application via tiny sensors decoratively embedded in his fingernails. Angela recognized the system because she had seen a prototype one of her colleagues had reviewed. She tried not to stare but looked long enough to catch a glimpse of electronics embedded behind his ear and an impossibly thin eyepiece hovering just above his eyebrow. A business traveler, she surmised. He must be staying in one of the corporate penthouses. Angela wondered what kind of business brought him here. Had he mag'd up the coast or did he rate as a flier? Few did since the passenger airlines had collapsed. She so dreaded facing her friends that she almost stopped to ask him.

But she couldn't keep Molly and Nate waiting, so she pulled herself away from the bar and strolled over to their table in the corner. Angela had barely sat down before Molly, her dark eyes blazing, spat, "Well, I hope you're satisfied. Arthur is frantic. And I've got to pretend I don't know anything about this whole thing. You know, this is just like you. You set out to do one thing, and then you end up doing another without thinking of the consequences. Only this time, what you've done is criminal. Literally. But also, you've tempted people. You set out to show people the risks of Cheating and instead you've glamorized it." Molly's face had begun to color and she broke with her standard, measured cadence. "I think, at the very least, you owe us an explanation."

Angela felt as if she'd been slapped. She had never seen Molly so irate. Unable to respond, she looked at Nate. "Your turn," she muttered.

Nate looked sheepishly into his glass. "Well, I guess I was pretty surprised when I read it," he started. He glanced at Molly quickly, then looked sideways at Angela. "But it was dead on. I felt like I was right there with you." Hearing Molly click her tongue in disapproval, he gave Angela an apologetic look and continued. "But Molly's right too. What you wrote is pretty dangerous. What happened?"

Angela took a sip of her beer. It tasted disappointing. Watered down. Standardized. She had always found modern drinks to be pleasant, if not distinctive. That was, until last night. One of the strongest memories of her dinner was that first sip of red wine that had been smuggled in from New York. Josh eventually told her it came from the Finger Lakes, a region a few hundred miles west of the Northeast City. It had been crafted by Outsiders who were part of a model alternative community. Delicious as it was, drinking it had been more frustrating than delightful. "Taste the plum and pepper," June had urged. But Angela hadn't been able to place either.

She sighed and looked back at Nate. "You're right. It is provocative. And it probably seems like a big leap to both of you. But this is how it works. I go in and I investigate. I make friends. I infiltrate. And eventually, I get to the truth. I've only just scratched the surface. This is just a tickler. A story to get people's interest going. To get the debate started. It's definitely not the last word. I mean, you should see the discussions it's generating. People are engaged again!"

"To get the debate started? There isn't anything to debate," Molly protested. "People are engaged because the story isn't objective! What you've written isn't based on science." Her face flushed again.

Angela was trying to stay calm. "Molly, I'm not a scientist. I'm a journalist. I've been writing about food for almost 15 years and this is my first story, my very first, that didn't mention the NArc. How is it that I've been writing about food for that long and it's always been about the NArc?"

"Because the NArc is *legal*. Because the NArc is safe," stated Molly, as if it were the most obvious thing. "Why would you promote something that is illegal and dangerous?"

"I'm not *promoting* anything," Angela argued back. She no longer felt guilty or calm. "Look, I'm writing what I saw. I'm reporting on *reality*. What I wrote is just the beginning. It's not the last word on the subject, okay?"

"Speaking of how dangerous the food is," interjected Nate, "how are you feeling? Did the NArc fine you this morning?"

"No." Angela waved him off. "There's a guy in the group who knows how to tap into the system and spoof it. He did something to my chip, to keep my stats in range—"

"You let them fuck with your chip?" he roared.

"Shhh!" Angela glanced around, but the bartender was busy flirting with her other customer.

"But you don't even *know* them," he hissed.

Angela dropped her chin to her chest. She wasn't doing herself any favors by insulting Nate, who seemed to be at least partially on her side. "I didn't have a choice once I got there," she said gently. "But don't worry. The engineer works for the NArc."

"So that makes him an expert?" Nate scoffed. Angela could see his nostrils flaring. "You have no idea what he did—"

"He used a back door to get in. When was the last time you built a system without a back door?" Angela stared at Nate until he admitted that he never had. He was about to argue back when Molly interrupted.

"That's not really Nate's point Angela. Do you know who these people are? Can you trust them?"

Angela trusted them, but could they trust her? She'd promised not to expose them, yet here she was, about to spill all to her friends. She looked from Molly to Nate and knew that she needed their insights. There was no other way. "I can trust them. And I need to be able to trust you, too. I need to tell you what I learned, but it's all got to stay between us, including Sage Weaver's identity. Okay?"

Molly and Nate exchanged glances, then nodded in unison.

"Here goes then. On the surface, my contact is Josh Salter. He went to Tech, graduated something like 15 years before us. He helped invent the robotic pollinators they use in the skyfarms and wall gardens, places like the orchard next to our apartment. Now he runs a company that maintains the pollination systems and monitors crop production. But I get the feeling he doesn't spend much time doing it."

She stopped and stole a look at Nate. He seemed a little less incensed. "Nate, would you mind looking into him for me, on the sly? He's charming, so I guess I'd like to be sure he's not dangerous underneath."

When Nate nodded, Angela let out a sigh. She felt relieved. More relieved than she'd expected herself to be. She wasn't just glad that her friends hadn't abandoned her. She had been more worried about Josh than she'd admitted to herself.

"Anyway," she continued, "it took me two hours to get to dinner, to an old house sitting at the edge of civilization. Big windows, clapboards, a front porch. I had to knock a secret code. The whole thing made me so jittery that my hands were shaking, even after going to all of those other places. This time I knew I was going to get in. This time I was going to have to eat their food. In front of them."

Angela paused and sipped her drink, trying to decide what to say next. "The people were just regular. Besides Josh, who seems like the ring leader, there was a teacher, a construction manager, and an engineer. They look healthy. Even Josh who eats mostly off the NArc. Not perfect, but well enough."

"So you're in with some sort of mob boss and a corrupt NArc engineer? And you needed a secret knock? This does not sound good at all," said Molly. "They are breaking laws left and right. If you get caught eating food, that's one thing. A fine you can't afford. Rehab in Food School that, as Nate knows all too well, you will not enjoy. But hacking your chip and trading on the black market? I don't even know what they do to people like that."

"They all seem to be normal, nice, intelligent people," protested Angela. "They just like eating outside the NArc. It's strange. Now that I've done it, it's hard to imagine why it's illegal. It seemed so…natural. After all, everyone used to do it all the time."

"But people used to be sick all the time too. You know how good the NArc has been for society," Molly replied. "We're healthier and happier and, don't forget, it was the NArc that saved us from economic collapse. Imagine if we had to feed all the people who are alive today with conventional farms. Imagine if half of them had chronic illnesses—"

Angela put up her hand. Molly had started to use her closure voice, but Angela had plenty more to discuss. "Look, I know all that. I've been writing about it for a decade, okay? The point is that underground food isn't about nutrition. It isn't really even about the food. Here's how they put it. Back before we were born, people had started to clean up agriculture. Little organic farms cropped up everywhere. Before it petered out in the late 20s it gave people a glimpse of an alternate future, one where people got healthy on their own. One where food wasn't dirty and unsafe. According to Josh, that future was stolen from them. From all of us."

"My parents were those little farmers," said Nate, quietly at first. "It didn't work. Maybe it would have if it weren't for everything else—the weather, the population, the fuel crisis. Either way, the history books are right." Nate brushed back his hair with his hand and leaned in, his voice more urgent now. "Technology saved us because those little farmers couldn't."

"So you think this alternate future was impossible?" Angela asked. "Aren't they doing it in Vermont right now?"

"Maybe its not impossible, but you can't compare a tiny country like Vermont to here. Even if you did, Vermont's system isn't so idyllic as you think. Growing up, my neighbors had cows and chickens. They also had a cesspit and a pile of chicken carcasses. It reeked. And their farm only fed a few families. That kind of cottage system doesn't scale." Nate continued, the frustration in his voice rising. "You know this already, Angela. This country needed industrial agriculture to support us all. You know what happened there. That system collapsed with the end of oil. The whole thing had to be reinvented. Maybe there was a missed opportunity. But going back to farming now? That's impossible."

Angela nodded. She'd had this same argument the night before. "Consider this, though. So the story we all know is that the NArc caught on like a fashion trend. It was expensive, but people lost weight, their cholesterol and glucose levels balanced. People didn't have to think about diets or what's for dinner. When the subsidies made it affordable, everything just tipped." Angela remembered that, by the time of the NArc mandate, almost 80 percent of the population was already tapped in. She also noticed that Nate and Molly had begun to ease back into their chairs. "But remember that all of that happened while we were young. Teenagers. College students. We didn't see it with a critical eye because we were already immersed in it. Josh saw things differently. He called the early NArc snake oil. He said that people only lost weight and got better because the NArc vendors cut calories."

When Molly and Nate rolled their eyes, she agreed. "I know. It's so much more complicated than that." Angela closed her eyes and pictured Josh, his face illuminated by the moonlight and his leather collar turned up against the wind. She heard his gravelly voice in her head and tried again to explain. "Josh said that people didn't line up willingly. They had to be coerced. It started in the hospitals. Anyone who checked in left with a NArc prescription. If you didn't fill it, your health insurance would cut you off. Anyone diagnosed with a genetic condition left with a prescription for her whole family. It wasn't long before companies started to require it as a precondition for insurance. Whole states followed. By then, since everyone was signed up anyway, the mandate made sense. By then, no one cared."

"If that had been the case, people would have rebelled," said Nate.

"Really?" deadpanned Angela. "Were you already on the NArc when you got to Tech?"

"Yeah. I had to for high school…" Nate closed his mouth and sat back, his eyes wide and glued to Angela's. She returned his gaze, but rather than an I-told-you-so expression, she looked as jolted as he did.

Molly shook her head in disgust. "Of course you had to. The NArc manages immunizations, which have been required for school for a century. These people sound like radicals. And you're playing right into their hands, Angela. But I don't understand why. You're smarter than that." Molly looked at Nate and then looked back at Angela. "Are you sure you're not letting your feelings for Josh cloud your judgment?"

Angela frowned. Where did that come from? "I just met him, Molly. If anything, my feelings about the NArc are in the way. I haven't thought about it critically for a long time." Angela rubbed her temples. This conversation was getting exhausting, but she gave it one more shot. "This is going to sound weird, but some of the foods made me feel different. Warm. Comforted. As if I could taste them all the way down inside my stomach. Like nothing I've ever eaten before. When I told Josh this, he said, 'You're starting to get the idea. Nature is smarter than we are.'" Angela looked up and waited for their reaction.

"That's it?" said Nate, his skepticism returned. "What does that mean?"

"That sounds like an allergic reaction," said Molly, looking relieved, as if she'd finally heard something that made sense to her. "You probably had something out of your NArciType and your immune system was reacting to it. That happens to me sometimes if I use a variety credit—"

"You're missing the point!" Angela fumed, causing both Nate and Molly to hush her this time. She went on, her voice muted but urgent. "This wasn't an allergy. I felt these things, but not so literally as you're taking them. We don't have words to describe what I felt. I will admit that a big part of it *was* emotional. The deep taste wasn't just from the food but from sharing it, preparing it, and eating it together. We were all tasting the same thing. We were all seeing each others' reactions. These are natural things..."—she groped for a word—"...connections. Connections that we don't experience anymore. His point is that engineering took all that away."

"Yeah. And engineering will keep it away. Along with the other stuff it keeps away like crop failures and viral epidemics," said Nate. "If we're lucky, maybe the weeds will grow up around them and their tomato vines and pull them all back to the stone age. I just hope they don't take you with them."

7

Molly hadn't planned to break from her Tuesday lunch routine. Despite the unsettling conversation with Angela the night before, she'd slept well. She'd woken at her normal time. She'd even had a productive team meeting. And as usual, she stood up to take a lunch break at the tail end of the normal dining hours hoping to avoid the crowds.

She walked to the NArcCafe and grabbed a meal. But then, on her way back to her desk, Molly's feet kept walking. She passed her lab. She traveled by two other research nooks, then three stories down to the subfloors. She waved her forearm over the sensor to identify herself at the security checkpoint guarding the Singer hold, then calmly donned the protective costume to keep the Singers safe from germs. And here she stood, arm extended, hand frozen on the door latch.

It wasn't that she had walked here unwillingly. It was more that, until this instant, she hadn't been conscious of how disturbed she felt. "Nature is smarter than we are," Angela had said. Molly had unwavering confidence in science, but she also knew that recent feats of engineering, like the Singers, had been around for a lot less time than nature. They might not work exactly as we planned, she thought. They might not keep working as we planned.

Molly shook this thought off. If the little bits of nature they had cobbled together to make the Singers ever did start to evolve, she and the other scientists would see it happening. We'll know, she thought as she pushed through the door and into the hold.

After her eyes adjusted, Molly stepped onto the steel platform circling the Singer, and looked down on the motionless creature. Its hum echoed in her ears. Over the years, the sounds had become familiar. Almost soothing. As the humming pulsed and peaked and dissipated into the dome, she tried to remember whether her team started calling them "Singers" because of the humming or because "Singer" was easier to say than "Synganium." She looked down, half expecting to see something moving, some obvious source of the sounds. As synthetic as she knew the Singers to be, she had to admit there was something natural about their songs.

But the Singer looked as it always did, like a twist of organs and veins that formed a heaping spiral inter-connected by tubes and signaling wires. The pumps and control circuitry—the Singer's heart and brain—sat at the center underneath the mound in a maintenance chamber. At the edges grew bands of harvestable flesh. Neermeat. According to a screen on the wall, the next cutting would begin in 20 minutes.

Molly felt a surge of pride at having been a part of this work. The Singers are a sustainable, elegant solution, she thought. So simple. *This* is intelligent design, she smirked. We took the complexity that evolved naturally and pared it down. We streamlined it to do one thing and do it efficiently.

Her mind wandered over the science and technology that went into synthesizing these living beings. She thought back to the discovery of DNA and how, after that, it took decades for scientists to tease apart the genome. Then the pace quickened. It wasn't long before scientists had the idea to synthesize their own genetic codes. Designer genes gave them the tools to make cells do whatever they wanted. At first, scientists and students used synthetic DNA to make designer bacteria that acted like miniature machines. Some computational. Some mechanical. By the time she got involved in engineering competitions in middle school, scientists were designing complex, multicellular systems. Then they started to engineer super-organs, still organic in nature but specially tuned with synthetic DNA. That work culminated here. She had been part of the team that had developed the first fully functional and sustainable designer synthetic-organic being. The Synganium.

She looked down again at the Singer below. So complex, yet so simple. These creatures actually reduce waste by using processed garbage as fuel. What they output fertilizes the local wall gardens. So much good is wrapped up in these tangled sinews. Maybe nature isn't smarter than we—

"What are you thinking about?" Molly jumped at the sound of Arthur Short's voice. He laughed and apologized, then gave her a speech she had heard many times before about coming here to think. "So, what *are* you thinking about?" he pressed.

"Oh, I don't know," Molly stammered. She hadn't expected anyone to find her here, let alone her boss.

Arthur patted her on the back. "Taking a mental break from your latest assignment, I imagine," he said. Earlier that morning Arthur had pulled Molly off another project and made her lead of a new one to make a simpler Singer. "Any ideas, or have I driven them all out of your head with my intrusion?" He chuckled lightly.

Molly, who never tired of talking about her work, latched on to the question. She had been asked to come up with miniMeat, a Neermeat that could grow in the simplest, smallest, most robust Singer possible. She had already thought through several ideas for eliminating organs, but each had fallen apart almost immediately. Her latest idea was nothing more than a notion, so unformed that she could hardly articulate it. "Well, I'm certain we can't eliminate anything but I'm thinking we may be able to combine some of the organs, to make a new kind of miniaturized system," she started to say, eager to keep talking but also wanting to get back to the drawing board.

Arthur nodded, making her feel like he understood her plans, but then he interrupted her. "This sounds promising, Molly. I look forward to hearing more when you're ready," he said. "You know how important this is. We've taken a big hit from that story glamorizing illegal food. It puts pressure on us to do better. But we're in a bind, Molly. We just can't afford to keep reconstituting these Singers every six months. Your project is going to make all of the difference."

"Reconstituting?"

"Of course," he said. "But then, didn't I explain? I sometimes forget that you don't attend all of the meetings. I suppose I should have mentioned it…" Arthur slipped his computer from his hip holster and, with a few finger taps, he projected a map onto the steel wall of the Singer hold. "Here we go," he muttered. "This should help."

Molly tilted her head and took in the data. The map showed the local city roughly divided into neighborhoods and crisscrossed by major traffic arteries. Arthur tapped his fingers again and up popped tiny nautilus-shaped icons representing the Singer holds within a 30-mile radius.

Molly gasped. The icons crowded the map, completely obscuring the neighborhood grid-work.

"Quite a sight, isn't it?" Arthur whispered.

Molly took a minute to admire the screen. She felt a surge of pride looking at this network of sustainable nutrition that she had helped make possible. She thought of all of the Singers quietly humming underground, just like the one behind her, unbeknownst to almost everyone who benefits from them. It had never occurred to her before just how large the network had become. It made sense, of course, with so many people to feed. She'd seen the numbers in product plans time and again. But she'd never before seen it laid out so strikingly.

Arthur tapped his fingers again. The image zoomed in on a 3-mile radius and the Singer icons changed color. Molly sucked in her breath. Nearly half of the Singer icons had turned to an alarming red, yellow, or orange hue.

"Now you see what we're up against," said Arthur. "The Singers grow old, just like us, but they seem to be doing it on an accelerated schedule. The red icons represent Singers that no longer deliver consistent product. Yellow and orange give us warning that quality or quantity are beginning to decline. We're starting to see real problems in the field. What's most alarming is that some of these Singers have only been in service for six months." Arthur swiped his hand across the image to close it and slipped his computer back into its holster. He turned to Molly and leaned against the railing. "We're hoping the miniMeat design will help solve the problem, or, at least, make the Singers cheaper to incubate. We need a solution soon. We've got those up and comers at Cellulix on our heels."

Arthur's earpiece beeped. "Selica Friedman. Another day, another emergency." He sighed and left Molly standing alone in the hold with the Singer.

When Arthur arrived at the Marketing suite, Selica's assistant shuttled him into her office and closed the door.

"Did you see the Cellulix announcement in the trades?" Selica asked him before he sat down. She flashed a smile, her straight nose and coiffed hair the picture of elegance, her painted lips and enameled teeth wolfishly dazzling. When he nodded yes, she continued. "They announced their protein strings. They grow like hair, only thicker. Spines too. They call it dense protein. It sounds fascinating. It could turn into multiple potential product lines. It's a whole new model for protein delivery."

Arthur had heard rumors about the new product, but he knew they didn't even have a working prototype yet. "It sounds better than it is because it doesn't exist yet. It's vapor. Nothing to worry about."

"I'm glad you're on top of this, Arthur. Did I mention that I got a call from Deshawndra over at the NArc Sourcing? She asked me about our plans for dense proteins. She said Sourcing is considering all of its options." Selica assumed a concerned look. "It's important that we stay ahead of the curve, don't you think? We need to define the cutting edge. SynEngra supplies sixty percent of the NArc's protein because we lead the field. If we want to keep our share of the sourcing, we need to keep leading." Selica tucked a loop of sculpted hair behind her ear and folded her hands.

Arthur shifted in his chair but remained silent. He knew what would come next.

"We need to make the miniMeat announcement," she said.

Against his better judgement, Arthur reacted. "But we're not ready. The first team crashed and burned, so I just assigned Tanaka. She's barely off the ground with it. She's not even sure miniMeat will be the right solution. Besides, you know the Singers make the public nervous."

"We won't mention the Singers. Only the miniMeat. We'll make it compelling and fresh. And you need to pull your schedule in." Arthur opened his mouth to object, but she talked over him.

"Remember, the government buys our products, like Neermeat, because we deliver reliable nutrition at the right price. If a competitor can deliver a better product at a better price, we'll lose our market share." Arthur opened his mouth again, but the discussion was already over. "I'll have Katelyn send you a draft by midweek." The twittering of Selica's chat window grabbed her attention. She answered it immediately. "Hello Stanley. How's your trip so far?" she simpered.

Stanley Withers, the CEO. Arthur groaned. He had never seen the man in person. But his likeness hung in the front lobby. A friend of Arthur's in the headquarters office said she saw him often, but only in glimpses. She described him as compact, smaller than you might expect, and always moving, barking commands as he passed through the office on his way to or from someplace else.

"Why did my lunch numbers drop, Selica? I was having a perfectly good round of ZeroG. Two under par at the turn. Then I get this blasted alert. Whatever it is, make it stop. I've got another round Thursday. On The Old Course, by the first lunar landing site. I'd like it to go uninterrupted. I'm playing with the Secretary of Health. You know how she worries. I need stable numbers. And something good to say. Something promising. Understood?" He didn't wait for her response before disconnecting.

Selica turned back to Arthur. "So we'll send the announcement out this week. And I'm glad you were here for this call. Withers doesn't like to see the NArc usage numbers dip. The slightest waver sets off alarms. The Health Department starts re-evaluating the whole supply chain. They want stable public nutrition, Arthur. It's in the best interest of the nation, don't you agree? They want consistent consumption of the NArc's products. And so do we. That's why it's so important that we put the brakes on this Sage Weaver woman. Right away."

Arthur raised an eyebrow. He hadn't expected this to come up.

"You of course saw her story yesterday. It seems as if everyone read it."

"I saw it. But—"

"Then you know what's at stake, Arthur," she said, employing her practiced smile again. "I really shouldn't keep you any longer, should I? You've got so much on your plate."

Molly hurried back to her desk. The new information Arthur had given her about her project had driven any silly ideas about Singers out of her mind. Now she just wanted to get back to work. She couldn't believe Arthur had not told her the root cause of the problem she'd been assigned to solve. He would never understand that the details, every single detail, had relevance. *I will have to be more vigilant in the future,* she resolved. Attend every meeting. Supervise every experiment.

As she turned down her hallway, she spotted Nate lurking outside her lab. *Not now,* she groaned to herself, planning excuses as she walked.

"Time to eat that upstairs in the SkyPark?" he asked, nodding at her lunch.

Molly sighed. He looked anxious, but her own anxiety won out. "I'm already behind today. Can it wait?"

"Me too. Sorry. I tried to get out earlier, but the algorithm I designed isn't working and I'm getting hammered," he said, shooting a look behind them. He leaned in. "Something's been bugging me ever since Angela started this, this…project."

"Alright. Fine. But just fifteen minutes, okay?"

He nodded and lead the way to the elevators.

When the doors opened, they were greeted by a cluster of lunchtime stragglers waiting in a neat row just wide enough for them to step efficiently into the elevator box. The group shuffled awkwardly to make room for them to pass.

Molly settled into a quiet grove of hanging trees. As Nate checked to make sure they were alone, she lifted her chin and let the sunlight beaming through the translucent roof warm her face. Then she unwrapped the meal the NArc had dispensed. Its extruded layers of Neermeat, starch, and vegetable cake were stacked to a convenient height. She admired the elegant multi-colored edges trimmed at crisp 90 degree angles before breaking off a bite-sized piece with her fork.

When Nate returned, he sat next to her. "I found something," he whispered.

The tone of his voice made her choke. "Did you learn something about Josh? Is he dangerous?"

"No, no. He checked out. No arrests. Everyone vouched for him. As much as he may be, what did you call him? A mob boss? Heh. As much as he may be that, he's a stand-up guy. He doesn't deal in violence. Far as I can see, he's an honest businessman, though, arguably, in an illegal business."

Molly felt momentarily relieved, then impatient again. "What is it then?"

"Well, what this connection told me, it didn't mean anything until Angela started talking about history the other night. Remember? She was telling us about our history, but then she was telling us they think that history is different."

"Yes, I remember. You didn't seem very impressed with their version of history last night. We both know it's absurd."

"Yeah, I guess. I think we might have been a little hard on her. Thing is, this guy online, one of the informants that told me about the drops, he also told me that Safe and Sustainable had all the answers. That was all he said. But it got me wondering. Answers to what?"

"I hardly think this is worth our time, Nate. This project of Angela's has already got Arthur worried," said Molly. "And I'm busy. So can you just please get to the point?"

"I looked it up this morning. Safe and Sustainable is the Safe and Sustainable Food Foundation. They fund research," he said, as if that explained everything.

"Yes, Nate, I know. They funded my first project when I was a grad student. They funded Sandy Philpot's lab. I worked on Neermeat prototypes there when I was still at Tech. They fund lots of stuff."

Nate seemed surprised, and Molly shook her head and looked back at him, waiting for him to give her one good reason why she should be wasting time on this discussion.

"Well, I guess I don't know as much about it as I should. But why did this person point them out to me? Of all the funding organizations, why point *them* out? I mean, shouldn't we try to find out where they got their money? Shouldn't we look at the studies they did and see if there's some sort of pattern?"

Molly shook her head in exasperation. "Look, Nate, science is science. It doesn't matter where the money comes from."

"But Angela's Foodie friends were talking about a conspiracy against food. You said yourself that they sound like radicals. What if they are? What if we can prove they're wrong? Shouldn't we at least try to make sure she doesn't get herself into something she can't handle?"

Molly sighed and looked past him. She knew Nate would pursue this no matter what. But she also knew he wouldn't be able to do it without her help. He simply didn't have the background. She dropped her chin. He had a point about Angela, too, she thought, sighing again. "Ok. I'll help. But I'm not going to be free until Thursday. Can it wait until then?"

Nate beamed. "I'll get everything set up. Thanks Molly. I feel better already."

In spite of herself, Molly smiled back. The simplest things seem to make him happy, she thought as she waved goodbye and hurried back to the lab.

8

Angela left her apartment late in the afternoon on Thursday. Four days had passed since her story came out. Since then she had spent most of her time responding to comments online, trying to educate her readers. She had also spent hours chatting with Josh and eating with him in person, mostly at tiny household kitchens.

Tonight he was taking her to her first speakeasy.

The place served one thing only. Pasta with meat sauce. It didn't sound that special to Angela, but Josh had assured her that it was. "The pasta is handmade," he'd said. "Plus they cook the sauce for hours, stirring it constantly over low heat. It changes the chemistry. The acid in the tomatoes neutralizes the fat in the meat. But only if you cook it slowly. And only if you stir it. It's an old Bolognese tradition. You're gonna love it."

Intrigued, Angela looked forward to quizzing the chefs about their methods. She did, however, still regret asking Josh about the meat in the sauce. Beef and pork were old hat by now, but chicken livers? Ugh.

She took the train south and met Josh on a quiet street corner set in an enclave that still had a small-town feel. She noticed the cries of gulls and, between gusts of wind, the smell of salt and seaweed invaded her nostrils. A block to their east, waves crashed into a concrete seawall. Just a few blocks west stood an apartment complex almost indistinguishable from her own.

Josh led her into an old two-family house that had been converted into apartments. They climbed to the top floor and a woman named Bella led them to a table on a screened porch hanging off the back of the house. Angela caught hints of cooking smells as they ascended the stairs but the sea breeze swept them away as fast as they arrived.

They sat down, taking the last two places at the oblong table, and Bella brought focaccia and oil. Angela was just about to try it when the door flew open. The room flooded with Food Cops, their faces shielded and their hands gloved. Their gun barrels bore down on the diners. Angela opened her mouth to scream but no sound came. Time slowed to a crawl and the scene unfolded before her in vivid detail: the blackness of a gun pointing her way; the hazard-orange glove stretched taught over an index finger poised on the trigger; the eyes of the man holding the gun wide and unblinking behind the plastic shield. For several seconds she couldn't register Josh's voice. She saw him, his arms raised, his face calm, his mouth moving, but heard nothing. Then, in a rush, the sound came.

"Angela? Can you hear me?" When her eyes focused on him, Josh continued. "Everything's going to be okay. Put your hands up and do what they ask. I'll contact you as soon as I can."

He got those last words out just before the cop behind him grabbed him and slammed his face onto the table. Angela shrieked. She instinctively reached out to help Josh when a firm but not unkind hand stopped her and pulled her arms behind her. "What are *you* doing here?" a voice rasped in her ear. "I told Frank to warn you off!"

The cop led her out a back door and away from the fray. He eased her into the back of a patrol car. It wasn't until he slid into the driver's seat that she recognized him. "I'm still going to have to bring you in. Too many people saw you there, kiddo," said Potente as he backed the squad car out of the alley. "You're just lucky I saw you first," he said, his harsh voice grabbing her attention.

At the police station, Potente led her to his desk, sat her down on a hard metal chair, and poured her a shot of whisky from a bottle he pulled from a drawer in his desk. Surprised but grateful, she accepted the shot with shaking hands and winced as it burned down her esophagus. She watched as he stowed away the bottle, avoiding her eyes, then she scanned the room. Each desk was manned by a cop interrogating one of her fellow diners. Without their face shields, gloves, vests and guns, the cops looked much less threatening. If it weren't for the raid uniforms, now unbuttoned and hanging loose on their shoulders, she would have had a hard time telling the cops from the criminals. She started to look for Josh but Potente's voice snapped her attention back to him.

"Do you want to tell me what the hell you were doing there today? There's no point in my sticking my neck out for you if you're going to ignore my warnings," he fumed.

Angela stared back at him, puzzled. She had regained her wits enough to hear him, but was still too stunned to understand. Warning? She hadn't gotten any warning.

Potente leaned back in his chair and shook his head. "You reporters. No loyalty at all." Leaning forward again, this time more sympathetically, his elbows resting on his knees, he said, "I passed a warning to Frank. I passed him this week's raid list. He said he would pass it to you. To keep you out of trouble."

"Frank didn't tell me," she mumbled, thinking that Frank had found a way to get her back for besting him. For breaking into the Foodie network and trampling his beat with her first food story.

"With the latest bad news, I thought you might lie low for a time anyway."

Angela slumped a little further in her chair. "What bad news," she droned, feeling defeated and out of touch. Whatever respect she had earned with the lieutenant during her first visits was eroding fast.

Potente shook his head again, but his fingers glided over his keyboard and he turned the screen toward her. She leaned in and read what was a very brief news report. So brief it didn't have a by-line:

Another Cheater Dies

Northeast City, May 16, 2063 — Thirty-four year old Felicity Merriweather died early this morning in her apartment in the Brattle Street living complex from apparent food poisoning. Her apartment contained scraps of illegal foodstuffs. Neighbors and immediate family members deny knowledge of her illicit activities. Officials at the scene, however, state the cause of death as poisoning from contaminated foods.

"This is a harsh reminder that illegal foods are illegal for a reason. They are not safe under any circumstances," said Henry Potente, a lieutenant in the food police at the scene of the incident.

"What happened?" she asked, looking to Potente for the inside story.

"You know as much as I do. As much as anyone will ever know, I suspect." He rubbed his hands together. "But what it means is that you should be careful." He held her gaze and then sighed. "I'm going to have to book you, Angela. I've got no choice." Potente patted her on the knee gently. "Don't worry. You're a first timer. No more than a fine and a mark on your record." He brought up a form on his old laptop computer, its top secured to the base with several layers of duct tape, and started typing. "This won't take long at all."

As Potente typed, Angela sat on the hard chair, surrounded by armed officers, and contemplated the news story. She felt as if someone had woken her from a dream. She hated to admit to herself that the Foodies had swept her away. But she got into this because of Martine Sinsky, a real woman who died a real death. She'd been having so much fun with Josh that, at this point, she had almost forgotten.

Angela thought back through the places he'd been taking her. She then remembered Josh sitting across from her in the speakeasy no more than an hour ago, his face just before he was... Wincing involuntarily, she ventured, "Lieutenant, do you know where Josh is? If he's okay?"

Potente waved her off without looking away from the screen. "Salter? He'll be fine. He's never been picked up before, either. Seems like he's got better friends than you do, kiddo." He gave her a quick wink, then went back to his forms. "Don't worry about him. He'll get the same treatment as you." Then, clearing his throat, he said, "The same fine, anyway."

9

Molly came home Thursday night completely wiped out from the long hours she'd been putting in all week. As she walked into her apartment, she wanted nothing more than to take a bath, go to bed, and not think about Neermeat or Singers for a good 8 hours.

But she had promised Nate. She dropped her bag on the floor and checked the time. Thirty minutes before she was due to meet him online. She had felt jittery all day, but now her brain felt muddy and incapable of the task he had planned for them. Normally she would relish the chance to review a bunch of old scientific papers, but this week had been such a strain. She needed a break.

But Nate had begged her. And Molly knew he needed her help.

"Angela?" Molly called into the apartment. Angela had hardly been home all week. Then again, neither had Molly. The last time they'd talked was just after her article had come out. Molly panicked for an instant. With everything going on at work, she hadn't even tried to keep track of her friend. How many times had she been underground since Sunday? She knew Angela would jump at every chance she got.

Molly flicked on a light and scanned her friend's room. It looked lived in enough, with clothes strewn about and makeup on the desk. When she checked her own room, the note Angela had left on her pillow jumped out as the only thing out of place. It read:

"Am fine. With Josh. Amazing stuff. Talk Friday?"

Molly sighed in relief, but then slumped in dismay. She had squandered all of her time. She promised Nate she would be in his secret online room by 8pm, but she had no idea how long it would take to get there. Nate had said that with his instructions it would "take no time." No time for him maybe. She was going to have to re-learn how to navigate cyberspace in stealth mode. Instead of a bath, Molly settled for a quick shower. Her hair still damp, she logged in. Even though she had given herself a head start, she still ended up being 5 minutes late.

"Is anything wrong?" asked Nate when she arrived. "Did someone follow you?"

Molly had no idea if she had been followed. She wasn't even sure how to tell. But she couldn't face going through all of that work again, work that to her seemed like overkill. She assured him that everything went well, just slowly. To change the subject, she commented, "Nice jacket."

Nate sat at a long mahogany table in a high-backed leather chair set inside a fancy conference room. His avatar this evening was a rockabilly version of himself, with a blond ducktail, a black leather jacket, tight jeans and black pointy boots.

"I, uh, I'm going to a concert later," he said. Just then, the sound of muted screams came through the conference room window, which looked out over a simulated amusement park with looping roller coasters and free-fall towers. "The place closes in a few minutes." he said.

Molly rubbed her forehead and hoped that meant that the screaming would soon cease.

"I've already split up the articles by topic and ordered them oldest to newest," he explained. "The piles include work funded by Safe and Sustainable, but only the papers with the highest bibliometric influence ratings. That should save some time."

"I still don't see why you're demonizing Safe and Sustainable," Molly interrupted. "You do realize who is on their board. Withers. You know he has *two* PhDs. Stanhope, the CTO at NutriArc. Sanguinetti from Cellulix. That woman from NuriVici, the one with the record-breaking number of patents. I mean, it's run by some of the most brilliant Nutritionists in town. In the world even."

"Yeah. I know who runs it," he replied, sounding undeterred. "Why don't you look at the Neerfoods papers and I'll look at the nutritional genomics stuff," he suggested.

Molly, still resisting the idea, pushed back the papers and suggested the opposite. "I've already read most of these. And I assume you've followed the genomics work. We'll find more holes if we look at the research we haven't seen yet."

Nate didn't argue. He took a paper off the top of one of the stacks and started to read.

Two hours later, Molly rubbed her eyes and stood up to stretch. She had taken breaks every half hour or so, and each time, she'd felt a little less revived. This time, she yawned a nearly endless yawn, as if she couldn't get enough oxygen.

Just as she was about to suggest calling it a night, Nate's avatar spoke. "I know what's wrong," he said, putting down the paper he was reading. "We've been looking for holes in each study. Aside from the obvious—a bunch of these studies are small and some of the data seems subjective to me—we haven't found any. But what's missing isn't small. It's so big, we can't even see it."

Molly's avatar blinked. In real life, she rolled her shoulders and stretched her neck, trying to wake up. "Okaaay," she said.

"What's missing is all the things that weren't studied. Look at this pile. It's study after study showing that engineered foods are nutritionally excellent." He flipped though them as he spoke. "These two show that mice thrive on prototype Neermeat. This paper reviews engineered plants loaded with anti-cancer micronutrients. Another one shows how to blend them for optimal nutrition. And yet another shows that tumors shrink when mice eat these balanced products. Don't you see? It's like these foods are running in a race by themselves. There's not a single study that compares these designer nutrients to regular foods."

Molly blinked again. She hadn't really thought of doing a study like that. No one had. The idea all along had been to do better than conventional foods. Conventional foods caused illnesses and people who ate them were sick all the time, so scientists didn't bother to study them, she reasoned. But how did she know that these foods were sub-par? She had been taught never to assume. It was one of the very first things she had learned in science. She grabbed the papers from in front of Nate and flipped through them. Where was it? It had to be here. "There was a paper…," she muttered, flipping to the backs of the articles and scanning the references.

"Ah! Here it is," she exclaimed. She pointed to a single line of one of the oldest papers Nate had dug up. The Dalyrimple paper. "This is the one. This is the source. I remember now," she sighed, satisfied and relieved. She explained to Nate that in the teens and 20s there had been lots of studies of conventional foods. Then in the 30s, pre-Migration, Dalyrimple had done a meta-analysis. She had crossed lots of different diseases with different foods and rated all of the risk and benefit factors. That paper had set the bar.

"After that, things changed," she told him. "Everyone's attention turned to engineered foods."

"Setting the bar is fine," countered Nate, "but it's only useful if people refer back to the bar. We've got 40 papers here and only one refers back to that paper."

Molly yawned again. Her avatar slumped as she sat at home trying to make sense of it all. Nate had a point, but to her it didn't sound like a conspiracy. It sounded like good sense. No one working on modern automobile technology would dream of comparing today's vehicles to 20th century gas guzzlers. Barely able to keep her eyes open, she said, "I think I need to sleep on this Nate." Her avatar gave a weak wave and walked out of the conference room.

When Nate arrived at his office the next morning, the first thing he did was send Molly a message. He felt guilty about having pushed her so hard. When she'd walked out, he'd called after her, but she'd already disconnected. He hadn't thought too much about it. They always debated. It was the one reliable way he'd found to connect with her.

It wasn't until later that he realized that she might have taken it personally. She saw things so differently. Nate had always known that the NArc had its critics. His own parents had fought against dependence on the NArc and delayed the family Migration as long as possible. He'd grown up listening to their protests, but their arguments hadn't stuck. When they finally did move, Nate had gobbled up the NArc. He knew he'd done it to spite them. Looking back now, he had to admit that there might have been some truth to their concerns.

Still, these arguments weren't new to him like they were to Molly. Her entire life had revolved around the NArc. She and her parents had a hand in pioneering several of the system's main components. He didn't want her to end up resenting him for being the one to point out its scientific flaws.

Nate typed his message: "Hey. Are you ok? Time to talk? – N"

He hit the send key and turned his sleep-deprived eyes to his code. Before he had a chance to refocus, his computer chimed. Molly's reply, he thought. He clicked back to his mail. The message had come not from Molly but from the system. The subject: "user communications blockade in effect."

To the sender,

The addressee cannot receive your message. Molly Tanaka, Consulting Scientist and Manager, Engineered Protein Foods Division, is temporarily isolated from all non-critical communications. If this communication is project-critical, please resend the message with the project-specific encrypted password in the appropriate format.

Please do not reply to this message.

Nate stared at the text. He'd seen mail blockades before, during crunch times. But for Molly, it was always crunch time. He considered asking his boss about it, but things had been weird between them ever since he had to take time off for Food School. He didn't want to have to tell Fletcher he was trying to chat with Molly on SynEngra's time. He read the message again and considered walking down to the lab to ask Molly about it.

Just as the thought crossed his mind, he caught a glimpse of Zoey Nordling reflected in the mirror he had clipped to his screen. Her approach cut his thinking short. Zoey assembled his team's code into easy to use Sim packages for the scientists. And today was a build day.

Nate designed Simulations that let the scientists try out different interventions on all kinds of biological imbalances. The Sims modeled the workings of individual cells, down to the very molecules that made them tick, replicating their chemical, electrical and mechanical interactions. Nate worked on the visualization package—much more fun than the internals he used to do. He had programmed data retrieval routines during a painfully boring internship at the NArc. Then SynEngra hired him to do chemical modeling. To test the models, he needed solid graphics and visualization tools, but the SynEngra VizKit sucked. So he ended up building his own. It wasn't long before the Sim group adopted his code—and him—to be the graphics core.

Seeing Zoey, Nate's project deadline came rushing back. Shit! He had spent the last few weeks working on better ways to show the electrical properties of cell surfaces. He'd finished tweaking the code the day before but hadn't tested it. He had planned to come in early and work through his final checks, but with everything last night, he'd forgotten. As his fingers danced across his touchscreen, closing his mail windows and bringing up his coding window, he caught sight of Zoey again in the mirror, much closer now.

Zoey's appearance, as usual, had forced a double take. Now that it was inexpensive to erase tattoos, she replaced hers as if they were clothing. She sometimes used her skin to advertise new products. She also used it to broadcast her mood. Today, between her eyes, just below her cropped orange bangs, glowered a third eye.

"Hunter, you're not checked in yet," she scolded. "Deadline's 3. Will you be ready?"

Nate murmured something unintelligible and waved her off without turning around, hoping not to have to face that eye.

"If you're not in, we're canceling," she threatened offhandedly, leaning on the cube wall and inspecting her black fingernails. Twice a week she had power and she never passed up an opportunity to use it.

"That's not fair," whined Barty from the next cube over. "I've been checked in since late last night. Why should I have to be punished? Can't we go without his stuff?"

"Shut up, Barty," Zoey chanted for possibly the hundredth time. She leaned in, and hissed, "I love making him sit through cancellation reviews. But not tonight, Hunter. I've got a date."

Nate shuddered. But then, he thought, better some other guy than me sitting across from that eye tonight. He set himself to work.

By the time Molly finished her day it was after 8 pm. Late for a Friday, she thought, but that was happening more and more often these days. After arranging her desktop so it would be orderly when she arrived the next morning, she gathered her things. Before clicking off her light, she made one last check of her messages. Still nothing from Nate. He forces me to stay up late, upsets me with some wild conspiracy theory, and then never calls to apologize? Not even to talk? Molly simmered inside. So unreliable. So inconsiderate!

She rubbed her temples and tried to relax her tensed forehead. I really don't need this right now, she thought. The long lab hours had seemed easier when she was younger. Still, Saturdays at work can be very relaxing. No interruptions. No meetings. She looked forward to getting a long night's sleep and returning for a day of laid-back weekend work.

But she had one more thing to do before bed. She had promised to meet Angela in the NArcCafe at home. It would be good to see her in person and verify that she was doing as well as she claimed. Besides, Angela won't mind if I don't stay up late, she thought, as the lab door closed behind her.

When she arrived at the NArcCafe, Molly grabbed her meal at the counter and headed for their usual seats. She faced the door, since Angela hadn't arrived yet, and began to unwrap her meal. This evening, the NArc had dispensed a sushi roll-up, strips of squishy omega3-infused Neermeat surrounded by green and orange cellulose all wrapped in a translucent pancake and covered with a tawny paste. As she arranged the food on her plate, she heard an unfamiliar voice.

"Molly?" it asked. She looked up into a pair of cool gray eyes. "I'm Parrish Knight. Angela sent me with a note for you." He handed her a slip of paper and then, after a glance at the sparsely populated dining room, added, "May I join you for a moment?"

"Please," nodded Molly. She waited for him to sit then opened her note. She recognized Angela's scrawl immediately. "I'm fine. Late night party. Join us! Parrish will take you. -A" After reading it twice, she looked back at Parrish, but remained silent. Each knew the other had some involvement in Angela's quest, but she didn't want to be the one to bring it up first. It was too serious, despite the light tone of Angela's note.

Besides, Parrish had Molly tongue-tied. There was something about him. His wide shoulders and long hair. And those eyes. Gray, but with a hint of gold around the pupil, as if they were lit from within. She couldn't stop staring at him.

Parrish broke the silence. "Angela didn't tell me you were Molly *Tanaka*. You are Kozue Tanaka's daughter?"

"Yes, but…how do you—"

"I worked in his lab years ago. In fact, I'm one of his biggest admirers. And I'm quite familiar with your work too." Parrish smiled warmly. "I had no idea Angela had such brilliant friends."

PUBLIC LIBRARY
PLAISTOW, NH

This made Molly blush and look down. When she looked back up, his eyes were still on hers. Finally she remembered the note, now limp in her damp hand. Why am I sweating? she thought, putting the paper down. "I'm glad to hear that Angela is fine," she said, wiping her hands and trying to get a grip.

"Yes, she's fine." He nodded at the note. "Would you like to join us tonight?"

For an instant, Molly was tempted. She looked at the note again and, seeing Angela's scrawl, thought better of it. "It really isn't my kind of thing."

"I understand. It isn't for everyone. It can't be."

Molly couldn't tell from his tone if he was lamenting that fact or bragging about it. She shook her head in confusion. "I'm sorry, but how is it that you know my father, that you worked with him, yet you're also involved in this?" She picked up the note again, then crumpled it.

"We all have our weaknesses, I guess. I got mine from my mother. She was a gourmet in her time. I've never been able to kick the habit completely." He let out a self-conscious laugh.

"I'm sure you must know what you're doing. But I still don't understand. How do you know the food is safe? How do you know that Angela is safe? How will she avoid being caught and fined? Or worse. Her mom...those deaths..." Molly's voice trailed off. She suddenly realized how grave a risk her friend was taking with her health. She hadn't thought it through before. Maybe she hadn't really believed that Angela would break into the underground. Of course, now that she had, nothing could hold her back.

"We test what we eat," he replied. "And you're right. Angela does have to be careful. Josh has taught her how to track what she eats. And I'm monitoring her feedback to make sure she doesn't raise any NArc Alarms."

"But how?" Molly pressed. She needed the details and wasn't willing to accept his word as authority. When Parrish started to describe the inner workings of the NArc, Molly interrupted. She knew how the System worked. She wanted to know how *he* worked.

"What I do," he explained, "is filter out the extremes. The chip will still report fluctuations in the normal range, but it won't sound alarms for abnormal swings. I check those manually. They aren't lost. If Angela overdoes it, we'll know."

His response made Molly feel that Angela was in competent hands. It made sense. And despite her exhaustion, talking to Parrish energized her. His self-assurance and directness felt refreshing. No longer dumbstruck, she found herself probing, wanting to know him better. "When was it that you worked with my father? Which project?"

"Decades ago. We did a few diagnostics projects together. He doesn't… He doesn't know about my outside interests. I hope it's not too much to ask you to keep this between the two of us?"

"No, not at all," she said a little too quickly.

Parrish looked relieved and smiled again, sealing their pact. "You seem as bright and curious as I would have expected you to be. And as concerned," he added with a somber look. "Is there anything else you'd like to ask me? I'm happy to try to help you understand, to help put your mind to rest."

Molly thought about the Dalyrimple paper and Nate's conspiracy theory, both of which still disturbed her. "Well, there is one. It's about science but also about the Cheater—sorry, I mean Foodie—world."

He chuckled. Rather than finding her gaff offensive, it seemed to Molly that he found her to be endearing.

She explained to him that a friend had concluded that the last 20 years of science was one-sided. Without a follow up on Dalyrimple, he'd said, the rest of science was somehow unbalanced. Maybe even biased. It worried her. "If Angela's stories catch on, and if my friend is right, I'm concerned that things might get out of hand," she confessed.

"I remember Dalyrimple. And I also have reservations about Angela's work," he admitted. "But what is your question, Molly?"

Molly felt flustered. He didn't sound impatient, but he should have been. She had been rambling. She wasn't accustomed to having jumbled thoughts and speaking off the cuff. She took a moment to let the key question form before stating it. "The question is, was the Dalyrimple work stopped because of a conspiracy against food or had it just reached a logical endpoint?"

Parrish nodded slowly and seemed to be thinking back to earlier times. "As I remember it, the funding dried up. All the money went to synthetic food studies."

"Right. But why?" she insisted.

Parrish eyed her as if she were too young to understand, even though, from the look of him, she guessed he wasn't more than ten years her senior. When he spoke, he used a gentle voice and softened his eyes. "You have to understand that it was a crisis situation," he said. "Food had become expensive and vulnerable. It lost out to engineered nutrition because society needed a reliable food supply during and after the crisis. What mattered was feeding people. Could we have learned more about food? Yes. Did the people with the money think we needed to? No. So we didn't."

Molly nodded. A crisis situation. She had read about it, and certainly she had heard about it as it unfolded during her childhood in the 20s and 30s. But she hadn't lived it. Not really. "So you don't think it was a conspiracy to eliminate food from the equation?"

Parrish shrugged but didn't dismiss her question. "Maybe it was. Maybe it wasn't," he replied evenly. "Dalyrimple studied an ideal, but we live in a world of compromise. I've learned to accept that and to enjoy what I have rather than regret what I've lost."

Sensible, thought Molly. Even if some outside force pushed things in one direction, it's too late now. There's no going back. And besides, the science we do now is good. It's solid. In her head, she closed the door on the topic.

But Molly wasn't ready for Parrish to leave. She liked being with him. With an equal, she thought. "I'm still bewildered that you can balance being a scientist and a Foodie," she said awkwardly. "How do you rationalize it?"

Parrish stared back at Molly, making her fear that she'd pushed too far. But when he spoke, his voice sounded serious. He held her spellbound again with his eyes. "I respect science. The thing is, Molly, that nature is better. Only right now, science is all we have." With that, he stood up and reached out to shake Molly's hand. "It's been a pleasure. Maybe we can meet again sometime?"

Molly's heart skipped a beat. She would like that very much, she thought as he turned and walked to the door.

10

Angela tugged her zipper up to her chin and shook out her hair. She checked her reflection in the mirror, dragging her eyes from her waist to her forehead, looking for bulges and flaws. She had always been curvy, with a round and soft body type so different from Molly's straight lines and sharp angles. But it wasn't curves that worried her. It was excess bulk, and she couldn't detect any. Satisfied that her new diet didn't show, at least not yet, she applied a final coat of lip balm, mashed her lips together and grabbed her bag.

Halfway out the door, she ran back in and grabbed a scarf. She suspected her journey would take her outside of the covered sidewalks and climate-controlled tunnels in the city center. Though still urban, the western edges of the city sprawled rather than climbed. Its outdoor walkways were always chillier or, in the summer, more stifling than downtown.

Despite the warmth of the scarf, she still shivered when she thought about Josh. When she'd seen him on Friday evening —for the first time after their arrest—he'd smothered her in a strong hug and then let go only to check her face and arms. Were you hurt? he'd asked. She'd assured him she wasn't, but as she said it, she'd reached out to touch his face. He had a black eye and a swollen lip. He shook it off and told her he'd split his lip on the table top and caught an elbow in the eye, but she didn't buy it. "I'm so sorry," she'd whispered, her eyes welling and her brain cursing Frank for setting her up. Josh hugged her again and, as he held her, she couldn't help but notice the strength in his hands and the way her cheek settled perfectly into his chest. But the embrace, having gone on just a little too long, had ended awkwardly.

Angela had tried to recover by bringing up the second dead woman, Felicity Merriweather. He hadn't heard the news either. She asked him if he thought it seemed similar to Sinsky, if he thought the two deaths might be related in any way. He said he didn't know, but that he would ask around. He had never heard of Merriweather, but if anyone had, he would find out. To Angela, the story seemed too similar to Sinsky to dismiss.

Angela tried to put Merriweather out of her mind by recalling the rest of Friday's events. Josh had kept close to her all evening. Alone, at the end of the night, he had kissed her. A sweet, luxurious kiss that they had lingered over, neither of them wanting it to end yet neither of them ready for it to go further.

I sure know how to find adventure, she thought, as she tucked in the loose ends of her scarf and stepped into the waiting elevator at the end of the hallway. The metallic cube dropped her to the 10th floor and the entrance to the train line that would carry her to South Station.

She boarded the train and, in another attempt at diversion, she eyed her fellow riders. Had the woman in the matte-black suit, sensible hair and orderly bag ever Cheated? An extra glass of wine, maybe some crafted beer from Vermont. Now that she knew such things existed, she found it hard to believe anyone could resist the temptation. What about the man in the navy work-clothes and scuffed boots? Did one of the three college students have a bag full of Junk? A report that came out the year before said one in five adults Cheated, but that only ten percent of those did so more than a once a month. If those numbers were accurate, odds were that her present company included at least five other sometime Cheaters. Angela, herself, made up the statistical half-person who took Cheating to an extreme.

These calculations comforted her, somehow. People wouldn't do it if they got slammed around by cops at every meal. Potente had told her that the raids were infrequent. His division had filled their quota for the month. She didn't have to worry. For now.

Turning her gaze out the window next to her, she took in the cityscape. The residential towers radiated outward from the old Avenue, forming arcs connected at odd angles. The patterns reflected the old neighborhoods they evolved from, almost as if the old triple deckers had sprouted upwards twenty stories and expanded to fill the spaces between them. Density had become one with efficiency. Angela had often thought it must have been tedious to have to travel several blocks to find a different neighborhood rather than just hopping from floor to floor. Now she wondered if the differences she detected in the modern neighborhoods were just illusions, each nothing more than a thin veneer on top of sterilized monotony.

The train crossed over the river. Below her, she could see the historic ironwork bridge. Sailboats flitted on the water below. The wind whipping in the sails made her glad that she had picked up her scarf.

The train stopped at the hospital. Several passengers departed, geared up in antibacterial smart fabrics. She hadn't needed any replacement surgeries or regrowth treatments yet, and dreaded the day she would. The procedures were safe, as safe as having your teeth cleaned, but she had never liked doctors or hospitals. She had seen too much of them with her mother. A new wave of passengers entered, looking ragged from their work or peaky from their treatments.

She turned her eyes back to the window and watched the cityscape grow increasingly dense. The train maintained its 10th story elevation, making two more stops at corporate tower hubs. As far as she could see there were skyscrapers. Some with lush, tranquil parks tucked into nooks on their sides, others with slick exteriors. The corporate names lit up the sky: SynEngra, EnerTec, GEknOwME, BankduChine, and so on. She craned her neck to catch a glimpse of the NutriArc buildings, twin towers further west that could be seen through the U-shaped gap of the Patriot Center. The NArc buildings formed two helical towers that linked together on multiple floors, like a DNA molecule. She had visited it once, years ago. When Nate worked there, he said the buildings looked cooler than they actually were. The infrastructure never worked. Some floors were too cold, others too hot. And it could take an hour to get from one place to another. Trying to design an efficient elevator had taken a team of mathematicians a year of effort but "the thing still sucked," he'd said.

The train continued its southern trajectory, hurtling its passengers toward South Station, the southern maglev gateway.

She followed the crowd down to the ground-level platform. People stood in single-file lines at the entrance to Track 3, awaiting a train leaving in twenty minutes. Her eyepiece display directed her to Track 7 and began a 5 minute countdown to departure. She jogged down the platform to the fifth carriage of the waiting train and stepped into line to board. It was filling up fast. Spotting Josh in the fifth row in a two-seater alone, she resisted the urge to make contact. Instead, she slid into the empty two-seater behind him.

With nothing better to do for the 30-minute ride west, she picked up where she had left off in an audio-book, hoping it would calm her nerves. A man in a black and orange fleece joined her and buried himself in his work. She wondered what it must have been like to share a bench this size with a 300-pound passenger like the villain in her novel.

The further the train traveled, the more Angela noticed how different the Western City felt from her MetroNorth home. The Western, like her neighborhood, was a mix of residences and businesses, but it felt more like a modern take on suburbia than an urban hub. Its towers formed an ersatz colonial landscape of double hung windows, synthetic clapboards, and moulded doorways. Like the rest of the city, the buildings interconnected, but with covered groundways rather than skyways. And instead of radiating in all directions, the Western gouged through the swamps like spikes that stretched westward for miles. Every once in awhile she could spy the marshes between the buildings and, in the distance, the lighted windows of another urban spur.

"Next stop, Borderlands West," the synthetic voice announced. The car reverberated with the sounds of rustling bags and slithering people. Noting the spittle on the window, she wound her hair into a knot and tucked it into her mother's old knit hat, still wedged in the bottom of her bag from the winter. Before standing, she stopped her book and filed it away. She had listened to several chapters but hadn't heard a thing.

Josh slid out of his seat and took his place in front of her, showing no signs of recognition. She coached herself to stay with the game plan. Blowing it now would waste a week of planning. Even though she knew Josh liked her, she still needed to treat work like work. She breathed in through her nose and stared at a spot halfway between her corneas and Josh's leather coat.

As the line of people exited the car, she put herself on autopilot. Without seeing, she turned right out of the carriage, marched past the two in front of it, then turned left into the station. She followed the route mapped out for her, projected through her eyepiece onto her optical nerve and updated in real time. The map showed a path out the front door and right again, then straight for several blocks. In one motion she snugged her scarf, swung her bag over her head and pushed open the door. In doing so, she almost knocked over a small, suited man carrying on a heated conversation with an invisible colleague. "Sorry," she muttered.

Every few steps she checked her monitor. Ever since her first meal she had become addicted to watching the vital stats in the bottom corner of the display. She had taken to walking as a way to burn off the excess calories and to keep her stats as close to normal as possible. But it wasn't always pleasant. The slat-covered walkway kept out the rain but wind lashed in from the sides, biting at Angela's legs. Walking briskly but not too urgently, she tried to remember if it had been raining at home.

The map on her display changed. She would soon reach an alleyway labelled 108. Here she would turn left. She slowed. To confirm her location she checked the label on the front of the nearest building, the only feature distinguishing one structure from the next. At Alleyway 107, her earpiece beeped. "Yes," she said into the mic just under her earlobe, still looking straight ahead.

"You're clear. Turn left down 108. Go to the end of the complex. I'll meet you there."

Alleyway 108 had no cover, but the towers blocked both the wind and rain. Most all of the foot traffic had dispersed, leaving her alone on the street. She eyed her reflection in the glass wall of the tower to her left and saw two people behind her peel off into a tower entrance. She breathed and pried her shoulders away from her ears, then scanned the upcoming intersection for Josh. The alleyway ended in a T formed by a boardwalk overlooking the bog. It, too, was uncovered and deserted. She spied a pair of joggers heading West into a cloud-muted sunset, their shoes squelching on the slats. To the East she saw more pedestrians scurrying in and out of buildings, trying not to get wet as they lived out a completely different lifestyle from her own. She turned West again and there was Josh, alone in a nook, leaning against a white clapboard wall. As she approached him, he looked directly past her, checked the opposite direction, then swiveled on his feet and disappeared into the wall.

Angela stared at the blank wall in disbelief then jogged over to it. On closer inspection she saw the edges of a hidden door. How had she missed them before? After checking both ways herself, she scuttled inside. The door sealed behind her. She stood on a landing at the top of a dimly lit, rickety staircase. The guide on her eyepiece went blank. She stowed the headgear and crept down the stairs. With each step, a hum grew louder. At the foot of the stair hung a heavy curtain of worn red velvet. She pulled it aside.

To her right, a woman counted cash out of a register. She wore black and white and had pulled her dark hair into an elaborate knot atop her head. To her left stood a short bar three deep with drinkers. A clutch of dining tables and diners nestled in between. Angela tugged off her hat and examined the room.

"You Josh's friend?" barked the waitress.

Angela nodded. The waitress tipped her head in toward the back of the room. Josh stood a head taller than the men with him, his brown jacket blending into the mushroom-colored walls. As she got closer, he intercepted her and led her to an isolated table. He offered her a seat with a view of the room.

"It's so noisy. I can't make out what anyone is saying," she said sideways to Josh, her eyes still collecting the scene.

"It's a Brazilian place, so a lot of these folks are speaking Portuguese. Down here they can be themselves, so they let go," explained Josh.

Angela nodded, though she wasn't sure what he meant. Before she had a chance to ask, the waitress came by and placed a piece of paper in front of her. She stared at it but none of the words looked familiar. Josh reached over and flipped it. This side made only a little more sense. It appeared to be a list of different dishes, organized into categories, and all with unusual names she had never seen before. She found a drinks section and what might be some kind of dessert menu.

"Do we pick one from each list?" she asked, still studying the paper.

"I recommend the churrasco," said Josh, directing her attention to a grill tucked into a back corner. On it sizzled rows of skewered meats roasting over an open pit of flames. The fat glistening on the browned meats hissed as it dripped into the fire. Leaning in close, he whispered, "According to Paolo, Sinsky's last meal was a heaping plate of churrasco, candied yams and mustard greens."

Angela stared back at him. Why hadn't he mentioned this before? Her mind raced. She wasn't prepared for this. There might not be another chance to investigate Sinsky's last moments. She needed to keep her wits about her and ask the right questions.

When the waitress arrived, Josh smiled at her and said, "I'll have the churrasco, and for my friend..." He gave Angela an encouraging look. She could see that he wanted her to try it, not just because of Sinsky but because he wanted to share the experience with her. She nodded her assent. "Make that two, please," he said, handing the menus back to the waitress.

By the time Josh and Angela were mopping up the last bits of food on their plates, most of the patrons had filed out into the night. Paolo and Rubi, the owners, joined Josh and Angela. They sat down with a fresh bottle of golden liquor they called cachaca, four glasses, and a bowl of tiny limes. Josh leaned back in his seat and interlaced his fingers behind his head. "Brilliant, friends. You've outdone yourselves again."

As Rubi crushed the limes and Paolo poured the drinks, Angela waited for an introduction. Rubi passed the glasses and Paolo made a toast. "A nossa saude."

Josh and Rubi repeated it and Angela, unsure of what they said, muttered a feeble "Cheers." The men laughed and Josh finally introduced her.

The tone of the table turned serious as Paolo explained that he did not believe Sinsky was poisoned by his food. He repeated what he had told Josh. Sinsky ate the churrasco. Meats roasted en masse. Meats shared by everyone who ordered it. Food ordered by over half the patrons on any given evening.

"If one is sick, all will be sick," chimed in Rubi.

Paolo beckoned Angela to follow him. He led her back through the curtain. Opposite it stood another door. She followed him through and squinted when he flicked on the lights. Before her was a 40-foot long 20-foot wide concrete and steel bunker that acted as a prep and storage room for all of Paolo's food. The smell of antiseptic from the evening cleanup still lingered. He led her to a small lab bench in the back. On the shelves were boxes of test kits. On the counter, an array of test tubes.

"Salmonella, E. Coli, Listeria, …" Paolo picked up each glass tube in turn. "We test every meat shipment," he said, then squirted an antiseptic into his palm and rubbed his hands together. "Miss Angela, this place is my life. These people are my family. I don't take chances," he asserted. "Murder, it was. But I don't know how. And I don't know why." He shook his head grimly.

Angela felt her knees give and leaned a hip on the table for stability. Murder. All this time, she'd been looking at Sinsky as the villain. The Cheater. But now, according to Paolo, she was the victim? And a senseless one, at that. Who would want to murder this ordinary sometime-Cheater? Tread carefully, Angela's wits told her.

She asked Paolo for details, but there wasn't much to his story. When Sinsky had left the restaurant—a few short hours after Angela had left her standing, disappointed on the sidewalk —she had seemed fine. Then later that night, he saw the story about her in the news.

Angela tried another angle, asking if he might have missed something that might have made her sick. Paolo launched into a detailed tour of every corner of his operation. He showed her where the shipments came in by skiff through a small door tucked under the boardwalk. He showed her his freezer room. Stacked from floor to ceiling were cuts of beef, pork and chicken. He told her about his suppliers. The vegetables and fruits came from farms and greenhouses in Vermont. The meat came in from two local farms on the Outside. In the old days he had his meat shipped all the way up from Brazil—"the taste, you would not believe. It's the grass. Different grass, different taste"—but the risks involved in illegal meat trafficking across so many borders had forced him to go local. He made a point to tell her that never once since going local had he found a bug in the meat. He vouched for his suppliers without reservation.

Puffing out his chest, he added, "Rubi and I make the rum ourselves." He tipped his glass then emptied it in one slurp.

Angela beamed at him over the rim of her tumbler as she took another sip. Though she'd barely made a dent in her drink, she could feel her skin glowing. She imagined the alcohol eating away at the wads of meat in her stomach. At this point, she didn't know what else to ask. Nothing here suggested that Sinsky could have died from food poisoning from this meal. But murder? She wasn't convinced of that yet either.

Angela thanked Paolo for his time and for his help. He nodded and then massaged his forehead, a look of regret clouding his eyes.

Angela placed her hand on Paolo's forearm. "Don't worry Paolo. Nothing I write will harm you. I promise."

11

"Anytime after eight," replied Angela, calculating the time it would take to make her way home from her office. "See you then."

It was Sunday night and Nate had invited himself over. An uncharacteristic move, thought Angela. Nate typically let others do the inviting. Angela had always attributed this to laziness more than to shyness. He never acted bashful, but he certainly didn't act like a go-getter either. Today, however, he sounded on edge. He had told her about the message blockade and his failure to see Molly in person. Apparently, she had spent the entire weekend in her office, behind the secured doors of her lab. Angela guessed from this latest call that he hoped to intercept Molly when she returned home that evening.

Angela didn't mind him coming over. In fact, she was looking forward to it. She had done so much that week, she had lived so much, that she wanted someone to share it with. Someone from her world. Someone to help her see things a little more objectively. She had been missing Molly and their talks and figured that Nate would be a fine, if less sharp, substitute.

Despite the long week, Angela was brimming with energy. She took the long way home, on foot, her steps springy on the concrete tunnels from her office, where she had spent the day alone writing, to the the main sidewalk near her living complex. She had just turned in her article and, instead of the jittery in-betweens, this time she couldn't wait for Monday morning. She couldn't wait to see if this second installment would get as much play as the first. Or perhaps even more.

When Angela turned down her hallway, it was a few minutes before 8 o'clock. Nate was approaching from the opposite direction. She acknowledged him with a friendly wave and tried not to act shocked. She had never known him to be on time for anything. He must be beside himself, she thought, but at least he's doing something about it. Nate had a tendency to let things slide, as if somehow, tomorrow, everything would be fine.

"Hi," said Nate sheepishly. "And thanks for this."

"No problem." She unlocked the door, walked in, and with a wave at the couch, she said, "Make yourself at home." She tossed her bag in her room and, seeing that Molly wasn't home, checked her desk for a note. She found one: "Out with Parrish. -M" Angela smiled. She liked the idea of Molly getting out and enjoying herself, even with Parrish. There's no accounting for tastes, she thought to herself. Then, seeing Nate through the half-opened door, her smile faded. He looked so hopeful and, at the same time, so concerned. She didn't want to have to tell him where Molly was.

She headed back out to the common room, kicked off her shoes and plopped on the opposite end of the sofa. She tucked her feet underneath herself and petted the blue microfiber. "I haven't seen Molly myself for days. I've hardly been home. And with her new workload, we just haven't crossed paths much." Molly had been working six-day weeks since grad school, but over the last month, she had added late nights and Sundays. "I'm sort of used to her being around more. Now that she's as busy as I am, I miss her. It's kind of lonely."

"I know what you mean," mumbled Nate, sitting upright and staring ahead at the opposite wall. "Did she tell you what happened? About Safe and Sustainable?" he asked, with a hopeful perk.

Angela shook her head, so Nate filled her in. He started with what he had heard online, then told her what he knew about Safe and Sustainable. He described the abrupt change in research direction, and how Molly had reacted when he pointed it out.

"Look at it from her perspective, Nate. Molly works on pure logic. Any gaps and she stops computing. When you factor in her emotional tie to the research you're condemning—which is basically her life's work—I wouldn't be surprised if she were angry at you. But she wouldn't tune you out. Besides, she's too busy to go through the effort of avoiding you. You'll be friends again in no time. You'll see."

Nate nodded glumly. "I hope so. I'm worried about her. Not just from this thing, but in general. She didn't seem like herself Thursday night. She was…slower than usual. And when I saw her at work earlier this week, she seemed out of sorts. Maybe it's nothing. But then, remember how I said there might be a bug in the NArc? What if there is? What if it's affecting her?"

"I'm sure it's not that," Angela said, a little too quickly. "I'm sure it's just the strain of her job."

An awkward silence filled the small room. He hadn't asked Angela if she knew where Molly was and Angela hadn't offered. She felt guilty about this. She felt even worse because what she really wanted to discuss was this conspiracy theory of his. But she couldn't bring it up, no matter how obvious it was to her that Nate and Molly were a lost cause. She picked at the edge of one of her fingers, trying to think of something to say. Then Nate brought the topic back up himself.

"So what do you think about what I found?" he asked. "Your mind doesn't work on pure logic. Do you think that this

Safe and Sustainable group rigged the system? Do you think they manipulated science to make things go their way?"

"I don't know," she said slowly, gathering her thoughts. "The Foodies would probably say yes. Their version of things could fit in with what you found. But then, they didn't put it in those terms, or name the group behind the lies. Hmm," she said, considering those last few words. "Lies is an oversimplification, isn't it?"

Nate nodded. "It does seem more complicated than that."

"I'll do some poking around to find out more. I guess I don't know what it means, though. I keep trying to balance my excitement about this whole amazing food world against reason. I mean, it *is* unfortunate that real food is illegal. But I'm not convinced yet that what we're left with now is wrong. After all, that research is still good science, right? So it's not like the NArc is a house of cards."

"No, I guess not." Nate shrugged. "I don't know why it bothers me so much. Something about it just doesn't feel right. Molly always picks on me for not knowing anything. She nags me to go to the SynEngra History Museum all the time. Of course, now, when I really try to dig in, that's when she decides to vanish off the face of the earth." He leaned his head back and covered his eyes with his forearm.

"Did you just say that SynEngra has a History Museum?"

"Yeah. For employees and their guests. Corporate BS," he replied, his voice muffled through his sleeve.

"I have an idea," Angela said, leaning in toward Nate. "One of Josh's friends is a history buff. A teacher, actually. She has a real handle on Foodie history. Maybe you can bring us to the museum and we can compare notes." She waited for a response. When she didn't get one, she tapped his knee. "Nate? What do you think?"

A muted "about what" came from under his elbow.

"Can you take us?" she asked, pulling his arm away.

"Sure," he said listlessly as he sat up. When he looked at Angela, he laughed.

Angela was bouncing on the edge of the sofa, eyes wide, hands clapping. She felt as if she could run out to the museum that very instant. Seeing his reaction, she smiled back. She had made him forget, even if just for a minute, all about Molly.

"We can go Friday if you're free," he said.

Angela leaned back and studied Nate's face. She'd always looked at him as if he were a little boy, like a know-it-all kid brother always tagging along. For the first time, she started to see the man behind the boyish flop of hair and smooth cheeks.

After a few minutes of relaxed silence, he finally asked, "How are things going for you? Your first story was great. Dangerous, but great. The whole thing has me thinking a lot. Remembering the way things used to be."

Angela knew that this was as close to an apology as she would ever get from Nate. In their conversation a week earlier, he had attacked her and mocked her. But he hadn't ignored her. He had listened. He had learned. And now, he wanted her to know that he was, at least in part, on her side. "Me too," she said. "Just wait 'til you read the next one."

"It's interesting stuff. Are you getting anywhere with the Sinksy thing? Weird news about that other woman, too."

"Very weird," she agreed. She filled him in on what she had learned. She had spent both Friday and Saturday mornings talking with people close to the dead women. After those conversations, she had started to wonder if there had been foul play. But murder, as Paolo said? It still seemed so unlikely. She decided not to mention Paolo's theory about Sinsky just yet. Instead, she told Nate that Sinsky's parents were consumed with bitterness and shame about their daughter's undignified death in a speakeasy. They claimed they wanted to forget about her and put the whole ugly business out of their minds. But at the same time their apartment had been filled with pictures of Martine at all ages.

"Putting her out of their minds was one of the last things they wanted to do," she said. "And Merriweather's family said the same things. They all used the same phrases to put me off, as if they had been coached." Angela shrugged. "I have no idea whether someone is pressuring them. Maybe it's just part of grief counseling these days. I don't know if they handle premature deaths differently from scheduled terminations but, according to Molly, scheduled termination counseling is all about moving on. At any rate, I didn't learn anything new from the families."

Angela paused, thinking that her theories probably sounded hollow. But Nate was leaning forward and appeared engaged and ready to hear more.

"There are a couple of Food Cops that have been helpful," she began, thinking back to a meeting she had with Potente and one of his detectives, a man named Roy, earlier that day. "We cut a deal. For now. I show them my articles before they hit the wires and they try to keep me out of trouble. Anyway, I asked them what they thought about some of the things the people in the story told me. Like, the owner of one speakeasy showed me his testing setup. It's incredibly safe. Simple but comprehensive."

"That makes sense. So obvious. It's what I'd do if I had a speakeasy."

"Well, when I told this to the cops, they just shrugged."

"That's it?" asked Nate.

"Yup. I didn't understand it either, so I asked them to explain again why they don't try harder to protect the NArc. Why don't they take down the Cheater network? I asked. They just laughed at me." Angela tried to imitate Potente's deep voice. "'The System?' he said. 'The System is a government-funded monopoly. They've cornered the market. And we're supposed to protect them?' He was completely disgusted with me."

Nate raised an eyebrow. "Aren't they called the Food Police?"

"Yeah. I was pretty surprised too. So I waited. Sometimes silence pulls the best confessions. In this case, it worked. Potente said, 'Look, we're here to protect the people. And we're doing all we can. Those little household kitchens and restaurants? If they start making people sick, maybe then I'll have something to say about it.'"

Nate sat up. "But what about Sinsky? And that other woman?" he asked.

"Exactly what I said, and not for the first time, either. 'They are dead,' I said to him. 'And you are on the record saying food was the cause.'"

"What did they say to that?" Nate asked.

"Roy laughed so hard he snorted. Just like this, he said, 'We're not homicide.'" Angela threw up her hands as if she had been asked the most ridiculous question.

"Jesus," uttered Nate.

"Pretty lame, huh? But I could tell that Potente had taken my question seriously. He didn't contradict Roy, but he didn't laugh. Instead, he closed down the conversation. 'Look, kiddo, we do our raids like the one you got caught in. We keep the Foodies on their toes. Just ask your Brazilian friend. His kitchen wasn't always as clean as it is today. And like I said before, we crack down on the Junk. It works,' he said. Then he warned me off a little. He told me to keep my eye on the calendar. 'You don't want a second offense and I'd hate to see you stuck with an overnight visit to the City Hotel,' he said."

Nate sat back, taking it all in. "You know, he's right, Ange. You need to be careful. You don't want to end up in jail, even if it is just for a night."

"I know," she agreed, relieved that he wasn't lecturing her for having been arrested in the first place. "I feel like I've hit a wall on these deaths. When I'm stuck, as a rule, I go back to what I know for sure. We know the name, age, time of death, and alleged cause of death for both women. That's about it. Nate, I know it's a lot to ask, but is there anything you can find out about them in your databases at work?"

Nate cocked an eyebrow but then nodded. No questions asked. "I'll start digging tomorrow," he said.

"It's nice to think this through out loud, Nate. Thanks." With that, Angela, suddenly drained from her hectic week, got up to go to bed. As she stood she said, as gently as she knew how, "Nate, you know, Molly might not be coming home tonight."

Nate pulled a thin blanket over his legs and rested his head on the arm of the small sofa. The door behind him hadn't opened yet, but he still had hope that Molly would return home. Alone.

A few hours later, Nate heard Molly giggle before she turned the latch. Still groggy, he couldn't make out her whispers. As she stepped into the room and flicked on the light, she spotted him. It didn't take long. The room was hardly large enough for three adults. "What are you doing here?" she demanded. She didn't wait for a response. "He's the one who upset me the other day," she declared to Parrish.

Nate lay on the couch stunned. Though his eyes were still adjusting to the light, his ears were clear. This did not sound like the level-headed, fair-minded Molly he knew. When his eyes cleared, he was struck by the sneer on the man's face. He blinked and looked again. Whatever coldness he had seen in the man's eyes had vanished. All that remained was an artless smile.

Meanwhile, Molly stood, arms crossed, waiting for an explanation.

Nate stood up slowly. "Molly, I'm sorry for the intrusion. I'd just like to talk to you for a minute. In private."

"You had your chance to talk, Nate. I haven't heard from you for days, and now you want me to drop everything at midnight for a little conversation. Well, it's too late." She tossed her hair and stepped back, making a clear path from Nate to the doorway.

Nate stared at her. He couldn't leave without talking with her. He couldn't just let Parrish win. And besides, he needed her. Angela needed her. So he tried a different approach. Nate faced Parrish, using his height to his advantage. "I'm Nate Hunter and Molly is a close friend," he said, holding his eyes fixed on the grey irises below.

"Parrish Knight," replied Molly's date.

Before Parrish had the chance to say more, Nate forced the issue. "Would you please give us just one minute? What I have to say is very important to Molly. I hope you'll understand." Parrish had little choice but to yield.

"I'll be right outside," he assured her, his hand on her cheek. Nate's insides churned.

Molly wouldn't even look at Nate. "Make it quick," she spat.

He still couldn't believe his ears. She had never been warm, but her meanness threw him. He didn't know where to begin. "Molly, I don't understand what's going on. I've been trying to contact you since Friday morning—"

She cut him off with a sharp laugh. "Please. Don't lie to me, Nate. I didn't sleep at all Thursday. And you know how stressed I am at work. Besides, your attack on Dalyrimple is totally unfounded. Parrish told me all about it."

Nate got out his flexscreen, flicked it open, and skipped his fingers over the display a few times before passing it to her.

"What's this. More conspiracies?" she chided.

"Just look at the messages." He had selected a list of 5 messages addressed to her both at work and personally. Each one had been rejected, either as a blockout or a bounce. As she started to scroll down, the angry lines on her face crumpled in confusion.

"Nate, I'm not under a blockade. There must be something wrong with these." She opened one, then another.

He knew what she would find because he had done the same thing. No flaws. No mistyped addresses. No suspicious attachments that might derail a transmission.

"But these are all fine," she said. "It seems like someone is blocking you in particular. I don't get it." She looked up and the look on her face made Nate feel hopeful for the first time in days.

"I don't either. I just wanted you to know that I tried to talk to you on Friday first thing, to apologize. I didn't mean to upset you." Nate stopped short of telling her how much he missed her and needed her. And how worried he was about her. "And when I couldn't reach you I tried to see you, but whenever I had a chance to duck out, you were shut in."

Molly's face flushed. She shook her head. "Wow. I was angry. I guess I let it build up. I haven't been feeling like myself lately." She yawned. "I'm sorry I yelled at you," she said, rubbing her fingers over her eyes.

Nate saw for an instant a glimpse of an aged Molly and wanted nothing more than to grow old with her. She represented so many ideals in his mind—intelligence, beauty, clarity—that no one else would ever come close. Other women might be kinder, but compared to Molly, they just seemed silly. And now, seeing Molly vulnerable even just for a minute, made him feel like he had something to offer her. That sometimes he could be the strong, stable one. Still, he decided, this was not a good time to tell her how he felt.

"Look, it's late and Parrish is waiting. I just needed to tell you. I'd like to talk about some other things that Ange and I decided tonight. Tomorrow morning?"

She nodded. Nate smiled when, on his way out, he overheard her make excuses to Parrish. As the elevator doors slid shut, he watched her close her door, leaving Parrish on the outside.

12

Barbeque
RealFood, by Sage Weaver

Northeast City, May 28, 2063 — For those old enough to remember backyard cookouts, the word barbeque alone is enough to get the salivary glands going. Now I understand why.

I visited two illicit barbecues in the past week and at each one, I sampled the flavors and aromas created through the magic of open air cooking and deep cultural roots.

The first kitchen, tucked into an apartment the size of a large closet, served 5 at a time. We sat, backs to the door, under dim lights at a white formica counter. The menu had two options: the Large and the Small. My "small" plate, a beige plastic oval, arrived laden with three heaping servings of meat: pulled chicken dripping with a smoky sauce, pork ribs rubbed with spices, and beef brisket with a tangy red sauce on the side. Buried under the meat I found a scoop of baked beans and a pile of runny cole slaw. "Southern style cooking at its best," my companion said.

What the meal lacked in presentation, it made up for in taste. Every bite delivered a burst of flavor. Spicy peppers, tangy mustard, sweet tomato and smoke topped the meats and fats, all cooked to supreme tenderness. I hardly needed to chew. To clear our palates we slurped down beer—something called an India Pale Ale brewed nearby that had such a flowery smell it made me sneeze. We sopped up the sauce with crumbly corn bread and accumulated obscene piles of greasy napkins.

The owner smiled at our indulgence. He winked at me and told me with the hint of a southern twang that he knew the first name of every person that had touched the food on my plate. Frankie, Shane, Marianne, and so on. When he started to tell me the names of the animals, I stopped him. It was only later that I realized that, by uttering these names, he was paying homage to their work and their sacrifice. He knew them, trusted them, and honored them, and he wanted me to as well.

The second place served food in the style of a more distant deep south: Brazil. On the other side of the street-level concealed door sat twenty boisterous men, women and children, all competing to be heard. Reading the menu, which included stewed and grilled meats, fish, and chicken, took over ten minutes.

We selected the Churrasco: meat impaled on three-foot long metal skewers and grilled over an open fire. Diners approach the grill to make their selections. I chose a well-done slice of beef and a hunk of chicken breast. As fat sizzled on the flames, the server lifted a skewer and sawed off oversized portions onto a stained board, then swept them onto my plate.

I tired of chewing my tough, over-done meat, so my companion urged me to try a less cooked piece. It made all the difference. I picked up hints of lime, salt and garlic mingling with the rich taste of beef and flame. We captured the drippings with spoonfuls of rice and sipped cachaca, a sort of rum mixed with lime and sugar.

The owner, a rotund man in his mid-fifties with a full ruddy face, brought me back to the kitchen. He told me he misses the days of imported beef from Brazil. "Different grass, different taste," he said. But he praised the "superior quality" he gets from his local suppliers. He trusts them and their husbandry—"these animals live like kings, nipping clover on lovely pastures." Nevertheless, he tests every shipment for contaminants, just to be sure. "You can never be too careful. I do it for them," he said, gesturing toward the dining area. "And if I ever find problem, everyone wants to know. Everyone wants to fix. We are all in this together."

"Did you see the latest from Sage Weaver?" Arthur's lips barely moved as he spoke, his head facing the center of the subway car, his shoulders touching his fellow passengers, his eyes focused on the image beamed into his eyeball.

"Yes," the half-real, half-animated face in the center of the image replied. "Nearly everyone has."

Arthur nodded. He imagined what his own face must look like, similarly captured in extreme close-up then repackaged by the technology in his headset as an animated talking head. He hoped the animation would tone down the panic in his eyes. This second review had shot to the top of the reading charts as fast as the first.

Arthur didn't like where this was going. He envisioned a return to the old ways and a future filled with suffering. He shuddered at the thought of good, innocent people falling to the whims of disease and the vagaries of genetics. He momentarily closed his eyes in an attempt to shut out his memories of food shortages, polluted crops, and worse, the disease. So many people afflicted and unwell. We can't let it come to that, he thought to himself. The NArc will eventually cure all ills. I need to help people remember that. They need to believe in it!

But it wasn't clear to Arthur just what he should do to stop his terrible vision from becoming a reality. He had to do something about this Sage Weaver. He still had difficulty believing what his informant had told him, that Weaver and Anselm were one and the same. He had never expected Anselm to turn on the industry so sharply. Even worse, her departure from the Nutrition beat had shut off his prime channel of influence over the public.

"Where is she going next?" he finally asked.

"She's going Outside," said the talking head.

Arthur felt a momentary sense of relief. Food resonated with people, but Outsiders got very little sympathy. Leeches, he thought to himself. Outcasts. With any luck the next installment will fall flat. With the NArc stats stabilized, he decided he could wait and see. He didn't need to make another move. Not yet.

"Is the other contained?" asked the talking head.

"Of course," shot back Arthur. He didn't like the tone of the question. He also didn't like being reminded that his best scientist seemed to be mixed up in the affair. He worried most about her.

Part of him feared her. She was too smart for her own good. And too persistent. If she started digging, it wouldn't take long for her to connect the dots. She had invested her life in this work and she believed in it, but could he count on her to understand how crucial it was for everyone else to believe in it, too? He couldn't risk it. He needed to keep her out of this mess and focused on her project. A project he was on the hook to deliver. He needed to keep her isolated from outside influences. Away from home and her roommate. Away from that fool from the Simulations group who always seemed to be lurking outside her lab and poking around in places he didn't belong. It's for her own protection, he rationalized.

"I'm doing all I can on my end," Arthur said. "Your continued help in that matter is appreciated."

"My pleasure," fawned the talking head.

Arthur shuddered again and changed the subject. "Any progress with your other assignment?" he asked. Arthur had been keeping tabs on Josh Salter for years. Rumor had it that he wanted a revolution and that he saw Sage Weaver as a way to begin.

The talking head shook side to side, its grey eyes grim.

Marcus leaned on the door jamb of Stew's office, trying to appear casual. But Stew recognized the look on his managing editor's face and braced himself.

"Your Sage Weaver column's got legs, Stew," he said. "Artful, Stew. Powerful stuff. Very powerful."

Marcus and Stew had reviewed the hit counts in an editorial meeting earlier that day. The column's popularity had doubled since the first edition and the rate meters showed that the story was still spreading. Like a virus, the Metro editor had said. Stew had ignored the left-handed comment and instead redirected attention to the content. Angela had penetrated deeper than anyone else had, he had reminded them. Despite the success, he had seen the concern on Marcus's face even then. And now he would hear why.

"Thing is Stew, it may be too powerful." Marcus stepped into the room, but didn't sit down. Stew assumed he wanted to maintain his authority. Marcus and Stew had been friends for a long time, but when it came down to it, Marcus was the boss. "I received a phone call this morning from the SynEngra public relations office. They want to know why we're glamorizing illegal substance abuse. They told me they see blips in their NArc Use Stats."

Stew didn't blink. "What does that mean?" he asked.

"It means more people are Cheating."

Stew stared back at Marcus but he didn't budge. He knew, from years of working for the man, that Marcus didn't like authority. He didn't like to restrain his staff. He liked real stories about real people doing real things. The idea that Angela's stories had influence, that they were changing the way people behaved, this was what Marcus and Stew both lived for. If Marcus wanted Stew to pull back, he would have to pick up the reins and put them in Stew's hands.

Eventually, Marcus blinked first. "I'm still behind you Stew. I told them that these are human interest stories. That they would continue to explore culture, and that surely the hits on the NArc would be temporary. I want you to pass that message along to Angela. She needs to make sure that Sage Weaver doesn't burn all of our corporate bridges, okay? The Well may be done, but SynEngra isn't. We still need their ad revenue. And remember, SynEngra dollars make up a big chunk of what funds the entire paper."

Stew considered this point. When SynEngra had real news, Angela would be there. Or some other reporter. He knew that SynEngra needed the paper's support as much as the paper needed SynEngra. They wouldn't be calling otherwise. They might control a big slice of Nutrition now, but if they pulled their ad revenue, some up and comer would step in to fill the space. It would take a long time for their blustering to turn into action.

"Sure thing, Marcus," he replied, filing the idea away in a dusty box in the back of his mind.

$$\neq$$

Josh sat in the 'SpaceCafe, his legs stretched out and crossed at the ankles. He leaned back in a chair that seemed a size too small for his avatar's large frame. Dressed in jeans, a leather coat, and work boots, he always appeared in animation much as he did in real life, though perhaps with fewer wrinkles and glossier hair. He had only been waiting a few minutes when June appeared. He watched as she opened the door and surveyed the room dispassionately. Today, her body was wrapped in turquoise spandex, her legs bound with leather straps attached to platformed sandals. Topping off the look, she had unevenly chopped pink hair that stood on end.

Though he had never felt more than friendship for June, Josh couldn't deny that he enjoyed her online creations. He also enjoyed the reactions of the other 'SpaceCafe patrons. Drinks dribbled. Napkins dropped. Customers collided. He knew that she enjoyed it too. It made her feel powerful without having to sacrifice her real-life self-respect. He let his avatar ogle as she sashayed across the room, placing one foot in front of the other as if she were walking a wire.

The bartender arrived at the table at the same time as June and set down two mugs of steaming coffee. "The usual?" he asked, sneaking a peek at June.

Josh waved him off and motioned for June to sit. "Nice shoes," he commented as she maneuvered herself into the chair.

"Thanks. When I first made them, I had to practice walking in them. They're tricky. And I don't really want to fall down in this dress."

"You seem to have mastered the art," he said, grinning. "Did you see this morning's installment?"

"I did. She seems to be getting it. The people, I mean. She seems to see what they're about. I'm pleasantly surprised." June sipped her coffee. "Interesting choice of places to take her," she added.

"Revealing, I think," said Josh. He had found Angela's latest article moving. It reminded him how connected he felt to the people he trafficked with, even people two or three steps away from him. She had captured the trust that held the network together, yet she knew she wasn't a part of the circle.

"Of what?" June clipped, snapping him to attention. "What exactly did she learn that you couldn't have told her yourself?" June put her mug down and leaned on the table. "This is the heart of what bothers me Josh. You expect us to trust her, but she can't trust you."

"You're making it sound like I'm feeding her a bunch of bullshit," Josh retorted. "Well, I'm not. If you were there, you'd see. She asks questions we'd never ask. She's better off without me telling her what to think. She's not an idiot you know."

June shrugged and bent down to tug at one of her sandal straps. "Have you talked to Bunny yet?"

At home, Josh shook his head and tore his eyes from the front of June's animated dress. "Between you and Parrish, I'm not sure who is pestering me more. You want her to see more. He wants her to see less. Two extremes harping at me at every turn. I don't see what the two of you are so afraid of. She's honest. She gets it. She's on the right track. Let's just see what happens next, okay?"

June sighed. "She asked me to meet her on Friday for a history lesson. Maybe I'll feel better about this after that." She set her mug aside and grumbled. "It's test week. I've got to proctor at 1. What a nightmare. An auditorium full of teenagers, their destinies on the line. Half them are jacked up, trying to raise their scores. The other half doped, trying to ease the pain of failure or, at least make the hours pass by a little faster. Wish me luck." As she stood up, she wobbled, then recovered, swiveling her hips and gliding away.

13

After a scant few hours of sleep in his own bed, Nate arrived at work early, hoping to download the data sets Angela wanted before his co-workers arrived. No one would think it suspicious of him to be setting up targeted data queries; he ran simulation tests on real data all the time. But he didn't want to start making excuses and end up buried under a heap of lies. Better to avoid it altogether, he figured. Besides, he and Molly had arranged the night before to review the data before breakfast. Before Arthur sequestered her in the lab.

When Nate stepped into the skypark, Molly was already there, nestled in the citrus grove and sipping a very large steaming beverage.

"You okay? Is that caffeinated? I didn't think you used stimulants," he said.

"I used an override. I'm exhausted. As you know, last night was a late night, but even still, I've been having trouble sleeping. And I've got another long week ahead. I know you and Angela want my help, but I hope we can be quick this morning. I've already had to dodge Arthur once to make it up here."

To Nate, she looked more than tired. She looked ragged. He apologized for taking up her time, then told her what he'd found. "I downloaded the records of everyone who died in the last 6 months. A pretty normal query for me. Then I processed it to narrow it down to the people who might be Sinsky or Merriweather. Since the records are de-identified, I can't just look them up. Anyway, I am pretty sure that this first record is Sinsky's and the second Merriweather's. I was hoping you could look through them and see if you find anything interesting," he said, handing his flexscreen to Molly.

She flipped through the records then transferred them to her own device. "So I can run some diags," she said, not looking up.

Nate figured that, with her medical and bioengineering degrees, few details would escape her notice. Molly had once explained that, though she'd never intended to practice medicine —hardly anyone did anymore with all the automated systems in place—the insights she had gained from the experience, as well as the basic skills, like reading medical records, had come in handy time and again. He watched her flip back and forth between the two women's records and her own medical diagnostic tools. He didn't like to burden her, but somehow the task seemed to trump her exhaustion, giving her something to focus on besides her lack of sleep.

"Hmmm," she said, flipping again and rereading the records, dragging bits of data back and forth. Nate shifted in his seat, but remained silent. He alternated his gaze between Molly and the skypark security videos streaming in through his eyepiece. He had tapped into the corporate surveillance systems so he could monitor the park entrances. *If only I could figure out where they programmed that email blockade,* he had thought to himself as he'd set it up.

"Merriweather's clean," Molly finally said. "Healthy except for the unfortunate food incident. But Sinsky's more complicated."

Nate snapped to attention. "What do you mean?"

"According to the record, she had some kind of cancer. It looks like the cancer adapted to her treatment late last year. Since then, this record shows no indication of her being treated for the resistant cancer. From the way this record reads, the NArc was ignoring it." Molly started to close up her files.

"Wait. What do you mean ignoring it? Isn't there some sort of intervention for this kind of thing?" asked Nate. Nate had never been sick. Not since he was a kid, anyway. Ever since the NArc, he'd been fit and well. Not even a head cold. He had no idea how the medical system worked.

"The NArc manages diseases with Nutrition. Take Angela. The NArc uses a special algorithm in her chip that knows about the predisposition to diabetes that she inherited from her mom. The NArc manages it for her. It feeds her the compounds she needs to keep her disease in check. Most of the NArc's work is preventive. Does that make sense?" she asked.

"I understand the basics, sure," responded Nate, knowing the question was rhetorical. Molly always walked people through things as if they were children.

"When prevention fails, for example, if someone ends up with a disease, the NArc takes the next steps. First it detects the disease using biomarkers or the monthly scans. Then to treat the disease, the NArc personalizes the standard treatment algorithm for that condition and uses it to prescribe treatments at mealtime. The NArc just integrates the compounds with the rest of the Nutrition, then monitors and corrects for side-effects. It's a system that still needs work, but most people continue on unawares. Then there are the conditions that can't be treated with Nutrition. Maybe the only cure that will work for the person is a small molecule to interrupt a chemical process in the body. And maybe that molecule can't be ingested. In those cases, the NArc injects compounds at the monthly scans. Do you follow?" Molly asked, her tone now dull, as if she'd been through this explanation many times before.

"Got it," said Nate, not looking up and disregarding her tone. He was listening, but she still hadn't gotten to the case he was interested in.

"For something unknown, a new disease like Sinsky had, I don't know what happens. I assume her case was under investigation, but it must not have been very far along. According to this record, the custom algorithm the NArc prescribed to monitor her disease hasn't been updated since it was first installed. They must not have anything more up to date yet," she said, tucking her flexscreen back into her bag. "I've got to get going."

"What does this mean, though?" persisted Nate. "And why do you keep saying 'according to this record?' Is there some other data we're missing?"

Still sounding like a doctor, Molly replied, "Sure. We could run pathology tests—a tox screen on a tissue sample. She might have been self medicating. Seeing someone outside the NArc, like an old-school medical practitioner. It's risky, but some people do it. She was, after all, a Cheater. It doesn't seem related to her death, though, does it? I mean, by all accounts she died an accidental death. Too bad. I'm sure a new treatment would have come out and cured her." Molly stood up, took another swig of her drink and grimaced. It had stopped steaming.

Nate wondered if this idea of pathology tests might be a real possibility. "Don't you know someone over at the hospital she died in? Maybe we could get in there and do the tests."

She raised an eyebrow. "Aren't you taking this a little too far?" she complained, sounding exasperated.

Nate felt abashed by her tone. The look on her face crushed him and he momentarily forgot why it seemed so urgent. He remembered Dalyrimple and the message blockade, the two unusual deaths and now this strange medical record, but he couldn't link any of it together.

Before he had a chance to back down, though, Molly relented. "I know you and Angela think this is important. So I'll call Tobin McGwire," she offered. "He owes me. I tutored him for hours in school. I'll call him today and see if there is anything left of Sinsky. I'm sure the data will confirm that nothing unusual happened. Maybe then you and Angela will be able to put this to bed."

Later that week, in the hospital lobby, Molly asked the guard at the desk for Pathology.

"Fifth floor. Badge in, please."

She scanned her wrist and Nate followed. They found Tobin in a back corner of a lab examining a tissue sample on a large screen. "Molly Tanaka!" he cried when he saw her. "Look at me now. I passed my boards and here I am. All thanks to you." He beamed at her then noticed Nate standing behind her. "Hey Nate. You still tagging along?"

Molly looked at Tobin quizzically.

"Uh, I've got a meeting upstairs," said Nate, sounding cagey. Tobin smirked.

Molly, not having the time or the patience for games, got down to business. "So, Tobin, you said that you still had some of that woman's tissue?" She brushed a stray hair from her cheek then quickly dropped her hand. She didn't want Nate to see how much it was shaking. She'd first noticed it a few days ago, off and on, an uncontrollable trembling. Today, she chalked it up to stress. Ducking out of the lab on a busy day had been hard enough, but now they'd already used half of the hour she'd budgeted for this trip just getting over here.

"Yeah," Tobin nodded. "The rest of her went out for donation or incineration late last week. But we always bank blood, skin and muscle for future studies. Uh, why did you say you needed this again?" Molly thought Tobin sounded uncomfortable challenging her, but he also sounded determined to do his job. She felt a touch of pride. She had played a big role in his education and she liked to see that he had, indeed, learned something. "It's a strange request. Not really something we do regularly. Or ever, really," he said.

"Actually, it is unusual. You see, I'm working on a project, you know, more engineered meats. And I'm stuck. The problem I'm trying to solve isn't making any sense. I need real tissue to remind me of how natural biology works. But I want fresh tissue. When I saw this story in the news, it just clicked. She would be perfect. She fits the criteria exactly," explained Molly.

Tobin's skeptical look made Molly pause. She hadn't expected him to hold the line.

To her relief, Nate stepped in. "You probably know exactly what she means. I don't understand a word of it," he laughed in self-deprecation, "but I bet it's perfectly obvious to anyone with a background like yours." Nate turned on his most ingratiating smile.

Tobin smiled back, nodding. Molly could see that it wasn't obvious to him at all, but he didn't want her to think he didn't get it. "Right. So, do you want some tissue from the other girl too?"

"Other girl?" Molly asked, trying not to look at Nate.

"She came in last week. Fresher, anyway. Same termination code. About the same age." He shrugged. "Can't hurt, right? Just let me know which reason code to use." He tapped a piece of paper taped to a door jamb, its edges tattered. It displayed a list of typed removal codes followed by a few more penned in by hand.

Molly pointed to one and Tobin said, "Thanks. I'll go get them out of the freezer for you."

"Well done," whispered Molly. Nate shot her a mischievous grin.

Half an hour later, Molly and Nate parted ways a block from their building, hoping to get back to their respective work areas without being spotted together. "I should have some results by seven tonight," said Molly without lifting her head, her hair hiding her lips from passers by.

"Paper only," instructed Nate, who kept walking as Molly peeled off toward the back entrance of the SynEngra research complex. They had agreed to avoid using the corporate network to communicate.

Out of his sight, Molly rolled her eyes.

That same evening in the office skypark, Nate watched Molly run her hands across a piece of paper, flattening it on the bench between them. The sheet contained a list of chemical names.

She looked up at him, and asked with her eyes if it was okay to begin. Nate checked again to make sure they were alone. The skypark appeared to be reliably deserted again and the cluster of trees he'd picked gave them good cover. When Nate walked back into the grove, he saw that Molly was yawning and rubbing her eyes.

"You okay?"

"Fine. Fine. Is it all clear?" she asked with an edge to her voice.

He gave her the go ahead to talk.

"What this shows," she said, referencing the reports, "is that Sinsky took several medications in the weeks before her death. Some very common. For instance, the NArc most likely gave her these to manage her cholesterol." She ticked the compounds off as she accounted for them. "Then there is one for pain, probably illicit. And two I don't recognize. Probably inhibitors intended to block the growth of the cancer cells. But from what I can see from her tissue samples, they weren't working."

Nate's head spun. "But you said the NArc wasn't treating her."

"Right. Like I said, she probably was self-medicating."

"But with unapproved compounds?"

"I checked for them on the approved treatments list, and they aren't there. But remember, there are lots of unscrupulous people out there. Would it be so outrageous to think that these drugs were experimental or had failed, but they leaked out anyway?"

"Okay, okay. What about the other woman. What about Merriweather?"

"Nothing special. Nothing out of the ordinary. She had a genetic risk that might have affected her later, but no evidence of any activity yet. Generally she checks out fine." Molly shrugged and folded up the paper.

She didn't seem to be taking this seriously. Nate knew she had a stressful job, and that it took most of her time and energy. But part of him was starting to blame her for her predicament. She did have a tendency to micromanage. "Let's go back to Sinsky. You explained the basics of how the NArc selects and delivers drugs—"

"Treatment. It's Nutritional Treatment. 'Drugs' sounds archaic," she instructed, making quote fingers in the air.

"Fine. Treatment. When did the NArc start to dispense Treatment? It seems different from the Nutrition they started with," he replied. He watched her think about it. He noticed that it took her longer than usual to process.

"It is, I guess." Molly shook her head. "It's too much to go into right now, this late. The short answer is that they had just started doing it when I started as a co-op student from Tech. That was around '45. They've been getting better at it ever since. You know," she added, "you really should visit the museum. It's fun, and you learn so much. I know you probably think it will be too dumbed down, but I think you'd learn a lot from it."

Nate nodded and muttered a half-hearted, "Yeah, maybe you're right." This wasn't the first time she'd brought it up. And it wasn't the first time she had implied that he would benefit by learning from this, as she put it, "dumbed down" exhibit. This time he didn't push back like he usually did, citing his disdain for corporate propaganda. She never seemed to hear him when he did, anyway. Even though it would make her happy, he decided not to tell her that he and Angela were going. For the first time since he'd met Molly, he thought that, this time, the trip might be better without her there.

Molly yawned again and dragged herself to standing. She groaned softly. "Arthur's expecting me back in at 7am to review the results of my two Sims."

Nate now felt guilty for being so hard on her. She looked exhausted. He wondered if maybe she micromanaged because Arthur micromanaged. Maybe some of her people weren't delivering. He thought of his own missed deadlines and his own manager's frustration with him. He wanted to make it up to her somehow. "I know how busy you are. Thanks for finding the time to look into this," he said. "How's your project going anyway? Any progress?"

Molly brightened. "Yes. It's exciting. I had this idea, and, well, I think it's going to pan out. It was a kind of eureka thing. You see, the Singers are aging, but not on the expected time scale. The real problem, which I just figured out, is that some organs are aging too quickly. So when I got these tissues, I did some screens to see what kinds of things were going on during the breakdown process. Anyway, I sort of rediscovered a cellular system that we had all but forgotten about. It enhances tissue preservation. When I saw it, it was so obvious."

"Wait. What?"

"Merriweather had a replacement kidney and I noticed that the sample wasn't deteriorating like the other organs. So I did a screen and there it was. The organ mills started using the cellular system a few years ago, boosting its activity to prevent deterioration. I found a bunch of articles in their journals about it. I'm thinking that in the short term, if we super-activate it, we can extend the lifetime of the Singers' organs maybe even twice as long as they're lasting now. Even better, I'm thinking that in the long term, we can add the human system that regulates this whole mechanism, so the Singers can keep themselves alive."

Nate felt his skin turn clammy. "You're going to add human parts to the Singers?"

"Sure. You do know that they already have human parts, don't you? Not the Neermeat we harvest from them, of course. But some of the organs are derived from human cells. They just work better in the system. Besides, at the level we synthesize them, it's pretty difficult to think of any of the parts as human or anything else. They're just components. DNA. Proteins." Molly didn't notice the look of horror on Nate's face. "It's really amazing technology, Nate. I thought you knew about it. I'm a little surprised that you don't, given that you've worked here for so long."

"So you weren't lying to Tobin when you gave him that story about Sinsky being perfect?"

"No. I mean, when we went there it was just a notion. I hadn't thought it through. But I figured it couldn't hurt to look. I probably wouldn't have done it had you not suggested the tissue scan to begin with. It is a bit unorthodox." Molly smoothed her pants and adjusted her bag. "Look, I've got to go. I'm meeting Parrish at eight. We're going to a dinner for my father. Safe and Sustainable is giving him an award. I'd have invited you, but, after the other night, well…"

Nate felt defeated. That's it, he thought. I've blown it. I pushed too hard. I argued too much. And somehow I managed to insult her father without even meeting him. He tried to smile. "Have fun," he croaked.

"Nate, I know you're disappointed. I know you wanted to see something more from this data, but it just seems to me that Sinsky and this other woman took big risks and ended up on the losing end." She shrugged and waved goodbye. "'Night."

Nate watched her walk away, but all he could see was the sneer on Parrish's face. What does she see in him? Why is he taking her out when she clearly needs time to rest? Maybe if she had time to clear her head, she'd see that she's got it all backwards. She'd realize what a jerk Parrish is. And she'd realize that this data doesn't really add up.

He tried to distract himself by thinking through the Sinsky data again. But he understood so little of it. His whole career had focused on algorithms, and most of it on Sims. Even when he did diagnostics for the NArc, he never saw the big picture. He had never really thought of the data he crunched as data collected from a real, live person.

He slipped out his flexscreen and called up his own records. Hardly anyone ever looks at this stuff, he thought. Who can make sense of it? And why would they ever look at it when they always feel fine? Scrolling through his own file, he found only one thing out of the ordinary. A single red flag with a countdown timer: two days, twelve hours, seven minutes. The time left on his probation.

Nate shook his head and closed the records. Molly had acted as if Sinsky's tissue report settled things. But Nate thought the opposite. Who were these outside medics Molly kept bringing up? And assuming they were practicing underground, where would they get experimental drugs that someone like Molly had never seen before? He wished she hadn't run off so fast. And he wished she hadn't told him where she was headed.

He stood up and began to walk the park. Moonlight reflected off of the algae pools. As the gravel crunched beneath his feet he stepped in and out of clouds of fragrance wafting up from the flower beds. He had never really noticed it before. But then, there were a lot of things he had never noticed before. At first, he had been angry at Angela for dragging him into another one of her capers. Now he almost felt grateful. He felt connected to it. He even felt connected to Sinsky, as if he were assembling a jigsaw puzzle that, once finished, would reveal the secrets behind her fate.

Only none of the pieces held together. No patterns had emerged. No commonalities. When his Sims felt this way, there was only one solution. Nate quickened his pace and turned back toward his office.

What he needed was more data.

14

A steady spring rain fell, filling the channels along the covered walkways that lined both sides of the street. Angela stood under the steel canopy fronting the SynEngra headquarters, watching the pedestrians pass by in front of her. The sound of the raindrops muffled their voices as they talked and walked, eyes forward, feet marking time.

She had stayed up late the night before to review her old stories. She'd also reread the food headlines from the years before she started writing, hoping to remind herself of the view of history the press presented to the public. She wanted to compare that to the picture SynEngra painted.

Late in the evening, she had happened upon an interesting retrospective on pre-Migration America in the *Spectator*. The author was a well-known, but recently deceased, journalist. His story painted a grim picture of the 30s, a time when food and fuel were becoming scarce and disease was rampant. According to his account, no one cared where the solutions came from. No one cared how extreme the remedies were. Desperation had taken hold. At the lowest point, he wrote, society had started to fragment. People had started to heed dogma over reason. The author, in the end, touted the NArc as a savior. The NArc, he wrote, had helped prevent society from slipping into another Dark Age.

Her eyes followed a stream of water as it trickled past the walkway with no choice but to flow into the grate. As she watched, she wondered what this same writer might say if he were still alive today.

"Hey," said Nate, startling her enough to make her gasp.

"Sorry," he said, then asked, "What are you staring at?" He looked down towards the grate. "Did you see something?"

"No. Only water. I was just thinking." She waved off her thoughts and looked at Nate sideways. She didn't want to pressure him, but she needed to know. "Any luck with your files at work?"

"We got data, but the NArc's in the clear. Merriweather's clean. Molly figures Sinsky was self-medicating. She says none of it has anything to do with why they died."

"Oh." Angela leaned on a nearby column. "Thanks for digging. Not too risky for you two, I hope?"

He brushed off the question. "I don't buy it though. The NArc would know if she had been self-medicating. Something's not right, so I'm getting more data." Nate glanced around him. "I'm still worried about Molly though. She's starting to look drawn. I know she's busy, but I don't think it's that. She seems to have plenty of time to go out with Parr—"

Angela touched his sleeve. "Look! June's here," she said with a wave, forcing her face into a perky smile.

Nate turned and eyed the steady stream of people.

June, still twenty yards away, gave Angela the slightest nod in response and then fixed her eyes on Nate. From afar, Angela was able to appreciate June's edgy yet natural beauty. Her asymmetrical hair accentuated her carved features and wide-set steel-blue eyes. As she glided towards them with long strides, her clothes fluttered with an effortless elegance. She carried herself with an air of sophistication that, even though June was only a decade Angela's senior, Angela thought she might never feel. She wondered what it was that made her feel so child-like in comparison. Before she knew it, Nate's hand was in June's. He stammered a greeting and she gave him a genuine smile.

She thinks he's cute, Angela mused. And he's completely flustered. With a not-so-subtle nudge, she encouraged Nate to sign them in, acquire guest badges, and lead them to the museum.

According to a placard at the entrance of the main hall, SynEngra had set up the museum as a service to its employees, to educate them on the history of the company, its technology, and its accomplishments. Selica Friedman, the head of public relations, had convinced the company to spend millions on the exhibit by telling them that good PR started at home. "Forget the press," she was reputed to have said. "If your people say the right things, the public will hear the right things."

The story made Angela chuckle. The thick folder of story tips she had accumulated from SynEngra PR reps over the years were proof enough that they had not forgotten the press.

The exhibit filled a cavernous room with a high ceiling. It consisted of several display panels, one for each decade since the company was founded in 2019. A glass cabinet displayed samples of the company's products. One entire wall was digitized, displaying charts that dissolved into one another. The graphs— each a steady or steep hill climb—detailed market share, profits, goods sold, and patents filed.

Nate led them to the beginning. The first display was a simple twenty-foot square panel titled "The 20s: Modern Medicine and the Age of UnWellness." The left side documented two major discoveries. It credited the invention of Fast

Genomics, in 2025, to Gibson Chaser, from Tech. It read: "He changed the question from 'What do my genes say?' To 'What are they saying right now?'" A translucent 3D rendering of Chaser, pale and hairless, filled the space around the blurb. Below that, the panel commemorated the 2027 invention of Nanobiognostics, a system to screen spit, urine and breath for miniscule but telltale signs of illness.

Nate looked more closely at the accompanying photo, a group shot of ten people standing awkwardly together on the steps of a granite building. "Is that…?"

"Molly's mom, Claire Doyle. A family full of brains," said Angela. She had seen the photo before, at Molly's parents' place, along with several other photos of her parents with other big name scientists.

June had already moved to the right hand side, which was topped with a single word: "Stagnation." Angela followed and saw that underneath it was a collage of disturbing video-stills with smaller captions. June touched an image and they all watched a series of shorts: children sitting in classrooms, fat hanging over the edges of their chairs; lines of elderly people waiting for prescription drugs at a pharmacy window, the lines extending out onto sidewalks and around corners; emergency rooms so swamped that some people were sleeping on the floor.

"It wasn't a good time to be sick. But so many people were," said June. She crossed her arms and frowned. "You know, the way they present this, it makes it look like people wanted to be unhealthy. But people hardly had a choice. Good food and healthcare were so expensive. And they were hard to find. Entire neighborhoods in the city had no access to fresh produce. And there weren't enough doctors. Most general practitioners had half-year long waiting lists. If you were rich, no problem. But the rest of us ate what we got. And we waited until we were sick enough to go to the ER." Bitterness permeated her voice. "You can see how well that worked out," she said, then started to head to the next display.

June stopped abruptly and turned back to Angela. Hands on her hips, she said through clenched teeth, "What really burns me is that it was companies like this one that sold us on the gimmicky stuff, the cheap empty calories that made people sick in the first place."

Angela and Nate exchanged glances—they'd already learned more than they expected—then hurried to catch up with June at the next panel.

This one, also split down the middle, was titled: "The 30s: The End of All Things…and the Beginning." The left side, "The End," listed a year-by-year account of failures. Angela touched 2033: 46 recalled meat shipments, 58 recalled vegetable crops, a hundred thousand cases of acute toxicity from seafood, 350,000 deaths from food-borne infections, 30 percent of crops wiped out by resistant pest infestation, 45 percent of fruit crops destroyed by erratic weather, and, after oil rationing started at the end of the decade, 60 percent of farmland taken by the government to be turned into fuel crops.

"That was a bad decade," said Nate. "I remember. We lived in a rural area. Crappy schools. But good food…until the rationing. We ate out of our garden. In the winter it was kale, kale, and more kale. And canned food. It wasn't so bad. Luckily the winters were mild so we weren't digging carrots out of two feet of snow or anything like that."

"My mom died then," Angela said quietly. Without giving June or Nate time to speak, she touched the same year on the right hand side, which chronicled a series of starkly contrasting beginnings. "I was telling Molly the other day that mom wouldn't let me get typed. She thought the early NArc was bunk. But after she died, dad took me. He didn't want me to end up like her. Sick, overweight, unhappy. He thought the NArc would help me." Angela looked at June. "I think it did."

June smiled sympathetically and sighed, "They were desperate times."

Meanwhile, Nate was reading a section about the formation of the Safe and Sustainable Foundation. "Funding science for long-term wellness," he read. A series of photos showed the board members over the years. "All PhDs, all scientists," he muttered.

June sidled up to him. Angela heard her add, "And all with corporate ties. The caption should read, 'Damn the conflicts, full speed ahead!'"

Angela scrolled through the rest of the decade, each display chronicling the spread of NArcCafes around the country. The year 2037 showed images of celebrities wearing T-shirts blazoned with NArciType slogans: "I'm a Wanderer" or "Hug a Hunter." The next two showed clips of rock stars playing benefit concerts on the "Fit World" Tour in '38 and then again in '39. A video showed a group of mothers called Bulge Busters marching through cities. They handed out pamphlets citing crippling statistics: Diabetes up 20-fold since the turn of the century. Over half the country obese. "Trim it down! Turn it around!" they chanted. A graph on the back of the pamphlets showed the same diseases dropping among NArcists. Nate had just opened his mouth to ask a question when June weighed in.

"The thing that is missing here is that the NArc was serving real food. The typing worked with real food," said June. "If we had invested in real food, and all the infrastructure needed to grow it... Well, who knows. The fact is, we didn't. We ignored the energy crisis until it was too late. And the climate crisis. We allowed ourselves to be distracted by more immediate problems —political posturing, economic downturns—things that might not have registered a blip in the history books today had we kept ourselves focused on the big problems. But instead they kept us from doing the real, hard, long-term work we needed to do to prevent this End of All Things." She let out a sardonic laugh. "We let things get so bad that we had to reinvent food."

Nate had been listening intently to June. In fact, Angela noticed that he had hardly taken his eyes off of her when she spoke. He smiled at her grim humor, so much like his own. "To me, this looks like a classic game strategy. You get a few people hooked, build the hype, and then let the demand force the changes that you need to take over. You get people to pave the way for you to come in and dominate them. The carrot, and then the stick," said Nate. "What I mean is, it seems like *we* didn't have to reinvent food. The NArc had to. Otherwise, its business plan wouldn't work."

"Exactly," said June. "And the people on Safe and Sustainable's board have made huge profits from the research that made those carrots."

Angela tried not to grin when she saw June's eyes meet Nate's. He seemed less flustered this time, up to the task of holding her gaze. And she seemed to notice him; she saw Nate as an equal, as a person to be respected. To give them a moment, and to give herself time to consider what they had just said, Angela moved on to the next exhibit.

When she arrived, she called out, "Hey, the Migration's next!"

When June and Nate joined her, Angela was watching an animation of the Migration. The clip first showed an abstraction of the countryside emptying and the city filling, then it ran a high-speed 3D video of the construction, showing formerly sprawling suburban areas literally filling with buildings.

She reran the animation. "How in the world did they do it?" she asked. "And so fast?"

"Most people can't survive for long on kale," remarked June. "When they cut off fuel and services in the suburbs and exurbs, most people had no choice. Plus, the government gave out financial incentives, but only for people who left during the scheduled window for their region."

"Another carrot," said Nate.

Angela glanced at him. She remembered that his parents hadn't wanted to move. She remembered at Tech how he tried to fit in with all the city kids. But no amount of swagger could hide how much he hated being in the city. She could tell that he hated the crowds. The buildings. The confinement. She wondered if that was why he spent so much time in cyberspace.

She grazed her fingers across the screen controls again and the image changed from an east coast map to a spinning globe. On the same timescale, country-sides around the world dimmed and urban areas lit up. When cheap fuel no longer existed, the whole world had to adapt. When the animation completed, the image zoomed into each continent and marked each of the NArc and SynEngra locations with a flag.

"There aren't many places left that aren't on the NArc, are there," commented Nate.

"A few. Vermont, of course," replied Angela. "Parts of Europe. New Zealand. They're the holdouts."

"Some parts of Africa, China, and India are also off-NArc, but it's because they aren't rich enough to afford it," added June. "A lot of these countries had no more choice than we did. When the fisheries collapsed, Japan's hand was forced. Australia had such terrible droughts, they had no alternative. Every region had its own driving force."

The three of them stared, mesmerized by the spinning globe. "I visited there once," said June, pointing to Japan.

"Really? When?" asked Nate, perking up.

"I was young. Maybe twenty. My uncle was getting married and I just went. There was this lull in fuel prices for some reason. The calm before the storm, I guess. So I went for it. Travel is kind of old-fashioned, I know, but I loved it. The Sim-tours just don't do places justice. Kind of like the NArc and food."

"The idea of climbing into a metal tube and rocketing halfway around the world for a meeting seems insane," said Angela. "I guess people my age are just used to Sim-tours and cyber visits."

"Yeah, we think we've been everywhere. But we've gone nowhere," cracked Nate.

June smiled and nodded. "When I was a teenager, my friend's mother came back from France with a model of the Eiffel Tower for him. He just laughed and then showed her an early Sim on his computer. He zoomed in so close to the tower that we could see the individual rivets. Then he took her to the top and dove off, landing on the green below."

"What did his mother say to that?" asked Angela.

"She said, 'I just wanted you to know that I was thinking of you while I was away.' I'm pretty sure he still has that little tower on his desk, collecting dust, and reminding him that there is a real world out there."

Angela stood silent for a moment, contemplating the shift. People taking steam ships across the ocean. People jetting around the globe. Now, bits flying through satellites, transmitting the world in 3D.

"So, what was it like" ventured Nate, looking at June with a curiosity that Angela had not seen in him in a long time.

June closed her eyes. "Let's see, what I remember best is the fish market. Horseshoe shaped, with a platform on the outside where the fish came in. Row after row of torpedo-shaped tunas, knee high and four feet long, frozen solid, their heads lopped off, and a tip of the tail cut open for a quality check. The flesh was bright red. They looked like giant figs.

"Then there were the porters, their carts roaring between the vendors and jamming up the pathways." June held her arms out in front of her like a bus driver, her face stern, concentrating. "They whizzed by, their heads banded with white towels. Warriors of the wharf."

"What were they doing, just carting fish around?" Angela asked.

"Yup, from seller to buyer, back and forth. The fish moved from the wharf to the market, from the market to shipping, then off to restaurants and onto people's plates. We ate sushi that morning. So fresh! They'd bring in a fish, still dripping wet, and cut it right in front of you. It wasn't fishy at all. Not the smell. Not the taste. The meat just melted in your mouth..." June moved her lips as if she were trying to recall the taste. "So good."

Angela beamed. "What did the fish look like?"

"They had flounder. An aquarium of them, laying like a brown mat on the floor. Shrimp leapt out of the water above them. They had squid immersed in pools of black ink."

"Ugh," said Angela. She'd reached her limit.

Nate smirked then gave June a sideways look. "Come on. Squid? Squid aren't real. Aren't they like sea monsters from some bad movie?"

"Nope. They were real. Squid was a delicacy. And so was the ink. Let's see. What else. Oh, yes. The eels. Long and metallic, as if they were gilded in silver. Some swimming, or I guess I should say not swimming, in pools of blood, their necks slashed. The workers had thin wire brushes they'd jam into the eel's body to pull out its innards before sending it out to the buyer." She pretended to hold up an eel in one hand and pulled back with the other to demonstrate.

"Now you're just trying to disgust us," Angela laughed. She looked back at the screen, which was now re-running the clip of the east coast migration. "These little blips left over, they must be the Outsiders," she said, dragging her fingertips across a space that used to be western Massachusetts. "How do they survive?"

"You'll see," said June. "Tomorrow."

Angela turned to her, wide-eyed, but June was watching Nate. They both followed his eyes, which were glued to an animation in the bottom corner of the panel. The caption read "2047: The first Neermeat is approved for human consumption, making Personalized Meals possible and making NArcCafes more affordable." The image of a much younger Molly stared back at them. Smiling and proud and standing awkwardly on the same granite stair, just as her mother had.

"She has her mother's eyes," commented June.

Though June had tried to sound amiable, Angela saw that the liveliness had drained from her face and her back had stiffened.

"That was just after I met Josh," June continued, pointing to a caption just above Molly's head. "When they started piloting the nanobot and implant system for personalized medicine, in '45, we still thought food could make a comeback. Then this story came out, and we knew it was all over. But Josh wouldn't give up. He's always been a little crazy, you know." June seemed to be directing her comments at Angela. "Charming, but crazy."

Charming, yes, thought Angela to herself. But not crazy. Smart, definitely. Ambitious. Caring. She's trying to tell me that I'm getting too close to him, she thought, following them to the next panel. She's probably right.

"The Golden Age. Jesus. I can't believe this crap." Nate didn't bother to keep his voice down. He never had, thought Angela. "So this is when it started," he continued, pointing to the panel chronicling the 50s. "With the drugs." He looked at Angela.

She gave him a sharp look to shut him up. As far as Angela knew, June didn't know about Sinsky.

"Right. I remember writing about some of this," she interrupted, planning to talk over him if he didn't get the message. She navigated the screens through each highlight in turn. "First the studies that led to the NArc mandate. Then the hospitals either shut down or turned into trauma centers. Body shops, we called them. Let's see, then the FDA joining with the DEA, one big Food and Drug Enforcement Agency. And here it is: the drugs. The FDEA-NArc partnership to fast-track drug approvals and funnel them into NArc meals. The Golden Age of Personalized Nutrition. You know, I think I might have written that in one of my stories. In hindsight, I guess it does sound a little overblown. Do you think they got that from me?"

Angela looked at her companions, but neither looked back. She didn't need to see their faces to feel the sting of their disapproval.

All three drifted to the final panel. They moved more slowly now, their energy sapped by the spin and their hearts heavy from the memories the panels had brought back. "The last panel," breathed Angela, relieved. "The Gilded Age. Wow. They've already got the new taste profiles on here. 'Decadence without the Guilt.' I wrote that, too," she said, her voice more subdued this time. A sinking feeling came over her, but it was interrupted by the bitterness in June's voice.

"Welcome to the 19th century," she spat. "They seem to have forgotten that the first Gilded Age ended with a depression. And so did the second."

"Only in this Age, people don't die at 23 from tuberculosis or at 35 from cancer," spoke a new voice from behind Angela. "When a person's time comes, it comes gently and mercifully. People believe in the NArc. They have faith in its benevolence, its omniscience. They no longer fear disease, pain, suffering, or even death." Angela turned and saw that the voice belonged to Arthur Short. "I do hope you are enjoying our exhibit. And I hope your escort, Mr. Hunter, is being a gracious ambassador for SynEngra." Arthur patted Nate on the back and first looked June then Angela in the eye. Holding Angela's gaze, he winked. "Enjoy the rest of your stay," he quipped as he turned to go.

The three stared after him until the door to the hallway closed behind him. "Do you know him?" Nate asked Angela.

"We've talked many times. He used to be one of my sources here."

"He's also Molly's boss. He's always skulking around. What do you think he was doing here?" Nate kept his eyes on the door as he talked.

Angela didn't know, but she didn't like it. She trusted Molly implicitly; she would never tell Arthur, of all people, about Sage Weaver. But she had a feeling that someone had told him. "No idea," she replied. "But let's finish up here."

The last panel was riddled with images of NArcCafes efficiently feeding smiling, healthy crowds. It showed glorious holographic mock-ups of rooftop orchards and wall-gardens. A long list of statistics ran alongside the renderings. Average life-expectancy: 120 years; average number of sick days per year: 3; percentage of people with terminal disease: 2; percentage of people outside the national health standard: 3;… After a few minutes, Nate interrupted the silence. "Funny. They didn't include a model of the Singers. Too creepy, I guess."

"They left out a lot of things," said June quietly. "Angela, I've got to get going." She glanced once more at the exhibit and said, "We can talk more about all of this tomorrow." June gave Nate a business-like handshake and a professional, "Pleasure to meet you," and walked out.

He watched her leave, with what looked to Angela like steely resolve in his eyes. Too bad, thought Angela. Too bad.

15

"Please do not tap the glass. It upsets the animals," called out the tour guide. Angela shuffled along with the crowd through a narrow walkway bounded on one side by a chain linked fence and the other by a low concrete wall topped with plexiglass. The crowd stopped and peered through the cloudy plastic into the meadow.

"See the cow, honey?" the woman beside her cooed to her child. The field was dotted with wooden cut-outs of cows, pigs, and goats stuck in the mud. Beside one of the cutouts stood a single black and white cow, her round lashed eyes staring ahead, a placid look on her face. Angela also spotted a chicken and, in the distance, either a cluster of sheep or a cluster of sheep-like statues. On a shack fifty yards away hung a roughly painted sign that read "Pig," but Angela couldn't see inside. Places like this had changed since she was a child. She had vague memories of reaching through wood slats and feeling the sheep brush past her fingertips. To protect against the spread of disease, the farm museums had been forced to eliminate human and animal contact years ago. Even though the muck the lone cow stood in made Angela crinkle her nose, she still wanted a closer look at the sheep. Part of her longed to reach through the fence and sink her fingers into their wooly coats.

She turned to ask Josh a question, but he had vanished. Looking for him, she caught the eye of June, waiting against the cyclone fence with Parrish. June tipped her head and Angela followed. Skirting behind the crowd, the three walked to the end of the tunnel.

"Do you see it? There it is! Look for his pink nose," the tour guide directed the crowd. As the visitors craned in unison for a glimpse of the swine, Angela followed Parrish and June out of the tunnel and through a creaky gate.

They passed by a demonstration barn filled with restored farm equipment, posters describing archaic farming techniques, and souvenir stuffed animals. Then they wound down a wooded hillside path. Several minutes later the path ended at a wooden gate. They stepped through the gates and into a meadow that sloped upwards to meet an old farmhouse and a working barn.

"A perfect New England day," Angela exclaimed, drinking in the fresh air, sunshine, and wide-open space. Like a daffodil, she tilted her face to the sun and then twirled around, laughing. *I almost forgot days like these were possible*, she was thinking to herself when a hand gripped her arm.

"This is serious," Parrish hissed. "This isn't a game, so stop acting like a child." His pale eyes shot daggers into Angela's.

"Take it easy, Parrish," June interjected, placing a warning hand on his shoulder as he let go. "You know, there are a thousand people up the hill right now who don't even realize the sun is shining on them. Let Angela enjoy it, and take heart that she appreciates it."

Angela adjusted the sleeve of her sweater, which had twisted under Parrish's grip. She wondered if he acted this way in front of Molly. But then, she thought, maybe Parrish never had to pull Molly back to reality. Then she saw Josh in the distance, waving from the front porch and holding a ceramic mug of coffee. She waved back and headed his way. Next to him stood a man, smiling and chatting, his hands shoved into the pockets of a pair of worn jeans. His pockets scrunched up the sleeves of his ragged turtleneck sweater and flannel shirt. When she got closer, Angela was surprised to see a youthful glint in the eye of this weather-worn, white-haired farmer.

Herb Walker smiled as he shook her hand. "My nephew here says you want a look around." Josh had told Angela that he had spent many summers working with his uncle Herb and learning about food and farming. As they stood there, sizing one another up, Angela noted the strong family resemblance. Though Josh towered over his uncle, she could see similarities around the eyes, and in the shape of their lips.

Herb looked down at her feet and said, "Let's see if we've got some boots you can use."

With Angela's flats and flowing microfiber pants replaced by a pair of Herb's daughter's canvas overalls and a pair of rubber boots, they set off for a tour of the farm. Herb led Angela across the field behind his house. "I've been here my whole life," he said. "My father farmed these same fields, and his father before him. Do you know, I'm the fifth generation here?"

Angela nodded, impressed, as Herb pointed west. "See those hills? They used to be covered with apple trees. Two families owned hundreds of acres. Even back when I was a boy in the twenty-teens people still drove for miles on autumn weekends to pick apples."

On the hillside, Angela looked for signs of the old orchard, but the trees had grown into a dense forest and formed a patchwork of spring-green hues. Here and there, scraggly evergreens poked out between the budding deciduous branches.

Herb continued to point, east, north, south; in every direction he saw former farms in his mind. "It started to change before the Migration. A hundred years ago. My dad used to tell me about the old farms, mostly dairy farms and orchards. He gave up the dairy some sixty years ago. Switched to meat. Used to tell me about all the hormones and drugs the farmers gave the cows, just to keep 'em milking. Just to keep their heads above water. It broke his heart. He used to say, 'What are we doing? We give 'em drugs and the bugs out-smart us, so we give 'em more drugs.' The other guys just sold out. Housing developments. Golf courses. Warehouses. A lot of good those are doing us now." Herb shook his head. Most of the land now lay fallow, covered with spindly trees and twisty vines. "Land here's too rocky for the big commodity farms they have out west." He chuckled. "That is, I assume they're still there. Never been there myself. If they are, they're all that's left of agriculture in America. Besides us."

He pointed south-east. "You passed the old Brigham Acres on your way here." Angela gave him a quizzical look. "The place where you can tour an old neighborhood, eat in the old style, with food cooked in a household kitchen. For the right price, you can stay in one of those old cookie-cutter ranch houses. I hear they play old television shows for ya." Herb laughed, but his eyes drooped in sadness. "Visit the relics. All museums now," he muttered.

Herb spoke quickly and had an odd way of dropping his r's. Angela sometimes had trouble keeping up with his slang. Josh filled in when he saw a lost look in her eyes. "Cookie-cutter means they all look alike," he whispered.

Herb explained that during the Migration, he and his family stayed behind, along with many other families, determined to make a life on the Outside work. The Walkers fared better than many. They had a hundred acres and already knew how to grow their own food. They slaughtered their own animals, grew crops, and used wood, running brooks, and an old biomass generator for power.

"At first, it was actually easier. Before the Migration, we had to follow all sorts of rules and regulations. We had government men out here once a week, sometimes more, checking the milk, testing the water, measuring the pens, making sure the cuts in the freezers had certified government stamps. The only slaughterhouse nearby was always backed up. Sometimes we just did our own and hoped no one would notice." Herb laughed. "Funny thing is, the biggest quality problems we had were with meats done on the up-and-up. Nowadays, now that we've got anarchy out here, we never have any problems. We all just trade with each other. If I slip up, it could hurt Bill, who sends our cheese, or Donna who bakes our bread. I'll tell you what," said Herb, tapping Angela's notebook with his gnarled fingers. "I don't slip up."

Herb said he still hoped that his son might want to continue the farm after him even though he left home at 18 for university training. "When he comes back now, it's only to visit," he said. Herb's daughter stayed to help out. She and her husband worked hard, but their first born had a medical condition. He needed treatment that Herb couldn't get without connections on the Inside. So Herb turned the farm into a museum. The museum acted as a front for his still working farm, he explained, but it also drew crowds of urban tourists looking for a dose of fresh air and nostalgia. He hosted bonfires, hay rides, and spring dances. Most of the money that came in went right back out again to pay his employees. He also paid Josh for supplies and medicines and shelled out hush money to keep the authorities uninterested in the activities going on behind the front barn.

As Angela scratched in her notebook, trying to capture everything her recorder was missing—her boots squelching in the mud, the way Herb's hair drifted across his forehead in the breeze, the smell of the wet grass—Herb stopped at a fence and continued his tour. "We move the animals in herds across the pasture. They eat for a few days, then we walk 'em to the next lot. By the time they come back to the first one, the clover and grasses have grown back."

"How do you keep them in one area?" asked Angela. The sheep seemed willingly clustered together in one corner even though there were acres of open fields around them.

"If you look close, you can see a thin rope surrounds the lot of 'em. Rope's got a bit of juice running through it"—"electricity," murmured Josh—"enough to sting their noses. They only need to get zapped once before they learn."

Herb turned and walked along the fence up a steep slope. They crossed a gravel road and climbed a shaded hill. Herb stopped them and gestured to the left. Three pigs foraged in the trees not more than ten yards away. A black sow weighing 600 pounds, according to Herb, dug her nose deep into the dirt and chewed the acorns she had unearthed. Her ears flopped over her eyes and her tiny tail wriggled in the air as she tottered on her toes. The other two, one pink and one a speckled mix, stood on either side. Both outweighed the sow by hundreds of pounds. "These guys 'll clear this hillside if I let 'em. I just like to let 'em dig the weeds out, eat some nuts, put on some good fat."

"What do you mean, good fat?" asked Angela.

"They're same as us. They eat good food, their bodies form good food. The fat on these pigs is good for you. When we get back to the house, we'll have some bacon and some berry pie made with lard. You won't ever want to eat those manufactured fats again." Herb smiled and led them up the hill for a view of the piglets. The big pigs in the woods, he explained, were his breeders, along with a few others they hadn't run across. "These little ones 'll be dinner for Foodies all over the city."

Angela winced then instantly regretted it. Herb had noticed. "Some people think it's cruel. But these piglets have a nice year and a half on our farm. When their time's up, we treat them with care. If we didn't eat 'em, these animals probably wouldn't even exist anymore."

Herb paused. "Least, that's what I used to think." He sighed and wiped his brow. "My son says all these animals exist in theory. They exist in DNA form. Digitally. He says that if we want to, we can just make 'em again. They use pig genes to make the meat in those Singer-thingies and whatnot. Mattie says that the engineered stuff they call Neermeat is the same as the muscles on these piglets, so I guess they exist that way too. He says that the modern way is more humane." Herb shook his head. "I don't like the slaughter anymore 'n the next guy, but something tells me it's more humane than cooking up piglet parts in a test tube. When I do a pig, I have to face him. Same way predators have been doing it since time began. To me, that's just life as it should be."

Angela looked out over the muddy field. The pink and brown piglets, the size of puppies, waddled around, snorting and grunting and tossing mud in the air with their noses. She wondered about the word humane. Josh had told her that morning that humans had never been humane. "Add humans to the mix and, throughout history, the first thing we do is destroy the life around us," he'd said. "Difference is that now we don't worry about destroying it. We've digitized it and stored it away. For later. But what we didn't bottle is all the intricate connections, the ecology, the balance. We have a catalog of all the parts, but we don't know how they fit together."

Herb led them along the edge of the field. "I'll take you past the garden on the way back to the house," said Herb. "Josh'll give you a garden tour while I round up some chow."

$$\neq$$

Angela and Josh strolled together across the yard and toward the garden. One of Herb's grandchildren, a boy of about eight, was running after a dog that had something in its mouth, though Angela couldn't make out just what it was. "Watcher! Watcher! Come back here!"

"The dog's called Watcher because she's part pointer. She stares at birds for hours. She's a big help when we go hunting," explained Josh.

Angela tried to picture Josh and Herb with shotguns slogging through the woods, but she couldn't come close.

As they approached the garden, Angela heard Herb's other two grandchildren arguing. They were picking beans and loading them into round wicker baskets, debating whether to pick the skinny ones or leave them until the next day. "You never see kids in the city," she remarked to Josh. "I guess they go to school and daycare, but if you don't have them, you don't really see them. There is something nice about having them around, though. It makes me feel…less serious, I think."

"I never thought of it that way," replied Josh, "but you're right. That's exactly how they make me feel." He looked at Angela. "Do you ever think about having kids yourself?"

"Oh, I…I don't know," she stuttered. With all of the assisted fertility technology, it was easy to put off thinking about it. Angela had been putting off the idea of children for so long that she had almost forgotten that motherhood was a possibility. "Molly always says she wants them, but in a perfunctory way, you know? I guess I'm a little less, umm…organized?"

Josh laughed at this. Then he put his arm around her shoulders and squeezed gently. His voice took on a more somber tone. "Since I'm not on the NArc, I don't have that luxury. All of our days are numbered, I guess, but my ticker will stop sooner than later." He squeezed again and looked at Angela with a sad smile that pierced her right through the heart. Now that she knew

Josh, she couldn't imagine her life without him. She wanted to beg him to go on the NArc, to let it fix everything. But she knew that wouldn't do. The lifestyle that was killing him was the one thing that made him feel alive. She wondered silently, as she slipped her arm around his waist, if she could handle being with a man who would inevitably get sick, suffer, and die before her eyes.

"Here we are. The garden," announced Josh. He waved her through the open gate. As they strolled the rows, he pointed out the different vegetables and explained how most of the plants in the glass-wall gardens in the city started out as traditional earthbound crops. "Add a few genes so they can suck nutrients out of the air, and you can hang them. Tweak a few more to standardize the pollinators and you've got mass-produced, robotically-pollinated plants. A few more, and you've got packable shapes, standard sizes, and color-coded nutrients. Grow them inside every building, and you've got an endless supply of Nutrition. Notice, I didn't say food," he added with a wink.

Angela stopped. "Wait a second. You act like it's engineering's fault that the food doesn't taste like anything. But genetic engineering doesn't *have* to change the taste." She remembered from one of her food history classes that people in Europe accepted genetic engineering when they realized it was the only way to save some of their regional specialties from the vagaries of the climate.

"No. You're right," admitted Josh. "When genetic engineering brought back the old varieties, it brought back the old flavors too. But only partly. Flavor also comes from the soil. The air. Grow root stock from the same grape vine in California and Australia and you'll get two very different grapes. That's part of the problem. That kind of variety is okay for wine, but when it comes to something like lunch, strong, unusual flavors made people nervous. Even before the NArc, most of the biotech foods in America were engineered to taste bland." Josh stopped and leaned against the garden gate. "Fact is, Americans care more about consistency than about taste."

"That seems a little harsh," she replied with a smirk. "Is that why you're helping me? So I'll sell the idea of taste to people?"

"Well, you are doing a great job of that so far," he said. "But no. What I want is for people to know the truth. Most people think real food isn't safe, sustainable, or reliable, but they're wrong. If this work we're doing together helps them see that, if it helps them see that there is value in our agricultural heritage, maybe that will be enough. It all depends."

"Depends on what?" probed Angela.

"On whether the NArc is—"

"Come'n get it!" called Herb, waving from the back porch.

"—to be continued," he said, waving back at Herb.

Angela couldn't believe he would leave her hanging. But he did.

The noon-time sunlight filtered through the trees and danced across the wooden slats of the porch. Angela sat in a shady corner. "I want to hear more about this good fat, Herb. For a story I did about four years ago, I had a nutritional geneticist analyze one of my NArc meals alongside my genome and other personal health readings. She showed me how the meal had 7 types of fats in it and she connected each one to a different biological function. All of these fats were designed to improve my metabolism, and I'll tell you, my metabolism needs all the help it can get." Angela accepted the plate of food Herb passed her, but didn't stop to eat. "I'll never forget what she said to me. She said, 'Honey, there's no natural food on the planet that is good for you. Your body? Well, let's just say it needs engineered food.'" Angela smiled and laughed. "My genes should have been selected out, I guess. Anyway, like I said, I know all of these scientific facts and engineered solutions. But I don't know anything about the kinds of good fats that might be in natural food. That's what I'm here to learn." Angela leaned forward, her plate resting on her knees, her eyes wide with curiosity, waiting for Herb to fill her mind with new ideas.

Herb, his mouth full, responded, "Eat your lunch before it gets cold. It's best when the bacon's still warm and the lettuce is still crisp."

So Angela ate, slowly and deliberately. As she did, the others dropped away, one by one, to attend to the rest of their day's work. When she finished, only Josh remained.

He reached over and wiped a dribble of tomato seeds from Angela's chin with his napkin. He hadn't tried to hide his fondness for her today, in front of his closest friends and family. He rarely allowed her to be seen with him in public and, when they visited speakeasies, he treated her as if she were a client or co-worker. But today, he'd let his eyes linger on hers. He'd dared to comb his fingers through her hair and let them dance down the space between her shoulder blades. Though she had met his first lingering gaze with uncertainty, she hadn't resisted.

Just as Josh started to bend toward her for a kiss, Parrish leaned out the back door and interrupted. "Josh. It's time."

Angela giggled. "Time to give Herb's daughter back her glass slippers." She slid out of the rubber boots and padded across the porch and into the back hall to change her clothes.

In the hallway, Angela ran into Herb. "Herb, you never did answer my question," she said, grinning.

"Good fats, right? Ok then. Let me tell you a story. Once upon a time, back in 1928, some guys in the United States agriculture department had three buckets of lard."

"Wait. Did you say *nineteen* twenty-eight?"

"Yes. So they had this lard. Each bucket of fat had come from three different pigs. When they tipped the buckets over, they weren't the same. One was solid, like candle wax. Nothing spilled out. One slumped, like thick oatmeal. These two were from pigs that ate feed. But the lard in the third bucket poured out on the ground like syrup. *That* pig had foraged in the peanut fields. *That* fat was as good for you as olive oil. Maybe even better."

"Huh. That is interesting. But aren't engineered fats better than olive oil?" pressed Angela.

"Sure. We've learned a lot since then. Lots of details. But the point is, we've forgotten a lot too. We've forgotten that nature's filled with good stuff."

Angela nodded. She couldn't argue with that point. In fact, it was one of the only things she had felt certain of recently. "Why do you think we forgot? How did it happen?"

"Back in 1928? Easy. They needed lard to grease the machines to keep industry going. Demand ramped up during World War II. So people engineered new fats." Angela cocked her head. "That's right. Even back then. Point is, sometimes we need to invent new things. But to me, the problem starts when we forget the old things. When we start to forget that we forgot, well, somebody's got to try to remember. That's what we do out here."

The blast of a car horn interrupted them. "Oh no! I've got to go, Herb. Thank you. For everything," she said, giving him a hug and a peck on the cheek. His skin felt soft, but his arms were like steel bands underneath the shaggy flannel.

"Anytime. Come back anytime."

When Angela emerged from the house, her companions were already strapped into Ken's truck, June at the driver's seat, its engine already running. Parrish had explained to her more than once that they operated under a tight fuel budget. The vegetable oil stocks they had needed to last until next harvest. "Bye! Thanks again," she called to Herb, ducking into the back seat next to

Josh. "Sorry," she breathed once inside the car. "I didn't realize… Herb kept chatting and, well, I hope you weren't idling long."

Angela's first thought when they arrived at Bunny's was that they must have made a wrong turn. The contrast between her place and Herb's could not have been more stark.

Herb's house, despite almost three centuries of use, felt sturdy. Its walls were plastered and painted. Its brick chimneys stood tall. Bunny's place consisted of a decaying double wide trailer with a shack, a greenhouse and a barn, each stuck to the next in a dimly lit labyrinth. While Herb's yard appeared pastoral, sown with tall grasses and wild-flowers, Bunny's yard was littered with old farm equipment, rusty hunks of metal, and abandoned windows and doors.

June knocked on a screen door that dangled, partly unhinged, in the frame. Bunny greeted them through the torn screen. A wisp of a woman, her cheek bones poked out from beneath the strings of hair that escaped from her messy ponytail, and her dingy t-shirt and work pants hung on her body as if she were a wire hanger. She motioned for them to follow, then darted through one of the back doors. Angela trailed the group, ducking under bundles of herbs drying in the rafters, dodging bins of dried beans, and finally arriving at a small barn.

Bunny seemed nervous, flitting like a bird from place to place. She kept moving and talking. "You need how much? Seventeen pounds? I've got a little extra for you in the freeze. Turkey. Deer. Rabbit. Boar. It's all there. Wrapped nice," she rambled. "Who wants a look around? Must be you." She gestured vaguely toward Angela and turned her head just shy of facing her. Angela noticed she hadn't made eye contact with any of them yet. "This is the barn. Got the feed in here, and the mulch I make for the garden. This here's the freeze." She tugged on a large metal bar and pulled open the insulated door. "Only room for two in here," she said, standing aside so Angela could step in.

Angela didn't want to step too close. The woman's clothes appeared stained and her hair dirty. But as she slid past Bunny into the freezer, she noticed that the woman smelled of soap. Even her fingernails were clean.

Then the cold hit her, followed by the shock of the sight before her. She expected to see cuts of meat, like she saw in Paolo's freezer. But instead, rows of animals hung from menacing hooks that slid across channels anchored into the ceiling. In the front were two pigs, larger than the pups she'd seen at Herb's farm that morning, only these pigs were frozen solid and cleaved in half from nose to tail. Behind the pigs hung a deer, it's antlers pointing toward the ground. Beyond that hung parts, some skinned, some boned. Angela covered her nose and mouth with her hand even though the room smelled faintly of antiseptic and nothing else.

"Full house today. Lamont got a few deer this week. One big buck. Been dolin' it out. See the rabbits in back?" She pointed and Angela saw the neatly stacked mauve-colored bodies on a shelf in the back. "Them's mine. I raise 'em. I'll show you. Good, rabbit is." Bunny stepped out and continued her tour.

As Angela followed her into the next room, she looked to Josh for reassurance. He nodded and ushered her along. Bunny was still chattering away and fluttering from one rabbit cage to the next. A stench, this time unimagined, hung in the air.

"—and some have this long fur. Good for sweaters, they say, but I'm not one for crafts. I just shave 'em in the summer and get what I can for it." Bunny shrugged and almost looked directly at Angela, then pointed in back. "We capture their poop. See the screen? Got that from an old abandoned barn and stuck it in last summer. Works miracles. Poop dries out and rolls down the screen. Lands in a heap down cellar. Turns into great mulch. Mix in some leaves, some grass. Great stuff."

Angela nodded, trying to take in the sights without missing too much of Bunny's ramblings. Bunny had started daring to take longer and longer looks at Angela. Through squinting lids she eyed Angela's shoes, her clothes, even her hands as she jotted down notes. Just as the lingering looks began to make Angela feel uncomfortable, Bunny spoke.

"You don't need no notes, seeing as these rabbits live just like you," said Bunny, who for the first time stole a look at Angela's face. "Babied, I mean. If one of 'em got out, she might make it a few months. Maybe a year if the snow doesn't fall again this winter. Most likely, she'd get ate up. In here, she gets to live nice and long and slow. Out there, everything speeds up. You get old fast. You've got to cram your livin' in before the coyotes get ya." Bunny cackled, revealing a rotten tooth.

Angela rocked back on her heels. All along she had been judging Bunny as inferior, looking down her nose at the squalor. Yet at the same time Bunny had been just as astutely looking down on her. Only Bunny's judgement ran more than skin deep. Angela steadied herself and wondered exactly how long she would last out here before the coyotes got her.

Bunny stepped into the final room in the labyrinth. Angela followed and watched her grab a blood stained apron from a hook and strap a belt around her waist, knives of all shapes and sizes dangling from its holster. She approached the center bench where a man stood hacking through a large hunk of meat with a saw. "This here's Lamont," she said. "He's cuttin' up some bear for smokin'. I gotta do a few more birds for your friends," she said, leaning inside the attached chicken coop.

"Hey there. You with those food dealers?" whispered Lamont. "I got some good Junk I'm mixing up out back. Maybe you're interested in trying it? Maybe, if you like it, you can bring it back and see how it does Inside?" Lamont's seedy smile faded as his eyes flitted to the door.

"Hi Lamont," said June, who had just walked in. "You know we don't deal in Junk. You should also know the Food Police are cracking down on it."

"I told you to keep your Junk out of this house, Lamont. I swear, if you mess things up with these nice people, you'll be hangin' in that freezer like a fat old hog!" Bunny waved a long sharp knife within inches of Lamont's nose and glared at him. She didn't have any trouble meeting his eyes.

He apologized but protested. "There's good money in it Bun," he muttered, then went back to work.

June repeated her bird order to Bunny and asked Angela to help her load the car. Once out of earshot, she said, "We don't really need your help. If you want to see her butcher the birds, you can. You just looked a little shaken and I thought, well, it's a lot to take in for one day."

Angela thanked her and leaned against a wall in the trailer. Across the room, a boy peeked out from behind a door at her. Underneath an ochre-colored afro floated two magnified eyes framed by clunky black glasses. Angela waved. The boy waved back. Angela recognized the glasses from the old medical device display at school. Myopia, like almost everything else, had been practically eliminated by the NArc. She couldn't remember exactly how. Something about gene therapy to slow the progression and surgery to correct it. She'd have to ask Molly.

At his feet circled an orange tiger cat. The cat traced figure eights around the boy's ankles then sat, pressing his forehead into the crook of the boy's knee, chin up, ears down, his face an expression of bliss.

"What's his name?" she asked.

"Marmalade," said the boy.

"May I pet him?"

The boy nodded.

As she scratched his ears, the cat nuzzled Angela's hand and head-butted her elbow, then meandered back behind the door. The boy pushed his glasses up and followed, shutting the door behind him. Angela could still hear the cat purring through the hollow veneer door.

A second later, Bunny walked in, four dead chickens dangling from her hands, their skin puckered and inflamed from the scalding water and pummeling of the plucking machine.

She held the birds out to Angela, who froze, unable to bring herself to touch the dead creatures. June bounded up the trailer steps, and cried, "These look wonderful! Sorry for the extra trouble," she said. Angela breathed a sigh of relief seeing that June's smile had charmed Bunny into forgetting any slight she might have caused.

Bunny nodded, and, noting a stack of packages on the table, said, "Well, I hope you've got all you need. Nice to see you folks. Come back again soon." She shuffled them out the door and shut it without another word.

Outside the trailer, Josh and Parrish hustled to finish packing the truck.

"June?" Angela ventured. "What did you leave for Bunny?

"I left her a new set of glasses for her son plus money and other supplies," she replied, carrying the birds to the truck.

"But why did she send us away so fast?"

June wiped her hands on the towel she kept dangling from her hip pocket and led Angela away from Bunny's trailer. In a soft voice, she explained. "Bunny is proud. She doesn't like to take handouts. She insists on trading food for supplies. It still embarrasses her that she's not self-sufficient. We insist on paying her for her goods but she won't take it directly. We leave it and Lamont takes care of their expenses. He pays the guys at one of the nearby factories to recharge their batteries and fill their fuel tanks so they can keep the freezer and the well pump running. She pretends he doesn't."

"Those glasses are so clunky," Angela remarked, looking back at the broken screen door.

"We've tried to bring her newer medicines, but she's set in her ways. She's happy to take those old lenses, but she won't take any of the new therapeutics. She thinks they aren't natural. I've tried to explain that plastic lenses aren't natural either, but she won't hear it. 'Good old-fashioned medicine is fine for us,' she says."

Angela nodded slowly but couldn't piece it together. "You wanted me to come here, but Josh didn't. He won't say it, but I can tell he's been trying to avoid it. What did you want me to see?"

"I did insist on bringing you here. And Josh has been avoiding it."

"He wants me to tantalize people, and then hit them hard. He wants me to shock people into change they can't argue with," said Angela. She watched as June tried to hold her face steady. Angela knew that June had been uneasy with her from the start, but now she was reconsidering. At the same time, Angela had also surprised herself. She hadn't meant to say these things out loud. In fact, the idea had only just started forming in her mind over the course of the day. I haven't found what he wants me to find yet, Angela thought to herself, but if I do, and I think I might, he may well get what he wants from me.

"Well, I'm relieved, I guess, that you know what you're into," said June. "For my part, I'm less radical. I believe in small steps. Incremental change. I want to bring things back into balance. And you can't do that through rapid change. If we push too hard, we'll just end up back where we were before." June cut herself off. Her voice had been ratcheting up. She took a breath and began again. "I wanted you to meet Bunny so you would see what the NArc has done to people who want to live independently. Bunny survives, but she has to do everything herself."

"But why so primitively?" Angela interrupted. "I just don't understand why Herb and Bunny and, presumably, all the others out here have to live like people did in the nineteenth century."

"It's because of what *wasn't* in the museum yesterday. Let's take fuel as an example, because it is a very important part of the equation. When the government shut off services to rural areas, the people left behind during the Migration were left behind forever. It's not just the laws that made it that way, but the world those laws created. Rationing changed the market. Corporate interests got fuel first. Individuals second. When alternative fuels came into play, they were expensive, so those market dynamics stuck. Even today, it's difficult to buy fuel unless you're industrial."

"But you and Ken buy it, for your house," Angela said, more as a question than a statement.

"We buy fuel for our house through a historical preservation cooperative. If it weren't for that, we'd be Outsiders, too. Or we'd be like the neighborhoods in the City where the line between the Outside and the Inside blurs. But what I'm talking about is bigger than that. The same way people out here have no market to buy fuel on, they also have no market to sell anything on. When I met Josh, when Neerfoods came out, we watched the markets disappear. So we created a replacement market. A black market. We smuggle their goods in and bring payment out. It's illegal, but it's their only option. That's what it means to be an Outsider. And that's what I want to change."

Angela had never given much thought to the Outsiders. She had always thought of them as flawed. Unfit somehow. And she had always thought of the illegal market as one based on greed. But June sketched out an alternative picture. One that made much more sense now that she knew more about the people involved. It made more sense having seen this family, this example of the people history had left behind.

"We've got to go," said June. "After dark, the gate into Borderlands West isn't always friendly."

On the ride back to the city, Angela sat quietly in the back seat of the truck watching the landscape fly by, the sun setting at her back. She had lost the feeling of elation that had filled her all morning. She felt nauseous. And it wasn't from the bouncing of the car over the rutted, curving roads. It wasn't from the sight of the dead chickens or the anxiety she felt about the checkpoint they would have to pass through to get home.

Angela felt sick because her views on the NArc, on her own health, on food, children, even death had, one by one, been turned upside down in the course of this project. She no longer knew which way was up. She felt so off balance, she wasn't sure she wanted to go home. Just as she felt about to pitch forward, her inner disorientation taking over, she felt Josh slip his arms around her and pull her close. He nuzzled her ear and spoke to her in a low whisper.

"I know you must be overwhelmed. I want you to know that I'm here for you. Whatever you need. You just let me know." He pressed his lips against her temple and she could feel him breathing in the scent of her hair. His arms felt so strong around her, she felt grounded and secure and certain that she didn't want him to let her go.

16

Despite the trauma of the previous day, Angela shuffled out of her bedroom late Sunday morning feeling dreamy. She shut the door behind her, then leaned against it. The skin on her chin was raw and her lower lip felt a little swollen. She shifted and her top brushed against her nipples, still tender. Angela hugged herself and shook her head. She'd never let herself go like that before. But then, Josh was the first man she'd been with who had actually seemed manly. Something about his hands. Something about the way he had moved her without making her feel big and clumsy. The way he held onto her and pushed her to the limits of pleasure, to the fringes of pain, commanding her yet not scaring her. Not at all. He made her feel like she was the most important thing in the world. Just the thought of him—the taste of cigarettes and wine mingling on their tongues, his beard on her cheek, the sound of his breath in her ear—made her knees give. Angela ran her hand over her camisole. Her fingers drifted between her breasts and down to her belly, stopping just below her navel. She felt softer, a little rounder than she used to. But he hadn't minded. She pressed down with her palm and let her fingertips dip under her pajama bottoms to brush the delicate skin there. She couldn't believe that she still wanted more.

As she made her weak-kneed way across the room and down the narrow passage between the sofa and the bathroom, she was so distracted that she tripped and nearly fell over a large bag blocking the way. Still groggy, she shoved it aside and moved on. In the bathroom, as she examined her inflamed chin in the mirror, it occurred to her that the bag was Molly's.

Angela had become so accustomed to having the apartment to herself that she'd almost forgotten about her roommate. With all of Angela's outings, it had gotten so that they only saw each other when they made specific plans. Even that had become hit or miss. She hoped Molly hadn't heard her last night; she hadn't even thought to keep it down.

Without thinking, Angela rapped lightly on Molly's door. Almost as soon as she had, she regretted it. Molly had been seeing a lot of Parrish lately. What if she hadn't been the only one indulging in a little male company? Molly almost never brought anyone home to stay, but the last thing she needed was for Angela to interrupt her when she did.

But when Angela heard the tremor of a feeble voice call out, she cracked the door and flicked on the light. Molly lay curled in a ball, her sheets tangled around her as if she'd spent the night in a restless frenzy. "Molly? Are you okay?" Angela asked with concern. She had never followed up on Nate's worries about Molly's health and now she regretted it.

Molly groaned and kicked the sheets away. "I can't sleep. I haven't slept for days. And my head is pounding. I don't know what's wrong with me. And I've got to get to the lab, but I just can't get up." She rolled onto her back, exposing a pale face with dark circles under her eyes, and groaned.

Angela ran back to her room. "Josh! Wake up," she said, shaking his shoulder. He had sprawled across the bed and was snoring loudly. She had to shake him again to wake him. "Josh! Molly's sick. I don't know what's wrong with her," she said, breathless even though she'd run only a few steps. Josh rolled over and rubbed his eyes. "Can you help? She's sick and I don't know what to do."

Angela could see him hesitating. She knew he was worried about being seen. He'd taken a big risk coming here the night before. He'd only done it because she'd assured him they wouldn't run into anyone. But now, Molly was here and she needed help. "You don't need to worry. Molly already knows about you. About everything. She's been dating Parrish all this time."

Josh stared back at her. She couldn't read his face but she didn't care what he was thinking. She didn't care if he wasn't awake yet. She just wanted his help. What was he waiting for? She was about to insist when he got up, pulled on his jeans, and followed her into Molly's room.

When they walked in, Molly sat up and clutched the sheets to her chin.

Angela touched her arm, "It's okay. It's just Josh."

Molly shot her friend a disapproving look. Angela looked sharply back. She didn't like being judged. Sure, she'd had more boyfriends than Molly had. Practically everyone had. But this wasn't just a one night thing. She had a feeling that she and Josh had something special. And she didn't like Molly assuming he was some cheap date.

Josh smiled gently at Molly. "Can I help at all?"

Angela explained to Josh that Molly hadn't slept and had a headache. Molly, meanwhile, had edged herself back toward her pillow. Angela was just about to urge her to let Josh help when he sat down on the edge of the bed and asked Molly to look at him.

"I know you're not used to being sick. But I help sick people all the time on the Outside," he said in a soothing voice. "I have some training. If you'll let me, I'd like to look at your eyes."

Hugging her knees to her chest, Molly inched closer to him and opened her eyes wide.

"May I feel your pulse?"

She offered her wrist.

"How long has this been going on?"

"About a week. It's been tolerable, just an annoyance, until last night." Her face looked scrunched. "According to my NArc stats, there's nothing wrong with me," she whispered, rubbing her forehead and temples with her fingertips.

Josh nodded and left the room. Angela sat down and patted Molly's back. She hadn't had to comfort her friend in a long time and wasn't sure how to do it. Josh had made it look so easy.

When Josh returned, he handed Molly a glass of water, and two pills. "Drink this," he said. Molly and Angela both gave him incredulous looks. "It's just water. I'll refill it when you're done. Tell me, have you been skipping meals?"

When Molly nodded yes, Angela couldn't believe her eyes. "Just this morning. And a few times this week. I'm not hungry at all."

"It's okay," said Josh gently. "But you need food and fluids. I'm going to go get a NArc meal for you. I'm going to give you mine." Molly shook her head, but Josh kept talking. "Once you eat it, take the vitamins. Then we'll let you sleep for an hour or so." Molly shook her head again. "Molly, you can trust me. I want you to pick up your own meal before you leave for the lab. I want you to screen it." A sudden look of understanding came over Molly's face. She looked at Josh and nodded. Angela had never seen her flip-flop so quickly. "Good. You'll have this problem solved before the end of the day."

$\neq$

Molly woke up an hour later and assured both Josh and Angela that she felt revived enough to go to work. She didn't feel perfect, but she no longer felt dizzy and her head had stopped pounding. Angela ceased her pacing. She was relieved and grateful Josh had been here.

But she was frustrated too. He wasn't telling her anything. When she asked him what was wrong and how he knew what to do, he sounded just like Molly: "We won't know anything until she does those tests," he'd said and left it at that.

After Molly left, Josh asked Angela a question. "So how long has she been seeing Parrish?"

Angela shrugged. "A couple weeks." Josh continued to sit, staring out the window through the vines hanging in the wall garden lining the outside of her building and into the tangle of skyscrapers beyond. "I don't know how she finds the time to see him. According to Nate, she's usually locked in the lab. She's under pressure to deliver some new Singer feature. Some kind of Neermeat longevity thing."

Josh continued to stare. A mist had formed between the panes of glass, watering the new seedlings dangling from their scaffolding.

"The Singers aren't the worst thing, you know," she clipped. She knew she was being unreasonable but she wanted to get some sort of reaction from him. "They're giving the land and the oceans a chance to recover. Plus the places you took me to are thriving. Sure, they can't grow food for everyone, but it's enough for some. And the NArc is keeping people healthy." Angela knew before the words came out that she was saying the wrong thing, but she couldn't contain herself. "*Most* people, anyway. And at least the people on the NArc won't become a burden on their families when they get sick."

Josh let the words hang in the air for a moment. Then he turned to look at Angela and spoke slowly. "Dying used to be part of living. I won't argue with you. It's true that caring for someone you love is a burden. It's hard work. But it is also beautiful work."

Angela felt her anger dissipate and a sense of regret began to creep in. She felt the tears welling up in her eyes and wiped them away with a pitiful, useless swipe of her fingertips.

"I feel like an idiot. Why don't I get it? What's this all about Josh? What are you really trying to do here?" she demanded. "I mean, we've spent all of our time talking about food. You've shown me how people grow it. You've shown me it can be nutritious and convinced me that it is, definitely, more delicious. But if it's not about food, what is it about?"

Still unflappable, Josh said, "You know."

Angela looked away. What did she know? Nothing. She didn't know what was wrong with Molly. And she wouldn't have known what to do to help her if Josh hadn't been here. And the food. What did she know about that? It hadn't turned out to be what she thought it was. Cheaters aren't who she thought they were. She hadn't gotten the NArc right either. And on top of all of it she faced the ugly truth she'd been avoiding thinking about since the museum. She had helped make all of this happen. Her column. Her words. Whatever I think I know, I can hardly trust it. "I want you to tell me. I want to know what *you* think it's about," she said without looking back at him.

Josh leaned in. "It's about everything." He grazed the back of his fingers along her cheek. She expected to see impatience in his eyes, but instead, she saw concern. "Angela, I…"

Angela let her frustration get the best of her. He's probably still worried about being exposed, she thought bitterly. She folded her arms. "Yes?"

Josh's face changed, as if a light inside had flicked off. "I should get going. We have another big day tomorrow. And you have a story to write."

He kissed her forehead and Angela felt the cold sting of her error. She knew that, at least right now, there was nothing she could do to turn that light back on again.

17

Several hours later, Angela sat across from Nate in the same corner of the upscale bar they had met in when Angela's first article had come out. Moonlight beamed through the window behind her and reflected off the wall. She idly watched as a pair of women sitting at the bar compared one another's skin resurfacing jobs. When the door opened, Angela sat up. Nate jerked around to see. False alarm, thought Angela, as the ladies at the bar shrieked hellos at a friend.

She and Nate had been sitting silently for several minutes, both impatient to hear what Molly had uncovered at work that day. When Nate turned back around, she saw that he was spinning his beer glass but not drinking it with his usual gusto.

"So your probation is over?" she asked him.

"Yeah. I'm trying to keep better track this time around." He lifted his glass in a halfhearted toast and took a sip. "How are things going for you? Any trouble with all the stuff you're eating?"

"No. So far so good. I've had to step up my workouts, and I'm still monitoring my stats like mad, but so far I've been fine. The biggest problem is portions. Some of these kitchens serve heaping plates. Josh has to eat half of mine sometimes. He's got one heck of a metabolism."

"Lucky him." Nate's forehead wrinkled involuntarily.

"Don't worry, Nate," she assured him even though she was worried too. "He knows what he's doing. And Molly really was fine when she left this morning."

"I knew it. I knew it. I should have—"

"Hey, she's going to be okay. I'm sure of it."

Nate nodded and looked out the window. "So I guess you have another story coming out tomorrow?"

Even though he didn't look back at her, Angela nodded, glad for the distraction. "Yeah. They're getting harder to write. Even the parts about food. There's something about it that's different. It's so, oh, I don't know, messy maybe? Something so imperfect about it, yet so good."

"Yeah. That's a good word," he replied, perking up a bit. He stopped staring out the window. "Messy. It's hard to design messy. Ever since we went to that museum I've been trying to create a Sim of my old house. I just want to capture the way the yard looked. We had these big maples. And a swing. Anyway, I have everything programmed perfectly, but it's still flat. It's still wrong. It's *too* damn perfect."

Angela thought about what Herb had said about his pigs and how, without farms like his, the animals might vanish, leaving nothing but a digital record of their genetic code. "I know what you mean—" She looked to the door. "Molly's here."

They both stood up as she approached.

"I'm still feeling good," Molly assured them. Angela breathed a sigh of relief, but she saw that the tension had not yet left Nate's face. "And I got the results. Josh was right." Molly pulled a folded rectangle from her bag. "He asked me to screen my NArc meal. I wasn't sure what he wanted me to look for at first, so I did some digging and it was pretty obvious. As soon as

Arthur left the office this afternoon, I started the analysis. I took samples of each component and screened them."

"Well?" said Angela. Both she and Nate leaned in closer.

"Amphetamines," she declared.

"But you don't need them," protested Nate. "Plenty of people do. But you? No way."

"No, and they aren't in my medical records either. The NArc is feeding them to me without my consent and without cause," said Molly, her voice calm and matter of fact. "My guess is that Arthur coordinated it. He tracks my every move. In fact, I ran into him on my way here. That's why I'm late. He backed off when I told him I had a date. He behaves so oddly sometimes," she commented, shaking her head.

Angela thought back to the museum and Arthur's sudden appearance there. What is he up to? she wondered.

"I think he is desperate for me to make a breakthrough on this project," Molly continued. "So of course he's hoping the speed will give me an edge. It's pretty standard. Poor performers get amped all the time in some industries."

"But you're not a poor performer," interjected Nate. "How can he get away with this?"

Angela could see Molly growing impatient with Nate. He will never win her over if this is how he shows his concern, she thought to herself. But then, he did have a good point. Had Arthur hacked the System?

"There's a logical explanation for all of this. I just don't know what it is yet," Molly insisted. "Like I said, when I looked in my NArc files, there was no record of this prescription. That got me thinking. When I looked at Sinsky's tissue, remember how I found traces of those drugs? Because they weren't in her record, I assumed she was self medicating. But if I'm not, maybe she wasn't."

Molly pulled out her flexscreen and opened up another set of files. "These are the files Tobin sent with the tissue sample. There are a bunch of records in it that are encrypted. I ignored them the first time, since I couldn't read them. The way they're organized, they look like part of the NArc records, only they aren't accessible by any means I know of."

"So what does that mean? Are you saying the NArc is hiding files for some reason?" asked Angela.

"We won't know until we decrypt them. I'm sure that will explain everything. For me, this is probably just business as usual. For Sinsky, she was most likely part of a study that isn't published yet. Wouldn't it make sense for the data to be encrypted until the research is done? A basic double-blind study. The subject can't see the data and neither can the investigators. But it's there, ready to be analyzed when the course of treatment is over."

Angela considered this explanation. It sounded reasonable. If it was true, she should be able to find a record of the study in the clinical trials database. She made a mental note to check as soon as she got home.

"These files might tell us what really happened to Sinsky and Merriweather," said Nate, turning to Angela.

Molly huffed and rolled her eyes. "You two keep jumping to conclusions. I don't see any reason why these files would tell us any more about their deaths than we already know. It's clear that they died from tainted food. And it makes sense with every statistic we've ever seen about food risks." Angela opened her mouth to protest, but Molly shook her head. "Please, let me finish. I know you've seen the food. You've eaten it and you're fine. But we all know what anecdotal evidence adds up to. Nothing. Studies, statistically significant studies, contradict your experience. If you ask me, you've just gotten lucky." Molly looked at Angela for a minute. "I'm starting to worry that your luck may run out."

Angela dropped her eyes. Molly had quoted studies before, time and again. But this time, Angela didn't feel trumped by them. She had more than anecdotal evidence. Maybe her work wasn't scientific, but it wasn't bunk either.

"We're not jumping to conclusions," replied Angela quietly. "We've just seen some things that make it hard to believe that the studies are complete. I agree that it doesn't add up to anything. But that's why we can't rule anything out."

"Fine. Keep chasing conspiracies then." Molly seemed impatient. She had barely even sat down. "Look, I've got to get going."

"Wait. But what about the amp? What will you do now?" asked Angela.

"Yeah. Molly, this isn't right," said Nate. "You can eat my meals. I'll eat yours. I could use the boost." Angela cringed on the inside at Nate's swagger. If he would just be himself, he might get somewhere, she thought.

"Thanks Nate, but we don't need to do that. I have to admit that Josh is pretty good. He said I'd have the problem solved by the end of the day. He might have been right. When Arthur first saw me—even though I felt okay, I still didn't look so good—he flipped. He didn't even ask me how I felt. He locked himself in his office for an hour. I have a feeling that my NArc meals will be clean from now on. Or at least he'll have fixed the dosage. Plus now that I know that I need to eat, I should be able to manage it if that's what he decides on."

"I don't like it," said Nate, pushing away the glass of beer in front of him.

"If it makes you feel better, I just ate and I feel normal." Molly smiled at him and patted his arm. "I feel great, in fact. You don't appreciate what it feels like to be well until you aren't." Molly released his arm then dropped a memory stick on the table in front of him. "Here are the files Tobin sent if you want to try

228

to decrypt them. I'd just transfer them to you but I can't remember how to get into your secure network. Anyway, I'll see you guys later."

"But where are you going? We haven't seen you in so long," Angela reached out to stop Molly and lowered her voice. "Are you meeting Parrish?" Molly blushed and turned to go.

As she walked away, Nate reclaimed his drink and drained it before she reached the door.

When Nate raised his hand to the bartender a third time, Angela reached out and pulled it back down. He frowned at her and jerked his hand away. At least she had his attention.

"Nate, you've got to find out what's in those files. For Molly's sake."

He glared back. "You have a lot of nerve, telling me what to do," he fumed. "You got us into this. You got Molly into this. And for what? A hunch about some woman we don't even know?"

"You know I never expected you or Molly to get hurt. I was just looking for a story—"

"That's right. A story. This was never about Sinsky or injustice. This is about you and your career." Nate seethed, hurtling all of the emotion he had bottled up and refused to show Molly full force at Angela. "How can Angela make a big splash? How can she get herself back on top?" he mocked.

Angela's eyes welled up. "I never expected something like this—" she began, but Nate interrupted again.

"I didn't like it when you started and I don't like it now. I told you someone was going to get hurt and here we are, safe and sound, and Molly has been drugged and followed. And now she's out there with some guy—someone I do not like or trust, no matter what you say—"

Wiping her tears, Angela cut in. "I'm not a big fan of Parrish either, and I've told Molly to be careful."

"He is filling her mind with… He's turning her against us. I can see it in her eyes. I can hear it. It's always, 'Parrish said' and 'Parrish explained everything.' She's not herself. Those drugs have her confused. And there's nothing I can do about it. Nothing I say registers with her anymore."

Angela pulled in an uneven breath and, despite the frown on Nate's face, she begged him for help. "I know, Nate. But there is something you can do. We have to know what's in those files."

He shook his head. "That's what gets me, Angela. All you can think about is yourself. All you can think about is how you can get me to keep doing your research for you. Well, you can forget it." Nate raised his hand and ordered another drink with defiance.

Angela reeled. "I thought we were in this together," she whispered. But Nate had tuned her out. She barely noticed when the bartender placed a fresh drink in front of him. Talking to him now seemed hopeless, so she stood up and headed for the door. Before leaving, she glanced back and saw Nate frowning into his beer, the memory stick still resting on the table in front of him.

Nate stared at his beer then took a big gulp. It didn't make him feel better. He considered going out to find Molly. He imagined himself walking up to her. Confessing his feelings. Reaching out his hand. He imagined her smiling back and then walking away with him, leaving Parrish behind without even a wave goodbye.

Nate downed the rest of his drink and stood up, shoving his inane fantasy into the back of his mind. He shot across town, cursing Angela and muttering to himself as the train stations flew by. Once home, he ducked into a loud bar in the basement of his building and had another drink. The noise annoyed him. He looked around with condescension in his eyes. How can these people stand around having fun as if there were nothing going on?

A young girl approached him and asked him if he wanted another drink. He looked at her the way he looked at all girls. Compared to Molly, her hair was too frizzy, her features too soft, her shoulders too narrow. "No thanks," he said. The music pulsed in his ears and he couldn't hear what she said next, so he ignored her. When she finally walked away, he felt suddenly alone. What am I doing standing around as if there's nothing going on?

He dashed out the door and up the stairs. He had work to do.

Nate poured a gel pack down his throat and gulped two ethanol antidotes. This will probably land me in Food School again, he thought. But then, as he learned in his last session, the metabolism booster in the gel pack sometimes masked the antidote, so maybe he would skate through. Either way, the combination would help him focus, and with any luck, he'd be stone sober in 30 minutes. He plugged in his headphones, turned up the music, and started to think.

The other day, when Molly had dismissed the Sinsky record as uninteresting, Nate had known that there must be more data. Even if Sinsky had been self-medicating, it would show up somewhere in the NArc record. You can game the System, he thought, but you can't hide from it. Not unless you hack it. And from the notes Sinsky had written to Angela, he was sure that she had not.

Following up on this hunch, over the past week Nate had downloaded large chunks of NArc data, brought it home, and stored it in a virtual trunk in his conference room by the roller coasters. Rather than downloading individual files and making specific queries, he had taken broad swaths of raw data home each night and locked them away.

At his desk, he rolled Molly's memory stick between his fingers. First things first, he thought. He needed to break the encryption code. He felt certain that the key that opened Sinsky's file would also open up the rest of the data he had squirreled away.

Nate logged into his work account and began to dig. He first checked the internal message boards the engineers used to collaborate with NArc engineers. There were a few mentions of encryption, but no key codes. He then scanned the source code. The only way to design a personalized meal is to read a person's NArc files, he thought. The only way to read the files is to open them. So he started with the test harnesses for the MealDesigner software. The MealDesigner taps into the NArc records and then designs different Nutrition combinations. The test harness taps in the same way, but with simpler code.

He typed in a search command and came up with a short list of files containing code to access the records. He opened each one in turn, scanning the lines around the access commands. After digging a few seconds, his search revealed a line embedded in a comment in the code:

```
*    NASCrypt:            *
```

"Bingo," he said out loud. He opened the file and, underneath that line, he found a detailed description of the decryption procedure.

A quick time check: it was already midnight. Fuck! Fucking Parrish. Making me waste so much time. I'll be lucky to have anything figured out before Arthur locks Molly in the lab again. He launched the decryption routine on Molly's files in one window, and in another, began navigating through cyberspace to his trunk and to the rest of the data.

≠

With each step away from the bar, Angela felt increasingly agitated. Her leg muscles twitched. And now her neck was cramped from holding in her stress. She needed to let off some steam.

On the way to the gym, she stopped on her floor. She might be crippled without Nate's help, but she had to do what she could. And one thing she did know how to do was check the clinical trials database. Once home, she logged in, brought up the search screen and typed in the typical searches. She looked for Sinsky. Nothing. Of course not. Participants would be anonymous. She looked for trials that mentioned the compounds Molly had found in Sinsky's system. Nothing. She broadened the date range. Still nothing. She couldn't think of another way to query the system. But she had to be missing something. Otherwise, she would have to chuck the only good explanation she had for the hidden records.

She rubbed her neck. It didn't ease the tension. I need to go for a run, she thought, as she grabbed her bag and headed for the gym.

Angela stepped into the CardioSphere and waited for the system scan to complete. When it recommended a vigorous cardio session, she felt reassured. She might not understand much of what was going on but at least she was starting to understand her own body. She opted for a trail run and programmed a 5 mile course. She set the first mile to slice through a meadow. For the next leg she selected a narrow path winding up a wooded hill. She added an exposed hilltop, a gradual descent, and a final mile back through the meadow to finish. She set the time to be 10 am and the weather clear, hoping to recapture a little bit of that feeling she had felt at Herb's place the other day, twirling in the sun.

She hit enter. The trail-surface belt clicked into place inside the sphere. She stepped onto the base as the belt spun up. The lights intensified and she was soon surrounded by elbow high grasses and wildflowers lining a mowed trail. Angela started to run, allowing the fabricated sounds of crickets and the faint floral smell to soothe her. A few minutes in, her heart rate stabilized and her breath settled into a rhythm with her feet.

As she pounded the uneven surface, coated with artificial rocks, roots, and ruts, Angela's mind began to wander. How had things gotten so out of hand? The idea behind the NArc had been so good, and so necessary. Even Herb Walker agreed that there really wasn't another way to feed so many people with such limited natural resources. What had gone wrong?

But then, she wasn't certain if anything had gone wrong. She had been through it all earlier that day while she was writing. But then, she had been crafting a human interest story. Now she needed to retrace *all* of the facts.

Sinsky hadn't been feeling well, and the NArc hadn't cured her. Then she died after eating in a speakeasy. But no one else died after eating that same food. And that food had tested clean. Sinsky had a terminal disease. She also had experimental, unprescribed drugs in her system. Now Molly had unprescribed drugs in her system. The NArc appeared to have no record of those either. But the NArc contains encrypted records that are hidden from view. And those records are not part of a registered drug trial.

What is in those records? And why?

She hoped that Nate would come to his senses and look into it. Soon.

As the treadmill tilted, the artificial light became mottled by the forest. The surface evened out and softened to emulate pine needles over dirt. Angela's heart rate increased.

The drugs Sinsky took were supposed to treat her disease, but they weren't working, she thought. They weren't working. What did that mean? If Sinsky was part of a study, was she a failed experiment?

Maybe. She tried to remember other failed experiments. But she had never run across one. Failures weren't news. She wasn't sure what happened when an experiment didn't work. What happened to patients with illnesses that had no cure? Did the disease simply take its course? As she thought through these questions, Angela felt that something else was missing. Some key piece of information she had learned along the way. One by one she ruled out conversations. Potente had said nothing about experiments, she thought. Nor had Herb. Nor Paolo or any of the other speakeasy hosts. Who was it?

Then it came to her. It was at Herb's. On the back porch. Josh had said: "The NArc is ..." How could she have forgotten all about that? With the trip to see Bunny, and all the things June had said that day, she had definitely been distracted. But why hadn't she come back to it? Why hadn't it come up when she and Josh got home? She frowned at herself. She knew why. Because it wasn't in her notes. She hadn't written it down. And she hadn't written it down because she had been too busy flirting.

Damn it, Angela! she chided herself. You're a professional. Your entire career rides on your ability to be an objective observer. Starting tomorrow, you're pulling back from Josh. If you want to break this story, you have to.

The trees gave way to a bald hill. The lights intensified and the ground leveled. Angela could still hear his voice: "The NArc is …" What? What is it? What had he meant? The evidence has shown for years that the NArc has improved health. Study after study has shown that people are living longer, that disease rates are down, that mortality rates from all kinds of illnesses have plummeted.

But then another voice came back to her. The voice of June, at the museum. "They left out a lot of things," she'd said.

Angela's legs lost their strength. Her feet stumbled beneath her. She grabbed hold of the rails and fumbled for the stop button, panting and shivering despite the blast of the lights overhead. She regained her balance and stared out at the ersatz hilltops in the distance.

They left out Sinsky. They left out her disease. But they hadn't left it out by accident. They hid it. And how many others? She needed to talk to Josh.

18

Caged Rabbits

RealFood, by Sage Weaver

Outside the Northeast City, June 4, 2063 — It has been called the ultimate sandwich. Years ago, many vegetarians claimed it as their downfall. It was the one food that they could not resist. The bacon-lettuce-and-tomato sandwich.

It is, as my host assured me, best when the bacon is still warm and the lettuce is still crispy. On lightly toasted crusty white bread with garden fresh earthbound tomatoes, mayonnaise, that magical emulsion concocted by French chefs to suspend eggs and oil in a smooth, tangy-white spread, romaine lettuce, again, grown in the soil, and, finally, slices of salty, smoky, chewy, crispy bacon.

With all that my host understood about this bacon—he had, after all, grown the pigs, slaughtered them, smoked the flesh and fried the slices—he could not understand my reticence. Tempted as I was by the aroma and the colorful and textured layers, I did not want to eat it.

By now, I have eaten plenty of risky foods. Fried, raw, oozing with juice and sticky sweet, almost nothing gives me pause. Except this. And it was all because of the fat.

My host had claimed that his pigs, because they forage for acorns, have "healthy fat." He urged me to eat. "It's good for you. Look at us! We eat like this every day!" he said. Though his skin was weather-worn, his body exuded a vitality that belied his years.

But I know myself. I know my body. It needs, as one Nutritionist told me, "all the help it can get." It needs fats engineered to keep its tendencies—toward high cholesterol, insulin resistance, and overweight—in check. When I looked at that sandwich, that ultimate sandwich, all I could see were clogged arteries and a fatty liver.

My host grew impatient. So I ate. And it was fantastic.

As I chewed, my host explained. But he didn't tell me about the composition of the fats in his pig. (I had a scientist friend do that later, and the fats she analyzed from bits I reluctantly saved formed a surprisingly healthy composition with some not so healthy elements mixed in.) Rather, he told me his philosophy. He said that he looked at his meals as part of his enjoyment of life. "Without this sandwich, what would I have to look forward to? Everyday, I look forward to lunch. BLTs. Fried chicken. Turkey sandwiches. Chili. We enjoy every bite because, maybe tomorrow, we won't be so lucky. Maybe tomorrow, we won't be here to enjoy it."

While I take for granted that I will live well into my second century, as does everyone who depends on the NArc, this farmer has no hope for such longevity. "We have to enjoy what we have while we have it," he said.

With this, I chewed in silence, savoring every bite of this precious and pleasurable food.

It wasn't until later, at another farm, that I realized what my host had been trying to tell me. The second farmer compared me to a caged rabbit. In my protected world, she said, life stretched out endlessly ahead. I encounter no threats to my health, so I never worry about them. In fact, I am so confident that I will live a long life that I have put off living. At 40, I have no children, no partner, no property, and, if not for this column, no drama. I live a life only slightly more interesting than that of her rabbits.

When I watched those rabbits hopping two hops to the right, sniffing, then a hop to the left, I licked my lips. The slightest hint of smoke, salt, and fat lingered. I savored it, thinking, maybe tomorrow, I might not be so lucky.

The sun had not yet risen when Parrish awoke to a twittering in his ear. He sat up and glanced at Molly, checking to make sure he hadn't woken her. Assured she was still sound asleep, he donned his eyepiece, stepped out of the room, and answered with an urgent "Yes."

"I'm so glad you're up. You've seen it, then. I'm so glad you're on top of this." Selica Freidman's voice chirped a quick staccato. She sounded as if she'd been up for hours and, given her immaculate hair and makeup, she looked that way too.

"The new Weaver piece?" Parrish hadn't seen it, but he knew what would be in it. He'd been with her the whole time. Worse, he knew there was more to the story. Molly had told him everything.

"Yes. Of course. I'm worried that our efforts to contain this aren't strong enough. We're just not doing everything we can to bring this to a close. I need you to take more aggressive action."

Parrish hesitated.

"I know you are as committed as I am," Selica continued. "I don't have to remind you that there are only three of us who know what's at stake here. We agreed to the current course of action. And we have a pact to keep the NArc in good standing in the public's eye. This is more important than ever now. We need to start moving the NArc into under-served areas. This is a critical turning point, as you well know. We need to be moving toward wider acceptance of the NArc, not increased doubt. Smithers and I are still completely on board with our original plan. And we agree. It's time for more extreme measures."

"I'm also committed," Parrish replied steadily. Inside his chest he could feel his heart pounding. Selica knew exactly how to make a person feel like an outsider. Or an insider. Whichever suited her needs best. Right now, he needed to convince her to let him back in. He had one shot at playing this right. "But there is new information. The problem with Sage Weaver has changed. I'm working on a plan to resolve it without extreme measures. I'm confident, but I need one more day."

"You know, I'm concerned that your time with these Cheaters has made you lose sight of our goals. I can't stress enough how important it is that we act swiftly and decisively here. Sage Weaver needs to be stopped. Today."

Parrish didn't want to give Selica the details. She wouldn't miss this opportunity to cut him down and accuse him of mismanaging his charge. But he had no choice. Her plans simply wouldn't work anymore. He pulled the bedroom door shut behind him before speaking. "Tanaka discovered the records. She's starting to ask questions. And she's not expendable."

Selica blinked. "No, she isn't. I won't ask how this happened right now. There's just no time. But you need to contain her. You need to give her answers that will keep her on our side."

Parrish nodded. "I could use your expertise there," he replied in his most ingratiating voice. Selica was the master of spin. And right now, he needed to stay on her good side. He'd let her seduce him into joining this inner circle with her promises of instant power. A shot at fame. An opportunity to change the world. But now he knew that he was her fall guy. The chump. He needed to play this right. And if things went south, he needed to hand her a better chump.

"It's all in how you frame your answers. She's a scientist. She understands experiments. Try putting it this way." Selica's voice changed slightly as she delivered the perfectly formed sound-bite. "When you think about it, personalized Nutrition is an experiment every day, at every meal. It's a constant nudging, like tiny taps that keep us in balance. The goal, of course, is prolonging healthy life. We're striving for perfect health for everyone. If we stay the course, we might eliminate disease and suffering by the end of the century."

Parrish nodded. "Nicely framed. I'd also like to refocus her attention away from the questions."

"Yes. I agree. You need to remind her how important she is to our work here. Champion her project. Remind her that it's vitally important and central to the future of the NArc. As a last resort, remind her that she's building on the hard work of her parents. That will help her refocus."

Parrish nodded again. "Very good."

"I think you've got what you need to wrap this up today." Selica smiled, her eyes sparkling. "I'm so glad we talked. I'm sure we won't need to speak of it again."

Parrish was about to assure her of his commitment, but before he could react, she was gone. Just as well. He heard the bedroom door latch click behind him.

"Morning," he said, disengaging his head gear as he turned. "You're up early." He smiled and kissed Molly sweetly on the side of her mouth. "Do I get a to spend a few minutes with you before you run off to the lab?"

Before Arthur finished reading Sage Weaver's latest installment, his fingers were tapping his keypad to call up his contact. In his windowless home office, the glow of the artificial light accentuated his pallor. Wraithlike shadows seemed to carve into his skin. Before the face on his screen said hello, Arthur bellowed, "Caged rabbits?! Where on earth did you take her?"

The gray eyes remained steady. "What Ms. Weaver wrote is not the half of it."

"You had better explain, and fast," said Arthur. But without leaving room for an explanation, he thundered on. "This story has already been read by more people than the other two together. She's egging them on. This isn't about the food anymore. I'm beginning to think it never was."

When Arthur paused, his contact spoke. "They know."

"What are you talking about?" Arthur demanded, still impatient for an explanation of Weaver's latest story.

"They don't have proof yet, but before long they will."

"Impossible," dismissed Arthur.

"You have underestimated your prized scientist," came the cool reply.

Still in denial, Arthur asserted, "She's barely been out of my sight or yours. Plus, she's been focused on her work. She hasn't had more than a few minutes to speak to Weaver, let alone help her uncover anything."

"You shouldn't have amped her," remarked the talking head.

Arthur's mouth opened and shut again quickly. He hadn't told anyone what he had done. He had figured that the drug would just boost Molly's natural focus. It would make it easier for him to keep her at work and preoccupied. No one was supposed to find out, especially not her. And certainly not *him*, he thought, looking askance at his contact. It was then, looking at those cold gray eyes, that he recognized his error. As much as he was dealing behind her back, she was dealing behind his. She was telling Parrish everything.

"When Molly discovered the drug, she also found the hidden records," said Parrish. "She turned them over to that computer hacker. With encouragement from me, she has dismissed all of it. But the others won't. It's just a matter of time now."

He paused for effect. When Arthur opened his mouth to speak, Parrish interrupted. "Just contain her," he instructed. "It's time for Plan B."

An abrupt change had come over Parrish's voice. To Arthur, it sounded alien. Stripped of its charm and sophistication, each syllable sent a chill down Arthur's spine. He remained mute, unable to respond.

"My work will be complete by close of business. Make sure yours goes without a hitch." The gray eyes vanished.

Arthur stared at the blank screen. Plan B. How had it come to this? All he had ever wanted was to help people. To make them healthier. To prolong their lives. The system had been a dream come true. An imperfect dream, yes, but every day they made it better. Every day that he worked he aimed at making it possible for yet another person to live longer and happier. He had convinced himself that all of the sacrifice would, eventually, pay off. It would all be worth it when the system reached perfection.

Plan B. Arthur sighed. It had to be done.

$\neq$

"Another nice piece from Weaver, Stew. Off the charts," said Marcus, leaning once again in Stew's office door early Monday morning. "That young lady is defining our time."

Stew nodded. Angela was pulling it off, alright. She still hadn't delivered on the news hook—the Sinsky story—but Stew was beginning to think it wouldn't matter. He had spent the morning drafting a proposal to keep the Real Food column indefinitely. It wasn't ready for Marcus to see yet, but Stew felt confident that his billing of the column as a resurrection of the old restaurant review format would be an easy sell. He just needed one more column to round it out. When she came in later that afternoon, they would talk about it. He'd see what she thought and see if she might consider letting go of Sinsky.

"The SynEngra folks called again. This time they complained about the hyping of Outsiders. Seems like they don't want anyone written about but themselves," Marcus chuckled. "In fact, they've got a new product they're announcing. Seems they've found a way to make Neermeat cheaper. Sounds like inside baseball to me, but they assured me that there was a story there. International market share. Increased NArc productivity. Cost savings for consumers. Who should we put on it?"

"How about Frank?"

Marcus raised an eyebrow, then shrugged. "I'll float it past him. As for Angela, if you're certain we're not going to lose SynEngra, I'm inclined to keep going with this column of hers. Maybe give Sage Weaver a little more runway to work with. No promises, but let me know how the next one shapes up."

Stew nodded again, stifling his smile. He couldn't wait to tell Angela. A new column. A gritty column of her own. She'll be tickled, he thought.

19

"Why do you need to go now?" June asked Josh. Still wrapped in her bathrobe, she stood in the doorway of the garage underneath her house. "If you wait a few hours, I'll head up with you. Angela might need an intermediary."

Josh, who hadn't looked up from his work tuning his vehicle for the trip, replied. "It can't wait June. Angela will be fine on her own. Talking to people is what she does best."

June felt anxious. The news about Molly and the hidden records had shaken her. She was having trouble accepting the fact that everything Josh had suspected was starting to look true, and there wasn't a thing she could do about it. "Ken's put together a map for you. He got the new coordinates last night."

Josh looked up. "Thank him for me, will you? And thank you for thinking about it. It slipped my mind that May's over already."

June leaned against the doorframe. "It's nothing. You know how Ken loves to track them."

The Vermont border markets, Josh's destination for the day, moved each month because of a compromise built into a food treaty to appease the nations on both sides of the border. The US wanted Vermont's border market to close. But Vermont had refused out of fear that US citizens would cross the border and raid people's farms instead. The nations settled on a compromise: temporary markets. Each month the yurts come down and reappear elsewhere. If people can't find the markets, the negotiators had reasoned, they'll be less likely to steal across the border and shop at them. Of course people still did—and Vermont's farmers still benefitted from their patronage—but the arrangement served its purpose. It kept the Cheaters in check.

"I wish you could wait. I was hoping to talk with you. About Parrish." June waited for a response but Josh didn't reply. In fact, he seemed to be purposefully avoiding eye contact. "There's something strange about him."

"Parrish has always been strange."

"I guess." June fiddled with the loose ties of her robe then scratched her forehead. "You know how he likes to tell his story. About his mother the gourmet and his oppressive father who forced him to be an engineer. I'm starting to think that's not his real story. The other day I asked him about growing up in New York. After that trip to that propaganda museum, I couldn't stop trying to collect real stories. Like it was somehow therapeutic to hear something true—" June waved her hand across her face, shooing that train of thought away. She didn't want to ruin another day stewing about it. "Anyway, he snapped at me. Accused me of interrogating him about his past. It was completely out of line. But then I've noticed that recently he's been acting colder. Meaner." She waited for Josh to commiserate, or at least to acknowledge that he heard her, but he didn't respond. "Ever since he went almost completely off-NArc." She waited again for a reaction.

"He's probably just tense." Josh didn't look up from his work. "Juggling our dual lives takes a toll. Ughh. Tire's got a slow leak." Josh, who was laying on the ground, got up and started fishing around in an old crate. "My guess is he just needs some time off."

"Well I did some research. There's no record of a Parrish Knight in New York. He didn't go to school anywhere in Manhattan. He wasn't born there, either. He did go college, just like he says he did. And he finished late, just like he says he did. At least, according to the records. But before that, as far as I can tell, the Parrish we know didn't exist."

"Maybe he was home schooled," Josh said as he continued to rummage through the crate. June watched him scrutinize each item before tossing it back in.

"Maybe. At any rate, he left a message late last night. He seemed anxious to tell me that he would be away for the next few days. But then he didn't leave any specifics. It was strange. Rehearsed, almost."

"Uh-huh." Josh was on the ground again, only now he seemed overly interested in a spot of dirt crusted on the rear fender.

June knew when she was being handled. She knew Josh had never trusted Parrish and she suspected he had noticed the same changes she had. But he didn't want to discuss it. Not now. Or not with her. Either way, she had said what she needed to say. She had warned him. She only hoped that the savvy she'd seen the other day in Angela wasn't just a one-time thing. "Just be careful today, okay?"

Josh finally looked up from the bike, a streak of dirt on his cheek, and smiled. "You know I always am."

Angela eyed the motorcycle.

"At least it's not a balloon," Josh joked.

She didn't laugh. She felt too out of sorts. She had contacted Josh the night before, as soon as she'd stepped out of the CardioSphere. But he had refused to talk. Instead, he'd instructed her to meet him here, in an industrial alley behind June's place, before dawn. She'd hardly slept. She'd skipped her Monday morning ritual of reading her column and compulsively checking the hit counts. She'd waited 20 minutes in the predawn darkness for a westbound train then walked, under an admittedly breathtaking morning sky, only to find this waiting for her.

"Trust me, it's faster and it's easier to get around the checkpoints this way. Plus it uses a lot less biofuel than the truck. You'll be fine," he assured her, handing over a helmet and a kevlar jacket. "This trip is cake." As she took them, she noticed a hint of strain in his eyes.

She slipped on the jacket, but it gave her small reassurance. Mostly she felt rushed. She needed to talk. "So Molly was amped. Just like you thought. Plus she found encrypted NArc records. Do you know what's in them, too?"

Josh didn't respond. But she could see from the look in his eyes, a look he was trying to conceal from her, that he was hiding something.

"I'm beginning think you've known all along. You knew when you first saw me. You knew when I brought up Sinsky on the train. Why didn't you tell me?" she asked. She was hurt. And angry. "Why won't you tell me now?" she said, stomping her foot.

"I *don't* know," protested Josh. "I have suspicions. But I don't have proof. And without proof, well, it's just outrageous, isn't it?"

Angela wiped her eyes, thinking that she'd been crying an awful lot lately. "Yes," she admitted. But she was still mad.

"I'm sorry. I should have told you." He squeezed her hand. "Would you have believed me if I had?"

Angela sniffed and wiped away the remains of her tears. "I'm not sure I'll believe it even if Nate decrypts those files. And Stew won't buy it." To convince him, she would need more than Sinsky's decrypted record and a printout from Molly. She needed a pattern. She needed the backstory. "I need to know not just how, but why, and for how long," she said. "I need to know who is responsible."

Josh nodded again. "I know. Let's go," he said. "There is someone you need to meet."

Angela climbed awkwardly onto the back of the bike, wrapping her arms tightly around Josh's waist. Even through the layers of kevlar and leather, she could feel a warmth emanating from him. Just being near him made her feel safe. So much for pulling back, she thought. She resigned herself to try harder tomorrow. Then, in spite of herself, she pulled her body just a little closer to his.

He gave her hand a quick press in response. "Try to move with me and not against me, okay?" he called through his helmet.

Josh wound the bike through the outskirts of the city. When they approached the urban border, he shunted the bike down an alleyway and into a dark tunnel with a muddy base, the empty shell of a river long ago redirected into a narrow concrete channel. At the far end of the tunnel, they emerged into a dead zone of empty streets, former neighborhoods now filling in with warehouses and solar collectors. With each mile, the buildings become more sparse and gave way to scraggly woods.

As the last traces of the cityscape dropped away behind them, the landscape grew wilder. Josh maneuvered the bike down old roadways pitted with potholes and wrinkled with frost heaves, dodging the hazards with the ease of one who had traveled these roads often. Within an hour, he ducked the bike down a dirt road. He had warned her it would be bumpy. She gripped what she could of his stiff leather coat and clenched her arms and legs, but still the bike tossed her out of her seat. She recovered each time, regaining her hold just to be flung out again.

They rode this way for an hour before Josh turned again, this time down a graveled drive that led to a small clearing. Near the back, where the ground sloped down, stood a single story building with double doors. Josh pulled around to the back. When he got off the bike, Angela realized that the single room at the top of the hill topped a three-story house built into the hillside. Josh walked over to the structure and opened a trap door built into the side wall. He reached inside and tugged on a thick, dangling rope. Above them, she heard the gonging of a bell. Josh climbed back on the bike and drove it slowly down a narrow lane, stopped at a gate, and waited.

"The Outsiders who live here have set up a surveillance system on the nearest Vermont highway. When they hear the bell ring, one of them checks the screens. When the roads are clear, they'll give us the green light to go." He pointed to an old-fashioned traffic light mounted atop a gatepost. The light burned red.

"So when the market is nearby, do they get a lot of traffic?" Angela asked.

"Not this time of year, but in a few weeks it picks up. The markets spread out to distribute the load. That helps… Hold on," he said.

The light had turned green. Josh launched the bike down the lane. It dipped then flattened and merged onto a smooth, well-tended roadway. Angela gasped. It was as if they had descended into a fairy-tale land. To her left ran a clear brook. Rolling hills of greenery and wildflowers rose from its banks. They climbed a steep hill and wound down the other side. To the right, coffee-colored cows gazed at them through impossibly long eyelashes, their swishing tails their only movement. An orchard of orderly trees sloped up to an old yellow farmhouse perched on the nearest ridge. Two huge maple trees shaded its front door. Around the next bend, the placid scene turned festive.

Josh pulled into the makeshift market and parked the bike alongside the other scooters and bicycles lined up in front. The market consisted of a series of yurts erected on the meadow a few days earlier. Dull fabrics draped the side-walls of each circular building, but the people streaming in and out of the entrances, their arms filled with bundles of goods, brought the makeshift market to life.

When Josh cut the engine and Angela pulled off her helmet, she heard a strange droning sound. She turned toward it and spotted a man in a plaid skirt and hat standing on the river's edge. "Bagpipes," said Josh in her ear. As the piper fell into a new reel, Josh led Angela inside. Behind the curtained door she found table after table of goods. The tables spiraled to form concentric circles. On one sat a display of home-baked breads, pastries, and cookies. On the next, jars of honey and pots of creams made of beeswax. After that, crates of freshly cut herbs, dried lavender stalks, and the first vegetables of the season: beets, greens, radishes, and carrots. Angela marveled at the assortment of colors and aromas. As they passed through the center, she smelled what she recognized as freshly brewed coffee. As they passed the vendor, Josh explained the trafficking routes. "The imported goods are more expensive than the local ones, but they should be given what it takes to get them here," he told her.

Once Angela got accustomed to the sights and sensitized to the smells, she started to notice the people. The Cheaters stood out. They looked so out of place in their wrinkle free and stain resistant clothing. They carried themselves with an aloofness that made Angela cringe. Most arrived in small groups that split up at the door. She saw one group congregate and depart without making eye contact with one another. They must come in on a kind of shuttle, she thought. They must be wary of one another. She suspected that, in the same situation, she would behave no differently. She would keep her distance from the others out of fear of being exposed.

The Vermonters, in contrast, came in all shapes and sizes. The purveyors, for the most part, seemed sturdy, their cheeks pink and their arms muscular. The shoppers varied. More than once Angela had to slide by a woman or man who took up the space of two or sometimes even three Cheaters. For each of these she counted, she saw an equal number of people who were rail thin. Yet these folks with their extreme physiques were the exception. Most people were just a little bulgy here and there, a bit thick in the center, a tad flabby in the arm.

People clustered in groups of three and four and chatted, their heads drawn together. Everyone seemed to know everyone else. Angela overheard snippets of chatter as she walked: one woman's husband had brought home yet another antique tractor that he wanted to convert to biofuel; a man shared grape vine pruning tips with a young couple; two women gossiped about their daughters' boyfriends.

Angela paused to examine some early strawberries. It surprised her how far the fruits were from perfect. From a distance, they'd looked so lovely, a mound of enticingly ripe and evenly sized teardrops. But up close, the fruits ranged from tiny to bloated. Some were still white at the tops while others were already showing signs of rot. Two children jostled past her to get to the counter. The older one loaded a bag with berries as the younger one pointed out the good ones. Angela wanted to ask them how they chose and what happened to the ones left over at the end of the day, but Josh tugged her hand, pulling her onward.

Eventually he stopped in front of a stand decorated with shelves filled with fragrant soaps. Angela sniffed one, trying to make out the spicy scent the label called "Patchouli." The look of puzzlement on her face increased when she read that the bar was made with goat's milk.

"Angela," said Josh, interrupting her note-taking. "I'd like you to meet Patricia Dalyrimple."

At first she gave the woman an indifferent wave, but then recognition flashed across Angela's face. Patricia Dalyrimple. The researcher Nate had told her about. The scientist who wrote the last paper about food. She peered around the shelf to face an elderly woman wearing a homespun linen tunic over cropped pants, her gray hair in a bob of short dreadlocks. She looked shrunken, but her eyes were clear and she gripped Angela's hand firmly in greeting.

"Let's get a cup of tea, or coffee if you want to splurge," said the woman in a throaty voice. She grabbed a shawl and, as she nimbly slipped between her table and the next, flipped up a sign reading "Back Soon. Self Serve." "Donna," she called to her neighbor, "would you keep an eye out for a few minutes?"

Over coffee, Patricia Dalyrimple told Angela the long and painful story of the end of her research career. The doctor began in a calm tone, one that had been soothed over the years by chamomile tea and meditation. "We studied plants, specifically food crops, and evaluated them to see what nutrients they had and what effects they had on health. It was fascinating work," she beamed. "Did you know that different beans—navy, white, kidney, northern—each one has different properties. They're practically the same food, but one is a real anti-cancer agent. Another anti-inflammatory. Everything we need to keep ourselves healthy just springs from the soil," she said, flicking her fingers like sprouting seeds. "It makes sense, of course, that we would evolve to benefit from a variety of foods. Evolution works. Or, at least, it used to," she added with disdain.

Angela guided the conversation back to the research. She had no idea how long the woman would keep talking and she wanted to get as much information as possible. I need to get a concrete example of the conspiracy to suppress food research, she thought, assuming such a story even exists. At first, Dalyrimple seemed cagey. She started her story several times then got sidetracked or jumped to the end without filling in the middle. Angela looked up from her notes in frustration. But when she saw Dalyrimple's face, she realized that the doctor wasn't dissembling; she was still angry.

"Let's walk through it once more," Angela counseled. "If I understand, you got funding for a pilot study of foods. That funding was from…"

"From Safe and Sustainable, back before those corporate bozos took control in the early 40s—"

"I see," Angela interrupted, hoping to stem the vitriol and get the story straight. "You then designed a system for typing foods, as a way to match meals with personalized NArc diagnostics? A kind of meal maker?"

"Yes, yes. It was a pilot. An example, if you will. Proof that it could be done with real food. No one else was doing this kind of work. No one."

"Right. I see. So, then, I'm not clear. You weren't able to get that published?" Angela asked.

"They rejected it. All the big journals sent it back. Nice. Cute, one even said. They all wanted more data. At first, I thought they had a point. But the reviewers didn't give us a target. So I looked at other papers that had been accepted. It turned out that the reviewers were hypocrites. Every last one of them."

"Why?"

"They were publishing all kinds of small studies from the Neerfood designers. The first Neermeat paper, in '42, had one sample. One! It had five mice eating it, and one of them died. The way the article read, it sounded like a resounding success. Meanwhile, 20 percent of their test subjects had died! It was scandalous!" she cried, thumping the table. "So many of those papers hardly passed the most basic scientific standards. Maybe, maybe there was enough evidence to justify funding a follow-on with a large cohort, like I was trying to do. But to derail all of our work and shift all of the attention and all of the funds to an unproven field? It was an obvious set-up."

Angela waited for the doctor to calm down and jotted a note to ask Molly about that paper. Her hand ached from writing, but she shoved away her inner lamentations at Dalyrimple's refusal to be recorded; she needed her wits focused on the here and now. "I'm sorry to put you through this," she said, regarding the woman with a sympathetic smile. "But then, I'm not clear here either. Your paper had how many samples?"

"We designed two meals and tested them against two engineered NArc meals using their standards. Five mice in each cohort. Our meals performed as well or better by their own measures. And don't forget, this was 2043. Our food was *food*. Theirs was engineered mush, not even FDA approved yet!" The scientist drew herself up in her chair. Despite her small frame and her lolling dreads, Angela felt that she had been and still was a formidable force.

"Did you apply for funds to expand your data or was it to build out the whole meal matching system?"

"Both, of course! Who knew what you could get money for those days. Some people got huge grants for the most harebrained ideas. I, on the other hand, got nothing. All of my applications were rejected. Even the companies that had supported me at first, companies that had data that I could have used to get the paper published, shut me out." She shook her head.

"I don't understand. Do you know why?"

"Of course I know why. Those companies were all making deals with the NArc. When I figured it out, I let go of any lingering thoughts that my own work was at fault. You see, they were selling products to the NArc. But the NArc wasn't buying food. They were buying *Nutrition*." Dalyrimple uttered the word with such derision that Angela looked up from her notes. "Those companies wanted to kill any data that might undermine their chance at latching onto the biggest bandwagon in town. And they did. When I went back a year later, my old colleagues were gone. The new people had no records of the studies we had done together. By the time Neermeat hit the market, the food data had been wiped clean."

Angela scratched frantically in the tiny notebook she normally used for recording sights, smells, and textures.

Dalyrimple explained that she had fought back. She wrote several review articles and worked, using her own funds, to discredit the papers that had corrupted the system. After two years, however, she still hadn't convinced anyone to back her work. As the engineered products started to hit the marketplace, she ran out of money. Her university denied her tenure. She left in disgrace.

For a few years she taught at a small college and followed the research closely. "The quality did not improve. It wasn't science," she said. "It was engineering pretending to be science. They made things work on the surface, put some weak statistics together to get them approved for sale, then scrambled to fix the bugs. That might have been fine for games and gadgets," she said, "but it's not okay when we're talking about the food we eat. I'm not against engineering mind you, but with this kind of work, engineers and scientists must work together."

Angela held a hand up. She needed to catch up, to capture every word. When she finished scribbling, she sat back and looked across the table. Dalyrimple appeared less fatigued than Angela felt herself. "Patricia, I need to ask you a difficult question. Could you tell me, looking back now, now that we know that the NArc is working, at least, according to their statistics, why does all of this matter?"

Angela watched the scientist shift in her chair. The woman frowned and crumpled a napkin in her fist. But Angela resisted her urge to soften the question and avoid the confrontation.

"That is not a difficult question," Dalyrimple finally said. "There are two reasons. First, with our system, small communities could have survived and improved their health. That might not seem like a big deal to you, but it might have saved many cultures around the world. The second is that the NArc still operates on the shaky foundations it built itself on. What they started then is still going on now. Invent it. Get it out. Then figure out what's wrong with it. It's a newfangled scientific method. And it is a recipe for disaster."

Angela felt giddy and repulsed at the same time. She had found it. The pattern. The backstory. And, if Dalyrimple was right, what she had found was appalling. She took a deep breath and continued the interview. She needed to understand her source. Dalyrimple had so far provided a cogent view, but Angela needed to know what had happened to her between then and now. Could her story be trusted, or was Angela just handing her a bullhorn and giving her an opportunity for revenge?

"And, Patricia, what happened to you. How is it that you ended up here, in Vermont?"

"Now that, that *is* a difficult question for me to answer," professed the woman. Dalyrimple was starting to look weary. Nevertheless, she told her tale. When the first NArcCafes opened, Dalyrimple hit rock bottom. She showed up at one dining hall with a basket of fruit and vegetables and harassed customers. She tried to get them to throw away their plates of mush and eat an apple or a carrot. The police took her away. After a night in jail, someone who did not leave a name bailed her out and left her a note. "Go to Vermont" it read. So she did.

"I found my peace here," she said. "I grow my herbs and make my soaps. I knit and trade with my neighbors. And I eat the meals I want to eat. I may not end up living as long as I might have had I stayed. I may not be as healthy. But at least I'm free." She plopped her napkin into her empty cup and rustled in her tote bag. She slid a packet of papers across the table to Angela. "This is the article. Or, I should say, the article that never was. I thought you might want to read it." Dalyrimple stood. "As much as it pains me to rehash it, I'm glad it hasn't been forgotten. You seem like a nice girl. Take care who you trust," she said, then walked away.

Angela stared at the table in front of her, sipping her now cold coffee. Though she wanted to look at Dalyrimple's research, she faced a scattered mess of scrawled notes. She had to tackle them before the woman's voice lost its freshness in her mind. She turned over Dalyrimple's papers to a blank sheet at the back and wrote down a few key points. Then she drew a line down the center of the page. On one side she chronicled history as the SynEngra museum had presented it, as best she could remember. On the other, she transcribed Dalyrimple's history, along with her best quotes.

When she finished that exercise, she flipped the packet over and read Dalyrimple's work. The scientist hadn't exaggerated. Her study showed that real food performed as well as or better than engineered food. If the rest of her data had come out, Angela thought, the public might not have jumped so readily on that NArc bandwagon. But was that the most important thing she'd learned? This story was about more than propaganda, but she still couldn't put it all together.

Angela shook her head, trying to clear it. She brushed her fingers along the side of her headgear, flipping through her messages. Her attention zoomed in on a note from Nate. Subject: success. She was about to open it when she heard a voice behind her.

"Hello Angela," said Parrish.

"Oh, Parrish, I didn't expect to see you here," she stammered. Though he couldn't possibly see the display projected onto her retina, she instinctively stowed her head gear.

He leaned over her, blocking the muted sunshine streaming in through the skylight overhead.

"Got some new leads you're working on?" he probed casually, nodding toward her notebook. He smiled, but she picked up a whisper of contempt in his eyes that, for some reason, emboldened her.

"Yes, in fact, I just had a very long and interesting discussion with Patricia Dalyrimple," she said. "I'm trying to make sense of everything she said, you know, and line it up with what I already know."

"Sounds like you could use a second cup of coffee. May I?" he asked, lifting her cup and offering to refill it. She nodded and felt a wave of guilt. Maybe she had him all wrong.

A few minutes later, Parrish returned with two steaming cups of dark liquid. As she breathed in a long whiff and savored the aroma, Parrish remarked that he'd lost track of time. "I have something I need to attend to. May I leave this extra cup for Josh? I assume he's here with you?" Without waiting for her response, he melted into a crowd that had gathered in front of a lunch cart.

≠

Josh had kept his distance throughout the interview, not wanting to influence Angela or Patricia and not trusting himself to keep quiet. He watched them from afar until an old acquaintance recognized him and stopped to chat about the late frost. He rambled on about how he'd lost a whole bed of strawberries and said more than once that that would learn him for trying to get a jump on things. Josh smiled and nodded distractedly but apparently engagingly enough that the man launched into a walk down memory lane comparing and contrasting the weather patterns of the last ten springs. Not a grower himself, Josh tired of the conversation.

In a lapse of attention, his eyes drifted over the man's head and between the nearby stalls. They focused in on the cafe where Angela sat, by herself now, reading. That's when he spotted Parrish.

Josh watched in horror as Parrish sidled up to Angela and leaned in to talk to her.

Putting his large hand on his acquaintance's shoulder, Josh said, "I'm sorry, but I've got to run. Nice seeing you again." He barely looked at the man's face as he pushed past him and squeezed himself into the flow of foot traffic between the aisles. The back of his brain registered the man's voice, fumbling and dejected, bidding him farewell.

When Josh looked up again, he could see Parrish carrying two cups of coffee toward Angela's table. He'd managed to take three big strides into the crowd, but the traffic in front of him suddenly stopped. He had no choice but to watch helplessly as Parrish placed the mugs down on the table next to Angela and smiled his wooden smile at her. Don't drink it, he willed Angela silently as he looked for some way around the crowd.

He ducked into an opening behind the next stall and weaved his way behind the purveyors, tripping over folding chair legs and knocking goods onto the ground. Without slowing down, he called out his apologies and craned his neck, hoping to catch a glimpse of Angela between the slats of the display stands. In a flash, he saw Parrish disappear into the crowd on the opposite side of the cafe. In another, he saw Angela lift the mug slowly and absently, her mind clearly occupied by the notes in front of her.

At the last stand just before the walkway next to the cafe, Josh grabbed a bundle of flowers from a nearby bin and tossed money on the table. He sprung into the walkway, apologizing as he jostled his way crosswise, nearly overturning an old woman's cart of radishes and greens.

When he saw Angela put the mug back down again quickly, he let out his breath then scanned again, unsuccessfully, for Parrish. Two more strides through the crowd brought him to the cafe entrance—a wide opening in a low wall surrounding the dining tables. As he bounded in, he saw Angela's hand circle the mug a second time.

Angela looked back at her notes, flipping through the papers to pick up where she had left off when Parrish had interrupted her. "Ah, yes," she mumbled to herself. She reached for the mug and brought it to her lips. She inhaled the rich toasty smell and noticed the intensity of the steamy heat. Still too hot to drink, she thought to herself as she lowered the the cup back onto the table.

Seconds later, her thoughts were interrupted again. This time by a kiss on the cheek and a bouquet of flowers thrust in her face. Angela gasped and then grinned at the bundle of dried lavender blossoms, breathing in the earthy aroma.

Josh whispered in her ear, breathing heavily and still holding the brittle lavender stalks in front of their faces. "You didn't drink any of that coffee, did you?" She shook her head no and looked at him, puzzled. Josh picked up the mug quickly and dumped some of it into a small vial he held between them. He then pretended to sip from the mug himself and said, "That hits the spot after a long morning." He put his arm around her and handed back the mug. Then he whispered, "pretend to drink, but don't let a drop touch your lips. We've got to go. Now." He smiled and started to chat about the mundane details of his morning. Bewildered, Angela mutely packed her things and followed him out to the bike.

Josh drove them back down the roadway, through the Outsider's gate, and then deep into the woods. He stopped the bike. Reaching into his pocket, he pulled out the vial and set it on a flat rock near the side of the path. He opened a compartment underneath the seat and pulled out a case the size of a shoebox. Still wearing his leather riding gloves, he struggled to work the latches and unlock the lid. He rustled around inside, finally retrieving a plastic cartridge the size of a matchbook and a tiny syringe.

Angela pulled off her helmet and watched as he dipped the tip of the syringe into the vial of coffee and then inserted it into the tiny cartridge. He slipped the cartridge into a slot in the case. The system bleeped twice. "Josh, tell me this isn't what it looks like."

He held up a hand, staring at the screen. Angela wanted to take a look at the screen for herself, but fear kept her frozen in place. She didn't want to go near the coffee or the syringe. Josh didn't seem to want her any closer either.

A minute later, the machine bleeped again. Josh dropped his chin to his chest and his shoulders drooped. "I should have known. But I didn't want to believe it. He came so close…" he murmured.

"What's going on, Josh? What was in that coffee?" Angela's voice sounded urgent but steady.

Josh regained his bearing. "Botulinum," he said. "A toxin. It's found in preserved foods, like the canned goods sold at the market. If you eat it, you feel woozy, blurry eyed. The infection eventually leads to paralysis and death. He wanted us to seize up on the trip home. Odds are, the coyotes would have gotten us. Our bodies would never have been found," he said.

"He? You mean Parrish? What are you saying?" The steadiness in her voice gave way to panic.

Josh just shook his head and said, "Angela, we need to go underground. And we need to stay there."

"Hold on. We were just sitting there, chatting. He got me a coffee, and one for himself. This can't be happening. How did you even… What made you stop me from drinking it? When did you start thinking he would do this?"

"I don't know. He's been trying to get me to stop taking you places since the beginning. And he said he was going to be away today. But then I saw him talking to you. I just reacted." Josh put the top back on the vial of coffee and tucked it into the case. "I've always thought of myself as a target, but I was sure I could protect you. Then yesterday, seeing Molly so sick, it hit me. I realized just how much danger I'd put you in." He latched the compartment and sighed. "Come on. We've got to get going."

But Angela didn't move. "Josh, I can't. I mean, Dalyrimple gave me the whole backstory. And Nate sent me some data. He's decrypted the files. I need to call him. I need to talk to Stew." She had already started drafting her story in her head. She had proof. She couldn't let it go. Not after what she had learned. Not after seeing her own naïve words glaring back at her at the museum. She wouldn't let it go. "I need to write this story," she insisted.

Josh had finished packing away the case and was now pulling at branches and crushing plants on the edge of the trail. He acted as if he hadn't heard her.

"Did you hear me? I've got it all. I just need to write—"

"This isn't a story," roared Josh, raising his voice to her for the first time and turning to face her. "Angela, I almost lost you in there today. Parrish thinks we're both going to die here in the woods. He expects it. If we don't, he'll just come after us again. They won't give up."

Angela tried to absorb it all. Parrish a murderer. Herself a victim. Her story more terrible than she could have ever imagined. "But if we stop now," she whispered, "all of this continues."

"Not necessarily," he said, pulling his helmet over his head. "He may try to follow. We've got to go. If we are going to stop them, we need to save ourselves first."

20

Nate sat on a bench in the skypark. His head hung low between his shoulders and his elbows pressed into his thighs. He no longer noticed the strong smell of citrus hanging over the grove of microdwarf trees and he had stopped compulsively checking the elevator. Instead, he stared at the gravel path, numb, turning the data over and over in his head.

He had succeeded in unlocking the files Molly had given him. He had also unlocked the data that he'd squirreled away in his digital trunk. They pointed to only one possibility. But he didn't want to face it. He wondered if he had been right to send a few examples to Angela. He had sent them without thinking, knowing that if he hesitated, he might hold back. But now the reality of his decision had sunk in. If she turns it over to the papers or the authorities, if she makes it public, what will happen to me? What will happen to the NArc?

Nate stopped thinking about it. Too late now. Instead, he thought about Molly. He didn't know how to break the news to her without crushing her. She had built her entire life on the principle that science is the pursuit of truth. It would be, he thought, if everyone else believed in the ideal the same way she did. He didn't want to have to be the one to tell her that everything she believed in was built on lies. His task would be harder now with Parrish in the picture. There hadn't been a time he'd seen her these past few weeks when she hadn't cited his authority. Nate had no evidence for it, but he suspected that Parrish knew what was in those files.

The sound of crunching gravel barely registered in his mind. It wasn't until Molly's feet appeared in his field of view that he slowly lifted his head. He had asked her to meet him here to review what he'd found. She had agreed, but had put it off until now, mid-afternoon. All day long he had watched a simulated sun rise and begin its descent on his monitor background, willing the minutes away. Now that the time had finally arrived, he wasn't sure where to begin.

"Hi Nate," said Molly. "I know why you want to talk to me."

Before he had a chance to respond, she continued.

"The experiments, right? I found out about them too. Parrish explained it all to me this morning. I've been thinking about it and it all makes sense. The NArc started out as an experiment. When you think about it, personalized Nutrition is an experiment every day, at every meal. It's a constant nudging, like tiny taps that keep us in balance. There's no difference between what we count on from the NArc everyday and these so-called experiments. It's all about prolonging high-quality life and reducing suffering. We're striving for perfect health for all, and we're getting there."

"So it's true then," he muttered. "The NArc is experimenting on people." But Molly seemed unaffected. Maybe Parrish only told her half the story? "Do you know what's in those encrypted files?" Nate couldn't help it. His eyes glassed over and his voice rasped. "They're killing the failed experiments!"

"I don't know why you always have to put things so crudely," responded Molly.

Nate closed his eyes. His heart sank. He hadn't realized how much he had hoped to find out that he had gotten it all wrong. All day he had agonized about showing the evidence to Molly. Secretly, though, he had hoped that she would point out some obvious mistake he'd made in reading the files.

But the data spoke for itself. Sinsky's files had detailed the experimental treatments, their failure, and her subsequent termination: "Type 3B," the file read; "Illicit food, tainted meat" according to the legend. In file after decrypted file he found evidence of drug trials, assessments, and death types. He had come to the only logical conclusion. But there were still so many questions. How many people know about these studies? How many people have they killed? And how can Molly be okay with it? There has to be something she knows that I don't that will make this all make sense.

"I don't get it. With all the Sims, why not check the drugs first? Why experiment on humans?" he asked, trying to filter the hostility out of his voice.

"You, of all people, know the answer to that question. Because the Sims are models. Imperfect approximations."

Imperfect, thought Nate. Or too perfect. Not nearly as messy as humans. "But they don't have to kill people. What does that serve? Why not just let them die in peace?"

Molly lifted her hands as if the answer were obvious. "To reduce suffering, of course. Would you prefer a long, drawn out, and traumatic death? Do you want to go back to the days when hospitals were jam-packed with people who were sick and in pain?"

The thought made Nate squirm. He knew Angela's mother had died a terrible death. He had watched his own mother suffer when she cared for his grandmother. He didn't want to increase people's pain.

"Nate, you're missing the key point. We're right on the cusp. With everything we're learning from this work plus the genetic controls that stop bad genes from being passed down in the first place, we could eliminate disease completely by the end of the century." She sounded exhilarated. Nate shrank to one side of the bench as she took a seat next to him.

"We need the NArc, Nate. We can't risk undermining it. Not this way. Not Angela's way. There are too many people like me who—according to the studies I've seen—can't tolerate real food. Almost a third of the population has never been exposed to it and all of its allergens and pathogens. There are just too many variables. The risks far outweigh the benefits. That's what I came up here to tell you. Angela's story will cause ripples that we won't be able to control. It could lead to an interruption in the NArc that would put many people in danger."

Nate looked at Molly. She still had that same transcendent face. That same self-assuredness. But something wasn't quite right. And it wasn't the speed or the long hours. Something had always been wrong. Only he'd been too dazzled to see it. She'd convinced him of things before with her flawless reasoning, every point lined up perfectly. But not this time. This time Nate believed in himself more than he believed in her. Even the worst case scenario, even a complete NArc failure would be better than letting this sham persist.

"I talked it through with Parrish," she continued. "He agrees that Angela's work has gone too far. He's going to talk to Josh today. I'll talk to Angela tonight."

Nate leaned back on the bench. He gazed over the tree tops and through the clear glass walls. In the distance, he could see the twisted towers of the NArc buildings. He wondered how it was possible that two intelligent people could view the world so very differently.

"I'm sure you agree it's for the best. It's for the greater good," he heard her say.

Nate snorted. "That takes me back," he mused, talking more to himself than to Molly. "Back to high school. I brought home an essay on bioethics and utilitarianism. An A-plus essay. I was so proud. Know what my mom did?" He glanced at Molly but ignored the baffled look on her face. "She tore it in half. Said I was parroting, not thinking. She picked every argument to pieces. Then she made me write it again. She sent me back with a new essay the next day—a much more controversial one—and of course you know what happened." Nate chuckled and shook his head. "The teacher read it out loud to the class. That sucked. Turned me into an outcast." Nate looked at Molly again. This time he wasn't laughing. "I hated my mother for that. But now I know. She was right."

Molly shook her head in disbelief. "You know, it's one thing to hear these kinds of cryptic stories from Angela. But from you? From you, they're just disappointing." The crease between her eyes deepened and she crossed her arms. "I have explained over and again why this whole thing is just a big misunderstanding. But you and Angela don't want to hear it." She stood up and took a few steps, then turned back to face him. "That on its own would be bad enough. But now I've finally made a breakthrough on my project, like I told you the other day. Angela should be reporting on that. She should be sharing this big advancement with the world. But instead she's off chasing ghosts and making up conspiracies. And I'm left talking to some reporter. Frank or some such. He didn't understand word one of what I told him. He's going to get it all wrong." Molly huffed and shook her head in disgust. "I'm hoping Angela will pick it up once we convince her to drop this other thing."

Nate sat in silence. He'd stopped listening. A strange sense of calm washed over him. He felt grounded. The path before him opened up and he felt excited about the possibilities. He wanted to call Angela. To get the rest of the files to her. To help her get the story straight. Strange that she hasn't called me yet, he thought.

"I'd better get back," Molly said. "I know you're disappointed, but you'll see. It really is all for the best."

Nate stood up and forced a smile. He placed his hand on her shoulder. Her bones pressed into his palm. She felt like a stranger to him. "For the greater good," he murmured, as she walked away.

As Nate watched Molly wind her way back to the elevators, he noticed a flicker of movement out of the corner of his eye. Arthur stepped out from behind a hedgerow and headed toward the grove, his short legs springing, his eyes blazing. "Mister Hunter," he called out. "I thought I might find you here." He grinned. "Did you have a nice chat with Miss Tanaka?"

Nate stepped out of the grove and strode toward Arthur, like a goalie coming out of the net, forcing the intruder to slow his pace and stop. "Good afternoon, Arthur," Nate droned. Meanwhile, in his head, he scrambled to make sense of this. Molly had told Parrish everything. How much had she told Arthur?

Arthur stepped close to Nate. "She's quite convincing, isn't she? Very smart. But even from behind the boxwood it was obvious to me that she was not convincing enough. I hope you won't make this difficult for us, Hunter."

"What are you talking about Arthur?" Nate stalled. "I know I missed another deadline, but I'll have the code in by tomorrow, first thing." Play it dumb, Nate coached himself. Make him talk. Nate shrugged and gave Arthur a sheepish smile. "I'd better head down to my office and get back to work."

Nate took a step but Arthur blocked his way. "Don't play games with me Hunter. I'm told you're quite smart, though I've never seen anything in you but arrogance. I'm told that you're needed here. As valuable to Sims as Molly is to Development. But don't let it go to your head. I'm prone to disregarding other people's opinions."

As valuable as Molly, huh? Doubtful. What he didn't doubt was that Arthur was threatening him. But with what? He no longer feared getting fired. Let's just get this over with, he thought to himself.

Arthur took Nate by the arm and led him to the overlook on the far side of the grove. "Do you see all of them down there?" he asked. Streams of people rippled through the skywalks crisscrossing in a latticework that reached from the 30th story to the ground. Arthur seemed to swell with pride. He looked down upon the masses as if they were zoo animals.

"Did you know that control of the food supply defined civilization? It still does. Even now," Arthur marveled. "Just look at them all," he breathed, gesturing to the throngs below and speaking without tearing his eyes from them. "All the farmland in the country couldn't feed them. They don't just want the NArc. They *need* it."

But Nate wasn't falling for it. He trained his thoughts on the people he knew. He forced himself to look past the streaming masses and identify individuals. One person's red hair stood out. Then a woman with a green scarf and a man with a shaved head. He gave them imaginary faces. This isn't a game, he repeated to himself. These are real people with real families and real lives.

Nate felt Arthur put an arm around his shoulder, as if he wanted to pull Nate back into the fold. "It is faith that holds everything together," Arthur professed. "We cannot allow the defects of a few to undermine the trust of many."

Though Nate's eyes had not moved, he had stopped watching. Is that what this is all about? he thought to himself. Keeping up appearances? All those people murdered—

"And we need you, Hunter," Arthur continued, speaking directly into Nate's ear. "You can help us improve the NArc, so we can eliminate suffering completely."

Arthur patted Nate on the back and gazed again at the moving figures below. "It must be difficult now that you are alone in this…quest. Such a shame about your friend Angela. Or do you call her Sage Weaver? Such a shame. And her friend too. To die so young. And so violently."

Nate gripped the railing to support himself. His knees had buckled. He tried not to look at Arthur. He tried to keep himself together. Then he realized that Arthur was holding him up. "I'm sure you don't want to suffer a similar fate," he heard Arthur whisper in his ear.

Nate wasn't sure how much time had passed, but he found himself sitting on one of the park benches. It couldn't have been long. The sun had hardly moved, and Arthur was still there, a satisfied expression on his face. "You've suffered a terrible shock. But don't worry. SynEngra has a wonderful program. A sort of retraining program. You won't be gone long. It's all been arranged. We've notified your connections. We've taken care of everything."

Nate numbly took the ticket Arthur handed him. They'd arranged for him to be on the 5 pm ferry to a northern harbor town, home to the SynEngra Training Center. As he gazed at the ticket, he wasn't sure what would become of him there in that remote location. But he had a feeling that it wouldn't be good.

$$\neq$$

The door latched behind Nate. Then he heard the lock turn. It didn't surprise him. He'd already surrendered his clothes, his headset, and his flexscreen to the guards.

Alone in his room, he stood, wearing a loose-fitting white jumper and slippers, and ran his fingers over his head through the space where his hair used to be. He scanned the room. No mirror, he thought, relieved. He didn't want to see if the buzz cut suited him. The one window in the room had bars on it. The only other furnishings were a small cot and a toilet and sink in the bathroom. In each corner he spotted surveillance cameras.

His stomach growled. Based on the travel time, he figured it had to be past 8. No wonder I'm hungry, he thought. In his left hand he held a bagged meal. He carried it over to the cot and sat down cross legged. He unwrapped the meal and broke off a piece. He brought it to his mouth then dropped it back into the bag. Bit by bit he pretended to eat the meal. When he finished, he stood up and dumped the contents of the bag into the toilet and flushed. As he threw the bag into the miniscule waste hatch built into the wall, his stomach growled again.

"Get used to it," he said. He didn't trust the food. He didn't know if brainwashing drugs existed. But if they do, he reasoned, they'll be using them here. Though he'd helped program the NArc's system of nanobots and sensors that coursed through his and almost everyone's veins, he was only vaguely aware of its presence. I need to feed it, he thought. But I need to do it without losing myself in the process. Nate made a point to slow himself down. To burn less. He could only starve himself for so long. He'd have to find a balance between keeping the NArc—and his body—happy and keeping his mind clear.

"Nathan Hunter. We welcome you to the SynEngra Refresher Course," chirped an enthusiastic voice through a set of speakers built into the ceiling. "We hope you enjoyed your meal.

Now we invite you to sit back, relax and enjoy your first evening of programming."

Nate walked to the window and stared out into the darkness. He thought back again to his mother and that essay. It hadn't been the first time she had done that to him. Nor had it been the last. He'd scoffed at her every time. His friends had called his parents radicals. Elitists. They'd teased him and several had abandoned him. But his parents didn't care. They hammered their ideas into his head. "Scrutinize the claims, Nate." "Always analyze the figures." "Question authority, son." But the more they hammered, the more he shut them out.

When the voice piped in again—"We invite you to sit back, relax and enjoy your first evening of programming. We will be happy to provide assistance if you need it."—Nate closed his eyes and tried to picture his mother's face. I sure hope some of it sank in, Mom.

He shuffled his slippered feet across the floor and sat on the cot. He propped himself up against the painted concrete wall with a flimsy pillow. As the lights dimmed, a small hatch above his head opened and a projector cast images on the opposite wall. He recognized some of them from the SynEngra museum. "This evening's program involves a series of self-paced videos. Use the remote control to view each segment and complete the quiz. Your performance will help us gauge your progress and direct your training."

Nate flipped through the menu. Only five segments. Two technical. Two historical. And one titled "Vision." As he watched, he played a side game with himself. He called it Spot. Spot the Propaganda. It started out as a joke. An easy way to keep his mind clear. During the first history section, Spot was a snap.

But then during the second one, things got tricky. He squirmed as the video showed interviews with several terminal cancer patients and their relatives. They were all in obvious pain.

Physical. Emotional. Relentless. Who was he to say that they should continue to suffer?

The technical segments also challenged his Spotting ability. He learned that before the Sims, people routinely took drugs that had been tested only on mice. They had no idea what effects the chemicals might have on humans. And lots of people got sicker or died while taking them. It seemed archaic. He couldn't believe this sort of thing had happened so recently. He worked hard to spot the lies, but found the whole thing confusing. He breathed a sigh of relief when he completed his final quiz.

"Congratulations, Nathan Hunter," chirped the voice. "You have completed your first program. Your next program begins at six am. Good night." Abruptly, the video stopped and the dimmed lights went black. Nate sat, frozen, waiting for something to happen. When nothing did, he slipped himself under the thin blanket and tried to sleep.

The next morning, the lights came up slowly. Nate had slept for a few hours, but had been awake for longer, puzzling over the videos. He'd worked out the tactic behind the cancer patient videos. The way they'd put it, there were only two choices: let people suffer or let the NArc handle it. The video made it seem black and white. But Nate knew that before the NArc, care had gotten better and many people had suffered less. The video had cut out that hope-filled gray area.

The whole segment on the Sims was harder to tease out. The video made him feel like an idiot for thinking that there should be more Sim testing done before giving people drugs. Of course Sim work was important, but human testing had to be done, the video argued. But when was a drug good enough to give to people? When was the risk low enough? Another gray area. He reminded himself that he didn't have to solve the problems to play Spot. He just needed to identify the flaws in the reasoning.

When his room was fully illuminated, Nate stood up and got ready for his next program. It didn't take long since he had only one jumper and no possessions. He didn't even have hair to comb. He put on his slippers and stood by the window. The sun hadn't come up yet but in the pre-dawn glow he could make out the road he had come in on. He worked out the shape of the building and determined that he was on the fourth floor, just over a sunken back parking lot with a service entrance. Below him and to the left the windows changed from small, barred boxes to a series of oversized panels.

A knock at the door startled him. He had been expecting the voice again. He pulled open the door. Three other inmates stood before him. "Ready?" asked the only woman in the group. She was tall and had long mousy hair. She looked thin and slightly pained.

"It's almost six! Let's go," said the young man next to her with a boyish enthusiasm. He had thick, wavy hair that had not been shaved. "We know you're Nate. The host for the week told us all about you. We're all here for orientation. Newbies to the SynEngra team! One of our projects is to help you through retraining. You'll be eating with us. Then after morning programs we're doing a ropes course. For teamwork! I'm Casey. That is Charlotte," he pointed to the woman. Her face remained expressionless. "And this is Raymond." Raymond waved, but he had already taken off down the hall. "Let's go. You are going to love the programs today. I've been here a week. I can't believe it's half over already. But then, I'm so excited to start working. It's my first job. I'll be in Development. I'll be working for legends!"

As Casey spoke, Nate wondered when orientation had changed. When he'd gone through it a decade ago, it was a few hours of paperwork, a safety video, and speech or two. He didn't remember the speeches very well. He had a vague recollection of an open bar during the break before that part of the program.

Nate fell back and glanced at Charlotte but she kept looking straight ahead. So he counted his steps and started stitching the insides of the building together with what he had learned about the outsides through his window. They took the stairs to the first floor. The stair continued down one more flight. To the sunken lot, he thought. To his right, he saw that the cafeteria had large paneled windows. Between the stairwell and the restrooms was one other door. Unlike the others, this door was locked with an ID scanner. Based on the size, he thought it must be a wiring closet or control center. It wasn't big enough to be anything more.

"Here we are," Casey called back. "We all grab our meals up front and then sit at table eleven. It's in the center. See it?"

At the table, Nate sat across from Charlotte. Raymond kept his head down and Casey continued to chatter. Nate learned that he didn't have to listen to Casey to keep him happy. Between nods, he scanned the room. Almost half the tables had a clear view of the doors to the restrooms, the stairwell and the closet.

As he calculated more distances, frowning to himself in frustration, he felt a kick under the table. Charlotte looked at him, her eyes dead. She put a bit of her food in her mouth and, even though she didn't chew it, it disappeared. She repeated this a few times and then she picked up her napkin and sneezed. She looked at him for a second longer, then looked away. Nate resumed his study of the room as he ate. When his cheek felt full, he sneezed or coughed or bent down to adjust his slipper.

Halfway through the meal, he felt another kick under the table. This time when he looked up, Charlotte was smiling and laughing. "Casey, you're too much." She gave Nate an encouraging look. He smiled back and forced a laugh. As he did, he saw a small contingent of official looking people pass by the head of his table heading for the aisle behind Charlotte.

"This week's host is here," breathed Casey next to him.

At first, Nate couldn't make out the leader's face. But when they rounded the corner, a jolt of electricity shot through his body. His eyes met Parrish Knight's. Instead of appearing surprised, Parrish looked wickedly amused. As Nate's eyes followed Parrish through the room, he saw that the other trainees were in awe of the man.

After breakfast, as the trainees made their way back to their rooms, Nate fell back next to Charlotte. "You know him," she said without turning her head. Nate gave her a slight nod. He felt her look at him. "You want out?" she asked. He dipped his chin again. "Good. We need your help." Nate raised his eyebrows, but before he could ask why or how, she disappeared into her room.

A few doors down, in his own room, the voice over the loudspeaker greeted Nate. As instructed, he sat on the bed and picked up the remote. In the back of his mind he was thinking about Charlotte. She looked young, almost as young as Casey. What could she possibly have planned? And why?

He brought up the first program and resumed his game of Spot. At first the game was easier than it had been the night before, but after fifteen minutes, Nate felt fatigued. No food for almost 24 hours. And little sleep. He didn't know how long he could keep this up.

He had just started the third of five programs when the video stopped. "Nathan Hunter, your programming has been temporarily interrupted," chirped the voice. His door opened. In walked Parrish Knight.

Nate scrambled to his feet. The tiled floor felt cold on his bare skin.

Parrish strolled into the room and looked around. "Nice place. Comfortable?" he mocked, though all traces of amusement had left his face. "I hope so. It is the last place you will ever sleep." Parrish wandered around the room as he spoke, examining the cameras and checking the window bars. "Arthur believes you can be retrained, but I disagree. I saw your face this morning. Steeled against us. It's too bad. They tell me you're gifted. It will be a shame to lose you." Parrish turned to face Nate and grinned. "Just like Josh and Angela."

The last words hit Nate like bricks. He still hadn't fully accepted that they were gone. But now, a rage rushed over him. He should have known. He should have seen it earlier. "How many people have you killed so far Parrish? How many friends? How many dead bodies is the NArc hiding behind?" he spewed, pushing out the words from the depths of his gut.

Parrish smirked. "Fear keeps the masses in line. They certainly can't be trusted to make decisions on their own."

"That's the stupidest thing I've ever heard," interjected Nate. "People lived for thousands of years making their own choices. Entire countries thrive on real food and real freedom no matter what your idiotic videos say."

"Not for long," Parrish replied from across the room. "When people hear about how Sage Weaver died a gruesome death in the woods after getting mixed up with the biggest Cheaters in the NorthEast, do you think they'll keep cheating? Do you think they'll keep buying food at these border markets?" Parrish shook his head in disgust. "These pathetic Cheaters, flocking like sheep to the markets. Mindless consumers. Demanding lower prices and driving down quality. They can't be trusted to think for themselves because they're too stupid to think for themselves." Parrish turned to Nate, his grey eyes gleaming.

"Fear will drive the masses back to the safety of the NArc. Then they won't have to think. The NArc gives them only one choice."

A look of understanding passed over Nate's face. "I see now." He smiled his most charming grin. "I understand. You're a snob. It's fine for you to Cheat. But the rest of us are just pigs." Then Nate's face turned dark. "You know, that is so much worse. At least Arthur and Molly think they're helping people. You're just saving yourself a place at the table."

Parrish's eyes narrowed. "It won't be long now. I suggest you try to enjoy what's left of your life." When the door closed behind Parrish, Nate sank back onto the bed. He was shaking. His feet felt like blocks of ice. When the voice instructed him for the third time to resume his programming, he rubbed his eyes. With unsteady hands, he picked up the remote.

An hour later, the Teamwork Director paired the trainees by height. He assigned Nate and Charlotte to work together. Their task was to scale a huge rope ladder made of beams between four and seven feet apart. Before they began, the Director gave them shoes. Even after just a few hours without them, they felt good on his feet. So good that Nate had to fight the urge to make a run for it. Instead, he followed Charlotte and scaled the first two steps easily. For the third, they had to work together.

Charlotte inched over to Nate and leaned in. "We're a go," she whispered behind her curtain of hair. "Today."

He blinked. So soon? He tried not to react. "Tell me what I need to do," he said, looking up at the next level.

"I'll use your leg as a step, then help pull you up," she responded, as if their other conversation weren't happening.

Nate nodded. As she stepped on his knee she leaned in again. "You need to hack the NArc."

He sucked in his breath. "Ready?" he asked. She nodded and he boosted her up. When she got herself positioned on the third step, she leaned down.

"We can get you in the closet. Can you get in the system?" Then, raising her voice, she asked, "Ready?" When he replied "yes" she pulled him up.

They sat straddling the beam, allowing the ladder to steady itself. "Two more rungs to go. They can't hear us up this high," she said. "Argue with me."

Nate looked at her quizzically for a second, then said, "It sounds risky," and pointed to one of the ropes.

"We have the host's ID number." As she spoke, she shook her head and pointed to herself and the lower beam and then the one above. "I'll send it to you during gaming, next. We need a NArc alarm."

He gulped down the surge of excitement in his chest. "That's no problem." He looked down. No one seemed to be paying any attention to them. "Then what?"

"We've got it covered. We go at noon." Charlotte swung her legs up and stood.

This time, he climbed on her knee. As he did, he felt her slip a plastic card into his sock before he clambered past her. "Why me?" he asked as he leaned down to help pull her up.

She smiled and for an instant, her eyes looked alive. "Because you're a natural," she said as he hoisted her up to the topmost rail. "And you're cute."

At noon, the foursome sat at table eleven. Nate looked up and said, "Pardon me. Restroom."

"No one goes anywhere alone," advised Casey as he started to stand, but Charlotte was already up.

"I've got to go too. We'll watch each other." She didn't wait for an answer and neither did Nate. Casey smiled awkwardly. "O-okay then! Great! You guys go." He waved. Nate could still hear him talking at Raymond when they reached the hallway. As they walked out past the guards, Parrish Knight was walking in. Nate kept himself concealed behind Charlotte's hair as Parrish passed, escorted by three officials. Nate heard applause erupt in the cafeteria.

"No time to waste," said Charlotte.

Nate strode away from her and walked directly into the men's room. He was gambling that if Casey and the guards weren't completely absorbed by Parrish's entrance, they might watch him go in, but they wouldn't keep staring at the men's room door.

Two seconds later, he slipped back into the hall. In one motion, he swiped the pass card Charlotte had passed him and slid inside. He flicked on the light and scanned the small space. He located the computer that acted as a local control center for the NArc. He flipped it open and logged in, chuckling at the recollection of Angela's voice taunting him: "When was the last time you built a system without a back door?" He had gone home that very night and found two.

He typed in the ID Charlotte had sent him during the gaming session. He chuckled again, almost giddy knowing that of all people, the ID belonged to Parrish Knight. His only regret was that he wouldn't be there to see the man's face when the klaxon blared. He hit enter and the record popped up. Nate went straight for the diagnostics and quickly tweaked the code. The data models were complex, but he just needed to swap one setting from LIVE to TEST to override all of Parrish's data and put a test sequence in place. He logged out and replaced the computer. He knocked twice and waited for the signal.

As the seconds ticked by Nate felt a bead of sweat run down his back. What was going on out there? Then he heard the klaxon and two light raps on the door.

Nate burst out and saw Charlotte's hair disappear behind the stairwell door. He followed, the alarm pounding in his eardrums. He took the stairs two at a time and flew out the service door on Charlotte's heels. Two other people he hadn't met stood in the lot, panting.

"Where's Jimmy?" demanded Charlotte. "Where's the effing van?"

Just then, a small electric van pulled silently into the lot. The back door slid open. They crammed in, Nate at the rear pulling the door shut as the van swerved around and back up the lane. He fell back onto a pile of laundry and tried to catch his breath.

"We each get an outfit," barked Charlotte, passing out bundles. "They're the best we could get so try to make them work." Charlotte tore off her jumper without the slightest bit of modesty. Nate followed, pulling on a pair of baggy green track pants and a matching jacket. The jacket was snug around his shoulders and too short for his arms, but he fared better than the others. One shorter guy had to roll his pants at the waist to keep them up and Charlotte had donned a sweater that fell to her knees.

"Everyone in for Vermont?" she asked.

Nate hadn't thought about a final destination. He had just wanted out. But he couldn't go to Vermont. "I have to go back," he said.

"Back to brainwash central?" the short guy asked. "That's nuts."

Charlotte, however, looked disappointed. She knew what he meant. "Jimmy, Nate needs passage."

"Damn it Charlotte. I told you, Vermont only. I fuckin' told you. I don't do this for fun, you know. I don't even know this guy."

"If you can just get me near a boat or a train or something, I can handle the rest," said Nate. He didn't know how, but he'd figure it out. With Angela and Josh dead, he was the only one who knew. He was the only one with the evidence. He had no choice.

21

Stew sat down at his desk Tuesday morning. He'd arrived early, eager to hear from Angela. Her last story had been fantastic, and he wanted more. But he also wanted her to be careful. When he suggested dropping the Sinsky story when he spoke to her Sunday afternoon, she wouldn't hear of it. "I'm right on the edge Stew," she'd said. "Give me until Monday night."

He opened his messages and scanned them for a note from her. Not seeing one, he changed his status to online and checked his chat icon. No contact attempts yet, but then, it's early yet, he thought. She'll probably come bounding in here in an hour or so with all kinds of stories and a handful of excuses. He smiled and began to tackle the backlog of work that had accumulated overnight.

He had plowed through a third of his messages when he heard someone knock on his office door. She's earlier than expected, he thought as he called out, "Come in."

But when he looked up, his face transformed from anticipation to puzzlement. Instead of Angela, two police officers entered, an older man and a young woman, both wearing blue uniforms and grim expressions.

The male officer spoke first. "Stewart Oakham?" Stew nodded. "I am Lieutenant Henry Potente and this is Officer Sheila Barnes. We have terrible news for you. Terrible news. About Angela Anselm and her friend Josh Salter."

Stew gripped the edge of his desk and closed his eyes. "What's happened," he asked flatly.

Officer Barnes opened a folder and read the report. "Between noon and two pm on Monday afternoon, Miss Anselm and Mr. Salter were attacked on an unmarked roadway on the Vermont border. Their remains were discovered by an Outsider who said he heard a disturbance, investigated, and then called the authorities. According to officers at the scene late yesterday evening, the couple succumbed to an apparent encounter with the wildlife. Most likely coyotes. They may have been disabled prior to the attack. Perhaps a spill from their motorbike. The neighbor recovered the bike, which showed signs of damage. Blood and hair recovered from the struggle provided positive identification." She closed the report.

Stew looked from Barnes to Potente but could not find words to speak.

Potente stood. "I am terribly sorry to deliver this news to you. Angela and Josh, well, let's just say I knew them. They were good people." He nodded to Barnes. She stood up, placed the report in front of Stew, and the two officers filed out.

The folder sat inches from Stew's fingertips, but he could not bring himself to touch it. He did not want to read it. He did not want to see the photographs it no doubt contained. He did not want to accept the truth. His best writer, his friend these past ten years, dead? He looked at his screen. No messages. No blinking chat icon. He felt the tears burn, then tumble down his cheeks.

He blamed himself. When she had come to him with the idea for this story, he'd thought it sounded dangerous. But she was good, he had reasoned. She could handle it. When she had come to him with her first report, he'd hesitated to let her continue. She'd already met with shady characters on isolated street corners. But she had survived. She had broken in. Then, when she filed her last story and told him what she suspected, he should have stepped in. He should have involved the authorities. Someone to protect her. Anyone. But she wouldn't hear of it. "If we can't trust the NArc, who can we trust?" she'd argued. "I only need a few more days," she'd assured him.

He had relented. It had been the worst decision of his career.

With the heavy hands and unseeing eyes of a man in shock, Stew opened a text window. At the top, he typed: "Angela Anselm, respected columnist and beloved colleague, 2023-2063."

The freight train slowed and entered the rail yard. Nate clung to the back of a biofuel tanker, suspended on the rungs leading to the fill cap. He eyed a clearing ahead and timed his leap. The landing was harder than he expected and he slid several feet on the gravel before rolling to a stop. Ignoring the pain in his knees and palms, he leapt up and wound his way through the maze of railcars.

From what Jimmy had said, this should be the Northern rail station. Nate figured it was between five and six pm. He oriented himself to the west, where Jimmy'd said the rail yard bordered one of the city's subway stations. From there he had a plan in mind. It wasn't a very good one. But then, the odds were stacked against him.

Jimmy had said that the Training Center would figure out who was missing within an hour. The quarantine bought enough time to get the group to Vermont, but that was all. "By the time you get to town, your face will be posted everywhere. They'll make you sound like a criminal," he'd said.

"I am," Nate had replied. Hacking a NArc controller was a federal offense. Nate was done for. He couldn't show his face in the city again without risking arrest.

He wound his way to an old cyclone fence. He decided to follow it south for 100 paces, hoping to find a way through. If that failed, he would backtrack and head north, farther out of his way, but also farther from the terminal and railway employees. The fence was littered with garbage and tangled with weeds and spindly trees. His paces weren't even, but he counted them nonetheless. At seventy-three, he started to hear the sounds of the terminal. Creaking doors, thudding crates, and barking voices. He had reached a large concrete structure. If he went any further, he wouldn't be able to get past it without being seen. He was about to turn around when he spied a hole in the fence just before the building. The bottom had been pulled up to form an arched opening just large enough for him to slide under. He dropped to his belly and slithered beneath it.

He scrambled up the gravel embankment alongside the building and found himself at street level. The subway station opening was twenty yards in front of him. He leaned back on the concrete wall and examined his hands. They were scraped badly from his leap from the train and the blood had run between his fingers and now mingled with the dirt crusted in his nails. He didn't want to wipe the mess on his clothes and draw even more attention to himself, so he scanned the garbage at his feet. He grabbed a few scraps of paper and set to work cleaning himself up.

It was then that he realized his head was bleeding. Damn! Must have caught myself on the fence. He wiped a scrap of paper across his face but it wasn't enough. He thought for a minute. Back around pace 54, he'd seen something. A scrap of cloth? He shook his head in disgust. I'm a dead man, he thought. It doesn't matter what I do anymore. He crawled back under the fence and retraced his steps. There it was, in a pile of leaves. A knitted black hat. It smelled of mildew but otherwise appeared clean. Nate scrubbed his face and hands with the damp insides then slipped it on his head.

Within minutes, he was inside the station. He jogged through the open turnstiles—petrified sentinels leftover from the pay-to-ride days—and leapt down the stairs. He'd planned to duck into the tunnels. But the inbound train was empty, so he hopped on it. He had no time to waste.

As the train approached the Tech stations, more and more passengers boarded. He kept his head down and gripped the scraps of paper in his hands to keep his blood from dripping on the floor. As the train pulled in to Tech, he stood behind a man as tall as himself, using him as a blocker. He trailed the man off the platform, past the turnstiles and into his alma mater's tunnel system.

Easy from here, he thought. He knew these tunnels inside and out. He picked up the pace and jogged, turning right, then left, then ducking into a bathroom. When he looked in the mirror he could hardly believe his eyes. He didn't recognize himself. His face looked drawn. He had dark circles under his eyes and the cap, pulled low, made them look sunken.

At least I don't have to find a disguise, he thought as he washed his hands and face. He pulled off the track pants and washed the blood out of the knees and cleaned up his legs. His scrapes had stopped bleeding. He dried the pants as best he could with the hand dryer and pulled them back on. He decided not to remove the hat. If he knew how dirty it really was, he might not want to put it back on.

Nate walked out of the restroom with a newfound confidence and headed straight for the library.

$\neq$

Stew had not moved for hours. Not since he sent the obituary to Marcus.

He had read the police report through once, then set to writing. The facts in the report had slithered through his mind and onto the page. He'd let them run, not stopping to examine them. They seemed amorphous and irrelevant. And too shocking to look at up close.

He'd finished the obituary just before the noon deadline. He'd worked on it in short bursts, numbly carrying out his other duties in between. The news had spread through the newsroom quickly. People stopped by to pay their respects. To commiserate. To speculate. But Stew had little to say. For the first time, he was wishing he didn't come into the office every day. Yet by the end of the afternoon, the office emptied, his story copyedited and gone to press, he couldn't bring himself to go home to his empty house.

He sat and stared out his window, struggling to stay awake. Unable to conjure the comforting images of days gone by, he instead saw only the sodden rubble of his old neighborhood. He preferred this view to what he saw when his lids closed. The rubble blocked out visions of Angela under attack.

It was in the throes of such a struggle against fatigue, a bleary-eyed attempt to focus on something tangible, that he noticed it. A blinking icon at the corner of his screen. Stew ignored it. He didn't want to talk to anyone. But the flashing persisted. And he had a job to do. That job is all I have left, he thought. So he hit the icon to connect.

"Hi Stew. It's Angela. Nice obit." Her voice filled the room and her face the screen. It was as if she were standing in front of him. Seeing Stew's condition, she changed her tone. "Stew, it's okay. We're alive. They think we're dead, but we escaped. We're okay. Please, we don't have much time on this line."

"But they said it was coyotes. I saw the blood. And the hair," he stammered.

"We left evidence to convince them they succeeded. Stew, they tried to murder us. But I don't have time to explain now. We have to talk about my story. It's ready. But it's not perfect. There is still one missing piece. But I need to get it to you and you need to run it. Soon. We're all in danger here. And we think they have my friend Nate. If we get the story out, he might have a chance."

Once Stew accepted that he really was talking with Angela, the adrenaline began to flow. "What do I need to do?"

"There's a man on his way to you. He's got everything you'll need with him. He's got old technology, but I'm sure there's a reader in the closet. Please Stew. Run the story. I've got to go. I'll be in touch again later," she said, then vanished.

He spent the next hour asking all of the questions that had eluded him earlier. He rechecked the death report and re-examined the photos. How had the Outsider who reported Josh and Angela missing known the exact location of the attack? There were hardly any signs of struggle. How had he known their names?

Stew was still reviewing the file and kicking himself for missing such obvious holes when he heard a tap on his office door. He peered through foggy eyes at a weathered man in old-fashioned work clothes. The man drew a gnarled hand from his jacket pocket. On the desk he placed a silvery disk and a business card. With a solemn nod, he departed. Stew picked up the business card and saw that Angela had scrawled GPS coordinates on the back. He tucked the card in his breast pocket then picked up the disk and spun it on a fingertip, gazing at the distorted reflection of his own aged yet determined face.

Stew had run big stories before. As a rule, he had always been in on the fact checking. He had always tipped off the leaders before taking them down. He had never blindsided anyone and had never run a story without a sense of what would come next. But this time, he thought to himself, he might not be so careful or so courteous.

He read Sage Weaver's story through once. It was good. Powerful. Shocking. But Stew knew Marcus wouldn't run it. He couldn't. The missing piece was the linchpin. Still, he had to try. He stood up, his legs stiff from sitting motionless all day, and hobbled to Marcus's office.

So far, Nate hadn't run into a single snag. He'd found Angela's obituary in the library and then tracked down the author who, it turned out, was also her editor. He'd braved the subway again to get to the news office. Then he'd found a door propped open in the back alley, the surrounding area littered with cigarette butts hand-rolled in paper that looked like used newsprint. He had to laugh. Nate hadn't seen a smoker since he'd moved to the city and had always wondered where they'd all gone. Once inside the building, Stew's office had been easier to find than his last Food School classroom.

From the hallway, Nate peered inside.

"I can't do it Stew. There's nothing here we can print. You need to go to the source. Get the rest of the data and we'll talk about it."

Nate let out a sigh of relief. He had gambled that he would find the man at his desk, reasoning that Angela had never worked a nine-to-five day in her life, so maybe none of these news people did. At the very least, he had hoped that here, of all places, he would find someone who would listen. Nate rapped on the door.

Marcus spun around and Stew stood up. Both looked alarmed. Nate realized he probably looked like a Junkie attempting a stick-up or something. He held up both hands, but the sight of his scabby palms didn't make things better. "I'm Nate Hunter. A friend of Angela Anselm's. I have information for Stewart Oakham. It would have gone to her but, well"—he gulped back his emotions for the umpteenth time in the last few hours—"now it has to go somewhere. I'm hoping you can help me."

The two men exchanged looks but Nate couldn't read their expressions. "I know I look bad. And you've probably seen the warrant out for my arrest. But please. This data. Angela's story. It has to get out."

The older of the two men stepped out from behind his desk and ushered Nate into the room. "You need to sit down, son." The man kept his hand on Nate's shoulder and talked over him. "Marcus, can you get the kid a cup of coffee? And one for me too? And if there's anything else... I have a feeling we're going to be here for awhile." Marcus nodded and left the room.

Stew sat next to Nate and leaned his elbows on his knees. "I'm Stew. Angela's editor. Nate was it? What have you got for me?"

Nate looked at his hands then back up at Stew. "I've got records. Hidden NArc records that show a pattern. Thousands of murders. Sinsky, she was murdered. It's all in the records. I..." Nate paused and started over. "Angela died for this. They murdered her to keep it quiet. And I've risked everything to expose it. I'm on the run now, too. But it doesn't matter. The only thing that matters is getting this out there."

Stew sat back and scrutinized Nate, looking at him in disbelief. It occurred to Nate that he had no idea who he was talking to. Without Angela or Josh around, he had no idea who to trust. Should he have tracked down that cop friend of hers instead? Crap. He sent Marcus out for coffee. Maybe he's out calling the cops now. I've gotta get out of here.

"Nate, I'm going to want to see these records," said Stew. "But before we do that, I have some news for you. Angela is not dead."

Nate stopped planning his escape. "But the obituary... You wrote it..."

"Yes, I did. I only found out myself an hour ago. Angela contacted me. They escaped, covered their tracks pretty well too. She also sent me a story. It talks about the records, but without them, without the proof, we can't run it. Maybe you've got what we need. Like I said, I've got to see it for myself first."

Nate pointed at Stew's computer. "May I?"

Stew cleared the way and Nate sat down at the desk. He couldn't log in as himself. Any presence on the Net might betray his location. Instead he logged in as an online character he used to borrow from a friend. Once in, his fingers danced across the screen and keypad. He barely registered Marcus's return. Until the smell of the coffee hit him.

"Mind if I take a minute? I haven't eaten in awhile..."

"Take your time," Stew said, chewing. Marcus had also brought donuts.

Nate crammed half a glazed donut into his mouth, then finished the rest. "Where did you guys get this stuff? It's Junk." He shoved another hunk of donut in his mouth and wiped the jelly off his chin. Marcus gave him a wink. "Stale Junk. And it's fantastic." He popped another bite in his mouth, slugged some lukewarm coffee, and resumed his cyberwalk.

Once he entered his conference room, he headed for the trunk. He held his breath as he keyed in the combination—Molly's birthday—then shook it off. "I'm in," he said. Stew pulled his chair back around the desk. "I downloaded these from SynEngra. Then I decrypted them. I organized them in a simple database searchable by date of death. So we can look up any date or just do a listing. There are other ways, but that seemed to make the most sense at the time."

Stew cleared his throat. "Look up January 15, 2060."

Nate looked at him for an instant, then keyed in the date. Two records came up. "We've got a teen-aged boy and a woman, about fifty-seven."

Stew pointed at the woman's decrypted file. Nate opened it and read. "She contracted an illness: Weakness Type 17." He flipped to a different screen. "An untreatable virus according to the legend." Flipping back, he continued. "The NArc took care of it for her. Termination Type 5A: Overdose, unapproved medication."

"She had been feeling tired. Run down," Stew began, staring at the record on the screen. "She said it was nothing. 'Probably just overworked,' she'd told me. But I was worried. Melanie had never felt overworked before. I knew something was wrong. Then I got the call. She collapsed on her way home. She died before reaching the hospital. Heart failure. They found evidence. A partially used pill pack in her tote. Said she'd gotten it from an illegal medic. But I didn't believe it. She trusted the NArc. When she got sick I begged her to consider an underground doctor, to see if there might be something wrong that the NArc was missing. But she said no. No way…"

Stew reached out a hand to stroke the cheek of his late wife, frozen in two dimensions in a frame on his desk.

Marcus put a hand on Stew's shoulder. "Why don't you take a minute."

Stew shook his head, his face set. "No. But I will need a few hours. We've got to get this story out. Tonight."

≠

By two am, the three men had finished editing Angela's story. They'd decided to keep it almost exactly as she had written it and to write a new piece about the NArc records. They framed this piece around the stories of Stew's late wife and Martine Sinsky. They linked the two articles together and then ran the lot through the standard editing process.

Marcus stood and stretched. "Well, boys, this'll hit the wires at 4 and be on desktops all around the city first thing this morning. I better start sending out the notices. The other news outlets are going to want to spin it. And I'm going to have to break it to the folks at SynEngra and the NArc. And to the Secretary of Health. It's gonna be a long day." He rubbed his forehead. Then he looked at Nate. "What's your plan. You available for interviews? Or you keeping it low?"

Nate looked from Stew to Marcus. "I need to get out of here. Out of the city. I started out as a whistleblower. But now I'm a felon. I guess that makes me an Outsider. That's probably where I belong."

Stew looked at Nate with real concern. He pulled the card the old man had given him from his breast pocket and eyed the coordinates. "Angela's Outside." He handed Nate the card. "Only I don't know how to get you there."

Marcus smiled. "Don't worry. We'll get you out."

Nate tucked himself behind a stack of printed newspapers in the back of the delivery van. Stew leaned in. "You okay back there?"

"Yeah. I'm alright."

"Good. Who knew we still delivered papers? And to Outsiders? Seems like I learn something new everyday. Makes me feel good, like the free press isn't as dead as I thought it was."

"Yup," said Nate leaning back on one of the stacks. He closed his eyes. "Compared to the train, this is comfortable."

"You're a trooper, son. According to the schedule, the van'll cross the city limits at 7am. Try to be as quiet as you can during the crossing. And stay down behind the stacks. The driver says they never check. Don't give them a reason to."

Nate gave Stew a thumbs up over the stacks.

"The driver says it won't be more than a few hours after that. He's got a bunch of stops to make. He'll let you know when it's yours."

Nate waved again.

Stew patted a stack of papers twice with his palm. "Okay then. You're off. Tell Angela when you see her that it was a hell of a job she did. Both of you. One hell of a job."

22

Unscheduled Mortality

By Sage Weaver, also known as Angela Anselm

Outside the Northeast City, June 5, 2063 — I wanted to believe. In fact, I did believe. It is recorded in these words, written by me a few weeks ago: "The NutriArc System is approaching perfection." Little did I know then that the NutriArc System — the system we all rely on for daily sustenance — was built not on science but on science fiction.

There is no doubt that we have benefitted from the NArc. I myself have fended off the disease that took my mother from me at an early age. The NArc keeps me healthy. But for those people whose troubles are more complex, the NArc is less kind. Indeed, for them the NArc is deadly.

In this, my last installment of Real Food as Sage Weaver, I will not tempt you by recounting my latest meal or entertain you with the graces of my hosts. No. This tale is one of murder. Because of what I know, I narrowly escaped murder myself.

My part in this tale started with the death of Martine Sinsky. Martine allegedly died after ingesting deadly bacteria during a dinner at a local speakeasy. Though none of the facts reported in the news were disputable, they did not add up. Why hadn't anyone else who had eaten the same meal gotten ill?

The answers were hidden deep inside her NArc record. So deep, even she couldn't see them. Martine didn't know it, but she had a form of cancer that was incurable by modern medicine. The NArc had detected the disease, but instead of informing her of her condition, the NArc secretly treated her with experimental drugs. When those drugs failed to improve her condition, the NArc eliminated her.

The operatives that carried out this crime tried to cover their tracks. They failed. A scientist inside SynEngra found traces of experimental drugs in Sinsky's remains. Another SynEngra employee, a computer engineer, found hidden records deep inside the NArc database. These files contain the history of experimentation on and subsequent elimination of Martine.

In the past year, according to these same hidden records, over two thousand people — twice the number of homicides last year — have met similar fates in the Northeastern City alone.

That such a thing could happen here in our safe and sound world is appalling.

But in a way, we are all to blame. Even I played a role in supporting this ruse. I embraced the NArc. I believed in its promise to make us flawless. We all did. The pristine became our principle.

Our culture wasn't always this way. The shift began long ago, during the first half of this century. Disease rates skyrocketed. Food plagues and shortages filled the headlines. People began to view nature itself as dangerous. And we increasingly felt a need for security and protection.

Scientists responded. They investigated ways to harness natural foods to improve health. By 2042, they were on the verge of defining a new, natural diet.

At the same time, however, engineers prototyped the first NutriArc cafe. They began work on the first Synganium. They had begun to craft designer fruits, vegetables, and meats.

The battle pitting nature against engineering had begun.

But one side had an edge. The engineers and the Nutritionists had all the money. A dearth of government funds for science had driven researchers deep inside corporate pockets. And those corporations funded only the ideas that promised the most profit.

As an example, Patricia Dalyrimple's research into the health benefits of natural foods went unpublished for lack of data. Meanwhile, engineered food studies of even smaller size and scope received public praise. Her research went unfunded while projects to develop Neermeat flourished. As a result, by the end of the decade, ninety percent of the food supply came from engineered sources dispensed by the NArc.

I don't deny that the NArc prolongs health and life. But it wasn't the only option, and it may not even have been the best option.

The deceit that squelched Dalyrimple's work was bad enough, but the fraud did not end there. The NArc fell short of perfection. Fearing that its flaws would hinder the transition to a NArc-based food system, its supporters conspired to keep those flaws hidden. They manipulated science. A corporate clearinghouse called the Safe and Sustainable Food Foundation funded studies designed to prove the NArc's effectiveness against a host of illnesses. The studies were small and the data subjective, and the results were always positive.

The propaganda worked. News stories (many of them written by me) championed the miraculous NutriArc System.

But some people still got sick. So a few individuals took action. They secretly tried to cure the unhealthy with experimental drugs. But medical science wasn't fast enough. So as a stop-gap, they launched a methodical and gruesome plot to eliminate the unwell. Even worse, they used the people they murdered as agents of propaganda to demonize real food, old-fashioned medicine, and anything else that competed with the controlling arms of the NArc.

Perhaps they rationalized that each victim would prefer a quick death to prolonged suffering. Perhaps they justified their actions by asserting that their work would, in the long run, improve science.

But these excuses do not justify murder. Surely those who perpetrated this great fraud will pay. But what's next for us?

I could incite you to rise up against the NArc. Indeed, after seeing the way the Outsiders live, after sharing natural meals with Foodies all over town, I am tempted to do just that.

But to do so would be irresponsible. The old studies showing that we cannot feed the world with traditional agriculture still hold true. And since then, we have only expanded the population and exacerbated the problem.

There is no turning back now.

But we can take back our health. We can demand that we be informed of our illnesses and given options about how we want to be treated. Perhaps, if we can get that far, we can begin to accept that a full life is also a life full of risks and flaws.

Angela woke to an unfamiliar aroma. She opened her eyes to see Josh sitting on the edge of the sofa holding a plate in one hand and a mug in the other.

"Is sleeping beauty ready for her pancakes?"

Angela sat up. "Cinderella," she yawned. Then, suddenly alert, she asked, "Is it out yet?"

"Minutes ago," he said, handing her the plate. "No reactions yet."

As Josh turned up the volume and settled in next to her, she breathed in the smell of maple syrup, blueberries and sausage. "Herb is a genius."

"I won't let it go to my head," he called from the kitchen. Angela, chewing, waved good morning. Then she stole a peek at June, still cocooned in a blanket on the same big cushioned chair she'd curled up on the night before. She looked withdrawn. She'd hardly said two words since she'd heard what Parrish had done.

She turned her attention to the streaming news reports captured by a small satellite dish on the roof of Herb's house and projected on his wall by one of the computers Herb bought to run the museum business.

The reporters were discussing the hidden NArc records, so Stew must have gotten hold of them somehow. Had he used the sample she'd sent to get a warrant or something? Or had Nate come through? She'd been worried about Nate since Monday evening, when he didn't answer her calls. She knew that Parrish would be after him too. Then, on Tuesday, his face had appeared on the news. The police wanted him for questioning about a case of vandalism at the NArc Training Center. It didn't sound right. Vandalism? It had to have been a cover up. But for what, Angela didn't know.

After another hour, with little new information other than a rehash of the facts in the article, Angela groaned. "It's fallen flat. All of that risk. All of that effort, and it's just going unnoticed."

"It's still unfolding," said Josh. "People are just waking up. Going to their first meals. We'll see the fallout soon enough." He patted her knee.

His attempts to soothe her worked. She settled back and waited. This story had taught her—or, rather, Josh had taught her—to slow down. To let some of her urges go. She still had ideas and ambitions—she wanted to write about the Outsiders and to follow up on the hidden records and the stories they told—but she knew she didn't have to start today.

Josh glided his fingers over the remote control. He selected a news stream from a grid of talking heads. The one he chose was airing the official reaction from SynEngra. When Angela heard the corporate statement, she felt as if she were listening to Molly.

"The NutriArc System has been a boon for society," spoke a silvery voice. "Before it, we were plagued with disease. Our food supply was unsustainable. But now, people are healthy. They live longer. Their food is safe and nutritious. We urge citizens to stay on the NArc and assure them that SynEngra is using every resource available to verify that the NArc is safe, as it has always been."

"Tripe," muttered June.

The screen switched to an anchorwoman with breaking news: "Police have arrested Arthur Short, a director in SynEngra's research division. According to SynEngra officials, Short masterminded the alleged Unscheduled Mortality program uncovered this morning by journalist Angela Anselm, also known as Sage Weaver. He acted alone to coordinate a scheme to eliminate people before their time had come."

"If they knew Arthur, they would know how preposterous that is. He's a yes man, not an idea man." Angela leaned in toward the screen. "What about Parrish?" she demanded. Then, sitting back, she turned to Josh. "You don't think he would come here to find us, do you?"

Josh opened his mouth to answer when a knock at the door made them both freeze. As Herb opened it, Josh stood up defensively. But Angela recognized the intruder immediately and she leapt past her guardians.

"Nate! You're okay," she cried.

He smiled weakly at her and barely kept his balance when she hugged him. She took a long look at him. He looked terrible. Gritty. And he smelled it too. "Nate, what's happened to you?"

He waved her off. "Another time. I'm fine. Happy to be here," he said. "What's going on out there? Is the story out?"

"It is," said Angela. When she told him there was no word yet on Parrish, his face darkened.

"He may still be detained…," Nate said, glancing between her and the streaming news reports. Josh had turned down the volume but was flipping through the channels, looking for an update.

"What do you mean?" Angela asked.

"Later," he said, waving her off again. "What else?"

"They arrested Arthur." Then, after giving Josh a look, she asked, "Nate, have you contacted Molly?"

"Molly? She's still… She's…"

Josh shushed them, turning the volume back up on the news.

A reporter stood in what looked like the lobby of the SynEngra museum. "We have with us Selica Friedman, the director of public relations at SynEngra. Ms. Friedman assures everyone that the NutriArc System will be safe by the end of the day. They have dispatched crews to test food across the city to assure it is free of unapproved additives. Ms. Friedman, can you give us an update on the secret experiments?"

"To be clear, these experiments were simply unregistered clinical trials. They were and always have been a fundamental part of our automated Nutritional Architecture. The terminations, however, are the work of one misguided man who is now in custody. We are working around the clock to define new checks that will prevent future abuses and allow us to continue to improve health. The NutriArc is not perfect, but we believe that, with everyone's help, it can and will be."

"Do you have any examples of these new checks?" the reporter asked.

"Certainly. We have begun informing individuals of their health conditions and alerting them of any ongoing clinical trials they may be eligible to participate in. We are proceeding with the best interests of our clients, our science, and our business in mind."

"Ms. Friedman, what about the allegations of murder? What about the attempt on the writer Angela Anselm's life?"

"The actions of one eccentric do not implicate the NArc or SynEngra. Mr. Short has been taken into custody and we will ensure that the System is safe from such extreme deviance in the future," she replied.

"But what about Par... Wait, Josh, switch over." Angela pointed to a miniaturized inset showing Officer Potente walking up to a podium.

Potente's face filled the screen. "We have reopened the Sinsky case, along with several other cases of poisoning found in the NArc's secret records, and turned them over to homicide," his statement began. "We have one suspect in custody, Arthur Short, and he has given a statement that he acted alone. All other suspects have been released due to lack of evidence. In particular, one Parrish Knight, who was accused of attempting to murder journalist Angela Anselm and her companion, Josh Salter, has been cleared of all charges. We found no record of a border crossing on the day of the alleged attack. Moreover, witnesses put him DownEast at the NArc Training Center Monday. Indeed, he has been quarantined there since Tuesday at noon when a vandalized NArc system raised an influenza virus alarm. Without further evidence, we have no case against him."

Potente looked at the screen and Angela felt as if he were looking directly at her, urging her to contact him with more evidence. Evidence she didn't have. "Parrish is going to walk. But he was there. The coffee vendor must have seen him," she complained, incredulous. Josh patted her hair, but she hardly noticed. "Vandalism. Nate, was that you?"

Nate shushed her and pointed to a different screen.

Josh switched the channel back and the screen once again featured Selica Friedman's face. "… announce that we have appointed a new Director of Research and Development at SynEngra. Please welcome Molly Tanaka, a scientist and trained physician with over a decade of experience designing our integrated protein products. Ms. Tanaka, in fact, has led the charge to design a new protein product that cuts costs dramatically, allowing the delivery of high-quality nutritionally dense product around the world. This advancement will open up opportunities for the NutriArc to reach more people, alleviating suffering in less affluent regions of the world."

The screen zoomed in on Molly's face. Her features were the same. Angela saw the same pale skin. Her kohl framed eyes blinked under the same matchstick bangs. She looked awfully together for a woman who had just lost her two best friends.

"Thank you Selica. It is my great pleasure to accept this new role. Our division is committed to designing the highest quality products and making the promise of long-term wellness accessible to as many people as possible."

"She's trumping the story," Angela said in disbelief.

"Interesting news from SynEngra this morning," droned the reporter. She touched her ear. "This just in. We now have reactions to the news of SynEngra's unregistered trials."

"And they've changed the conversation. Murders, thousands of murders are now unregistered trials?" Angela whispered.

At the bottom of the screen scrolled a listing of the NArcCafe's cleared so far. In the place of Molly's face, the screen changed to show photographs of people interviewed on the street, their comments captured in text and audio:

> Noble Sinclair, age 56: "Will I go back to the NArc? I wouldn't dream of leaving it. Look at me! I feel great—better than I did when I was 20. Who cares how they do it. Just keep doing it!"

> Marcia Walters, age 47: "I was happy with things as they were. I'd just as soon they keep their experiments secret. Who wants to know they're sick? Who wants to spend their time in a doctor's office?"

> Jordan Michaels, age 23: "Why would we go backwards? Are we seriously talking about going back to farming? That technology is 4000 years old!"

Dr. Uri Obamoff, age 72: "Clinical trials should remain the domain of the System. There is far too much data for humans to make sense of. We cannot add to that by factoring in each individual's desire. The NArc, with all of its digital intelligence, is the most reliable approach."

Padma Reynolds, age 98: "When the NArc can't keep me healthy anymore, I expect it to pull my plug. Saves me the trouble of doing it myself."

Josh turned down the volume.

Angela couldn't move. She couldn't speak. This was all too much. Parrish free. Molly the new Arthur. And now, public apathy. She knew it was her fault things turned out this way. She had written only half of the story. She had done only half the reporting. Her audience had wanted icing and she gave them cake. She had done it again. She had worked so hard to tell a fair story that acknowledged the NArc's benefits and admitted the limited alternatives, but she had still missed the most important part: the people. She sunk deeper into the sofa.

She couldn't bring herself to look at Nate. He had lost everything—his work, his home, even Molly—and it was all because of her. Her *story*. When she finally did look his way, she was surprised to see that he somehow, despite the grime and fatigue, seemed more alive than she'd ever seen him. He didn't seem upset at all. She continued to eye her friend as Josh pulled her closer and whispered in her ear.

"You've made history. Only no one has realized it yet. Just wait until tomorrow," he said.

Tomorrow. Where would she be tomorrow?

She looked at Josh, half terrified and half hopeful that he would dump her. She hadn't turned out as he had planned. She hadn't delivered his revolution after all. If he ditched her, she thought morosely, then at least she could blame some of her mistakes on him.

But Josh kissed her forehead. He brushed away a tear on her cheek with his thumb and asked her if she wanted more coffee. And then he smiled at her, his eyes gentle and warm.

Angela smiled back and blinked away her tears. Tomorrow, she thought. Tomorrow might be better. But maybe today isn't so awful. She pulled herself closer to him and rested her head on his shoulder. "Hey Josh?"

"Hmm?"

"Do you know how to bake cookies?"

Nate, still standing, was unmoved by Molly's appearance and unsurprised by comments from the public. The reporters probably found just as many people who were appalled, he thought. But those people don't have as much power as Selica Friedman does.

Nate's thoughts were interrupted by Herb, who coughed awkwardly and stood. "Well, it's about time I milked those cows."

Nate looked at Herb. He felt like he already knew the farmer. The old man appeared exactly as Angela had described him. She's good at what she does, he thought. She really gets it. She really gets people. Too bad no one else out there does. But then, given how skeptical he had been when she first started down this road, he figured it was way too soon to know what the full effects of this story would be. For now, though, he was happy to see that Angela still had Josh to depend on. And he was happy that, at least for the time being, he was safe.

Herb put his hand on June's shoulder. "Why don't you come with me. The work'll do you good."

Nate couldn't say what, exactly, compelled him to do what he did next. It might have been the lack of sleep. Or the exhilaration he had felt from moving around in the real world, struggling to keep himself alive. Or the look of peace that came over June's face at Herb's suggestion. It didn't matter that he had no experience, and until that instant, no interest in milking cows.

"Mind if I help too?" he asked, directing his question more to June than to Herb. He reached out his hand to help her out of the chair, not thinking about his blood-stained palms, shaved head, and acrid smell. She smiled at him. As soon as his hand touched hers, he knew that he'd made the right choice.

Acknowledgements:

Special thanks to my sister Meghan Dougherty and my sister-in-law Anne Marie Phillips for diligently trudging through many versions of my manuscript. Without your help, I might never have kept going. Thanks also to my many readers along the way: Elizabeth Emery, Dorothy Dougherty, Cory Sawyer, Steve Glassman, Alyssa Kneller, Courtney Humphries, Laurie Phillips, Laura Sugano, Teresa Katuska, and Carolyn Montie. Each of you provided me with unique insights, thoughtful suggestions, and invaluable moral support. Your time and thoughtfulness meant the world to me.

I also want to thank the members of my online writers group, who read many chapters, asked tough questions, commiserated about the writing life, and who most importantly inspired me with their own in-progress novels. Every writer I have met along this journey has been an inspiration and a joy to know.

A special shout out to Luke Strosnider, my brother-in-law, who designed the cover and who put up with me as I struggled to give him useful comments. I just love the way it turned out!

Finally, I want to thank my parents, Paul and Dorothy Dougherty, for being my biggest fans, and my husband, Mike Phillips, for believing in me.

About the author:

Elizabeth Dougherty is a science writer, a runner and a former engineer who likes to cook and loves to eat, especially when it involves food she's grown herself. She lives and writes in an old house in central Massachusetts. *The Blind Pig* is her first novel.

7225509R0

Made in the USA
Charleston, SC
06 February 2011